Danny Dowdells

Angel Jo and the Brackish People

Danny Dowdells

Angel Jo and the Brackish People

Cresson McIver

**AN EXUBERANT TALE OF COLOURFUL
ULSTER FOLK IN THE 1950s**

Appletree Press

This edition produced by
The Appletree Press Ltd.
Roycroft House
164 Malone Road
Belfast BT9 5LL
Telephone 028 90 24 30 74

First published
by Appletree Press
2021

Text copyright © 2021 Cresson McIver
Quotations copyright © as acknowledged

Typesetting, design and layout copyright © 2021 Appletree Press
Cover design and illustration Rob Torrans

All rights reserved. No part of this publication may be reproduced or transmitted in any form or by any means, electronic, photocopying, recording or in any information and retrieval system, without prior permission in writing from the copyright holders.

987654321

AP3835

Danny Dowdells Angel Jo and the Brackish People

Acknowledgements

Danny Dowdells and his world would not have materialised had it not been for the help and encouragement of my wife, Linda, my children, Annalies and Daniel, my son-in law, Harry, daughter-in-law, Heather, and my good friends, Dr Richard McMinn, Lorraine Thompson and Dr Jonathan Bardon [now. sadly deceased]. Their scrutiny of the text and advice at various stages was invaluable, though any blemishes remaining are down to me. I also owe special thanks to John Murphy of Appletree Press who patiently and skilfully guided me through the publishing process.

I wish to thank Ards & North Down Borough Council for awarding me a 'Tyrone Guthrie Centre Bursary,' also the staff at the Tyrone Guthrie Centre at Annaghmakerrig, Co. Monaghan, for making my stay in this creative place so worthwhile and enjoyable as I continued to work there on the text.

The reference materials listed in the annex greatly helped with the dialect episodes in the book, and in capturing the spirit of rural Northern Ireland in the 1950s. I have also drawn heavily on the rich often distinctive dialect usage and varieties of speech that I heard around me in the Ulster countryside over half a century ago.

> "The whole landscape a manuscript
> We had lost the skill to read,
> A part of our past disinherited;
> But fumbled, like a blind man,
> Along the fingertips of instinct."

Extract from 'A lost Tradition' by John Montague from Selected Poems 1961-2017 (2019) by kind permission of the author's Estate c/o The Gallery Press. www.gallerypress.com

> 'Overheard.'
> "It's all wrote down," said Patrick,
> "What happens ivery day,
> The stories they be tellin',
> The things that people say;
> The chat at wakes an' weddin's,
> The thrade[1] that's goin' on,
> It's in a book," said Patrick.
> "Yir a liar!" stuttered John.
>
> Said Pat, "The clargy praiched it,
> As plain as plain cud be,
> An' I don't see no raison,
> Why you should liar me."
> "I'll let you know the raison,"
> Said John, with scornful look,
> "The best horse in yir country
> Cudn't dhra'[2] the book

I am grateful to Caroline Marshall for permission to quote from 'Overheard' by W F Marshall 'The Bard of Tyrone.'

Ballybracken is a fictional Irish townland surrounding a small town of the same fictional name somewhere in Northern Ireland in the 1950s. The characters in the story are not based on anyone living or dead.

1 **Thrade** – the chat about local happenings
2 **Dhra'** – draw/carry

For my wife, Linda, and my children, Annalies and Daniel, also for my parents, Cresson and Tansy McIver and my brother, Edmund, to all of whom I owe so much.

Contents

Part I   Ballybracken - Opening Pandora's Box   11

Episode 1:	At 'The Meeting of the Waters'	13
Episode 2:	Danny Dowdells – Mystery Boy	34
Episode 3:	Angel Jo Pays a Visit	38
Episode 4:	Pigs, Sponge Cakes and the Boys in Black	45
Episode 5:	Cherries, Bribes and Wrong Answers	53
Episode 6:	At McKnight's Shop	62
Episode 7:	Dreams Can Come True	69
Episode 8:	Packie to the Rescue	77
Episode 9:	The Milk Bottle Kiss	87
Episode 10:	Problems in Paradise	97
Episode 11:	Smuggling on the Sunday School Express	102
Episode 12:	Crime and Punishment	121
Episode 13:	China Tea with the Dowager	129
Episode 14:	'Strolling' and 'Scrabbling'	138
Episode 15:	Danny Clams Up	145
Episode 16:	Tantrums and Betrayal	152
Episode 17:	Revolution in the Air	157
Episode 18:	Money for America	164
Episode 19:	The Donkey Derby	173
Episode 20:	Madam Catalina's 'Little Cherub'	182
Episode 21:	The Knights of the Round Table	191
Episode 22:	The Evictions	200
Episode 23:	The Quest for the Holy Grail	215
Episode 24:	Vengeful Fire!	238
Episode 25:	The Big Reward and the Bronze Halo	244

| Episode 26: | The Dangerous Diaries | 250 |
| Episode 27: | The Football Match | 264 |

| Part II | Cupid Fires His Arrows | 269 |

Episode 28:	Love and Betrayal	270
Episode 29:	Wedding Plans	285
Episode 30:	The Canon's Conundrum	292
Episode 31:	Virginal White and Virginal Questions	296
Episode 32:	Robbie in the Doghouse	302
Episode 33:	Awaiting the Angel of Death	306
Episode 34:	Jessie gets the 'Cure'	317
Episode 35:	Maisie's Big Day	325
Episode 36:	'Holy' Daniel Malachy	337
Episode 37:	Big Bertie's Bounty	354
Episode 38:	The Bishop's Table Talk	363
Episode 39:	Danny's song of Love	378

| Annex | | 386 |

Part I

Ballybracken: Opening Pandora's Box

Episode 1

At 'The Meeting of the Waters'

The Lonely Journey

This account of the earthly and heavenly sojourn of our little hero, Daniel Malachy Dowdells, his guardian angel, Jo, and the good people of Ballybracken over half a century ago, does not get off to the most propitious start. Daniel Malachy is nearly six months old, a happy, gurgley sort of baby, but, much as his mother, Rosie, loves him, she has resolved to drown him this sunny Sunday afternoon, and herself with him, where two rivers meet in the pleasant Irish townland of Ballybracken.

We will shortly learn Rosie's reasons for this lamentable decision, but we must first join the dismal pair as Rosie pushes Danny's dinged and battered pram along under the tall beech trees that line the main road through the townland. She is crying bitterly at the prospect of what she is about to do but has the route to her death and little Daniel Malachy's carefully set in her mind. She will go to the meeting place of the waters, where the gently flowing Ballybracken river joins the much broader and grander river Mourne marking the boundary between the two great estates of the local gentry, and there she will wade out into the whirlpool where the rivers aggressively embrace and drown them both. She will commit this terrible deed in this beautiful spot, chosen because it is well away from any roads or cart tracks, a place where only the gentry exercise their horses or labourers working on the estates are ever seen. As a precaution against second thoughts, she has with her a naggin of poteen[1] to give her courage in case her resolve falters. She looks down at the sleeping baby. He was surely a lovely little lad but it's far better to deliver him out of this wicked world into the peace of the next. His innocence will bring him straight to heaven; for herself, she knows, as a devout Catholic, that she is heading straight to hell for what she is about to do. Doesn't Father O'Kelly tell them often enough at Sunday Mass that the only unforgiveable sin is the sin of despair. Well, Rosie is in despair right enough, is never any other way these days, and has now decided on her own way

---

[1] ***A naggin of poteen*** – *a quart of illegal homemade whiskey (Irish 'Moonshine')*

out, for how could hell be worse that what she is suffering?

She has reached the gate lodge to the great Roxborough estate and sits down for a minute to take a swig of the liquor. Then she settles the baby in the pram to make him comfortable for his last journey. As she crosses the road and enters the grand gates, she feels the pram pulling her forward down the steep drive seeming to be hurrying her to the fate that awaits them both. There is nothing that anyone can do to stop her now, such is her resolve, such is her despair.

Robbie and Adeline's Tryst

On this same Sunday afternoon, Miss Adeline Roxborough too is bound for a spot overlooking the beautiful 'Meeting of the Waters' for she has a fateful assignation there this sunny afternoon. Her reason - though such a grand lady didn't need to give reasons – for setting off without a maid to carry her painting materials would have been that she wanted to sketch the soulful view of the 'Meetings' in solitude and without distraction from the vantage point of the 'Ladies' Bower'. This ancient Celtic earthwork has loomed over the confluence of the rivers for over a thousand years. It is ringed by aged oak trees that add grandeur to the location but also afford concealment, and it is concealment that has drawn the grand lady here today, for what she has in mind must be hidden from prying eyes. Now, we should be aware that Miss Adeline's beauty is a talking point well beyond Ballybracken, and no one is more experienced or adept than she at using it to her advantage. She is a glorious gadfly, superficial and flighty, and the men flock around her. She could have any of them she wanted, and some of her lovers would have been considered suitable to her station as the eldest daughter of a Peer of the Realm and British Colonel, but none of these gentlemen are to Miss Adeline's taste. No, the great lady has a penchant for the 'rough and ready' sort. And on this sunny Sunday afternoon, just as we are accompanying Rosie and baby Daniel to their watery grave, Miss Adeline has a date of a very different kind above the sparkling rivers. Her impending liaison is with a young farm labourer, the handsome Robbie Elliott, late of the Royal Enniskillen's, veteran of D-Day, and now a casual labourer on the broad acres of her father, Sir Thomas Roxborough. Robbie had caught her eye as indeed she had caught his, and she quickly grew to desire him but only, of course, for a little 'fun' this sunny Sunday afternoon in Ballybracken. So, both Adeline and Robbie are heading for the 'Ladies' Bower' overlooking the 'Meeting of the Waters,' but we will forbear at present to speculate on what they may get up to in that beauty spot if only, in the meantime, to spare our blushes.

Instead, let us dwell for a moment on the handsome Robert Elliot to acquire a more rounded acquaintance with this gallant fellow, for he is fated to feature largely in our story. He was one of the lucky ones who had survived the horrors of the war without a serious scratch. The ferocious initial training, the Dunkirk evacuation, parachute training in Scotland, the D-Day landings, Arnhem and most dangerous of all, as he frequently joked in Cobain's pub, drinking the required amount of vodka with the Soviet soldiers when his unit met up with them in liberated Germany. He had fought gallantly reaching the rank of Sergeant Major but although returning to Ballybracken unscathed in body, he was back greatly changed in mind. Clever and shrewd, he had compensated for a patchy early education by avid reading in the periods of 'hanging about' that were much more typical of life in the army than the bouts of gung-ho action. And he had learned a lot especially about politics and had come to espouse socialist – even for a while Communist – ideals, and, horror of horrors for the 'holy folk' of Ballybracken, had totally rejected the religion of his youth. When he reflected on the horrors of the Nazi camps he had helped to liberate he could not but wonder 'Where was God?' and that got him thinking about the 'Christians' back in Ballybracken who, he now perceived, had turned the wondrous creed of the simple carpenter of Nazareth into a crazy nightmare of bigotry, prejudice, often even hate. His early admiration for Communism had faded too in light of what he had gleaned from its outworking in Russia from the Soviet lads in Germany. Both great ideals he now considered to be impractical creeds neither of which could be made to sit squarely with the actions of selfish man. Someone, he had read, had summed it up admirably - 'great ideals, wrong species!'

So, when our new companion marched up steep Ringsend brae in his demob suit on a Spring day in 1948 to resume life in this remote part of Mid-Ulster, he paused to survey the beauty of the place, but now with a cynical eye. Below was the ancient bridge spanning the Ballybracken river shimmering in the sunlight, the gentle countryside and bog-land anchored by the parish church and his old primary school, and the whole valley framed by the dramatic Sperrin

Mountains. He was home safe and sound, and the tranquil countryside that Spring day should have warmed his heart but instead he was suddenly beset by resentment for all that Ballybracken stood for. Worldwide Armageddon had just been averted but, *'sure as shootin,'* the Ballybracken folk will not have changed one iota. Their old bigoted certainties on both sides of the religious divide would be as rock solid as ever. The local 'big bugs' would now be feeling even more secure and set in their ways. He could predict the Protestant and Unionist side would be assuring themselves that God had won the war for Protestant British Ulster, as they always knew He would. And on the other side, the Catholic Nationalists would be assuring themselves that God and his Blessed Mother had saved the Irish Republic from invasion and preserved its precious neutrality. As he passed Ballybracken Orange Hall, he was running over in his mind Ballybracken's 'big bugs' that were the cause of his unexpected resentment. There were the religious zealots and the Loyal Orders who dominated the Protestant side of the townland, the powerful Catholic Church and its minions in the Legion of Mary and Knights of Columbanus on the other, their iron control over Catholic working folk as firm as ever. Presiding over all were Ballybracken's small-time gentry like the Roxboroughs on this side of the river and the McKendrys on the other with their big houses and cars, fancy accents and education, box pews in church and their grand air based on their broad acres, high cotter-house rents and poor labourers' wages.

But Robbie Elliot is now his own man, and on certain matters he was firmly resolved as he strode homeward. He would not fall into any of Ballybracken's political and religious traps that he knew would be poised to ensnare and rebrand him, for even a blade of grass in Ballybracken had to be designated either 'Protestant' or 'Catholic.' Nor would he take to drink like many of the townland's old soldiers from the First World War, his own father included. He remembered them from his youth; there they were, paid by the day by the local farmers so they could satisfy their boozing addiction all night and every night, and who, when sober or nearly sober, provided cheap labour for those same hardnosed farmers.

But, happy to relate, by the time Robbie had reached his family home he had succeeded in putting his bitter thoughts to the back of his mind as, with a loud cheer, he threw his kitbag through the open door of the tumbledown cotter house on the Ballybracken Esker where his widowed father lived. After all, wasn't he home when so often out there he had thought he would never again see it or his old man. Hadn't he somehow survived when so many good mates had not, so why the dark thoughts! The welcome was warm and heartfelt, the kettle was soon boiling for the tea, the soda bread was amply buttered, and he had a glass of Guinness in his hand. Sure, wasn't it great to be alive, and now every day a bonus.

So that is the young man who was strolling out, smoking a 'Woodbine,' dressed in a clean shirt, well pressed trousers, German leather jacket - a macabre trophy of his war – who is now bracing himself to enjoy his assignation with Miss Adeline Roxborough, and whatever she was offering, that sunny Sunday afternoon.

The Language of the Cottage and the Hearth

Let us continue to resist the temptation to succumb to prurience just yet and, however sadly, return to Rosie and our little hero, Daniel Malachy Dowdells. They have reached that part of the long stately drive to 'Grovehill Manor' where the servants' entrance branches off to the right. Rosie is going to have to go carefully now, and if she meets anyone, she needs to have some sort of story ready. If she can get across the estate yard without being spotted, the back lane leading down to the 'Meetings' should not be a problem. She has just reached the yard when she is spotted by Cassy Heaney, a kitchen maid, who is loitering with a couple of farm lads over by the old flax mill. And here we must attune our ears to the rich dialect of Mid-Ulster - 'the mark of history on our tongues'[2] - with its older forms of spoken English, for the good Ballybracken folk slip easily from 'school-room English' to the dialect of the cottage and the hearth. Let's pause then and listen to and enjoy this form of English, enriched by Ulster-Scots and Gaelic, that is at times close to that spoken at the time of the First Elizabeth and James, cadences of which may also bring to mind the language of Shakespeare.

"Well, wudn't yeh know it," Rosie muttered to herself, "jist my luck."

"How're yeh, Rosie?" shouts one of the lads who she recognizes was a Maguire from over the Ballybracken Esker.

"I'm rightly[3], son," answered Rosie, "an' how's ye'rselves this nice warm day?"

"Ach, sure we're al gran, Rosie," replies Cassie. "What brings yeh down here

---

2 ***Dialect, the mark of history on our tongues*** – *Professor John Braidwood QUB.*
3 ***I'm rightly*** – *I'm doing all right*

an' is that the wee wain[4], wee Danny? Go on, let's see the wee darlin. I'm sure he's gittin bigger bay the day," and Cassy made to lift Daniel Malachy out of the pram.

"Don't Cassy, I've jist got him over tay sleep so maybe ye'd leave him be[5] for now. If hez wakened, he'll make strange[6]. Sure I'll wak over way him yu'r way some evenin on may ceili[7] tay let yeh give him a wee cuddle, an' you an' me can have a good shanagh[8] for I hiven't seen yeh this good while."

"We'd lake a wee cuddle too, Rosie," said the other lad who Rosie didn't recognize. "Any chance aff that?" and both lads sniggered.

"Now don't yuz-uns be takin a han out aff[9] a poor woman." Rosie went to move on knowing well enough that she wouldn't get by without more quizzing about why she was there?

"Where is it ye'r headin anyway?" demanded Cassy. "Wud yeh not hiv time for a wee drap aff tay[10] here in the kitchen?"

"Day yeh know, I cudn't get him tay settle for he's havin that much bother way hez wee teeth. I'd jist come out for a wak tay get him over way the rockin aff the pram maybe, an' we got as far as the lodge when it come tay may min[11] that nettle broth wuz a remedy spoke about bay the owl folk as good for wains' sore teeth. An' isn't there the quare stan aff nettles beside the 'Ladies' Bower' down the back lane that I thought I'd away down an' pick a bunch tay have a go way them. I'm that scunnered[12] sitting up al night way him girnin[13] and lamentin."

She had surprised herself for thinking this story up on the spur of the moment.

"I niver herd aff nettles as a remedy for teeth but maybe ye'r right for the toothache is the divil, an' worse on a wee wain. Sure I'll come way yeh for the wak now I'm redd-up[14] an' ken slip away. I'll go an' get gloves an' scissors from the kitchen for them nettles can give yeh a powerful stingin."

Rosie plans for the drowning were disappearing fast as Cassy headed back

---

4 **Wain** – *young child*
5 **Leave him be** – *don't disturb him*
6 **Make strange** – *he will get upset and cry if lifted by someone he is not used to*
7 **Ceili** – *a friendly visit to a relative, friend or neighbour*
8 **Shanagh** – *a chat*
9 **Takin a han out aff** – *make fun of*
10 **Drap aff tay** – *some tea*
11 **Come tay may min** – *I remembered*
12 **Scunnered** – *annoyed*
13 **Girnin** – *complaining*
14 **I'm redd-up** – *I've finished my chores*

across the yard to the kitchen door. What was she to do now? She had got herself in the frame of mind to go through with the dreadful deed, and she never wanted to see her home again with all its bad memories. Was she now going to have to go back there - to him - clutching a bunch of nettles?

"That's a powerful black eye yeh hiv there, Rosie," said the Maguire lad. "Did yeh get a drap too much an' wak inta somethin or is the owl fella bad tay yeh?"

This was too near the truth for Rosie to bear but she rallied to say, "Nether. Sure where wud I get the money tay drink?"

Cassy now appeared at the kitchen door and crooked her finger to call Rosie over.

"I've been cornered," she whispered, "I can't go way yeh. McKendry's son, yeh know the very smart wan that's a big doctor in Dublin, hez arrived unexpected an' the Colonel wants me to put on a nice tay fir them al. Between you an' me, I think the young doktor come roun on the aff-chance that Miss Caroline might bay here but sure she's not back yit from that fancy school she's at," and she cocked her head to one side and gave a knowing wink. "Sure, I'll be seeing yeh anyway. Come over some evenin soon, and I'll save yeh a few fancies from the bread-cart for our tay." And with that, to Rosie's relief, she disappeared back into the kitchen.

'Nobody Cares on Earth or in Heaven'

Rosie had been badly thrown by this encounter for it had brought a breath of the normal into her troubled head – lads laughing, teasing, and having a smoke, and Cassy with her promise of fancy buns and an evening's chat. Could she go through with it now at all? But it was the pain that shot through her right hand and arm when she took the handle of the pram that again stiffened her resolve. The memory of yesterday evening came flooding back, and it would not stop until it had swept her and Daniel Malachy down the back lane to their fate at the 'Meetings' – *'him comin home that drunk, goin mad when he smelt the bacon cookin... throwin it out aff the pan into the fire an' it, with the dry bread, the only thing she had in the house for their tay... accusing her of squannerin money he only wanted for more drink... beating her black and blue an' howlin her bare hand an' arm over the burnin turf in the grate, an' then grabbin the wee wain an' throwing him on the floor jist because he was crying way hez wee teeth.'*

She had done all she could to bear this treatment, had even asked Father O'Kelly what she might do, and all he could say was to stick faithfully by her husband and pray to the Virgin for things to come right. But the Virgin didn't seem to be heeding her prayers. How could Our Lady not see what she was suffering and do something to help her? The drinking went on, the beatings went on, they were hungry half the time. It was no life. She had come to the conclusion - sinful though she knew it was - that the Virgin didn't care about poor people like them, with her sitting up there the 'Queen of Heaven.' Why would she care? Nobody up there or down here seemed to care. Rosie had made her decision. She wheeled the pram out of the yard and sets off down the back lane.

The Naughty Liaison

Time for us now to re-join Adeline Roxborough setting up her easel in the 'Ladies' Bower' taking care to do so in the leafiest part of the glade where she is least likely to be spotted. She fixes her foldable stool, opens her paint box and, sitting down, makes a swift attempt at a painting of the pretty river scene below. It would be best to have something to show when she got back to the house but, in truth, painting is furthermost from her mind right now. She was just beginning to get impatient, for she was not used to being kept waiting, when suddenly she is caught in a pair of strong arms from behind.

"Oh, there you are," we hear her gasp as she felt Robbie's stiff bristle on her cheek. "You have given me a fright. I didn't hear you coming."

"That's the good army training," Robbie whispered in her ear. "Creep up on them silently and take them unawares with your bayonet."

"Well, I hope you are not planning to take me with a bayonet," Adeline gave a naughty little laugh as Robbie pressed his bristle still closer to her face.

"I've brought a rug... in case the grass is wet," she explained, for a look of apparent surprise had crossed Robbie's face and she didn't want to appear too eager or too brazen. He must be made to work for his reward for, after all, he was only a farm hand even if a very handsome one.

They spread the rug out in the middle of the bower and lay down side by side safely hidden from prying eyes by the circular bank of the ancient earthwork, the ferns and the surrounding oak trees. Robbie began to caress her beautiful soft auburn hair and put an arm round her elegant neck. Her perfume began to fill his nostrils and stoke his desire. Now this was living as he had never expected it in Ballybracken. His hand began to explore further.

Adeline of course wanted liberties taken, but not too soon and in her own good time.

"Give me a cigarette," she pouted.

He fished the packet out of his jacket pocket, put two in his mouth, lit them and put one between her moist lips.

"That's better, even if all you can offer a girl are these ghastly 'Woodbine coffin nails' as my father calls them." Her voice was deep and sensual. "You are an impatient man," she continued teasingly. "Have all the girls this effect on you?"

"I don't know any other girls," he said resting his head on his hand and smiling down at her, "sure you know I'm virgin territory."

"Just like me," laughed Adeline blowing smoke in his face. "We will just have to learn together, won't we?" She stubbed out her half-finished cigarette and so did he. "No time like the present to get on with our first lesson," and she now pulled him towards her and ran her fingers lightly across the dark hair on his chest. Then when this and other experienced caresses had the desired effect, she said huskily,

"My, you are a big boy, aren't you?"

"I thought you said you didn't know about such things." Robbie was now expertly caressing and teasing her where it was obviously giving her intense pleasure.

"Oh I don't," she said, "It's just I'm such a fast learner, "and her voice trailed off to a whisper as she gave in to enjoying him.

Very soon he was getting impatient, "Oh not on top," she pleaded, "your too heavy. I prefer it," ... she took a sharp intake of breath," ... I like it ... side saddle," and she moaned with pleasure.

"You will like it the way a bit of rough like me likes it," Robbie snarled in her ear, for he knew exactly the mastery she really wanted from him that sunny afternoon ... and indeed, that is what she got.

Afterwards they lay side by side on the rug smoking. "You're a rough, tough big boy," she said smiling. "Where did you learn those engaging little tricks? From the naughty girls in Paris?" And she ran her fingers across his hairy chest again.

"But surely you are such an innocent you would have no idea what naughty girls get up to in Paris," he said kissing the tips of her well-manicured fingers.

They were both satisfied and happy, and back in teasing mode, "I was at a finishing school in Switzerland, the one my sister, Caroline, is now attending," she said, "I learned such a lot about… shall we say little dalliances… on our unsupervised weekends out… that was real living… you'd hardly believe… you never know, maybe I could teach you a thing or two next time."

"Och I'd believe it OK," Robbie said. "Did I hear you say, 'next time'? Who says there will be a next time? Sure, I'm just a common labouring boy led astray by my mistress."

"Indeed you are just that," she said, "my piece of 'rough and tumble', and I will certainly want more of what you have to offer. But I don't want to meet you here. We will have to find somewhere more comfortable. Life in Ballybracken is so very dull, so boring. I need you, Robbie, to make it bearable."

"Well," he said, "how could I resist a second helping at what you have to offer me, Lady. Be assured I will do my best to compete successfully with those Alpine peaks you still long for."

Again he took her in his arms, his passion rekindled by her eager kisses and immediate surrender to his rough embrace when suddenly there was the most frightful commotion and shrieking from down where the rivers meet.

"What the hell…!" exclaimed Robbie jumping to his feet.

"I think it's somebody in the water," cried Adeline now standing on the bank of the earthwork and shading her eyes against the brightly setting sun. They both set off down the steep slope to the rivers following the direction of the horrible continuous screaming.

The Bird of Ill-Omen

Now let us rewind the clock a little so that we can re-join Rosie as she gets to the end of the back lane and is avoiding the rough path leading up the hill to the 'Ladies' Bower.' Instead she is taking the grassy track along the hawthorn hedge that will eventually bring her and her little son to the 'Meeting of the Waters.' The rough ride in the wonky pram has wakened Daniel Malachy but he isn't crying and is gurgling happily and chewing on his plump baby hand. As she arrives at the edge of the riverbank, Rosie is struck with how lovely the place is. Both rivers are twinkling with watery stars in the spring sunshine, the fresh leaves on the oak and beech trees make lovely silhouettes on the grassy banks and the silky green water weeds are drifting languidly with the rivers' flow. Fleetingly she thinks that it seems a pity to ruin all this beauty with so dark a deed, but quickly recollecting what she is escaping from, she is suddenly more determined than ever to put an end to her own dark existence and to drown it here. And there were the big stones under the hawthorn hedge, just as she remembered them, that were used long ago by the scutchers to weigh down the flax in the nearby flax dams. The May hedge is in full bloom, and in the light spring breeze is spraying the riverbanks with delicate white petals as pure as the Virgin's cloak in St Brigid's chapel. In bloom too is the prickly whin testifying its love of life in a riot of bright yellow. But such beauty and vibrancy only help to provide a contrast to Rosie's terrible life – no love from anyone, no respect from anyone, only grinding poverty, a husband brutal in drink, neither understanding or any comfort from her religion and, worst of all, no longer any hope for the baby.

It must be done! With some difficulty, she lifts some of the stones from under the hedge and puts them at Daniel Malachy's feet in the pram to weigh it down in the water. Some of the smaller stones she puts in her cardigan pockets. Then, for some reason she doesn't fully understand, it seemed right to break off a few branches of the May blossom to cover the big stones in the pram, maybe it was to remind heaven of her child's innocence, who can tell? All this complete, and with difficulty due to the weight of the stones, she now pushed the pram into the bigger more fast-flowing Mourne river, and then waded out herself.

Robbie and Adeline had no trouble finding the exact spot on the riverbank from which the frightful screams were coming for they seemed to hover in the air never changing location in their terrible intensity. Robbie arrived at the rivers first and looked in disbelief at the sight before him. The fully clothed body of a woman was lying head down in the water and ahead of her was a pram with a baby crying piteously. The pram was being drawn into the centre and towards the whirlpool but was tilting backwards and taking in water fast. More outlandish still, overhead, flying round and around in circles and occasionally diving down towards the sinking pram, was an enormous bird shrieking and screaming like the tormented in hell.

"Jeezes Christ," Robbie shouted, throwing off his jacket and pulling off his shoes as Adeline reached him.

"Oh my God," she said, "what is it? What has happened?"

Robbie to the Rescue

But Robbie was already up to his chin in the water and making for the pram which seemed in even more immediate danger than the woman. He was swimming now, and the pram was nearly within reach when a forest of slimy green water weeds wrapped themselves round his legs and pulled him back. With difficulty he broke free and somehow succeeded in taking hold of the pram handle with his right hand just before the pram reached the turbulent whirlpool where the rivers met. He turned towards the bank one hand holding on to the handle when it suddenly came away in his hand. Released from his grip, the pram shot forward, a shower of water raining down on the baby, and then lurched drunkenly backwards pulled down by some weight. It quickly disappeared below the water. Robbie's only thought now was to do his best to save the baby at whatever cost, so he dived after the pram, somehow succeeded in catching it by its rotten hood just before it settled on the riverbed. He made a last desperate grab for the baby's head, his relief at feeling the soft baby flesh in his hands tempered by the feeling that he may already be too late. He reached the surface, struck out for the bank, found his footing and waded ashore carrying the baby above his head. Until now the child had been deadly silent, but suddenly there is a long intake of breath and it began to scream blue murder. Seldom had Robbie been so glad to hear anything in his life.

A woman was sitting on the bank, a bottle in one hand, her rosary beads in the other and mumbling 'Hail Marys.' Wet and bedraggled as she was, Robbie recognized her at once as Rosie Dowdells.

"What the hell happened tay yeh, Rosie," he asks gasping for breath. "How did yeh fal in?"

"I didn't fal in, I did it deliberate," she said, and continued in a flat unemotional voice, "I'm that heart sore an' he's that bad tay me. I wanted tay do away way mezself an' the babby too. An' now I haven't done it an' I'm no better aff. Ye'r woman is over there," she continued in the same flat voice, pointing to the exact spot where the two rivers meet, "I doubt she's in a bad way. She slipped when she pulled me out, an' I hadn't the strength tay dale way hir."

Robbie looked to where the woman was pointing. Dazed as he was, the full horror of what he saw struck home. There was Adeline lying in the reeds and slimy mud her beautiful blue eyes staring heavenwards, blood in a steady trickle issuing from a gash in her forehead mingling with her long auburn hair now spread out like a fan by the fast current. Robbie realized at once that Adeline was dead, and that this beautiful woman had paid the ultimate price for another's madness, whatever its cause?

He clumsily carried Adeline's body up the bank and did all in his power to revive her even though he knew it was hopeless. He was oblivious to the half-drowned wretch beside him chanting her prayers while her baby lay on the grass screaming incessantly. At last he gave in to the inevitable and, sitting down beside the body, thought about what he must now do?

'Stroll' don't 'Scrabble'

Robbie's soldiering life had taught him to be cool and calculating, qualities we can now do no better than to sit back and admire. When confronted with life's crises great or small, he has learnt that, as he put it, to 'stroll' is better than to 'scrabble', so he has already taken control of his thoughts and is carefully pondering how to square the story he will tell with the facts. For Robbie, survival is always the name of the game, and to try not to make bad worse. If it now takes lies to achieve that, that is what it will take.

He looked across at Rosie, "Did anywan see yeh comin down here, woman?" he asked.

She didn't answer, her confused mind somewhere else.

"Damn yeh, Rosie," he said dragging her to her feet and spitting out the question again into her ashen face.

"Aye, I think so," she said. "Maybe Cassy up at the big house an' wan or two others in the yard. I can't rightly mind, I've been knocked that throughother."

"Yeh'll bay more throughother if it iver gits out what yeh wur up tay the day," he snarled.

But he knew Rosie for what she was, a poor woman of Ballybracken's cotter class who had done something stupid for some reason he had not yet grasped. The first thing to do was to get her away from the scene and so out of the story that was taking shape in his mind.

"What are we goin tay do?" Rosie asked, appearing at last to take in the seriousness of the situation. "If they iver get tay know, they'll jail me or put me in the mental asylum an' take the wee wain away from me," and she started to weep uncontrollably, the whole tension of her terrible day suddenly overwhelming her.

This was exactly what Robbie wanted to hear. "Aye, they will, Rosie, so from here on yeh must keep ye'r mouth shut about what happened here the day an' don't bay bletherin[15] about it efterwards lake a ha'penny book. If it git's out, sure as God's in heaven, they will cart yeh aff[16], and what will happen to ye'r wain then? Ye'r story from now on is that yeh mind nothin for yeh wur that knocked sideways way what yeh happened-on down here at the 'Meetins' when out for ye'r wak way the wain. Do yeh hear me. Say feck all – ever. It's ye'r only hope tay save ye'rself an' ye'r wain from even worse."

"I'll say nothin – iver." Rosie repeated, "Fir I know I've acted stupid and sinful, an' luk where it's got meh."

"Now", Robbie continued, "you sit there for a minute, take a slug aff whatever's in that bottle tay settle ye'rself, an' I'll bay back. Try to keep the wain quiet an' pray God nobody else is out for a dander[17] along the riverbanks here the day. An' don't bay tryin tay drown yourselves again or any other stupid antic. We'll git it al sorted out if yeh give me a chance."

He left her nursing the baby and rushed back up the hill to the 'Ladies' Bower.' Experience had taught him that simple explanations are the best so, *'Miss Adeline had met with an accident of her own making,'* would be the line to take. He must now arrange the 'evidence' to substantiate this alternative story to explain the catastrophe. He grabbed Adeline's easel, paint box, pallet and brushes and carried them back down the slope to the rivers. Picking a likely spot, he scattered them randomly along the bank of the Ballybracken Burn.

"Now, we must get back tay the big house," he said to Rosie. "Mind now, yeh say nothin fir ye'r that shocked!"

There was nobody in the estate yard when they got there so Robbie headed for the back door and threw it open.

"Where's the Colonel?" he shouted to Cassy who was sitting by the black range reading the 'News of the World' which she unsuccessfully tried to ram behind the turf basket.

"Why, what's happened tay yeh, Robbie?"

"I must see the Colonel immediately," he said. "Where is Sir Thomas? I hiv bad news, an' he must bay the first tay hear."

"Yeh can't see him in them clothes, sure ye'r wringing wet," said Cassy. "Wait an' I'll see if he'll see yeh at al for he hez a visitor. Stay where yeh are. Yeh can't

---

15 **Bletherin** – *talking nonsense*
16 **Cart yeh aff** – *ignominiously take you away to prison or a mental asylum*
17 **Out for a dander** – *out for a stroll*

go into the parlour in that state. He'll maybe come out tay yeh."

She rushed out of the kitchen dropping pages of the newspaper as she went.

The post-mortem recorded accidental drowning due to the victim having sustained a blow to her head rendering her unconscious when she lost her footing trying to cross the Ballybracken river using the ancient foot-stick which had become dangerously slippery. Recorded too were the gallant though sadly unsuccessful efforts of Sergeant Major Robert Elliott, MC, to revive the victim when he happened upon the incident while walking by the river that sunny Sunday afternoon. There was no mention of a woman and her baby.

Frankie McSorley's Ghosts

"So yez hiv waken the owl ghost aff the 'O'Nails Mor'[18] down yonder at the 'Meetins'. Bay God, it'll be the divil's job tay get that settled again. I'm tellin yez." Frankie McSorley took a sip of his Guinness and gazed at Robbie through the smoke of his cigarette as they sat at the counter in Cobain's pub.

"What are yeh takin about?" asked Robbie. "Are yeh drunk, man?"

"Och divil the bit drunk," said Frankie, "but hiv yeh niver h-eard tell the yarn[19] about the pagan ghosts that frequent them 'Meetins'?"

"Naw, niver heard tell aff it[20]," said Robbie, "but I'm sure you're gonna tell me."

Frankie continued in a low voice. "It's been passed down bay the owl folk[21] that the 'Meetins' wuz thought a sacred place bay the pagans in times past, an' sure isn't there an owl pagan fort jist up above it? Aye, that 'Ladies' Bower' contraption the gentry cals it, an' isn't that where they say some aff the Great Gaelic O'Nail Clan lies buried with not a stone kine markin their graves now. Yeh know, them O'Nails that wuz hunted from their lan at the time aff the English Plantations. An' why is some aff the great Tyrone O'Nail's buried at yon spot? I'll tell yeh for why… they say that the 'Meetins' be tay lie[22] at the

---

18 **O'Nails Mor** – *The Great O'Neills, the most powerful Gaelic chieftains before the Plantation of Ulster*
19 **A Yarn** – *a story*
20 **Niver heard tell aff it** – *Never heard of it*
21 **The Owl folk** – *our ancestors*
22 **The 'Meetins' be tay lie** – *the Meeting of the Waters is situated*

very heart aff wan aff the holy forests aff owl pagan Irelan an' in that Bower place above the rivers grew the scared tree, one of the five holy trees aff Irelan, the 'Mother Tree' it wuz.... real sacred to the owl pagan gods an' tay the Great O'Nails... till yuz Protestant Planters hunted the lot aff them some time back. Are yeh still way me?"

"Sure, I'm followin ye'r ivery word, Frankie, but don't bay too long about it for I'm hefted for a pish."

"Ach well, they say that ivery seven years a big stallion rises out of the water at the 'Meetins' way somethin ridin on its back – betimes it's a beautiful woman, or an angel or I've even heerd aff it bein a big snow-white bird. Aye, yeh may laugh but there's them that hez seen it, an' day yeh know what the thing says before the horse an' it vanishes again back inta the depths? Now, let me get this right. Aye that's it... " and, in a quavering voice rising steadily for effect, Frankie said, *'Cursed be they that stole the lan aff the O'Nails, banished us their guardian spirits an' brought shame on this sacred place. Vengeance will be heaped on them in ivery generation till the end ah time,'* he finished breathlessly. "An' hezn't it al come tay pass way the drownin of ye'r woman? What more proof de yez need?"

"Ach, git away outta that[23], man, aren't yeh the quare owl eejit," said Robbie, headin for what passed for the pub lavatory.

He smiled to himself. He had indeed seen a big bird all right - 'skreekin[24] worse than a banshee[25]' - but it was just a bird. Nothing more. If there had also been a big stallion or the angel, he must have missed them. Maybe he'd been too busy in the water that day with other things on his mind. Shame! It would have made a good pub yarn if, like Frankie, you were into that kind of stuff. But Robbie wasn't...

"What a rail owl eejit[26] that Frankie is. Haunted my ass! Just an' owl pishogue[27]."

Don't be too sure, Robbie, there are more surprises of a similar kind ahead!

Willy Dowdells Shown the Door

Robbie's robust soldier talk we will, I fear, have to tolerate throughout our story

---

23 **Git away outta that** — *Stop talking nonsense*
24 **Skreekin** *-screeching*
25 **The Banshee** *-the death fairy*
26 **Owl eejit** – *an old fool*
27 **Pishogue** *–a superstition*

and so, I also fear, must we accommodate the lustful side of his nature already witnessed when we earlier looked in at the 'Ladies' Bower.' For, deplorable as it will seem to tender consciences, when we next encounter him it is largely lust that is driving him along the road in the direction of the Dowdells's cottage, no more than a week after the episode at the riverbank. For the more he thought about her, the more Robbie reflected that Rosie was a very attractive, desirable woman. And what was that she'd said about her man being so bad to her that he had driven her to that madness down at the rivers? There might indeed be more to be had than a good 'curt', agreeable as that would be, for he was also on the look-out for a more permanent billet than his father's cotter house, so further exploration was called for. Mustering what was left of his soldier's luck, he is strolling out ostensibly to see how Rosie and the little lad are faring but, you never can tell, maybe there might be more to be had, then or later, as a reward for his gallant effort in saving their lives that Sunday afternoon.

"Naw, I hivn't ventured a word so yeh needn't bay comin here tay tackle me." Rosie was on the defensive before he had got through the half door of her cottage. "I'm skard[28] aff even mentioning it in may sleep. I pray fir that poor dead lady ivery night, an' will light a cannel for hir in the chapel ivery Sunday, fir I know rightly I wuz tay blame for al that happened tay hir."

"Wheesht[29], woman. No wan wuz tay blame. It wuz a tragic accident. I'm not blamin yeh. I've ony come roun tay see how you an' the wain's doin?"

"We're rightly" Rosie said. I've jist wet the tay, Yeh hiv a sup, will yeh[30]?"

"Aye, work away[31]," Robbie said casually. He had more than a mug of tea in mind as a thank you, but he'd work on that after the tea. He sat down by the turf fire on the only safe-looking chair.

"Is this hezself's chair?" he asked. "He'll not want tay come home an' fin a strange man sittin in it. Is he due home anyway soon?"

This by way of preparing the ground. Rosie had her back to him putting the black kettle on the crook.

"Niver fear," she said. "Sure he's niver home till he's threw out aff the pub at

---

28 **I'm skared** – I'm scared
29 **Wheesht** – be quiet... hold your tongue
30 **I've jist wet the tay, ye'll hiv a sup, will yeh?** – I've just made some tea. Will you have some?
31 **Work away** - that's fine, carry on

closin time, an' sometimes not even then."

She turned to the table under the window and began to cut slices of bread from a stale-looking loaf.

"Ye'r limpin, Rosie," Robbie said. "What ails ye[32]?"

"What always ails me?" she replied. "The same thing took may tay the rivers that day ails me still an' always will till the day I die that I hope will be soon."

"Now yeh'v surely got over the notion aff dyin… but is it Willy that bad to yeh, woman?" Robbie asked directly.

"An' what if he is?" she said. "What remedy hive I? A cotter woman[33] way a wain an' a man that drinks ivery penny we hiv. Not that he's a bad man when he's not on the drink, but it's got such a howl over him[34]."

"Boys-a-dear," Robbie said thoughtfully and then, "well, he still hez no cawl tay bey beatin yeh. You're a fine lookin-woman that any man in Ballybracken would be proud aff. Maybe I cud hiv a wee word way him. Him an' may Da is very great[35], an' I get on rightly way him anytime we come across wan another[36]."

"It'd do no good," Rosie turned to the singing kettle. "No good at al. Sure didn't Father O'Kelly hiv a word way him way back but he ony come home that night drunker than iver an' beat me even worse. Said how dar I be goin squealin about us tay any priest. That wuz a sore night. I had tay close mezself in the turf shade yonner an' sleep there tay get away from him."

Genuine concern prompted Robbie to say, "what kinna life is this for yeh, Rosie? An' worse still, for ye'r wain? I now understand what driv yeh tay the rivers that day, I'm heart sorry fir yeh. Wud yeh leave it tay me tay put manners on[37] Willie."

"Och Jeezes, Mary and Joseph don't do anythin, Robbie," she begged, snatching back the mug she was about to hand him in her anxiety. "Yeh'll square up tay him, an' he'll say he'll quit, an' when yeh go he'll be worse than iver. "

Robbie stood up, took the mug from her and put it on the table. "An' what if I didn't go? What if I niver lave yeh?" he asked, taking her in his arms and

---

32 **What ails yeh?** – what is the matter with you?
33 **A cotter woman** – a poor working-class woman living in a cottage on a country estate
34 **It has got such a houl over him** – drink has got a hold over him… he is addicted to alcohol
35 **Him an' may Da is very great** – they are good friends
36 **Get on rightly any time we come across wan another** – we get on well any time we meet
37 **Put manners on** – teach him a lesson that will make him stop

kissing her long and deep.

"This is not right," she said making a sham at pushing him away. "Not right at al."

"Maybe it not right," he said, "but I think yeh cud bay doin way more aff it."

❖

Willy Dowdells came home that evening earlier than usual for the money had run out. He was in a bad way. He banged on the door with his fist, the top half flew open, and he had difficulties focusing on the latch to open the lower half.

"F*** yeh, yeh bitch," was his drunken greeting to his wife. "Yeh hiv may lukin a right fool in Cobain's yonner way yeh squannerin may wages so I can't h-owl may own in the public house or meet may rounds. Ye'r a right cute hure[38], woman. Ye'r hidin money on me again. Now, give it tay may, an' yeh'll not see me no more the night. Come on, hand it over or I'll give yeh another right good keekin."

It was only then he spotted Robbie sitting by the fire. "Ach, yeh'v got a ceilier[39], hiv yeh? How're yeh doin, Robbie?" he said, trying to focus on the visitor and not slur his greeting. "This woman aff mine hides may money, day yeh see, an' if she'll han it over, you an' me can still have a quare night aff it in Cobain's."

"I think maybe yeh've had enough, Willy. Maybe it's time tay quit for this evenin, an' leave ye'r woman be."

Willy's mood then swung swiftly from drunken bonding with Robbie to drunken rage."

"Ach yeh do, do ye? Troth an' sowl[40] yeh'll not come into my house an' tell me what's what, yeh big bastard. Get out aff here an' don't come back," and he staggered across the kitchen to make a grab for Robbie.

"Ye'r too drunk tay put up a fight, man," said Robbie. "Away outside an' try tay sober up for I don't want tay take advantage of yeh in that state."

"What state?" roared Willy "Yeh'll not tell me what state I'm f***** in."

"Listen tay me, Willy, ye'r heads away way the drink[41], now go out an' try tay sober up an' then we'll see… " he tailed off for Willy had reached the hearth,

---

38   **Ye'r a right cute hure** – *you are devious… sly… deceptive*
39   **A ceilier** – *a visitor*
40   **Troth an' sowl** – *by my soul! (an oath)*
41   **Ye'r head's away way the drink** – *You are not thinking sensibly because you are drunk*

lifted the tongs, and would have brought them crashing down on Robbie's head if he hadn't leapt up to avoid the blow.

"Och Holy Jeezes, will yez quet." Rosie was sitting on the outshot bed[42] in the kitchen, her apron up to her face. "I'll go an' get Constable Mc Crum tay separate the pair aff yez. If yez is gonna fight, go outside for yez hiv wakened the wain."

True enough, Daniel Malachy had been wakened by the noise and was crying wildly from somewhere behind Rosie on the bed. Still with the tongs in his hand, Willy made another swipe at Robbie whose blood was now well and truly up. He caught Willy by the wrist that was holding the tongs and forced him to drop them. Then he pulled him towards the fire and, with a steady grip, forced his hand over the roasting turf flame and held it there for some seconds while Willy screamed with agony.

"Now yeh know what it feels lake, yeh bastard," Robbie snarled in his ear. "An' how's this for a bit of ye'r own medicine," and he kicked Willy very hard on his shins. Willy fell backwards into the fire scattering the live turf over the hearth and unto the clay floor.

"Oh Jeezes, he's gonna kill me," Willy cried, trying to get up. "Help me up, Rosie. The greesagh[43] is scaldin[44] the ass aff may. I'm sorry… I'm sorry… "

"Ach, lake al feckin bullies ye'r sorry when ye'r squared up tay[45], yeh get[46] yeh. It's a bit late tay bay sorry," and Robbie hauled him out of the hot embers, propelled him to the door by the collar of his coat, dragged him across the yard and threw him face down on the cottage's filthy duchill[47]. "That's where shit lake you belong," he said, aiming a final kick at Willy upturned backside "… an' don't come back. I'm boss here now, isn't that right Rosie?"

She had followed them out into the yard and was staring at Robbie in a

---

42 **Outshot bed** – *a bed recess in the back wall of a cottage kitchen*
43 **The greesagh** – *hot embers*
44 **Scaldin** – *burning and blistering*
45 **When ye'r squared up tay** – *when you are challenged*
46 **Yeh get yeh** - *you despicable fool*
47 **Duchill** – *refuse heap… dunghill*

mixture of fear and awe. "Ach I donno… but yeh surely ken't leave him there sprachlin[48] on the duchill?"

"Ach let him be. What are yeh gawpin at[49], woman? Day yeh not think I deserve another mug a ye'r tay?" Robbie took her by the arm and led her back into the kitchen to the sound of Willy struggling to rise and flee.

That was the night that Robbie moved in never again to leave, and that was how Daniel Malachy Dowdells ended up with two daddies, neither of them his!

An Audience with Sir Thomas

When ushered into the parlour, Robbie had stood to attention before the Colonel.

"Just wanted to thank you in person, Elliott," the Colonel said, "for all you tried to do on that dreadful day. We speculate constantly about how it happened, what was in Adeline's mind, and why she was there? Lucky you came along or the body might have been carried away in the current given the thunderous downpour later that evening. Very grateful anyway for all you did. You'll have a drink with me? Whiskey? Good man. What's became of that woman and the baby boy? I hear she was down there to gather nettles for toothache! Extraordinary! Some old country charm, I suppose."

"She is OK, Sir," Robbie said in a non-committal way. All that mattered was that a line appeared to have been drawn, and that there would be no further questions. As Robbie accepted another drink, and the Colonel changed the subject to enquire about Robbie's war, he was impressed by the Colonel's calm acceptance of his family's tragedy. This man is an impressive 'stroller,' Robbie thought. Pity there are not more of us to make the world a saner place.

As he left Grovehill Manor, he saw a young woman getting out of a taxi at the front door.

"Miss Caroline home from that fancy school the girls went tay in Switzerland," Cassy whispered to him without being asked. "More work fir us poor skivvies but sure where's the use complainin, an' anyway she's very nice an' aisy tay git on way."

'Sure is a 'good looker' too," Robbie mused, and couldn't stop himself wondering if she has the same taste in men as her dead sister?

---

48 **Sprachlin** – *sprawling awkwardly*
49 **Gawpin** – *Staring in a stupid manner*

Episode 2

Danny Dowdells – Mystery Boy

Speculation Round the Hearth

"If it wuzn't for that damned stutter[50], I think Danny would be a brave smart wee lad. He seems tay hiv a good head on him[51]," Robbie said, laying aside Daniel Malachy's school exercise book that he had been scrutinizing beside the hearth. "He luks good on paper with his spellins an' tables an' that but sure he can hardly get a word out."

"Aye," Rosie answered. "The teacher says he's right an' smart, but sure way that stutter, however he come bay it, he'll niver get no road.[52]"

Robbie had now been living with Rosie for several years and was the only permanent man in young Danny's life. Willy Dowdells had stayed away after the beating that evening and had, in a strange Ballybracken sort of twist, moved in with Robbie's father on Ballybracken Esker.

"Them two owl droughts[53] can drink away tay their hearts content," was Robbie's verdict on the arrangement, and so they did even after an evening's drinking in Cobain's pub. Everyone in Danny Dowdells's young life seemed happy with this irregular arrangement, though in a fragile sort of way.

Rosie would sometime say, "Ach, Willie not that bad a man except when hez on the drink," to which Robbie invariably answered, "yeh wur gled tay swap him fir a better wan when he drew up alongside yeh[54]."

And so she was. She felt lucky to have such a good-looking big man around for she loved him and he her, even if he might not always be faithful about which she turned a blind eye. He worked for local farmers when there was any work to be had, collected his army pension, drew the dole – *fir hadn't I helped save the friggin country from Hitler so it's the least they can do fir meh* – and gave it all to Rosie every week, except for a pound or two he kept back for a few sociable

---

50 **Stutter** – *Speech stammer*
51 **Good head on him** – *a clever, questioning and thoughtful boy*
52 **He'll niver get no road** – *he will never be successful*
53 **Them two owl droughts** – *Those two old drunkards*
54 **Yeh wur gled tay swap him fir a better wan when he drew up alongside yeh**
  – *You were glad to swap him for me when I came along*

drinks and his Woodbines. His erstwhile flirtation with socialism had all but vanished except for a merest vestige when he called master Daniel Malachy his 'little comrade' which pleased Danny, and made him feel a big man even though he didn't know what 'comrade' meant.

Rosie had two children by Robbie, a daughter she called Dorry and a son, Bobby, after his father. With Robbie's money, the cottage improved a bit. The kitchen and bedroom were freshly whitewashed every year, there was better second - hand furniture, a little more on the table, and Rosie took immense pride in keeping everything including her children neat and clean. But despite that, her cottage, with its clay floors and leaking windows, was never more than a hovel and, sadly, folk like her in Ballybracken never expected more which was, in practice, what made their condition bearable. Robbie still chaffed under it, and frequently sang the praises of the British Labour Party to the discomfiture of almost everyone in the townland. But he had long since decided that, though his soldering efforts had contributed to changing the world, Ballybracken's world nobody could change.

Who is Danny Dowdells?

"So who's hez Da?" asked Robbie one evening, with nothing on his mind more than idle curiosity, and to tease Rosie which he delighted in doing. "Surely he's not Willy's? He's far too smart a wee lad."

"What day yeh main"[55]? Rosie countered. "Aren't yeh very pass-remarkable[56]. Sure, amen't I'm right an' smart mezself. Maybe he gits hez brains from me."

"I know ye'r a powerful smart woman, but Danny's even smarter than you. Come on, who is he?" and he winked at her. "Sure yeh know I'll keep ye'r dark secret."

Caught off-guard, Rosie said, "I'm not that sure but, naw, ye'r right, he's not Willy's. Sure he wuz niver sober enough to do the trick though it didn't stop him tryin.'"

Rosie's candour had surprised Robbie, so he pressed home his advantage.

"Well, whose then?" Robbie persisted.

"I think maybe hez daddy wuz wan aff them young sodgers[57] stationed in the army camp on the Colonel's lan.' They wur on some sort aff exercises roun here

---

55 **What day yeh main?** – *What do you mean?*
56 **Pass-remarkable** – *making impertinent uncalled-for remarks about things that are none of your business*
57 **Sodgers** – *soldiers*

about that time an' one of them got lost... an' it wuz teemin[58] way rain on him when he called at the dure[59] tay ask directions... so I brought him in out aff the wet tay dry hezself... an' he wuz a real nice wee fella... an' I wuz that desperate for a wee wain... an' Willy was jist a drouth an' no good... so I think maybe... " She tailed off, aware that she had dropped her guard, so quickly continued, "but its hard tay know. I suppose he might be Willy's efter al." She was now scared that Robbie would accuse her of being a bad woman, "… for, lake, now and again he was nearly up fir it."

"So, some smart squaddie or officer's maybe. Whose iver he's is, yeh got ye'rself a real owl-fashioned[60] wee lad there."

So, the mystery of our little hero's parentage remained just that – a mystery! But however he came by it, Daniel Malachy Dowdells was indeed a very clever boy, as we shall see.

Even though Rosie was a devout Catholic, Daniel Malachy was brought up a Protestant, and was sent to Ballybracken's Protestant school. Robbie saw to that. Rosie's parish priest, Father O'Kelly, tried, in his gentle way, to persuade Rosie to switch Danny to the Catholic school but Robbie would have none of it. All three children would attend the same school, and it would be the Protestant one.

"Sure they will get a better chance way the Prods," he insisted, "for they are dying out in this townland because aff them thin-lipped, tight-assed Protestant wemen that are too busy prayin an' makin money tay hiv any wains so the Protestant school has far wee-er classes. Naw, our wans will stan a far better chance there than in the Catholic school that is bustin way scholars. Sure them Papishes breed lake rabbits."

Rosie ignored this slur on her religion with its crude allusion to her Church's taboo on contraception, but she accepted that Robbie was a smart man who read everything from serious books, newspapers and magazines to the football papers. Because of this, and because she loved him, all her children went with the Protestants, even though it often bothered her conscience. He never said it, but Robbie, at best an agnostic, also thought that the Protestant questioning

---

58 **Teemin** – *pouring with rain*
59 **Dure** – *door*
60 **Owl-fashioned** – *precocious*

kind of religion, with its greater appeal to logic of a kind, was easier to shake off later in life than, as he saw it, unquestioning Catholicism with its dogma, indoctrination and strong appeal to emotion.

But, thoughtful and clever as he undoubtedly was, Robbie hadn't reckoned with Ballybracken's powerful evangelical 'holy brigade,' the teachers in the Protestant school being in the vanguard of this assault on the minds of their young charges. Neither had Robbie reckoned with Danny's consuming interest in religion as he grew older. Maybe it was just in the Ballybracken air, but Danny was forever asking questions. Robbie's strategy was to tell Danny to direct his questions to the 'God squad' as he called Ballybracken's devout Protestants. He hoped their shallow answers would put a clever boy like Danny off but in fact, it only encouraged him to ask more questions.

"Are you sure you didn't go tay bed way the Priest or yon Anglican Canon?" Robbie laughingly teased Rosie one night after Danny had raised a few difficult queries arising from his Sunday school lessons.

"I'll kill yeh fir thinkin such bad things," Rosie said crossly.

"Ach sure yeh know I'm ony keepin yeh goin. Who iver hez daddy wuz, I wouldn't bay surprised if we don't hiv a theologian on our hands. Isn't that right, Danny?"

Daniel Malachy didn't understand any of this, and went on learning his catechism hoping he wouldn't stutter too much reciting it in Sunday school next day.

Episode 3

Angel Jo Pays a Visit

Cats and Angels

Danny was in bed scratching his hives and reciting the eight-times tables when a large cat appeared at the end of the bed. This was somewhat unexpected for the Dowdells didn't own a cat, Rosie declaring that she had enough trouble looking after her family without adding 'live-stock' to her care. But it was a nice white cat that was now licking its paws and giving every appearance of settling in for the night. Danny knew that his mother would blame him for its presence, that her reaction to it would fall short of welcoming so he struck at it with his foot to dislodge it but missed. Then a strange thing happened, leading Danny to think he must be dreaming. The cat stood up on its hind legs at the bottom of the bed, purred calmly and slowly turned into an angel. Well, that's what it looked like anyway for it was the spitting image of the angels pictured in the Bible Daniel Malachy had got as a Sunday school prize last December.

His first reaction was to scream the house down, but that would waken everybody up and most likely get him a hammering for his '*owl ardiks*' as his mother called any of his wilder behaviour. So, he just kept calm behaving as if this was a regular nightly occurrence, and said without stammering, "who are you?"

The presence at the end of the bed, who had been smoothing down its long golden hair with beautiful china-white fingers, now straightened itself up and said in a soothing voice, "Oh Hello! I am your heavenly guardian… or your guardian angel as you 'earth-grubbers' call us… my name is Angel Jo… I've come to see how you are getting on?"

"Oh," said Danny, which was all he could think to say for it was news to him he had a guardian angel. His next question had to be, "so, what are you guarding me from?"

Angel Jo gave him an indulgent little smile.

"Oh, you'd be surprised. I saved you from drowning for a start when you were a tiny little baby, I was called forth by your screams and appeared as a beautiful heron because I have always fancied a long elegant neck... mine is so... short," and here Angel Jo looked as though he wanted Danny to contradict him and admire his neck. When he got no response, he continued sharply"... but you won't remember that, and that's really why I'm back now, to see how you are? Only people like you who have had a near death experience can see and hear their guardian angel or communicate with us, and not all of them either, so you are very lucky boy even if the drowning has left you a bit, shall we say...'odd'... even for an 'earth - grubber.'"

Being nearly drowned and left a bit 'odd' didn't seem too lucky to Danny but he didn't want to appear ungrateful, so he said,

"So, you watch over me... like the 'holy' people in Ballybracken say Jesus does. Should I be praying to you then instead of Him... or God?" for Danny grasp of the complexities of the Holy Trinity was... well, truthfully, non-existent... but he is still a small boy and can't be expected to have our mastery of it!

"No, certainly not," said Angel Jo. "Just go on doing what you've been doing on the prayer front and leave me out of it. For, you know, we angels are on a 'work- to- rule' at the moment so I certainly don't want to be pestered with any prayers. I simply can't take it," and he rolled his lovely blue eyes.

"What's a 'work- to- rule'?" asked Danny.

"It means we only do the barest minimum within strict working hours," explained the angel. "Well," he continued crossly, "they were taking advantage of us up there. 'Go here, go there, look after this one, that one, write this report, write that report'... it's too much! Our wings can't take it for a start. Have you any idea how hard it is crossing between universes to look after silly creatures like you. You haven't a clue, have you? And neither have they... Oh yes, it's a strict 'work- to- rule' until they get the heavenly work rotas sorted out. That why you haven't seen much of me since that unfortunate drowning episode."

Angel Jo paused, unfolded his wings and looked balefully at Danny who now felt, in his good-natured way, that maybe he needed to cheer the angel up a bit.

"It was nice of you to save me," he paused for the angel looked surprised at this clumsy vote of thanks, and then, wanting to change the subject to something lighter, Danny said,"... you have nice wings."

"Oh, do you like them?" asked Jo. "Yes, this style is now back in fashion up there. Nice and glossy and well-trimmed. The shabby chic was in last millennium but it didn't suit me at all though one does one's best with whatever fashion comes along. Yes, I do think these suit me." And he spread them out for Danny to admire.

Since the angel now seem in better humour, Danny felt he could ask a few questions that had occurred to him about angels and heaven and God and Jesus at school and Sunday school but didn't dare ask, not even Robbie.

"Ah," he faltered and then continued, "does God not care that you are... not working real hard? We are caned in school if we don't work hard."

"God!" exclaimed Angel Jo," "God!" "Haven't you 'earth-grubbers' heard? God's has disappeared. We haven't seen hilt or hair of God for years."

Danny should have been shocked by this news given his mammy's belief in never ending prayers, Ballybracken's churches storming heaven day and night with their prayers, and the holy Ballybracken folk who attended the Reverend Quigley's mission hall where they prayed about everybody and everything from the King and Queen to the weather. But he was not really surprised at all. From his experience of his own simple prayers asking for this and that like that God might take away his stutter, that the Dowdells might have a chicken for their dinner more often - for eating chicken was, in Danny's view, the height of luxury - but no matter how hard he prayed, none of it ever happened. So now he learned that God had disappeared… well, that explained it, and it also explained why Robbie was forever reading bits out of his paper about the world being in a terrible state. So little use continuing to say 'Our Father, who art in Heaven' for according to the angel, He wasn't there at all.

"How did it happen… God disappearing, I mean?" Danny asked in a totally matter of fact way and out of genuine interest, for, as we now know, our little hero was a very inquisitive boy.

"Well, there are lots of theories of course," said Angel Jo, "one is that He may have blown Himself up... just went too close to the big bag of universe mixture and BANG... He was a gonner! Of course, he is God, so my own view is that He is still knocking around somewhere out there. After he had created a universe, he always took the seventh day off to rest up and sometimes that got a bit extended to a rest cure of a few million years, so I suppose He may pull himself together sometime, and get back to us."

The angel gave a little giggle at his own joke. "It was odd really," he continued, "there He was rolling out perfect universe after perfect universe, some real master pieces, all exuding sweetness and light and not an awkward 'earth- grubber-type' living on any of them when suddenly He seemed to just… well… lose his touch. Result was at least two of the last universes He created were deeply flawed… I daren't tell you what goes on in them… and then their yours, the most awful mess of the lot! We know that you earthlings really depressed Him big time, which may be another reason why he disappeared. Acute depression brought on by your ridiculous antics down here. He just couldn't bear to watch so may just have decided He'd had enough and went 'walk-about.'"

Angel Jo now looked accusingly at Danny as if he was somehow to blame for the failings of mankind and the disappointment of the Almighty.

"With God away, who's the Big Boss up there now?"

Angel Jo gave a sharp intake of breath as if bracing himself for another awful revelation.

"Would you believe, little man, heaven is now run by a committee!" He ran one of his delicate white hands across a wing as if to comfort himself.

"What's that?" asked Danny. "A committee, I mean?

"Well, it can best be described as a bunch of self-important folk who think they know it all, holding never ending meetings, circulating long boring papers about everything under the stars and planets, setting up consultation groups who never consult anybody worth consulting, working groups that sit about squabbling all day about their agenda, sub-groups of working groups that forget what they were asked to do and so do anything that comes into their heads. Committees! Hopeless! The road to nowhere! Ours is called the 'Brilliant Organizers of the Angelic Kingdom' or 'BOAK' for short. If it ever makes a decision, which is seldom, it is either unintelligible, unworkable or both. They haven't a clue what it is like out there in the universes or the problems we labouring angels face. Is it any wonder we are on a work-to-rule!"

"I suppose not," said Danny. "Are there not a lot of very holy saints up there who could help the… the committee?" Danny struggled with the unfamiliar word. "My mammy is always praying to them like to St Anthony, I think it is, when she loses something or to Jesus's mammy, Mary, when she's really desperate, which is a lot of the time. She's even got a plastic statue of Jesus's mammy filled with holy water on the fire-board in the kitchen."

"Oh, the Holy Saints are all up there looking for their great reward, some more worthy of it than others, let me tell you! Actually, you never met a more boring crowd… and now they do nothing but complain since BOAK has reallocated them to other duties on top of listening to people's prayers. They have now been made chairmen of all the working groups, sub-committees, drafting councils and all that carry on. And believe me they are not a bunch of happy haloes. Well, would you be if you had denied yourself lots of nice thing here on earth and had gone around caring for everybody and generally being sickeningly good only to find that your reward in heaven is to chair a committee? Like us angels, I think they have every right to be really cross."

He paused as if trying to remember something. "Your mother prays to St Anthony, you say. I think he might not be in charge of helping to find things nowadays. That may have been reallocated to another one of them. It's hard to keep up really since I'm so busy and seldom there, and it's impossible to read all the papers BOAK flings at us across the universes. Half of it never arrives since Gabriel was relieved of the post of messenger and reallocated to 'Heavenly Co-ordination' whatever that is? But I'll find out about Anthony and let you know next time. It is a disgrace if your mother is praying to the wrong one just because nobody has been notified of the changes."

"It doesn't matter to me," Danny said. "I think I'm a Prod... something; anyway, whatever I am, we don't have much to do with saints, but I suppose they don't care since they are all so busy. They wouldn't have time for us anyway."

"All very confusing, this Catholic Protestant thing," mused the angel, "but I suppose it's just part of God getting your universe and you earthlings so wrong. However, enough of this. I can't stay here all night. I am breaking the work-to- rule by coming after working hours, you know, but I'll do nothing at all tomorrow to keep myself right with the Angels' Guild. Now, is there anything I can do for you, Daniel Malachy Dowdells?"

"I wonder if you could cure my stutter?" said Danny. "That's all I want really. Then I might get a good job and help mammy pay the rent and for the groceries, and maybe have a really big chicken for the dinner now and again."

"Oh, I'm not too sure about that," said the angel. "There is a strict rule from BOAK that we must never interfere with anything that would change you 'earth-grubbers' fate. We used to be able to have great fun messing around with all of you but, after that disaster of over-egging the Ancient Greeks that had them inventing all those dangerous inquisitive 'ologies', BOAK put a stop to it. 'Never interfere' is their current motto. One of the few things they have ever firmly decided. You see the thinking up there is that, in cases like yours if you could speak clearly, who knows maybe you'd end up shouting and screaming like, well, that Hitler fiasco and we all know how that ended! Oh, dear me no, little man, BOAK is bound to find out sooner or later that I've been tinkering with you, as it calls it, so I daren't. Really sorry, but no can do."

"Oh well, "said Danny, "that was all I'd like really but if you can't do it, that fine."

In fact, it wasn't fine. It was very disappointing but what else could our little hero say? He just curled up in bed and started to suck his thumb.

Angel Jo looked taken aback at the thought that his powers might be finite for, even on this our first acquaintance with him, we will have deduced that he is a somewhat self-admiring celestial body who has clearly been thrown by Danny's suggestion that he might not be able to do something. He said,

"Oh, I can do it by just snapping my fingers, but I'd be taking a big risk what with me hoping to be on the next list for promotion to arch-angel." After a moment's reflection, he continued, "I tell you what though, Daniel Malachy, since you admired my wings, I WILL ask them about curing your stammer! Now how's that! I'll put up a paper to BOAK and tell them that you are a little nobody and that I'm convinced that curing your problem won't make you any more of a nobody, so we won't really be interfering with fate down here at all. Now I can only try. Mind you, BOAK will put it out to one of the saintly sub-committees who will set up a working group and maybe a consultancy group and on it will go as I explained a minute ago. We may not get an answer for a while; in fact, we may not get an answer until long after you're dead, you earthlings live such a ridiculously short time."

"Thanks for trying for me," said Danny. "It's just that for the first time ever I have been able to talk to somebody without stuttering and it's great, so if you could ever get my stutter fixed for good, I could talk to everybody the way I have been talking to you. "

"I'll see what I can do. Let's live in hope that I might get approval to change it permanently but whatever happens, you will always be talking to your old guardian angel pal in proper English without your 'stutter' and not in that awful Ballybracken-speak. Won't that be great?"

This limited transformation in his speech seemed to Daniel Malachy something of a one-sided blessing since it benefitted Angel Jo mainly, but he said nothing.

"Now I must away," said the angel beaming and spreading his wings apparently for Danny to admire again for it wasn't to fly as he seemed to be disappearing off the end of the bed in a sort of drizzly mist.

"When will I see you again with the answer about my stutter?" said Danny hurriedly.

"I'll be in touch when I have time whether I have an answer or not," said Angel Jo, and with that he shimmered into nothingness on the bed end.

"Oh well," said Danny to himself snuggling down, "I suppose it was a dream.

Pity, I liked the angel, but if he was real wouldn't it be great if he got permission to cure my stutter."

Real or not, as he went to sleep, Danny decided to tell Robbie the interesting things he had heard about heaven, but he wouldn't tell nobody else. He knew they would only laugh at him.

Episode 4

Pigs, Sponge Cakes and the Boys in Black

The Rich McKendrys

"Come on, little comrade, get in step with the workers." Robbie was marching down Ringsend to the McKendry estate, a large wooden mallet over his shoulder and a bulging knapsack on his back with Danny hopping and skipping along behind him trying to keep up. They were going to kill pigs this morning, and though Danny didn't know what exactly that entailed, he was feeling good for wasn't it big men's work 'killin' pigs.'

The McKendry Estate yard was in much better shape than the Roxborough's on the other side of the river, the latter dependent on old money fast running out, the former riding high on new money with apparently no end to it. As they entered the yard through the arch in the old bell tower, a large Bentley nosed its way into the yard from the wider entrance opposite, a bespectacled man at the wheel, and with two lady passengers.

"Good mornin, Boss," said Robbie touching his cap, "an' good mornin, ladies."

George McKendry - Commander of the British Empire, Justice of the Peace, Unionist County Counsellor, Worshipful Master of the Royal Black Preceptory Lodge, District Commandant of the B-Special Constabulary and something equally big in the Masonic Order - greeted Robbie with a welcoming smile.

"Ah, good man, Robbie, I'll be with you in a minute."

"Good morning, Robbie," gushed his wife adjusting her large picture hat as she stepped from the front passenger seat, "and is this Rosie's boy, young Daniel? My, he's getting so big, I'd hardly know him. Now you'll both come in for some tea when you're finished, won't you?"

"Thanks, mam, we'll be glad to," said Robbie, and Danny felt a glow come over him at the thought of maybe buns, cake and biscuits with the promised tea.

The passenger who had been sitting in the back seat of the Bentley had emerged slowly carrying a bulging shopping bag and a large brown parcel. She gave Robbie and Danny a bleak smile, and said to her two travelling companions,

"I'd better go and check that mother has got her morning coffee." This was Mina McKendry, the Boss's spinster sister, her voice as ever one of martyrdom, and her disappointments in life etched on her strained wintry face.

"Right, Mina," said Mrs. McKendry. "You'll find those marshmallows that she likes in the pantry, and don't forget her glass of sherry. I forgot it yesterday, and she was not well pleased."

Danny was standing on a three-legged stool with only his eyes visible over the half door of the pig sty as Robbie went about the pig killing. But they are lovely pigs, Danny thought as his big hero cornered them, hit them over the head with the wooden mallet before cutting their throats with a big butcher knife. There was blood everywhere, and before long Danny could watch no longer though he could still hear the poor pigs squealing with terror. One of them even put its snout over the half door trying to get away and from the look in its terrified eyes, Danny thought it was pleading for him to help it. After that, he sat on the stool with his back to the sty door and tried not to cry as the pitiful loud grunting and screaming continued. At last there was silence except for Robbie casually whistling and sweeping up. As he pulled back the bolt on the half door, Danny jumped off the stool and turned away to hide his tear-stained face as Robbie emerged with his overalls covered in vivid clotted red blood.

"Well, how did yeh lake me murdering the poor wee pigs?" asked Robbie as Danny stood staring up at him in a sort of horrified wonder.

"It wuz good," Danny lied for he must appear to be a big man, and then added, "do yeh lake killin them, Robbie?"

At that precise moment, our hero was really in a state of shock at what he had just seen Robbie doing, and badly wanted to recapture in his mind the man who was his big war hero, and not a pig murderer. Robbie might be restored to the place Danny held for him in his heart if he would only say "Naw!" and that he didn't like killing the pigs. But Robbie only said,

"It has to be done, Danny, may owl comrade. Your mammy wudn't hiv them nice slices aff bacon for ye'r dinner, an' sure fried bacon is wan aff yeh'r favourites, isn't it?" And he began changing into a fresh pair of overalls that he had taken from the knapsack.

With himself tidied up, Robbie said,

"Right, Danny, we'll wash our hands at the pump yonner, son, and then we'll go an' get that tay we wur promised."

The McKendry's kitchen was big, warm and smelt of baking bread. Hanna McKendry, a plump woman her face a little overdone with lipstick, powder and rouge from her shopping expedition greeted them again with a warm smile.

"The tea is just on the draw," she said, "and Mina made sponge cakes yesterday, so you can both try a wee taste of that if you'd like. Help yourself to milk and sugar, Robbie. Maybe Daniel would prefer a glass of milk instead of tea. Would you, Danny love?"

Danny knew that big boys drank tea, but he decided to postpone his ambition to becoming a big boy with the prospect of milk and the delicious-looking cake. Robbie winked at him as Mrs. McKendry placed a big slice of the sponge on his plate, and an even larger slice in front of Robbie.

"Do you know," she continued, "I do believe I have some apple tart left over from yesterday. Maybe you would both like a slice of that too."

Robbie didn't demur much to Danny relief, and the apple tart was duly produced from a new fridge under the draining board at the sink.

"Isn't this the great new gadget?" Hanna remarked as she made a show of opening the fridge door. She would like the new acquisition to be talked about around Ballybracken, and what better way than to show it off to visitors. "Of course, we can only have these wonderful gadgets, and the Godsend of electricity all around the place, because the Boss had the vision to install that generator so that we could make our own. But it is such a pity that the television signal still can't reach us down here. George was going to buy a set so that we could enjoy watching the Coronation but sure there's no point. Will the government up at Stormont ever get us up to date with mains electricity, do you think? It would be such a blessing for the farmers. Where would we be now, with such a big milking herd, if we didn't generate our own electric to run the milking machine? They do say that the farms in the Republic are nearly all electrified now but, as usual, our politicians lag behind. Do you know, I sometimes wonder if they ever think about us farmers here west of the river Bann up there at Stormont?"

'Aye,' Robbie thought, *'an' that's not the ony way the self-satisfied Unionist tribe up in Belfast neglect the country an' do all in their power to resist any of Westminster's social reforms that might improve everybody's lot, especially the poor. But wuzn't that*

the real purpose of this wilful neglect! The poor, both Protestant and Catholic, might get above themselves an' begin to question their lot in holy loyalist Ulster. An' the Catholic boyos were no better, the 'big bugs' with the turned collars an' fancy rigouts up in Armagh an' down in Dublin all hell-bent on wrecking the government welfare reforms both North and South. What a country!'

These thoughts welled up from Robbie's past, but he knew better than to voice them. Instead he launched himself at Hanna's delicious apple tart.

Just then, Selina McKenna, one of the maids threw open the door leading to the servants' hall. She was followed by Mina McKendry.

"I've been giving these hard-working men some of your sponge cake, Mina, for you know it will not keep."

Miss McKendry pursed her thin lips, gave a dry little cough which was apparently meant to indicate her approval, and then disappeared into the scullery. Selina staggered after her carrying a big basket. When she got to the scullery door she placed it on the kitchen floor pretending it was to get a better grip but really because she wanted to catch Robbie's eye. His gaze had been following her, and he now took his cue and gave her a knowing wink. Danny noticed that Robbie winked and whistled a lot at girls so that must be something else that big men did. Now and again Danny practiced winking and whistling when there was nobody around but so far, he had to admit that he wasn't much good at either and certainly couldn't do both at the same time.

Hanna bustled over to the table with more tea for Robbie and to top up Danny's glass of milk. Robbie looked at her and pondered, as he now started on his second helping of apple tart, on how this nice generous woman was so bitterly resented in the townland. Of course, he knew well enough that her background told against her, something you could never escape in the narrow society that comprised Ballybracken.

And here, in pursuing our quest to learn all we can about Ballybracken folk in all their colourful variety we must leave, however briefly, Robbie and Master Daniel Malachy enjoying their sponge cake and apple tart in McKendry's comfortable kitchen to learn of Hanna McKendry's former perilous existence, and the quirks and turns of fate that had her serving such culinary delights that morning as the wife of the most prominent and the wealthiest man in Ballybracken, and indeed much further afield. Hanna's is a story that must surely alert us to the strange tricks quirky fate can play on us sometimes for better, sometimes for worse.?

Hanna – Poor Little Rich Girl

For Hanna was a foundling retrieved from the Church of Ireland Adoption Society in Dublin, and this background she was never allowed to forget in censorious Ballybracken. After a girlhood skivvying unendingly for her adopted parents, she got a lucky break when George McKendry fell head-over-heels in love with her. But a woman with her background marrying into such wealth caused resentment of the most malicious kind among Ballybracken folk, and even her mother-in-law let it be known that she did not approve of her son '*marrying a foundling so far beneath him,*' and that she had set her heart on him marrying one of Sir Thomas Roxborough's genteel if impoverished sisters. Hanna's bulwark against such envy and hostility was George's unshakeable love for he was that somewhat unusual male, a one-girl guy. Also shielding her was his unassailable position as the leader in the Unionist community and the wealth he commanded for, as always and everywhere, money means power, security and respect however grudging. And Hanna herself showed spirit and great resolve. She had no intention of apologizing for her existence or donning sackcloth and ashes to atone for the so-called sins of others, and worked hard at endearing herself, through acts of generosity and kindness, to those who did accept her. Those of the brackish folk who did not could look elsewhere for a victim; she was resolved to enjoy the comfortable life that fate, in its capricious way, had vouchsafed to her, and to carry the day.

So that is Hanna's story as we observe her putting a large roast into the Aga cooker in McKendry's kitchen where Daniel Malachy has found it impossible to refuse another slice of the delicious sponge cake. For Robbie's part, our soldier man has just had the odd realization that he probably understood Hanna McKendry better than anybody in Ballybracken. Despite their differences in wealth and position, both she and he were outsiders to the good folk of the townland, she because of her recherché background and the begrudged good fortune of fate, he because of his experiences in a world beyond Ballybracken's comprehension and now living unchurched in sin with a Catholic woman.

"She is a nice woman, isn't she? I like her… and her nice cakes," Danny said as they walked home, our little hero feeling overfull and mildly sick.

Danny Dowdells

Joining the Boys in Black

Before they left McKendrys, the conversation had inevitably come around to everybody's current pre-occupation with the latest IRA campaign and the recent attack on the local army barracks. George had reappeared in the kitchen and had stood listening for a few minutes. He said,

"Speaking of which, Robbie, I'm wondering if you could be persuaded to join the B-Special Constabulary? As the local Commandant, the wonder is that I didn't think of asking you before for it is men like yourself we need if it comes to an all-out fight with the Irish Republicans, as I think it might. A well-trained army man like you would be a godsend to my platoon. You know, our Unionist grandees in Belfast and the east of this Province don't know the score here west of the Bann. The Unionist majority in the east can rest easy but here in the west, where we are fifty-fifty at best, it is a different story. We are under siege and could be overwhelmed by one type of Irish Republican or Nationalist group or another at any time. As in the past, we mustn't give in or show signs of wavering or we are done for."

"I would certainly consider joining the B-Specials for it would be good to be back in a uniform and hold a rifle again."

"That's great," McKendry said, "the next drill night is on Thursday next. Come along and we'll start signing you up, and getting you in."

"Are you really gonna get a uniform an' a gun?" Danny enquired as they neared Rosie's, his admiration for Robbie knowing no bounds at this prospect. Able to kill pigs with a mallet and knife and now maybe kill people with a gun. Wasn't Robbie great!

"Looks like it, may owl comrade," replied Robbie. He was pleased to be asked to join for the present IRA campaign had been worrying him for some time. As an Ulsterman and proudly British, he had come to the view that the Irish Republic into which the 'freedom-fighters' were so keen to sink the Six Counties was an even worse country to live in than the bigoted North if you weren't a Catholic and fully signed up to kowtow to all their particular religious strictures. Where was there any semblance of the true republican spirit of '*Liberty, Equality Fraternity,*' that any sensible man could support? His reading had led him to the view that Irish Republicanism had long since parted company with its 18th Century liberal enlightened roots and was just narrow Catholic Nationalism by another name. *'In every way, a good match for the narrow Protestant Unionism on this side of the border,'* he thought but at least the Northern blaggarts were his own blaggarts, and that made a difference. The B-men he knew genuinely felt they were defending their country so why hold back? A United Ireland might be worth considering if there were safeguards for his Britishness, but he was damned if he was going to be forced into the existing sectarian Republic by IRA bombs and bullets.

Only Dreams?

Danny decided it was now time to impress Robbie and show him he was a big important man too. The moment had come to tell him about the angel in the hope that Robbie, who read so much, thought so much, and had so much to tell him about everything, would be impressed by what Angel Jo had told him about heaven and all that. So he told him. Robbie stopped in his stride, stood listening leaning on his mallet and looking at the ground so that Danny could not see his reaction. When he looked up he was smiling. He said,

"Listen, little comrade. I wouldn't bother tellin anybody about your angel... ony me. Do yeh hear me? Sure you're the best man I know at tellin good stories, an' haven't yeh the quare imagination. That a great story but yeh put it out of ye'r min for yeh niver know where it might lead. Will yeh do that for me, wee comrade?"

This hadn't gone as Danny had wanted.

"I didn't make it up," he said, sorry now that he had told Robbie, and disappointed at his big hero's reaction.

"I'm sure yeh didn't," Robbie could see he had hurt the boy's feelings and wanted to put it right. "But yeh know, Danny, sometimes we have very rail dreams that seem so rail when we waken we think what happened to us in them really did happen. Do you think I might be right about your angel?"

"Well... maybe I wuz dreamin. Aye, I think I might hiv been," he said reluctantly.

"Good lad," Robbie said putting a reassuring hand on Danny's shoulder, "... but sure wuzn't it a great dream. And wudn't it be great if it was true. I'd love to see the faces of this townland's 'Holy Rollers' on both sides if they ever got to hear that God hez gone walkabout!"

"I wudn't tell nobody else," Danny hastened to reassure him. "I ony wanted to tell you. But what happens if Angel Jo is allowed by his Big Bosses up in heaven to cure may stutter, you'll hiv tay believe it wuzn't a dream an' is true then?"

"If that happens, I will, Danny, I promise I will believe in your angel."

They walked on and were rounding the gable of Rosie's house when Robbie said, "Be God, is that bacon I smell fryin? Are yeh still sorry for the wee pigs now, Danny? Yeh can't have ye'r pig and ate it, wee comrade!"

Episode 5

Cherries, Bribes and Wrong Answers

Yielding to Temptation

On the Sunday afternoon after the pig killing, Robbie and Danny were walking along the banks of the Mourne River with fishing rods and nets, for Sir Thomas Roxborough had given Robbie permission to fish and shoot on his estate anytime he wanted. Robbie had selected a good location near the 'Meetins' where they had already spotted the odd fish jumping much to Danny's excitement.

They were sitting on the bank having cast their lines when two figures appeared walking arm in arm just where the two rivers met but on the opposite bank. They recognized one of the young women as McKendry's maid, Selina McKenna. The other was a stranger.

"How are yez, girls?" Robbie shouted. "Yez is out for a stroll."

"Aye, we are surely," said Selina, "but what's it tay you, Robbie?" And they both took a fit of giggling.

"Ach sure it always nice tay see good-lookin girls dannerin[61] about on a sunny day," said Robbie. "Who's your friend?"

"She's may cousin home from Englan come over tay see me for the day."

"Englan?" said Robbie. "I'm sure she'll be able tay tell yeh a whole lot about the capers of the fellas there, a good-lukin girl like that. Not that she's a patch on yourself, Selina, for yeh know rightly I have eyes for nobody else but you."

"Ye'r an owl cod, Robbie," Selina said, "an' ye'r putting bad into that wee lad's head. Come on, Siobhan, we'd better get back. Sure there nothing for us here."

They turned, pretending to go, when Robbie said, "Siobhan is it? That's a quare good Irish name fir a fine-lukin blade[62]. Wud yez not lake tay come across here over the foot-stick[63], an' I'll show yez aroun?"

"What's over there that wud bay aff interest tay us?" Selina demanded.

"You niver wud know. I might be able to surprise yez. Sure, wudn't yez lake

---

61 **Dannerin** – strolling
62 **Blade** – attractive young girl
63 **Foot-stick** – improvised wooden bridge for pedestrians only

tay take a skelly[64] roun the 'Ladies' Bower' up yonner? Ach, come on ahead. Wat's howlin yez[65]?"

The girls turned away, again making to leave. Robbie rose saying to Danny,

"You stay here, son, whatever happens, an' watch the lines. If they come across, leave them tay me an' don't follow me, sure yeh won't. I'm off tay pick a few cherries if I get the chance."

"Come on, girls," he said, "I'll give yez a hand crossin the foot-stick for it can be a bit slippy but the watter bez low this time a year so yez'll harly get wet-shod even of yez fal in[66] ... an' sure I'm here tay save yez."

He positioned himself at the end of the primitive contraption and held out his hands to encourage them.

"Naw, Robbie," Selina said, "we'd be heart skared tay cross. Sure, isn't this where that grand lady fell in an' got drownded some years back? Sure, why don't yeh come over tay this side?"

That was invitation enough. Robbie expertly crossed to the McKendry bank and immediately positioned himself between the two girls, quickly and expertly putting an arm round each. They put up a pretence of objecting, but clearly didn't really mind. After a few minutes chatting, they all headed off upstream on the far bank with Robbie their man of the moment. They had only gone a few yards when, looking back, Robbie saw our little hero's crestfallen face.

"Danny, I'll be back soon. If it comes on tay rain make for the shelter aff the 'Bower' up yonner."

"Aye, Danny," Selina shouted over her shoulder. "He might be back sooner than he thinks."

And with that, all three disappeared into a stand of trees preserved by the McKendry's gamekeeper as cover for game fowl.

Danny was cross with Robbie for deserting him for the girls. He would have liked to help them pick cherries, though it was news to him that there were cherry trees somewhere over on the far bank. With the two fishing lines dangling listlessly in the water and never a bite, our little hero was bored. The afternoon

---

64 **Skelly** – brief look at
65 **Wat's howlin yez** – what is holding you back?
66 **The watter bez low at this time a year so yez'll harly get wet-shod even if yez fal in** – you will hardly get your feet wet even if you fall in

sun was shining through big watery clouds, it was sultry and hot and soon Danny felt sleepy. He lay back on the grass, his hands clasped behind his head and his eyes closed imagining picking and eating cherries somewhere over there across the river.

BOAK's Decision

He had not been musing long when something with a sharp point was dropped into his mouth. He sat up abruptly spitting out a feather, and ready to do battle with Robbie who he thought had returned and was playing tricks on him. Then he saw it… a beautiful snow-white dove hovering just above him, its wings beating furiously. Danny jumped to his feet and made a grab for the bird's legs. But there was nothing there. Instead he found himself looking up at the angel.

"At last," said Angel Jo plopping down beside him on the grass. "I thought I'd never get your attention. How have you been? Going on fine? I don't think I need to worry about you, do I? Oh good, for I'm so busy I hardly know whether I'm coming or going."

"Did you have to waken me that way?" Danny said crossly, spitting out the remains of the feather. "I don't like feathers, they make me sneeze."

"Oh, you're never satisfied," said Angel Jo crossly. "Much more of this sulking and I'll never come back at all to hear about your problems." And he went into a sulk his head to one side that reminded Danny of the stone angels that adorned some of the headstones of the rich people in Ballybracken graveyard.

"I'm sorry," Danny said limply, for he never wanted to offend anybody in heaven or earth.

The angel turned towards him and spread his wings. "How do you like them now? he asked, his previous pout forgotten. "Notice the difference?" And he paused, waiting for the admiration he expected was on its way.

Danny didn't notice any difference, but he thought he had better say something, so he just said, "Oh… yes… they are… very nice."

"Very nice!" exploded the angel, "'very nice!' Is that all you can say after I've had the tips singed and curled? And all you can say is 'very nice.'"

Danny could only reply, "very… very… nice," again, and after a pause "… very nice indeed."

"Oh well," said the Angel, "what can I expect from an 'earth-grubber.' I told them up there it is all a total waste of my time being assigned to this silly earth place, and do you know what they said? 'Write us a paper on it! Put it into the system!' And we all know what that means! Nothing will ever happen. Nothing at all. So, I just couldn't be bothered. Leave it, Jo, I said to myself… just leave it. So here I am again on mission impossible to guard you. I hope you realize the trouble you are."

"Have they given you permission to cure my stutter? If I had it cured, you really wouldn't need to be bothered with me again."

"Oh YES!" exclaimed the angel suddenly drawing himself up in his self-important way. "I do have news for you about that. I am really surprised for they can take literally ages to get back with a decision about anything. But, yes, I have got an answer for you."

"What is it?" said Danny, the simplicity of his question concealing his anxiety and raised expectations.

"Well now," said the Angel, "I put it up in a long paper about you to BOAK, I suppose you don't remember that they are the heavenly ruling committee just now."

"I do mind that," Danny said. "That is what Bobby used to do when he was a babby and mammy gave him too much milk. He boaked all over her blouse."

"Be that as it may," said Angel Jo sniffily, clearly not too taken with this glimpse of domesticity in the Dowdells's household, "well, I put your case and, as I predicted, BOAK passed it to a sub-committee chaired, would you believe, by St Malachy himself, after whom I assume you are named. Great piece of luck, I thought, for surely Malachy would look favourably on this little problem of his namesake who is such a pathetic nobody stammering around here on this ridiculous piece of rock. Bit of luck for me too really. None of my papers have ever been considered by so grand a committee before. St Malachy! … imagine him scrutinizing my work! At last I'd hit the big time. And that sub-committee has a lot of other Irish Saints on it too… I think St Brigid's there… St Aiden certainly but not St Patrick unfortunately. He's on the committee that has to do with bits and pieces in the USA. And has he made a job of that! I'll say he has. He's peppered them with a real propaganda blitz all about himself and, naughty saint that he is - for hardly any of it's true - he has succeeded in going down big over there. Just goes to show what blowing your own trumpet can do. Mind you, I understand the others on his committee aren't too happy about his US ego trip, but he's such a presence, they daren't challenge him."

This lapse into heavenly politics annoyed Danny, and he wanted to shout, "but have they allowed you to cure my stutter?"

If the Angel sensed Danny's impatience, he was ignoring it intent as he was on milking the situation and keeping our hero in suspense. "So anyway," he said, "back to your little problem."

"It's not a little problem to me," Danny said. "Everybody makes fun of me, and teases me and bullies me, so if you could get on with it and cure me that would be great, and then I'd show them all."

But the angel was not to be hurried." Mind you," he said, " the problem with having a lot of Irish on anything is that they will talk - never-ending debates, useless arguments, and they love sub-groups and splinter groups and all that kind of timewasting nonsense so, although I was in high hopes of us getting the answer we want, I thought it might take even longer to get a decision and you might be dead a thousand years before we got a reply from them, which wouldn't be much good to you really, would it?."

"No, it wouldn't," Danny agreed, "so, anyway, they haven't told you the answer yet," he ended bleakly, and felt like crying.

"Oh, they have, they have, they have," shouted the angel triumphantly, "and their answer is emphatically NO! I'm sorry, Daniel Malachy, I did my best but they wouldn't hear of it. Tinkering's OUT! And BOAK said I should know better than even to ask... though St Malachy wrote such nice things on my proposal paper so it wasn't all a waste of time. I think I've finally caught their eye and just might be on my way to becoming an Angelic Supervisor, and all because of your stammer. Isn't that great? It's an ill wind... or heavenly zephyr as we say up there."

The angel ended on a high note clearly oblivious of Danny's disappointment. He felt very cross.

"That all right for you, but I'm very disappointed. You're supposed to be my guardian angel, but you do nothing for me."

"Well, if I hadn't saved you from being drowned at this very spot years ago, you wouldn't be here at all... just think of that... it was 'tinkering' big-time and could have got me struck off but I took a chance with you, I was going to say 'heaven knows why' but actually heaven doesn't know about that bit of forbidden tinkering, and I need to keep it that way if I'm to get on up there. I don't know why I bothered saving you but, as I say, I'm just an old softie. And what thanks do I get for all I've done for you? None at all. You are a very ungrateful boy, Daniel Malachy, very ungrateful, and I'm very disheartened."

"And so am I." Our hero was beside himself with anger, all his disappointments of the afternoon welling up. "What good is it if you can't cure my stutter which is all I need. You might as well go away and never come back. I'm sure you never told them everything, like that I would try my best not to turn into Hitler if you cured me. I'm sure you never said all that in your paper."

Danny had enquired from Robbie who Hitler was, and he really didn't sound like the kind of man Danny would want to turn into.

"Oh, I did, I did, I put it all down. Said you were unlikely to turn into a rabble rouser, and pointed out to them that, anyway, Ireland already has so many of them you'd be lucky to find a slot to start shouting even if you wanted to. I emphasized that I was certain you would not try to take over anything and that you would always be an earth-grubbing nobody. I even got St Francis to sign my paper for he loves nobodies and animals and plants and all that sort of thing. It would have helped if he had been on the committee but unfortunately, he's been banned from all committees because he's no good at the paperwork. Just couldn't get the hang of agendas and minutes and action plans and all that stuff that BOAK think is essential up there now. Anyway, it was no good, you'll just have to stammer your way all through life. Pity, but there it is. If it hadn't been for Malachy liking my paper – 'elegant' he called it – I'm sure I would have got a severe wrap over the knuckles for writing on such a trivial nobody as you. Believe me, I tried everything and got nowhere so… " he tailed off "… did I say nowhere? Well, not quite. I have one piece of good news that I hope will cheer you up. They have agreed you can be a beautiful singer and not bad as a musician either. Now, isn't that good news?"

It was not good news for our Daniel Malachy.

"I can sing already," he protested, "for I don't stutter a bit when I'm singing. But I hate singing. The boys say I'm a sissy cos I can sing. I don't want to be a good singer."

Big Bella's Bribe

And here we must again digress briefly to learn why the heavenly musical gift, which would be so welcome to most of us, was such a sore point with our little hero. We need seek no further than the local Anglican Canon as the cause of Daniel Malachy's antipathy to all things musical. Canon Pretyman, for such it was, had been tormenting Danny to get him to join the church choir. This was simply because Danny had shone forth at the last 'Harvest Thanksgiving' service in church when the organ had broken down and everybody had been asked to sing their loudest to compensate. The organist, Big Bella, for the moment redundant, was not to be done out of her moment of the week so she had raised her ample frame from the organ stool, turned around to face the congregation, and had conducted the hymns, her plump arms punishing the air and large white furry hat leaping up and down on her head reminding everyone of the animal the fur must once have graced. As ill fortune would have it, Danny happened to be stuck in front of Big Bella in the row that served as the Sunday school pew, and where all the Sunday school children were held captive to force them to attend the church service that followed Sunday school. By this means, the Canon was guaranteed an audience every Sunday, however small in stature and restless in attention, for his less than stimulating sermons. At this harvest service, few of the hapless children were singing loudly enough despite Bella's baleful glares. At the end of the dismally executed second verse of the first hymn, Bella decided, against her Christian scruples, to resort to crude bribery. She bent down towards the children and whispered loudly:

"If yez will start tay sing up, I'll give yez al a sweet and the best singer will get a shillin."

Now a shilling was not to be sniffed at especially for Danny whose finances were always in an acutely perilous state. He had learned that particular hymn off by heart for Sunday school and right boring he had thought it, but once Big Bella had started the congregation off again he found the tune strangely easy to pick up. There was not a hint of a stutter as he sang out loudly and clearly, and so it was with all the other hymns to the point when it came to the last one the whole congregation had fallen silent to listen in admiration and amazement to Danny's angelic voice. He duly got the promised shilling, and the Canon had there and then declared Danny's was - *'a voice from out of heaven itself'* - while the boys in the school playground next day had said Danny was a *'real owl sissy, an' that ony girls laked singin,'* and then they threw half a bottle of milk over him in the boys' lavatory to make him look powdery white like the sissy girl he was. So Danny never raised his voice to sing beyond a whisper ever after, avoided being in the choir by saying he had a sore stomach or toothache or some other excuse, and beating a hasty retreat out of church after Sunday school to avoid the service, and any further attempts to make him sing. On those Sundays when his excuses worked, he lay low under the arch of Ballybracken Bridge, putting in the time trapping sticklebacks in a jam jar, and then made his way home when he heard people crossing the bridge indicating that church was over, and the coast clear. Rosie had no reason to suspect he was 'mitching,' and he had never told her about the singing incident at the harvest service.

Danny Dowdells

The Unwanted Gift

So now we know why the very last thing Danny wanted to hear from the angel was that he would be a great singer.

"I think it is really very ungrateful of you," Angel Jo was now mightily annoyed too, and going into another of his huffs. "I managed to slip the singing and music bit in at the end of my... 'elegant'... paper and, hey presto, landed it for you. I may tell you I was at considerable pains to get the support of St Cecelia, a lovely woman who just lives for her music but who hasn't time to practice a note these days since she has been lumbered with chairing the 'Celestial Transport and Highways Committee.' And not content with Cecelia's support, I went out of my way to sign up the leader of the 'Multitude of the Heavenly Host,' Angel Rhapsody, one of the most talented angels up there. He hasn't been back much to your planet since the Host sang at Bethlehem a while back. It was very widely reported. I'm sure you must have heard of it, and indeed I believe there are still repercussions from the event they were celebrating then. I tell you, little man, the trouble I have gone to on your behalf, and I say again what thanks do I get?"

"I've told you, I don't want to be a good singer," Danny insisted. "Get them to take that present away from me. I'm never gonna sing again. I hate singing. And I don't play music. I haven't anything to play on – a flute or the bagpipes or an accordion or anything – and I don't want any of them things anyway."

"Now, now, naughty Danny," Angel Jo was attempting to assert himself. "I can't ask them to take these musical presents back from you. Can you imagine the amount of paperwork that would entail for me for a start? I'd be grounded writing it all up for weeks, and I have such a lot on. I shouldn't even be here now. I should be away acting as guardian angel to a little chap on the planet Hysteria in another of God's dreadfully flawed universes before He made your even more dreadful one. You wouldn't believe what is going on there! They have all turned into cannibals and are devouring each other. I ask you! Last time I was with him, my little chap was in danger of ending up in a crusty pie. Plump little thing, I can see why he's caught their eye."

"So, you can save him from cannibals, but you can't cure my stutter. Is that not ...tinkering... like you're not allowed to do?" Again Danny surprised himself by his determination to catch the angel out and put him on the spot.

"Certainly not," said Angel Jo. "We are absolutely forbidden to tinker anywhere in any of the universes. No, I'm only there to take a record of what happens to the poor little chap. Lots more paperwork I'm afraid. Got to be all written up in triplicate and submitted to BOAK, circulated round the relevant sub-committees and lodged in the 'Heavenly Madness Archives.' So lots to do, places to go and madnesses to record. I'm a bit like your United Nations forces I suppose really; *whatever you do, do nothing but always get the paperwork right.* It's not easy holding back at times given my soft heart but there it is, we are where we are. Now, is there anything more I can do for you before I go?"

"No, there's nothing. Will you ever be back?" Not that Danny now cared one way or the other given his big disappointment.

"Certainly," said the angel breezily. "You will always be on my books... unless there is a change of management up above, and then who knows what might happen? Us poor overworked angels are still hoping for a full-blooded uprising to sweep away awful BOAK. There have been rumblings especially from St James and some of those other smouldering Spanish saints. St James has a great track record in slaying people, so that might be promising and could lead to great and terrible things if only he and the Spanish holy brigade up there could agree what language to speak. Hey hum... the devil is always in the detail. Anyway, I'll keep you posted if there is any high drama for you seem a reasonably intelligent little thing... for an earthling that is. Well, I'm off. Bye for now," and he disappeared in the usual misty cloud.

Our little hero lay back on the grass again to wait for Robbie now even crosser with him – indeed with everything - than before. It had been an afternoon drenched in disappointments. After a while, Robbie appeared not looking too pleased with himself.

"Bloody waste aff time," he muttered in Danny's direction as if he had to relieve his feelings on somebody even if only to his little sleeping friend. "But there will always be another day. I'm not beat yet way that Selina wan."

Then he became conscious that Danny was now sitting up and listening, so he said,

"So, how've you been, Danny? Caught any fish?"

"Naw," said Danny coldly. "Did you get any cherries?"

"What?" said Robbie, puzzled.

Episode 6

At McKnight's Shop

Piano Pressure

Fateful for Master Daniel Malachy and his resolve never to sing another note, gift or no gift, was the strange notion his mother took around this time that what she most needed was a piano to move her family up in the world. Pianos were expensive but, by a strange coincidence, she got to know exactly where to lay hands on one that might be going cheap, and nothing was going to stop her acquiring it.

Every Saturday Rosie scrubbed, brushed, dusted and washed, and was generally a maid-of-all-work in McKnight's shop and their adjoining dwelling house. Danny always came with her to polish all the family's shoes for church next day, and do other odd jobs as required. On these Saturday mornings, Helen McKnight practiced her pieces for her music lessons and, as her wonderful playing echoed through the house, Rosie's resolve to acquire a piano for the Dowdells grew in intensity. As we know, sometimes determination coincides with opportunity, and her determination that her daughter, Dorry, would one day play as well as, if not better than, Miss Helen and be *'a lady'* was unexpectedly matched with a possibility. This came in the form of a death and an auction and it was these events that just might get the Dowdells family their piano and, as Rosie saw it, on to the first rung of Ballybracken's social ladder.

"I'm sure you must be nearly finished in the parlour by now, Rosie. Don't let that girl distract you with her music." Mrs. Effie McKnight brooked no loitering. "Get the potatoes scrubbed for the dinner. They are in the sink in the scullery. Then head on up to the shop store and give it a good sweeping out, and I think James will have some other jobs for you in the shop as well."

Rosie picked up her basin and dusters and headed for the scullery.

That Covert 'Petticoat Power'

The fancies and foibles of Mrs. Effie McKnight will now provide us with an instructive case study of selfish tyranny masquerading as selflessness and sweet reason. Effie had recently been widowed and had summoned her only other child, James, home from University, where he had been studying for his BA, to take over the running - however temporarily - of the McKnight's country shop and their substantial farm. James – or Jim as everyone called him except his mother - had returned very willingly for he appreciated his mother and sister's need for immediate support, but he hoped the break in his studies would be temporary and that he could persuade his mother to sell up and move to live with her sister, his aunt Myrtle, on the North Coast. However, as we shall see, Effie had other ideas. This willowy woman with a gimlet eye had unshakable views, and judged the world in general, and the Ballybracken world in particular, through a very narrow focus. Hard work she saw as good for the heaven-bound soul, and earthly profits a sign of God's favour. In girls, she admired 'modesty' and could pay no better compliment than to describe a local girl as 'a modest wee cutty.' This meant, in practice, that the girl in question wore no makeup, had her hair in a Puritan bun, dressed in the fashion of ten years ago, was 'biddable' and 'holy' so never went to dances, and was good at milking and housekeeping. This was the kind of wife she envisaged for her James now she had got him back in Ballybracken and well and truly trapped.

Both her children were clever, but Effie had decreed that girls were in no need of anything but the most basic education so when Helen was trying to study in bed for the entrance exam to get to grammar school, Effie would go round and turn off the gas light *'in case she would ruin her eyes for the sewing.'* Helen never got more than primary education but her competence in music was different in Effie's eyes. Her thinking here was that if Helen was good enough– and Effie was going to see to it that she was more than good enough - she would soon oust Big Bella as church organist, and wouldn't that be a feather in the McKnight's cap! To triumph in church was to triumph where it really mattered in Ballybracken.

Conditioned from her earliest days to her mother's view of the world, Helen, after just one act of defiance involving a tragic affair of the heart, had finally acquiesced, and went under before the tidal wave of her mother's self-serving narrowness. She had long since accepted her role to be the nice 'modest' country girl of her mother's making.

But Jim was different. A spirited boy, as he grew up he refused to bow before the various secular and religious 'altars' in Protestant Ballybracken, and excelling at school had been his way up and out. As he shut up the shop and settled down to his lunch with his mother and sister shortly after one o'clock that Saturday, even he could not have anticipated the web his mother was subtly weaving to fix him permanently in her Ballybracken world.

Effie left Rosie and Danny's lunch on the hatch between the big kitchen and the breakfast room. Rosie brought the beef stew and potatoes over to the breakfast room table and sat down. She forgot to close the hatch, and it was the conversation between Mrs. McKnight and her son that finally landed Rosie her piano.

Rosie's Big Chance

"I hear that old Mrs Ballantine, her that had the farm up there on the edge of the Crockins bog, was got dead by Arty-the-Post last Wednesday. Poor soul, she had nobody... and nobody knew her for she never went out," Effie said, setting the floury potatoes and butter on the kitchen table. "She even got all her groceries from that mobile shop fella that does the rounds. I'm sure he charged her over the odds for she wouldn't have known any difference. Such a terribly lonely life. Arty tells me he found the poor soul lying at the bottom of the stairs, her neck broken. She was a big age of course. Arty had a chance to take a look round while he was waiting for Doctor Johnston to come on the scene, and he tells me that she had a few nice Victorian pieces and a lot of that ruby glass that I like. He also says there is an old wreck of a piano and some other odds and ends of furniture dumped in an outhouse, but it doesn't sound if that would be much good. Still, if there is an auction, I'll be there."

'... an' so,' thought Rosie in mid bite, '... will I. Wrecked or not, I'll hive that piana for it sounds lake nobody else I'll want it. Sure Robbie or somewan cud maybe get it fixed up for me an' it'll do us rightly.'

Fortunately for our Danny's state of mind, given his recent determination to resist all things musical, he had heard none of the McKnight's conversation or knew nothing of his mother's musical ambitions even if, as yet, they were not specifically for him. He was just intent on laying into the nice tasty beef stew.

Effie Springs Her Trap

But Effie McKnight had other things on her mind more important than the death of a lonely old woman away up near the Crockins bog, and a possible auction. She began to spin...

"… I hear that the election for your daddy's seat on the Local Council will be held very soon," she said casually as she harpooned a forkful of beef. "Now James, I know it to have been his deathbed wish for you to stand and to win it in his memory for the Unionists as well as keeping it in the family. Not that I want to put any pressure on you but that was the sort of your father, he always put your and Helen's welfare and advancement first."

"Mother, how many times do I have to tell you, I want to go back to Queen's in the autumn. I don't want to spend my life here in Ballybracken. University has been the greatest thing ever happened to me, I've made good friends there from all sorts of backgrounds, and I just can't wait to get back."

But Effie had carefully rehearsed the line to take to have her way for in this, as in everything, there was her way and the wrong way.

"Well, James, I'll allow[67] of course that it's your decision, and now that your poor father has gone, you are the man of the house. Go back to university certainly if that's your wish. Helen and me will struggle on here as best we can but it won't be easy. The flyboys[68] round here will delight in putting their fingers in the eye[69] of a widow -woman with no man about the place, and as for getting anybody to oversee the work on the farm, well, I don't know? There's nobody suitable comes to mind, and I've thought long and hard about it. It will be a bitter day if we have to sell up especially since I promised your daddy on his deathbed that I'd do my utmost to keep it all together, and do you know what he said: *'Sure you can always depend on James. He's the best son anybody could have, and I know he'll do his duty by you an' Helen and the business.'* That's what he said, sure as Goodness."

She paused to let this piece of blackmail sink in as she wiped what might just have been a tear with the tail of her apron. "Now Helen, get yon apple crumble out of the Esse and the custard in the saucepan. Pass two saucers of it in to that

---

67 **Allow** – *agree*
68 **Fly-boys** – *devious individuals*
69 **Putting their finger in the eye** – *deceiving & cheating*

pair in the breakfast room and bring the rest over."

Jim sat looking down at his empty dinner plate. "If I stay, Mother, I can see the future mapped out for me here as clear as daylight. Do you really want me to spend my life like my father did, a sort of patron saint to the Protestants around here? Getting them a council house over the head of more deserving Catholic families, getting them this and that wee job to keep them out of poverty again over the head of even poorer Catholics. Is that what you really want for me too by trapping me here?"

"There are no traps set by me, James dear, and I'm glad your father's not here to listen to what you've just said. I doubt you have forgotten your Christian duty to your family and indeed to the staunch Protestants and Unionists here in Ballybracken who, whatever you say, have always looked up to our family to give a lead. I only know it would be your daddy's dearest wish for you to take his place on the local council looking after the Protestant interest… and… yes… for that matter his place as well in Ballybracken's Orange and Black lodges. He would have been so proud that a son of his would step forward to fill his boots. I can tell you now that he was never that happy about you going away to Belfast, for he felt that was the danger in highfalutin university education. Our young Protestants going East and never coming back when we need the numbers here west of the Bann to keep us British."

Jim had feared this moment from the hour of his return. The moment when he would have no convincing answer to the charge of family betrayal except to simply walk away. And it was not in his nature to do that. In his heart he knew there was no escape but, in his frustration and anger, he could not resist striking out at his mother.

"Let me tell you something, mother. By getting to Queen's I thought I'd finally escaped all this Ballybracken pressure to sign up in the Orange, the Black, the Apprentice Boys, the B-Specials, the Local Council, for do you know what all these outfits are… poor deluded Protestants are for that matter… all my father was? Stooges and lackeys of Mother England and her fast vanishing Empire. And I can assure you, mother, that the English ruling classes don't give a damn about us and neither do the big - house ruling Unionist hacks up in Stormont. We think we are holding the fort here in Protestant Ballybracken for King and Country against a tide of Irish Nationalism and British socialism. But it's a lost cause. The Catholics are outnumbering us by the day, and socialist measures are just what poor Protestants and Catholics need to lift them out of the poverty that the big - house Unionists and, disgracefully, the Catholic hierarchy too want to keep them in to copper fasten their hold on power. Look around you, and you'll see I'm right."

He pushed the remains of his dinner away and was angry with himself for he hadn't wanted to turn on his mother. But his outburst told Effie she was winning though she was shrewd enough not to be triumphant. Far be it from her to lay herself open to the accusation of exercising 'petticoat power.' No, it was the men, of course, who made the decisions, guided to the correct ones by those who knew the right course to take. To Effie, having her way and winning was all that mattered. Her son's hopes and ambitions – inconceivable in her narrow view of the world - were as nothing compared with her's. She had bent him to her will skilfully invoking his dead father's alleged hopes, reminding him of his Christian and filial duty, and deploying just the right amount of artful blackmail. He was now safely lodged at the centre of her web.

All she said was, "I know that like your father you're easy riz[70] and sure that's no bad failin. I just hope you don't come to regret that university smart talk."

Jim got up from the table and opened the door between the kitchen and the shop. 'Smart talk!' Yes, he got it! Perish the thought that any fresh thinking might challenge the status quo in Ballybracken. But he was beaten and he knew it, so why hold out? Looking back at his mother, and though still very angry and resentful, he said "I'll stay... I'll tell the university I'm not coming back... but I'm not joining anything or running in any elections. Let that be clearly understood. Now don't go harpin-on[71] about it anymore, mother."

"Och you're a good son, and your father would be the happy man this day. Now go on, son, for I see there a car at the petrol pumps and we can ill afford to be turning away customers."

Jim returned to the shop outwitted and boxed in. And he knew in his heart that this was only the start. There would be no escape. He would of course shortly be joining the Orange and Black Lodges and all the other British bastions in this outpost of the vanishing Empire for, whatever history had taught him about the steady demise of that Empire, Protestant Unionist Ballybracken dare not let itself believe so. To do that would be the start of surrendering to 'them', and that was unthinkable.

---

70 **Easy riz** – *quick tempered… quick to get angry*
71 **Harpin- on** – *continuing to raise some issue when it has already been resolved*

Rosie had heard all of this through the open hatch, and Danny too, as he finished his dinner, had become aware of the man's angry voice rising and falling. He was puzzled why anyone who had a shop full of penny chews, gob stoppers, brandy balls and so many other nice things could get so cross? What had he to be cross about?

Helen dutifully rose from the table glad to escape from the tense scene that had ruined her dinner. She loved her brother but from past experience had good reason to fear her mother, so there could be no question of not acquiescing in whatever she decreed.

Effie started to carry the dinner dishes to the pantry and for the first time noticed the open hatch between the kitchen and the breakfast room. She put her head through and said, "Right Rosie, dinner times over. Give the potato peelings to the dogs and then continue your work in the shop and store."

It was a pity Rosie had heard the conversation but what odds. The Dowdellses were nobodies in Ballybracken.

Episode 7

Dreams Can Come True

The Auction

The auction of Mrs. Ballantine's goods and chattels was held late one wet afternoon very shortly after the funeral. Rosie and Danny picked their steps up the wet boggy lane from the main road to the tumbledown farmhouse sitting under the two little hillocks that peeped out of the bog called the 'Crockins'. There were very few there when they finally arrived at the house, and the few that were seemed pleased to see the likes of Rosie for where, they said quietly, would she get the money to outbid them on anything. More folk arrived in dribs and drabs including Effie McKnight intent on getting hold of the ruby glass. There was much speculation as to who was going to pocket the money raised by the auction for, as far as anyone knew, Mrs. Ballantine had no known relatives. The broad consensus was that Frank Mooney, the auctioneer, would get most of it for, '*that owl divil wuz surely always on the make when he wuzsn't chasing the wemen… an' him a married man way six wains… an' poor Brigid, the wife, not knowing what he wuz up tay half the time, an' havin tay turn a blind eye when she twigged what he was about… an' wuzn't his car often seen parked up at that hovel in Ballybracken Upper where al them loose hussies lived way Teezie Knox… .an' they al knew what went on under that roof…*' and so on until Mr Mooney himself stepped out of his car and was warmly greeted by all who had just been scurrilously maligning him.

Mooney said he wanted to make it clear that the proceedings of the sale, and indeed of the farm when it came on the market, were going to the British Legion, and that he had been told so by the Canon who had taken the deceased's mind on the matter just before her tragic accident. So that cleared that up, causing the speculation to take a different turn: '*The British Legion'! What connection had the dead woman way the 'British Legion?*' But anyway wuzn't it great owl Mooney wuzn't gonna get his hands on it… 'And so the bidding began. There turned out to be considerably more nice furniture and bits and pieces than anyone had thought, and there were still so few bidders that great bargains were to be had.

With the auction of the contents of the house in full swing, Danny could not understand why his mother seemed far more interested in what was in the outhouses, and why she kept wandering round into the back yard. He wouldn't have minded all that much, for the auction bored him rigid, but he was getting wet in the soaking mizzle[72] that was now blanketing the Crockins.

"When can we go home?"… and "Is it not over yet?" he kept demanding, and when that didn't work… "I'm wile tired an' I'm wile hung-ery."[73]

He only stopped this whinging when Rosie hit him a smack on the ear accompanied by the exhortation to *'quet creakin an' keenyin*[74]*.'* His ear wasn't really sore, but he now thought a bit of loud crying might be more effective and was about to try this when his mother seemed to find what she was looking for, and it didn't please him one little bit. There, sitting in an outhouse in the middle of a jumble of old broken chairs, tables and cupboards was just what Rosie had her heart set on. The piano! It too was in extremely poor condition but then she always knew it would be.

'That wud do us gran', she thought, *'but sure I'll never get it if there is anywan else efter it. I'll be heart sore if I don't get it.'*

"I wanna go home. Robbie said he was gonna take me snaring rabbits this evenin. He'll go way out may[75]. I wanna go home… NOW."

"Will yeh wheesht an' give a body paise,[76]" Rosie said. "I want the piano for Dorry, for I think she might be right musical."

This was news to Danny for Dorry had never shown much interest in anything except her rag doll, hop-scotch, skipping and sissy things like that. At that moment Mr Mooney, his raincoat flapping as he rushed in their direction to get out of the rain, led his phalanx of bidders in the direction of the outhouse.

"I think," he said loudly, "that there are a few items out here, so yuz that hiv been disappointed so far will get ye'r chance yet," and he smiled his gombeen-man[77] smile.

---

72 **Mizzle** – *light rain*
73 **I'm Wile tired an' I'm wile hung-ery** - *I'm very tired and very hungry*
74 **Creakin & keenyin** – *complaining & wailing*
75 **He'll go way out may** – *He will set off without me*
76 **Wheesht an' give a body paise** – *Keep quiet and give me peace. Stop annoying me with your behaviour*
77 **Gombeen-man** – *an exploiter, usually of the poor… someone on the make at the expense of others*

'I'm finished!' Rosie murmured to herself. *'I thought they wudn't bother auctionin' this owl stuff. Sure it's not for the likes of them gran folk.*

But Mr Mooney was intent on getting rid of as much as possible.

"Now these items may not luk much…," and they all murmured that *'the wee runt wuz right there'*… "for the deceased - 'God rest her'- "and here all the Catholics crossed themselves and all the Protestants scowled - "she lost a lot of slates wan winter an' it rained in on this furniture so she moved it out here intending to get it repaired but niver got roun tay it. Now you well-doin people can surely see that none of it is beyond repair, an' al know a bargain when yuz see it. We'll take the few chairs first. Who'll start the biddin?"

And to Rosie's great disappointment, bid they did. The chairs went to Cassy McCrystall… *'an' what need had she fir them?'*… the table to Arty-the-post, and other items sold as well. At last, only the piano and one or two items were left. Danny very desperately wanted somebody –anybody – to buy the piano so long as it wasn't his mother and, in a daring moment, he hit on a plan. He sidled his way through the assembled bidders just as Mr Mooney moved into position in front of the piano, and was saying,

"Now this instrument may not be in the very best aff condition at present but I'm assured it's playable, an' I'm sure…" he tailed off as he detected something wriggling through between his legs which at first he thought might be a mouse. But no! It was the bold Danny determined to get to the piano to show just how good it was so that somebody would bid for it and foil his mammy's musical ambitions.

"Och," said Mr Mooney pretending he was amused at the antics of the boy as Danny got to his feet between him and the piano, "… we seem to have a keen customer already? Are yeh goin tay demonstrate for us what a good instrument this is, lad?"

That was just Danny's plan, but he said nothing. Instead he opened the lid. It creaked ominously due to having swollen in the damp, then came away in his hand and slithered unto the cement floor where it lay at a tipsy angle. It was not a good start as far as Danny was concerned but, nothing daunted, he struck the keyboard to show that it played. Nothing happened so he struck it again and again nothing happened. Not a sound. Then something did happen; the vibration caused one of the pedals near ground level to dislodge itself and fall off with a loud clatter at Danny's feet. That put paid to the sale! The bidders muttered that it was *just an' owl piece aff junk… an' wud yeh be wise at al even bringin it into the house? An' sure it wud take a fortune tay fix it even if it wuz worth* it, which they greatly doubted... an' wuzn't it great the wee caddy[78] had showd it up for the piece of owl rubbish it wuz before anywan squannered good money on it.'

To retrieve his auction, Mr Mooney hastily gathered himself and said,

"... now don't yuz'ens be heading away home yit, any of yez, for there is some farm machinery in very good order in the hay shed over there, an' a d-ale of hay[79] tay bay disposed aff too."

The bidders headed for the shed, their enthusiasm waning fast with Mooney taking up the rear but not before saying to Rosie out of the corner of his mouth, "You shud keep a better eye on that wain. If yeh ask me, he'll come tay a powerful bad en." And then to himself, *'I donna what'll be done way this owl rubbish now? You cudn't even burn it fir it's that wet. I'm taking nothing more tay do with it. It can sit there for iver for al I care.'*

So saying he hastened after the bidders who had taken shelter in the barn and were now busy running down the quality of what they saw in there too.

"Ach yeh wee darling love, yeh saved it for me, Danny," and Rosie clutched Danny to her dress and kissed the top of his head while he struggled to get away.

'Why,' he asked himself, *'did everything turn out the opposite of what he wanted?'* He'd have a few questions along those lines to put to the angel if he ever showed up again.

Stolen or Rescued?

"What the hell day yeh want a piana for?" Robbie was standing with his back to the turf fire in the cottage as Rosie explained it was there for the taking.

"I think our Dorry might be musical," Rosie said, "so I want that piano to give her a chance. Now, are yeh gonna help may get it or not?"

"I suppose so," Robbie said. "I've seen no signs of the cutty[80] bein' musical, none at al, but if you think so an' the piana is lying there, sure we'll away up an' get it. But I'll hiv tay borrow a tractor an' trailer tay get it home fir it's a bulky item an', what with the owl doll's farm not that near han[81], lake we cud harly wheel it down the road. Maybe Jim McKnight wud let me borrow his tractor an' trailer for an hour or so."

---

78 **Wee caddy** – *small boy*
79 **A d-ale of hay** – *a good quantity of hay*
80 **Cutty** – *a young girl*
81 **The owl doll's farm not that near hand** – *the old lady's farm is some distance away*

"Naw, it wudn't wheel. It needs a bit doin tay it," Rosie thought it best to prepare Robbie for the challenge ahead.

"Try not tay tell Jim why yeh want it. His mother wuz at the auction, an' I want no tak about it. They might think we were stailin it[82]."

Danny was listening swinging his legs on the outshot kitchen bed, and now in an acute state of anxiety.

"I think it is stailin," he said. "Isn't it stailin something if yeh hiven't paid for it. Your stealin that piano, mammy, an' it's not right."

Robbie went across to the bed, caught him under his arms and swung him round in the middle of the kitchen.

"So, you're the fella that out tay keep us al right. We'll make a priest or a parson aff yeh yet, little comrade, an' there wuz me hopin tay turn yeh into a Communist."

"I'll go up to McKnight's this evening and see what's what. I need tay cal in the shap anyway for a packet aff fags. Tell us, where are you going to put your gran piana when yeh get it home?"

"Down there in the room," Rosie said, "then Dorry can practice away on it well out aff sight. We'll have to get somebody to give her chep[83] lessons. That'll be the nixt problem."

Rosie had given our hero a shilling for his 'good work' in helping her get the piano, and if ever there was a bitter-sweet reward, that shilling was it. But a shilling is a shilling and, like most small boys with money to spend, the shilling was now burning a hole in Danny's pocket, so he persuaded Robbie to take him to McKnight's shop. They arrived as Jim was just removing his shop boy's coat and closing up for the night. The shop smelt of boiled sweets, cloves and soda bread. To Danny's disappointment Jim agreed immediately that Robbie could borrow the tractor and trailer, no questions asked. When Robbie had got his cigarettes, he offered one to Jim, and they both stood chatting casually about the weather. Then Jim said,

"It would be great to hear about your war experiences some time, Robbie. Maybe we could go to Cobain's for a pint and a chat if you are content to do that? My studies at university are, I'm afraid, behind me now for my mother and Helen need a hand with the farm and the business. I'm sorry not to be able to finish my degree. I hear you're a great reader yourself."

Robbie told him about discovering Shakespeare's plays and other literary

---

82 **Stailin** – *stealing*

83 **Chep Lessons** – *inexpensive lessons*

gems as his unit battled from Normandy into the heart of the German Reich, and what an eye opener reading that great literature had been for him.

"... not," he said diffidently, "that I'd be up tay discussin Shakespeare or history or anythin else way an educated fella lake ye'rself an', tay tell yeh the truth, Jim, what I know about the blood and guts of war you might not want to hear. Few want to know but if you still want to hear my side aff the war an' how I beat Hitler single-handed, I'll sure enjoy tellin you over a pint or two."

"You're on," said Jim laughing. "We'll arrange an evening when you get back with the tractor. Oh, and bollocks to your talk about me being educated. Sure the more education you get the less confident you feel about saying anything, man dear. Now this young fella of yours has been very patient What can I get you, young sir?"

Danny was a bit overcome at being addressed as if he was important but he rallied to whisper, "I'd lake a penny chew an' bubble gum please... sir."

Both men smiled at the little boy's attempt at formality. Danny moved from behind Robbie and, reaching up, placed his shilling on the shop counter.

"Do you know," said Jim, "I think it wouldn't bankrupt us to give you a few penny chews and bubble gums and maybe some of these jelly babies without taking that shilling from you," and he put a mixture of confectionary in a paper bag, handed it to Danny who immediately retreated to sit on the high step leading from the shop to the meal store. He started to shovel the sweets into his mouth two or three at a time, as small boys will.

"What do yeh say tay Jim, little comrade?" demanded Robbie.

Danny placed his bag solemnly on the step and, with a mouth full of jelly babies, stammered, "Thank you very much... sir."

"... and keep some of them for Bobby and Dorry," Robbie warned.

"Ach sure we might just pull together another bag for them too without breaking the bank," Jim said unscrewing the top of the sweet jar and tipping more jelly babies into another paper bag.

With such small generous gestures lifetime friendships are often formed, and so it proved between Robbie Elliott and Jim McKnight.

"Holy Jeezes, woman," Robbie was looking in amazement at the piano in the late Mrs Ballantine's shed. "Is this the owl wreck aff a thing yeh have us traipsing[84]

---

84 *Traipsing* – *trudging around without much purpose*

up here for? Hiv a titter aff wit[85], woman, surely yeh wudn't give that houseroom?"

"I towel yez it wuz no good," Danny said in a loud voice trying not to stammer. "I said it's al rotten." And with that our little hero kicked the side of the piano hoping it would disintegrate further before their eyes.

The instrument emitted first a bright tinkling noise and then a dull thump as if something vital in its interior had been dislodged and had fallen through the base.

"Yeh wee ruffin yeh. Ye'll hive it wrecked before we git it home," Rosie said angrily, "I'll give yeh a good cuffin[86] in a minute."

She turned to Robbie. "Didn't I tell yeh it needed fixin up but, if yeh can't do it, I'll git somewan else. Now, come on, let's get it home. Oh, an' there that wee piana stool, Danny, we'll take it too. Sure they're al goin tay loss in here[87]. Nobody else wants them."

"I think it stailin... an' that a sin!" Danny said this with great emphasis hoping it would weigh with his mother who never stopped warning her family about how sinful nearly everything was from stealing her biscuits, cogging your homework, tormenting the goat or even picking your nose. But it was to no avail. Robbie had let down the back of the trailer and between them he and Rosie hoisted the wrecked piano up unto it laying it down with a crash on its back. Rosie went back to get the piano lid which had completely parted company from the instrument, and also to collect the piano stool.

"Is there anything else in there yeh want tay plunner[88]?" Robbie said. "We might as well be hung for a sheep as a lamb."

"Ach, will yeh quet. It's not stailin," Rosie said to convince herself. "Come on. We need tay get home."

Once there, the piano was carefully maneuvered through the kitchen door and then sharp left into the one and only bedroom where it sunk into the clay floor. Dorry immediately took possession thumping the keyboard to try to get something to happen. When nothing did, she quickly lost interest and retreated to the kitchen. Robbie took his first careful look at the wreck.

"Seriously, Rosie, it's in real bad shape. Yeh need tay git somewan who knows what they're doin to fix it up, if it can be fixed at al."

---

85 ***Hiv a titter aff wit*** – *have some common sense*
86 ***Cuffin*** – *smacking*
87 ***Sure they're al goin tay loss here*** – *They are all going to wrack and ruin here*
88 ***Plunner*** – *material taken without permission*

"I know rightly who ken hiv a go at fixin it," Rosie said. "Packie-the-Banty is the man for it. He's powerful musical an' can turn hez hand tay fixing anythin, an' he's not ill tay pay[89]. When he's done way it, yez will al bay sorry yez had so little faith."

They all retreated to the kitchen leaving the piano to settle in its latest damp location.

---

89 **He's not ill tay pay** – *He doesn't charge too much*

Episode 8

Packie to the Rescue

Dead Hens & The Resurrection Man

Packie-the-Banty was indeed a man of many trades. He did the rounds of Ballybracken on a rusty bicycle about once a month with no one knowing from whence he came or whither he was bound, and he was not to be drawn on his possible destinations no matter how many cups of tea he was plied with. He had a heavy tool bag on the carrier of the bike, a fiddle attached by some means to the handlebars, and usually a couple of dead hens tied to the bar which he had culled from the poultry stock of some farm due to them having stopped laying or dropped dead from some unknown cause. These carcasses he would beat with a stick to fluff up their feathers so that they would pass as healthy birds and then would try to sell them to the less discerning or the short-sighted. With Danny's passion for chicken dinners, our little hero would plead with his mother to buy one of the hens when Packie called but Rosie had the good sense never to do so saying she didn't want to have to rush them all to the County Hospital *'with God alone knows what affliction.'*

But it was Packie's other talent, that of general handyman and musician of sorts, that Rosie now wished to avail of. About ten days after the piano had arrived in Dowdells's, Packie rounded the corner of the cottage on cue and propped his overladen bike against the front wall. He always expected and got a mug of tea and a round of loaf bread liberally covered in jam. This time Rosie also placed a packet of digestive biscuits in front of him *'tay butter him up.'* He immediately abandoned the bread in mid bite devouring the biscuits three at a time. Thus softened up, Rosie ventured to mention her piano project to him taking him down to the lower room and showing him the job. Unlike everyone else who had seen the piano, Packie seemed nothing daunted claiming that he had successfully repaired one or two nearly as bad.

"I'll take a while, an' a wile lot[90] a money too tay fix that," he said after a cursory examination. "But I'll give it a go if yeh lake[91]. I'll hiv tay fine the

---
90 **A wile lot** – *a sizeable sum*
91 **I'll give it a go if yeh lake** – *I'll try to fix it if that is what you want*

missing bits an' I'll have to bay comin and goin for maybe up tay a week or more. In the m-iantime, ye'll hiv tay get a tilly lamp goin in the daytime down there sittin near-han it tay git it dried out."

Rosie was delighted. "When can yeh start, for our Dorry's mad keen tay get goin on it."

"It'll bay late nixt week," Packie said "Now, we'll hiv tay tak 'turkey.' How much hive yeh tay spen on it fir a'ment I after tellin yeh it's not goin tay be chape.[92]"

Rosie told him.

"I'd say that's about a quarter aff it. Can yeh not ask himself tay pay the differs?"

Rosie asked Robbie that evening.

"Day yeh think that owl hobo[93] ken make any kina job aff it?" was his reply. "I wudn't trust the knots aff straws tay him[94]."

But he could see Rosie wanted it done and, even though he thought she was mad, he parted with some funds which Rosie put carefully in a tin box high up on the fireboard[95]. Packie took up residence in the lower bedroom a week later, and work on the piano began. Every time Rosie took him his meals – *'an' he cud ate fir Irelan'* - she could hardly see him through the fug of cigarette smoke which hung in the air, lingered all night, and which the three children ingested as they coughed themselves to sleep. When asked did he think it would ever play again, which Rosie did constantly, Packie's answer was always the same – *'It'ill bay touch and go. I'm promisin yeh nothin.'* The only good thing, from Danny's point of view, was that Rosie felt obliged to buy Packie's dead hens – to keep him *'sweet'* as she put it - which he produced from somewhere most days. The house was soon coming down with these slowly rotting carcasses which were strung out along the kitchen dresser. To Danny's great disappointment, they never materialized as chicken dinners, for Rosie remained deeply suspicious of what they had died of, and eventually Robbie got fed up with the smell, gathered them all up and buried them in the duchill. As the week progressed, Packie seemed to be making a truly surprising success of the repairs. He would disappear from time to time on the bike and return with yet another odd-looking piano part, where he had got it, best not to enquire. As the piano slowly took

---

92 **Chape** – *cheap*
93 **Owl hobo** – *a unreliable worker*
94 **I wudn't trust the knots aff straws tay him** – *I wouldn't trust him with the most menial task*
95 **Fireboard** – *mantelpiece*

shape, our little hero's strange dread of it grew for to him it was an evil presence standing there against the lower bedroom wall.

Just over a week after Packie had started work, Rosie had set the bacon, cabbage, and potatoes on the kitchen table, and was trying to get everybody to gather round and start their dinner, when she heard the sound she had longed for coming from the lower bedroom. Packie was playing the piano! They all rushed down and, to her children's dismay, Rosie threw her arms round Packie and hugged him.

"Get away outta that!" Packie exclaimed, "fir I'm not used tay weman!" But what passed for a smile on so wrinkled a face clearly indicated that he could get used to them quite quickly.

"Ach, ye'r an angel, Packie," Rosie said, and there were tears of pure joy running down her cheeks. "Sure I niver thought I'd see the day that the Dowdells wud hiv a piana the lakes aff the gran folk."

"... an' you ken take that cearr[96] aff ye'r face, yeh wee rapscallion[97]," Robbie whispered to Danny "an' be happy fir ye'r mammy fir wance."

"Now ye'll need tay get it well tuned," Packie said, "for I can't do that for yeh fir I'm near deef. The Darkie is the man that'll tune it for yeh, for he has a powerful good ear."

The Darkie's many Talents

Mr Chatterjee was a travelling clothing salesman, always referred to as 'the Darkie' in the houses he called at to sell his wares in Ballybracken. The title was used without a hint of prejudice, for all in Ballybracken had their own cherished prejudices about their immediate neighbours so hadn't room for any more, except to wonder occasionally *'if he was a Protestant or a Catholic Darkie?'* It came as news to Rosie that the Darkie was musical as well as having such good value in clothes.

"How day yeh know the Darkie is musical?" asked Rosie as Packie was pocketing the white fivers for his services.

"How do I know iverything?" was his sour reply. "Now before I go, can I

---

96 **Cearr** – *insolent look*
97 **Rapscallion** – *rascal*

interest yeh in these wheen⁹⁸ a hens for they are powerful good val-yeh."

His main job done, Rosie now felt empowered to resist buying any more poultry living or dead so Packie peddled off down the road muttering that *'some folk didn't know good valye when they see it.'*

"Ach, God in heaven," Rosie exclaimed as she went down to view her pride and joy in the lower room, "I forgot tay get him tay fix up the wee piana stool."

But on closer examination, she thought the stool shouldn't be beyond Robbie's ability to fix.

That Terrible Telegram

That evening Robbie brought the stool up from the lower room. The cloth cover on the seat was damp and rotten but otherwise it was sturdy enough with only one loose leg. He opened the lid to see if there were any sheets of music there. There was nothing except a faded envelope only part of its flap opened. Robbie fished around inside with two fingers and felt a flimsy piece of paper. He gently eased it out and unfolded it. It was a telegram and read,

'The Army regrets to announce that corporal Frederick George Ballantine died in action on July the First 1916 at the Somme. He was a brave soldier who died serving his king and country.'

Robbie read it out. Rosie stopped washing the dishes and came to look over his shoulder to read the telegram for herself. The poignancy of this only slowly sank in.

"Does that mean he wuz shot?" asked Danny innocently from where he and the others were playing marbles on the kitchen floor.

"It does, love," said his mother quietly.

"How did you not get shot, daddy?" asked Bobby.

"I was good at dodgin bullets," Robbie answered without looking up from the telegram.

"I want tay be a sodger when I'm big," said Bobby, "an' I'll not get shot ether."

His parents said nothing both slowly taking in what must have been the terrible story that lay behind this cold communication.

"The tak wuz that Mrs. Ballantine wuz widowed about a year efter she got married for they tell about her man dyin from a kick from a horse, and that she was left with one wee wain. I niver knew what had become aff the lad till now but sure nobody knew her, or ta-ked much about her, stuck away up yonner on the edge aff the lonely Crockins. Did yeh know he had joined the army, and what had become aff him, Robbie?"

"Naw, I niver even knew he existed. So he died in the First World War on the first day aff the Battle aff the Somme as so many men from roun here did."

"So... that poor widow woman gets that telegram... tay say that her ony son had been kilt... an' from that minute she has tay work the farm hirself not a man tay help her, an' she's up there on her own for near forty years. It must hiv been a lonely do fir hir[99]. God rest her now, for there's some gets it hard in this world."

Rosie turned back to washing the dishes. Robbie said thoughtfully, "I must ask my owl fella about the lad for they might have sarved together in the First War."

Widow Ballantine's lonely Furrow

"Ach Aye, young Freddie Ballantine. I knew him well," Robbie's father rolled a cigarette and spat into the hearth. "Real good fella he wuz too. I herd-tell he wuz workin at the harvest way a pair aff horses in that field aff theirs that lies along the roadside when a bunch aff fellas shouted over the hedge tay him that they were goin to join the Enniskillen's at Omey barracks[100] an' wud he not join too? There and then he took the horses up tay the house, towel his mother he was away to join up and headed aff. Och Aye... young Freddie... I think it was at the Somme he got blew up. I would doubt if there was much tay bury for lots of the lads wur blew tay smithereens that first day aff the battle. It wuz poorly managed by the f***** Generals."

"Did yeh niver think aff goin up tay the Crockins tay see hez mother, you that had survived it al? Sure yeh might have been able tay say something tay comfort her even if it wuz a lie... lake that he didn't suffer... or something lake that."

"What comfort wud I hiv been tay hir? In our war, the fellas died worse nor animals, Sure I stood beside mates an' seen their heads blew aff... or worse still, there wuz the gas. Naw, man dear, there was nothing tay bay said that wudn't hiv made hez mother feel worse, or any comfort tay offer anywan. The only comfort I iver got iver since is outta a bottle. Will ye'll have wan way me now ye'r here? I

---

99 **It must hiv been a lonely do** – It was surely a lonely existence
100 **To join the Enniskillens at Omey barracks** – the Royal Inniskilling Fusiliers HQ was in Omagh, the County town of Tyrone, Northern Ireland

don't think Dowdells I'll be back for a while for I know yeh an' him don't pull[101] since yeh took up way hez woman."

But that telegram had troubled Robbie. A hardened soldier, he had long since steeled himself against feeling too deeply about anything for he too had witnessed destruction and death on an unimaginable scale in his own war. But somehow this was different. This lad was an innocent drawn into a stupid war where thousands of young men, millions even, had been slaughtered like his father had said… and for what? At least Robbie's war had been about something worth fighting for, though he had to confess that for him and his mates it was mainly, in the end, about surviving with all your vital parts intact.

But that lad, a decent young man by all accounts, all he had succeeded in doing was grieving his mother and leaving her to toil on her own on a wee hungry farm in Ballybracken for the rest of her days. And there was nothing to mark the passing of mother or son. They might as well never have existed at all. There was no plaque in the parish church for the lad, no gravestone for her. And worse still nobody cared. Well, it wasn't good enough! Robbie Elliot cared.

But what could he do? Anything by way of memorials in Ballybracken had to be either Protestant or Catholic, and he was resolved that the lad's sacrifice would not be tainted by either if he could help it. Then he thought of something, a very simple thing but it would do, and would bring ease to his usually untroubled conscience. The next day he took a knife from the kitchen drawer, found his sharpening stone and set to work on the blade until it was razor sharp. Then without a word to anyone he set off down to the rivers and the old Celtic fort encircling the 'Ladies' Bower.'

"That woman, Ballantine, an' the young lad hiz been troublin me iver since we foun the telegram," Rosie said a night or two later.

"Well, bother yourself no further," Robbie said looking up from the football results in 'Ireland Saturday Night,' "for I've tuk care aff it in a fashion. I'll show yeh the morrow if it's a good day, and if you're up for a wak down tay the 'Meetins'."

Rosie looked at him with tears in her eyes. "Sure you know I can niver go back down there as long as I live efter what I nearly done tay wee Danny. You above al people know why."

---

101 **Yeh an' him don't pull** – *you and he are not on friendly terms*

He gently held up her face to his with his finger and kissed her. "I know, love," he said, "I shud niver hiv mentioned it. Let me tell yeh what I've done."

When he had told her she looked him straight in the face and said, "That's great... yeh've done a great thing, the right thing, Robbie."

"Ach sure I'm a powerful fella," he said pretending to brush aside, but glad to have, that simple appreciation from the woman he loved.

She said, "Now, you an' the wains go tay see what ye've done, an' they can tell may al about it. An' maybe someday I'll pluck up the courage an' go an' see it for mezself. But not now, Robbie. I'll give youz a couple aff sandwiches an' apples, an' yez can hive a picnic down there."

Sadie's Headless Ghost

Unfortunately, Rosie plans fell apart when Bobby and Dorry learned that their mother was going somewhere far more exciting than down to the 'Meeting of the Waters.'

Sadie Greer, who lived on the snout of the esker, had been proclaiming loudly for weeks that her house was haunted by a headless man dressed all in black with a book – she thought maybe a Bible – in his hand, and she couldn't be left alone in the house day or night till the ghost was got rid of. Neighbouring women were taking it in turns to sit with her though to their disappointment no man, headless or otherwise, had yet materialized. Local lads, however, keen to prevent the watchers being disappointed entirely, saw to it that doors flew open apparently of their own accord, windows rattled, footsteps were heard, moaning and groaning came from various rooms in the house all accompanied by much suppressed laughter and shrieks of "Ach, bay Jeezes, there he's now!" from Mrs. Greer. "He's drivin may clian wild. Nothin fir it but I'll hev tay flit[102]."

On that Sunday, Rosie had agreed to sit with Sadie, and the prospect of seeing a headless man, however terrifying, was of consuming interest to Bobby and Dorry, so they opted to go to Sadie's with their mother. Initially Danny too found the idea of the headless man thrilling and terrifying in equal measure but on further reflection he decided he didn't want to see any more other-worldly apparitions, headless or otherwise, for he had more than enough on his plate dealings with the other-world in the form of Angel Jo. So in the end he was more than happy to go walking with his big hero, Robbie, but only so long as

---

102 *He's drivin may clian wile. Nothing fir it but I'll hev tay flit* – He is driving me mad. I have no option but to move house

he didn't desert him and go off with any girls. This was bothering him as they walked along the road under the beech trees and, by the time they turned into the Roxborough's avenue, he decided to have it out with Robbie.

"If them girls appear," he said, "sure you wouldn't go away with them to pick cherries." He was very firm and solemn.

"I promise, my little comrade," said Robbie looking down at him and trying not to laugh, "sure how could I leave you?"

That was all Danny wanted to hear so he changed the subject "Do you think there is a ghost in Sadie Greer's?"

"I'll tell you what I think, Danny Boy," said Robbie. "I'm thinkin that Greer woman wants wan aff them new council houses beside the church, an' I'm thinkin a lot aff the fly boys round here ur havin great craic[103] helpin get that ghost on her side. It's a right teed-reel[104] fir al concerned if yeh ask me."

"So, there is a ghost," said Danny not understanding Robbie at all.

"Ach, sure there is, Danny," Robbie said running his hand through Danny's mop of curly hair. "Sure hiven't you got an angel so why shudn't Sadie Greer hive a ghost?"

Saluting the Forgotten Dead

They arrived at the 'Ladies' Bower' overlooking the rivers.

"Now," Robbie asked, "Can you see anything new around here?"

Danny only saw the ancient earthwork ringed by the tall old trees and inside the large ferns waving in the breeze looking as if they were trying to escape from the bower.

"Naw," he said. "I can't see nothin."

"Luk at the trees," Robbie said.

Danny went round the outside of the earthwork looking up at the trunks and branches of all the magnificent trees. Then he spotted it. Carved deep into the trunk of one of the biggest trees was some beautiful fresh lettering.

"Is that it?" he shouted to Robbie.

"That's it, my little detective. Can you read it?" And he held Danny up to take a closer look at the engraving.

"It's too hard for me," Danny said. "You read it for me."

Still holding the boy in his arms, Robbie read,

---

103 **Craic** – *harmless fun… a lively time*
104 **It's a right teed-reel** – *it's a mischievous carry-on*

'In memory of Frederick George Ballantine who died fighting for his family, his friends and his country on the First of July 1916 at the battle of the Somme in the Great War of 1914-18.'

He let the boy slip from his arms unto the grass.

"So, what do you think, Danny?"

"I think it's great that you've cut the sodger's name into a tree. He was a brave man that got killed to save us all from bad men. I'd like my name on a tree sometime too if I wuz iver that brave, an' I think the music is lovely too."

Robbie stared at his small friend. "What that yeh say about music, Danny?"

"The nice tree music," Danny said. "It's lake the music I hear from the rivers down there or the nice bog music or the coloured music the moon plays some nights when it wakens me an' I look at it from our bed-room windey. But the tree music was nice an' sad because the trees is sorry for the brave dead man too."

All this said in the most matter-of-fact way, and with great earnestness.

'Music from trees an' rivers an' visits from an angel... what next?' Robbie mused, and realized, not for the first time but now with raised bewilderment and some alarm, that he and Rosie had a remarkable little boy on their hands. That said, all this must surely only be the result of the boy's prodigious imagination. Surely that must explain, mustn't it, angels an' music where there was none? *'Aye, that must surely be it.'*

Danny's voice brought him back from his reverie asking,

"Robbie, is that another man's name on the tree, a wee bit higher up, but not as bright?"

"Well spotted, young sir," said Robbie, glad to refocus on something tangible, "for it was that other name that giv me the idea. The other wan wuz a school pal aff mine, Jimmy Galbraith. Him and me joined the army on the same day, an' before we did we come down here to the 'Bower' and the 'Meetins' for they were always favourite places aff ours tay swim in the whirlpool an'... " here he lowered his voice "... now and again we corned the odd pheasant to take home for the dinner. Well, that day Jimmy produced a pen knife an' carved his name on the tree. He handed the knife tay me to do the same, an' I wud hive done but it come on to teem with rain, so we had tay run for it an' I niver got back tay it."

"Is he still ye'r friend?" Danny asked.

"Naw, Jimmy was killed at a place called Dunkirk in France, Danny."

Danny now felt sad that Robbie had lost this friend and thought how sad he would be if Robbie ever died, and he never saw him again. That gave him a lump in his throat.

"But these lads wudn't lake you an' me tay be sad, Danny. They'd just want us to remember them an' be happy."

Robbie then did what to Danny was a wonderful thing. He went in front of the tree with the two names on it, stood stiffly to attention and very slowly saluted the two names. When he had finished, Danny said quietly,

"Wud you show me how tay salute?"

So Robbie stood him in front of the tree and brought the boy's hand and arm up to the salute. "So, Danny, the proper way to salute is 'longest way up, shortest way down.' Don't forget that, will yeh."

… and Danny never did, nor that unusual 'memorial' for two forgotten soldiers at the ancient earthen fort overlooking the 'Meeting of the Waters.'

Exit Sadie's Ghost

"Well, did yez see the ghost?" Robbie asked"… I suppose he had a head under ivery arm."

"We seen nothin," Bobby said. "Dorry an' me wish we'd come way you tay the 'Meetins', daddy."

"He's right. There wuz nothin at al," Rosie said disappointed. "It's jist some galoots aff fellas up tay shenanigans[105] aff al sorts tay skar the wits outta Sadie. Runnin mad roun the house dunnerin on the dours an' windeys[106]. Jessy Craig wuz there too way yon big handbag aff hir's howlin it up tight tay hir lake she had the crown jewels in it. She allowed that there is no such a thing as ghosts but that she's a great believer in demons an' that they come tay torment them that done somethin wrong. So, wud yeh believe, she asked Sadie to tell us what she had been up tay that had brought the demons down on her? She said that Sadie shud examine hir conscience there and then, an' come out way it. We al didn't know where tay luk. Sadie didn't take it well, an' is it any wonner?"

And did Sadie Greer get possession of one of the new council houses by the church to remove her from the noisy ghostly presence? Sad to say, no, she did not, and as her hopes of flitting vanished so too, mysteriously, did the ghost.

---

105 **A lock a galoots a fellas up tay shenanigans** – *some young men clowning around and playing tricks*
106 **Dunnerin on the dour an' windeys** – *banging on the door and windows*

Episode 9

The Milk Bottle Kiss

'The End is Nigh!'

It was on a Saturday in high summer when Danny decided he was a very wicked sinner, and he had better do something about it quick before he landed up roasting in hell.

Rosie had packed him and Bobby and Dorry off to Ballybracken's mission hall every Saturday afternoon where the latest Christian Crusade was underway because '*Yez can't get too much religion tay set yez on the right track,*' but her motives were mixed for it also got them out of the way so she could, as she said, get her '*head shired*'[107] and some modicum of peace after spending all morning cleaning for Effie McKnight.

The Reverend Quigley was the prime mover in all things evangelical in Ballybracken. A powerful 'Hell's Fire and Damnation' preacher himself, he nevertheless co-opted guest speakers during his periodic crusades to reinforce his own robust message. Mildred McBain, though suspect of course as a woman, was redeemed up to the hilt so could be trusted to lead in prayer - just about. She was a '*dab han*'[108] at bringing all Ballybracken's sins before the Lord many of which, as described by her, were so deliciously dreadful that some of the congregation got excited, and the good Pastor had to calm them down when Mildred had finished. It remained a mystery to some of the more sceptical as to how Mildred had such a comprehensive knowledge of such wickedness but nevertheless all must surely rejoice that she had exposed it, and that it was on its way to being purged.

Mr Quigley, for his part, was great at picking out some of the more terrifying bits from the Old Testament, where God seemed less than accommodating to them that crossed him, and used these lurid passages as a terrible warning to Ballybracken folk as to what lay ahead of them if the end of the world were to come that very night. In the Reverend Quigley's view 'that very night' was a lively possibility for God couldn't fail to be fed up with them and their sinful

---

107 **Get her head shired** – *get some peace and quiet*
108 **Dab han** – *skilled*

ways. The only modicum of comfort for his listeners was that 'the end' did seem to keep getting postponed from Saturday to Saturday, but Mr Quigley explained that this was to give them all every chance to repent and confess their sin there and then, *'out good an' loud.'*

After one of the Reverend's more terrifying sermons, poor Danny couldn't get to sleep worrying about the 'End of the World,' and where he would end up if it happened, so was greatly relieved when he woke up the next morning and yet again there seemed to have been a delay. Of course, he didn't dare tell any of these God-fearing folk what Angel Jo had told him about the state of heaven just now since Robbie had told him not to, and had cast doubt as to whether the angel was real at all. And anyway, how could all these holy people be wrong about God and Jesus and heaven and hell and all that? They apparently spent all their time thinking about it, worrying about it, and getting more and more holy at every meeting so that they would end up in the right place.

Shocking Revelations & Much Muttering

The Reverend Quigley was in the habit of inviting Ballybracken people, recently redeemed, to give their testimony, encouraging full confessions of past sins with the exhortation – *'come on now, don't be howlin back*[109]*, spit it al out* – and *'spit it out'* some did, often giving vivid accounts of past improprieties and misdemeanours. Needless to say, in a society short of much daily sensationalism – except for the stimulation provided of a Sunday by the 'News of the World,' - Mr Quigley's congregation took a prodigious interest in these frank revelations, accompanied by disingenuous dismay at what they were hearing*'… cud yeh believe that him an' her were at the lakes aff that*[110] *when everybody's' back wuz turned?... an' did she really say she stole money from the church collection? ... surely he didn't say he watered the milk regular! … where did she say she did it way an' airman? It was surely niver on the Sunday school excursion tay Portrush! ... sure yeh niver rightly know what's goin on under ye'r very nose!... them at it lake rabbits... an' her actin that innocent, lake butter wudn't melt in hir mouth...* 'and so on.

The Reverend also had a regular go at the Pope, Rome and priests, and all that Catholic stuff. This upset Danny for his mammy believed in the Pope and had a picture of him staring across at the 'Sacred Heart of Jesus' picture on the opposite wall in their lower room. The Pope was wearing a lovely white suit which Danny

---

109 **Don't be howlin back** – *don't delay… don't be holding back*
110 **Were at the lakes aff that** – *that they were doing such a wicked thing*

thought would brighten the place up if everybody wore one. Rosie said it must be the *'divil tay keep clian'*[111]*.* Anyway, it was pretty clear from the Reverend Quigley's account that the Pope and the Catholics had better see to themselves, get *'redeemed good an' proper'* or they would all end up in hell too.

It was on the Saturday afternoon that the Reverend Quigley had lined up some of the newly converted to give their testimony that occasioned our little hero's most serious spiritual panic attack. In the course of one of the testimonies Danny realized that all was definitely far from secure regarding his eternal destination, and indeed his physical well-being. A fellow Danny vaguely recognized as being one of the big boys who used to be at Ballybracken school described how he had been *'washed in the blood'* recently but, before that, seemed to have had a whale of a time doing all sorts of wicked things associated with what Danny in his innocence had come to call 'it.'

'IT' & the Milk Bottle Kiss

Now suffice it to say our hero had no accurate working knowledge of what 'it' really was, he only knew that it intrigued him if for no other reason that it seemed to be a pre-occupation of the oldest 'big-boys' at school, and was spoken of by them in furtive whispers, accompanied by much sniggering and smoking, behind the boys' lavatories. Danny realized immediately that what the fellow was now confessing to in considerable detail was all to do with 'it,' and how sinful it was even to want to know about 'it,' to think about 'it', never mind to speak of doing 'it!' Understanding very little of what was unfolding, he nonetheless understood enough to know there and then that the game was up as far as he and God were concerned.

Because it was a 'Big People's thing', his curiosity, like Adam and Eve's of yore, had got the better of him so he listened more carefully in the playground for mentions of 'it' and, when further enlightenment was not forthcoming from that quarter, he even tried, surreptitiously and unsuccessfully, to get a book on the subject in Ballybracken library. And now he was hearing that seeking such knowledge was itself sinful but - and this was the knock-out blow - hadn't Florence Hunter kissed him and held his hand when it was their turn to wash the milk bottles at the sink in the school porch! While Florence's attentions had been unsolicited with Florence making the running, that sink event must surely be a manifestation of 'it' at its very worst. Danny was doomed!

---

111 ***The divil tay keep clian*** *– it must be very difficult to keep clean*

And now the Reverend Quigley words brought him even worse news. The holy one got to his feet, once the young fellow had finished, saying he just wanted to underline that God knew they were at 'it' in some shape or form and if they went on doing 'it' -unless you were married when, for some reason, God didn't seem to mind - there would be nothing for you in the next life but to burn in the fiery furnace. It was such a bad sin that God sometimes didn't wait to get even with you, and sometimes started your punishment in this world by striking dead people who did 'it' in the wrong place in the wrong way at the wrong time. The Reverend then read from the Bible about people who had been caught doing 'it' all wrong, and how God had not hung about getting even with them in various unpleasant ways. He finished with a cry of triumph, *'There yeh hiv it! Chapter an' verse!'*

Danny's Dilemma

There was obviously nothing now for poor doomed Danny but to get God sweetened up immediately for hell sounded desperate, even worse than school, and he didn't want to be dead as well as having a stutter. But how did you go about joining Ballybracken's holy folk that didn't involve you standing up and talking about seeing the light, kissing Florence in the porch even though it might be worth pointing out to God that it was Florence had kissed him. Even if he could pick up the courage to give a testimony, he would stutter over his words, and he had noticed the Reverend Quigley's congregations got impatient if anyone went on too long, especially if they hadn't much of interest to confess. There must be some other way of telling God he would be good from now on like not thinking about 'it' anymore and making amends by carrying buckets of water from the well without complaining, not fighting with Bobby or hiding Dorry's doll. But above all, he definitely must give up any further interest in 'it' in case God already had him written up in His 'Bad-boy' book, was planning to do for him any day now, and was watching out for any further sinful kissing episodes. He tried to ease his anxiety on this score by reminding himself that Angel Jo said God hadn't been around for a while but then hadn't the Reverend Quigley said he personally knew of people God had struck down recently in one way or another, so it would be better to take no chances with the Almighty.

Inspiration from Africa

Robbie had recently brought the children a bundle of old comics that Jim McKnight had given him in the shop, and it was from one of them that Danny got the inspiration as to what to do next to square things up between him and God. The comics were mostly about 'Corky the Cat' and 'Desperate Dan' and funny people like that but a couple of them also had religious stories in pictures. One of these was about a tribe in Africa or some other wild place, and when they thought their gods were cross with them - and their gods seemed even harder to get on the right side of than the mission hall one - the tribe set up a big stone and got a sheep or a goat or, if none of them was available, a chicken seemed to do at a pinch, then cut its throat and sprinkled the blood over the big stone. That seemed to do the trick with their gods, and generally seemed to cheer them up. The story finished with a bunch of missionaries arriving in the jungle who told the tribe they were doing it all wrong, that they should be worshipping the proper God, told them to stop sacrificing things and throwing blood around, and generally get themselves tidied up by wearing nice suits and ties. The tribe immediately saw the sense of all this, stopped their carry-on with sheep and goats and hens, became good Christians, joined the British Empire, whatever that was, and were seen in the last picture standing round their altar wearing nice suits and ties, waving Bibles and union jacks, and looking very happy.

As he studied the pictures, it slowly dawned on Danny that maybe what he needed to prove to God he was a changed character was a stone altar. Didn't both the Canon and his mammy's churches have big altars around which a lot of boring stuff seemed to be going on every Sunday which must please God in some way or other that Danny couldn't rightly fathom. But now he got to thinking that altars had some connection with stopping God striking people down and packing them off to hell. If he set up an altar of his own, somewhere quiet where nobody would know or laugh at him, maybe that would prove to God that he had turned over a new leaf and, above all, had given up thinking about 'it.' Surely that would do instead of trying to give his testimony in Mr Quigley's mission hall with all the terrors that held for him. So he decided an altar was the answer, and he immediately set about looking round for a really big stone. It would need to have at least one flat side so that he could sit on it and tell God how good he now was, and would He mind rubbing his name out of His 'Bad Boys' book as soon as possible. To speed things up, Danny was even prepared to lend God his school rubber in case He couldn't find His own.

The Altar in the Fort of Silk

Our little hero's plans did not go smoothly at first for he soon discovered that suitable stones were in short supply in Ballybracken. All he could find were either too big to be carried or too small to be any use for the kind of altar he had in mind. It was the school holidays so, although he had lots of time on his hands, the matter of the altar was urgent for God could have a go at him at any minute. Also to his dismay as 'nearly holy', the more he thought about how bad and wicked and sinful thinking about 'it' was, the more he couldn't stop thinking about it even, horror of horrors, that it might be quite nice to kiss Florence again and hold her hand! But surely once the altar would be set up, and he was properly holy, all thoughts about 'it' would be banished.

One morning his search took him along the Ballybracken lower road to where it began to wander crookedly and steeply up the Scroggy Brae that skirted round the edge of the ancient Lisnaseedy Celtic ring fort at the top of the hill. To avoid embarking on the steep slope, Danny dodged under loose barbed wire into a low-lying field where there were two disused flax dams. These were covered in slimy green sludge with tufts of grass sticking out of it but between the two dams was exactly what Danny was looking for, a pile of reasonably sized stones that had originally held the flax down in the dam water but were no longer of any use to anyone. Danny immediately knew what he must do. He would set up his altar inside the Celtic fort at the top of the Scroggy for he was certain nobody would ever find it there but, more to the point, God would be able to see it. The fort too was within sight of his home so every time he might be tempted to think about 'it' he had only to look up at the fort, remember his altar stone and surely all such bad thoughts would go away.

But first he must get a suitable stone up to, and inside, the fort. The slope from the dams to the fort was very steep, but that was good too because maybe God would give him credit for the great effort it would take to get the stone up there. He selected a stone with one nice flat side, but which, unfortunately, was about half the size of himself, and started to carry it up the slope. It was dreadfully heavy. He hadn't got very far before he dropped it, and it clunked its way down to the bottom again. He tried again, got a little further this time when the same thing happened. Reluctantly he went back to the pile and chose a smaller stone. He had managed to carry this one about halfway up, the sweat now blinding him, when he dropped that one too. He was about to start crying, for his body ached in every joint from the exertion, when the stone was arrested in its downward journey and fell into a deep muddy rut just below him. Maybe it was not so hopeless after all, he told himself. He would rest for a while and then try again.

And try he did, all morning with the sun beating down, sometimes carrying the wretched stone and sometimes rolling and pushing it until at last he came to the top of the hill and could see the earth wall that ringed the fort. This was his last hurdle but it too was very high. Then the thought occurred to him that the people who had lived in the fort long ago might have had an entrance cut in their big bank if he could find it. He was right. Abandoning the stone, he walked round the circular bank, and there it was. The fort entrance had got filled in somewhat over the centuries but it was still much lower than the rest of the bank. All he had to do now was carry or roll his stone round to this entrance, and he was ready to set up his altar inside the fort. After another rest, sitting on his stone this time, he half-rolled half-carried it to the entrance, pushed it up and through and, with victory in sight, he then carried the stone to the centre of the circle where he dropped it on his foot. He let out a scream of agony, fell on top of the stone and started to cry in pain and frustration. It had taken him hours and he had no strength left to even straighten the stone from the awkward angle at which it had fallen. He was now crying so hard he put himself to sleep.

Robbie Sorts Out the Almighty

He was wakened by somebody lifting him bodily and setting him on top of the stone. It was Robbie. Danny was tear stained, covered in mud and grass, his right foot was badly swollen and very sore.

"Well, may wee champion. What's al this? Yeh'r mammy an' me hiv been very worried about yeh."

Robbie was both puzzled and anxious. Danny didn't answer, stared straight ahead, then buried his face in his hands. Eventually he said in a distant voice,

"I jist fell asleep," and then he continued, "I'm sorry you an' mammy wuz worried."

Robbie knew the little boy well enough by now to realize there was much more going on in his head than taking a walk up to Lisnaseedy fort on a summer's morning and falling asleep.

"Come on, little comrade, sure yeh know yeh ken tell me anythin'. Aren't we great mates, you an' me? What's wrong way yeh?"

Danny still stared straight ahead. How could he tell anybody, even Robbie, about his sinful interest in 'it'?

"Where did this big brute aff a stone come from?" Robbie was trying a different tack. "Some big strong man must hiv humped it up here in the last day or so. I wonder who it wuz?"

That did the trick. It would be great to tell Robbie that he was the big strong man who had put the stone there.

"I brought it up from the dams at the bottom," Danny said proudly.

"That wuz fantastic, Danny, I knew you wur a big strong man. Now wud yeh tell me why yeh did it? Were yeh plannin on building a castle inside the fort or what?"

"Naw," Danny said and, after a long pause, "... it's my... altar."

"Ach, it's an' altar! Sure that's what it is right enough," Robbie tried to sound as if that was no great surprise, "an' what wud yeh bay wantin way an altar, Danny?"

"I jist... " Robbie waited..."I jist wanted to show God I was a good boy so he wudn't kill may an' sen may tay hell."

Again Robbie waited and then asked quietly, "an' why day yeh think God wud want tay send yeh tay hell, Danny? Sure you're a great boy."

"The Reverend Quigley says that if you think about 'it,' God punishes yeh an' sends yeh straight to hell unless you stop."

"And what is 'it' Danny? Come on, tell me."

The little boy buried his face in Robbie's tunic and said through his tears, "I can't tell yeh. It's too bad."

Robbie eased the lad's face back and looked him straight in the eye. "So, let me guess. Wud it maybe be something tay do way... maybe... girls? Is that it, Danny?"

"Aye, it is," Danny whispered. "I'm not sure but I think it's somethin tay do way kissin an' howlin hans an' thinkin about them sorta things that the Reverend Quigley says is al sins an' that yeh go tay hell for... when the world ends any Saturday." The tears were rolling down his cheeks as he immediately buried his face again in the tunic not able to face Robbie in his shame. "Please don't tell mammy... an' please don't stap bein my friend even though I'm so bad," for he was now scared of losing everyone he loved in the world.

Robbie lifted him gently and set him on his knee.

"Listen to me, Danny," he said, "an' now stap cryin. Are yeh listenin tay me?"

Danny took his thumb out of his mouth just long enough to say "Aye," dismally, waiting for his world to crash round him.

Again, Robbie looked him straight in the eye and said in a low but very clear voice, "that jist means you're growing up, Danny, an' startin on the road to becomin an' even bigger strong man who someday will hiv a wee family aff ye'r own, an' then you'll know that there is no need tay be skared aff 'it,' as yeh call it. For now though, forget about al that stuff, for that God aff yours dizn't want yeh tay bay skared aff Him, He loves yeh an' wants yeh tay enjoy ye'rself, an' the great big man Hez made yeh. Sure, how cud yeh hive humped yeh'r altar up that big hill if God hadn't helped yeh, an' yeh wuren't the strongest boy in Ballybracken?" And he gently tweaked Danny's nose between his fingers. "Sure that Quigley is a right owl blether[112]," he continued. "Don't bay listenin tay a word he says. His cruel God doesn't hiv tay be your God. He's takin a lot aff balderdash. I donno why ye'r mammy sends yez tay hez owl getherins[113]."

A wave of relief swept over Danny that instantly changed his mood from one of bleak despair into a surge of the greatest happiness. Sure, Robbie was never wrong. He wanted to put his arms round Robbie's neck but he didn't... *'cos big strong boys don't do that kind aff thing.'* A slight worry remained though. "Sure, yeh wudn't tell mammy... she might not lake me growin up tay be a big man ' leavin home for a wee while yet."

"Naw, sure that 'it' business is a wee secret yeh keep tay ye'rself, may wee comrade, so I wudn't bother tellin anywan else about it. it's something private. A bit lake yeh'r chats way that angel an' the music yeh hear sometimes. Al I'm sayin is that yeh mustn't worry about it anymore. Will yeh promise me that?"

"I'll niver tell nowan else." Danny had no trouble making this promise.

"Good man" Robbie said, lifting the boy off his knee and standing up to look at the stone.

"It's a great altar, Danny, but we'll not cal[114] it that anymore. We'll just cal it, 'Danny's Stone', an' when yeh want tay think or get away from the rest of us for a while, yeh can come up here an' sit on your stone an' think things over. Sure iverywan needs a quiet place lake this tay go tay think now and again. Let's turn it to see if we have the smoothest side on the tap for we don't want yeh hurtin

---

112 **Blether** – *he talks nonsense*
113 **Getherins** – *meetings*
114 **Cal** – *call... describe it as*

your bum every time you sit on it."

Robbie turned it over, decided which side should be upright and straightened it to lie flat "… now it's al yours, Danny, for nobody else ever comes here to my knowledge. But come on home now or your mammy will think we're both lost, an' sure yeh must bay chap-fallen[115] efter al ye'r hard work the day."

"How did yeh know I wuz here?" Danny asked as they headed out of the fort.

"I met Liam Owens on the road an' he said he thought he had seen a young man aff your description going into the dam field. After that I jist followed may nose. I knew a sensible big man like you wudn't hive fallen in the dam," though that was exactly what Robbie had dreaded.

They clambered up the high bank at the side of the old entrance to admire their handiwork.

Robbie said, "somebody in the pub towel may that 'Lisnaseedy' means the *'Fort of Silk'* in the Irish language, so there you are now. Your stone is set in silk, you know lake that silk scarf I bought ye'r mammy from the Darkie a while back, and that Dorry runs about wearing when your mammy's not lookin."

They slithered down the steep slope to get back to the old dams and the road.

As they strode back to the cottage, Danny said suddenly, "Robbie, mammy says that Father O'Kelly towel them in the chapel that Communists don't believe in God at al. Do you believe in God… an' his mammy… an' the divil an' al that?"

"I don't believe in votin God in or out," was the unusually curt reply, and then more gently, "believe me, little comrade, everybody believes in God when they come under machine gunfire. At all other times, I believe in keeping out of God's way. If He doesn't bother me, I won't bother Him but if He's there, I have a few hard questions tay put tay Him at the pearly gates. Now are you gonna come with me this evenin to check the rabbit snares or not?"

---

115 **Chap-fallen** – *very hungry*

Episode 10

Problems in Paradise

Angel Jo's Temper Tantrum

Danny took Robbie's advice and sometimes when the weather was nice he retreated to his stone in Lisnaseedy fort telling Bobby and Dorry, who wanted to come too, that it was far too high for them to climb, and that it was only for big boys who were brave enough to see off the bad fairies and demons that were up there jumping all over the place. It was during one of these visits to the fort that Angel Jo put in another appearance. Danny was lying beside his stone in the ferns squinting up at the sun when suddenly, and apparently coming right out of it, there was the angel.

"Oh, there you are," Angel Jo began in a bad-tempered way. "You 'earth-grubbers' are great at lying about. But I suppose better that than robbing and stealing... invading each other... hacking down forests and jungles... wars here, famines there, all those dreadful things you are so good at. No, better by far to just lie around all day... I've said it before, this hunk of rock is a no hoper. No wonder God went walk-about when He realized what a mess He had created down here. I have just come from one of His early creations... a thing of pure beauty... not a cloud in the sky... Mind you, it can be a trifle boring... a bit like your Sweden."

After this outburst, the angel seemed to calm down. He sat on Danny's stone and said with a condescending smile, "Don't mind me. Visiting this dreadful world of yours always gets me in a bad mood when I think what might have been but, as I always say, 'we are where we are.' Anyway, how've you been? Sorry I haven't been to see you lately. Just been so very busy. Any little problems or questions for me?"

Distant Times & Distant Planets

"What happened to the boy on the planet where they are all eating each other?" This had stuck in Danny's mind, and was the kind of chilling prospect that interests many small boys for, now that our hero was out of mortal danger from the wrath of the Almighty, he was keen to have news of the fate of others under threat of extinction or worse.

"So well you may ask!" exclaimed the angel. "He's a gonner I'm afraid. Dished up with fried eggs and a light sauce. But we must always look on the bright side, it gave me the opportunity to write another quite beautifully crafted report on it all, though I say so myself. By the way, where did this stone come from?"

"It was my altar. I brought it up from the dams down there when I thought God was going to kill me and send me to hell for being bad. But Robbie says I'm not bad so it's just a stone again. Robbie says he is not sure if there is such a place as hell or a Judgement Day or any of that stuff, but maybe that because he's nearly a Communist. Is there a Judgement Day or hell?"

This seemed a highly appropriate question to ask an angel.

BOAK adds to the Heavenly Work Loads

"That man should mind his own business. With what he gets up to, it will certainly suit him if there is no hell or Judgement Day. Well, since you ask, hell and, worse still, Judgement Day have both been in a bit of muddle of late. You see, it goes back to all of us in heaven being so overworked and the most overworked of all was St Peter. Now you know, don't you, that he has got the keys of the kingdom - heaven alone knows why - but he has them so that's that. Nobody gets past without him giving them the thumbs up. But the trouble is, you see, when God took a hike – still no word by the way – and BOAK started doling out more and more jobs to everybody, St Peter was no exception. Oh, he protested, of course, that he couldn't cope as it was, what with the throngs he had to deal with, day and night, all standing round the pearly gates to be judged and rewarded... or not as the case may be... and keeping records of who got what and why in heaven, for the goody-goodies squabble terribly over their heavenly rewards once they are in. Then, to cap it all, BOAK introduced an appeals committee for the ones Peter had damned so he had to chair that and listen to them whinging on about *special circumstances that made them do this or that or it wasn't them at all and they weren't even there at the time*... and so on. Then BOAK put him in charge of the heavenly archives which are in a complete mess, and of the woman saints who can be very demanding... and he got something else... oh yes... hermits who are a real headache what with never knowing where they are or what they are up to."

St. Peter Pulls the Chain

The angel paused to look sternly at Danny who was trying to stifle a yawn. "I hope I'm not boring you," he said sharply and without waiting for an answer, as was his wont, he hastened on,

"Anyway, BOAK doesn't like anyone up there doing their own thing. They like everybody accounted for, and everything recorded in triplicate. So there was St Peter beside himself with stress, and he was never great at coping with that... remember the cockcrow episode... yes! ... not one of his better moments I think! Anyway, he decided to take drastic action. It was a crowd called the Puritans that finally pushed him over the edge. They arrived saying, if you please, they wouldn't let him judge them because only God could judge them, that He had already done so, had found them whiter than white, and had told them they would go straight to heaven, no 'ands,' 'ifs' or 'buts.' Well that did it... the last straw! Peter told me himself it was one thing cluttering up heaven with the Catholics for at least they had staggered though life having a bit of fun and were always good for a laugh, and the Anglicans – that's your lot – added a touch of class to the place... though there are dreadful exceptions... but the heaven-bound Puritans! A sour-faced self-righteous lot wandering round condemning everything and everybody, and saying heaven wasn't exactly to their mind, not like what it says in the Bible, and questioning the right of priests, nuns and monks and even some saints to be there at all! I ask you!"

"Are the Puri-ans a bit like the holy people that go to the Reverend Quigley's meetings for they don't laugh much or tell jokes or do anything except sing hymns, pray, and scare the wits out of people like me."

"Very similar. Glad to see you are keeping up. Now you are surely wondering what St. Peter's solution was? Well, it was a bit naughty of him, and I have to say I think there were definite signs of a nervous breakdown, but since the Puritans seemed to want to be disappointed anyway, and hell is good at providing that big time, why not send them there straight away since they couldn't be more miserable than they are already. So as batches of them approached the pearly gates singing hymns and telling each other how holy they were, Peter just pulled yon big chain that opens the hatch in front of the gates and down the chute they all went, no exceptions."

"So... since St Peter started to pull that big chain, everybody is now in hell... even the ones that should be in heaven?" queried Danny now wide awake and trying desperately to make sense of it.

Cromwell to the Rescue

"Yes, that was how it was for a short while, until Peter's drastic action was discovered due to there being no fresh intakes. But he's a wily old boy so got away with it claiming pressure of work, headaches, stomach pains, the sort of excuses you use when you don't want to go to school. Of course Peter's solution to Judgement Day could only ever be temporary anyway so drastic steps had to be taken to correct matters, and the upshot was that BOAK had to step in. At first, they assigned St Theresa of Avila to help Peter with the judgements but that only made bad worse. I mean that woman's a mystic, so mystical in fact she can float around! And float she did... in ecstasy... over everybody's' head... waving a palm leaf... singing hymns in Latin... and asking people to shoot arrows at her so she can suffer a bit more. I mean what good was that in helping Peter with his problems? It all very well being other-worldly but not if you are already in the other world! I tell you, Daniel Malachy, you don't know your living down here. Not a problem worth mentioning compared with up there."

Danny was about to argue that he personally had lots of problems but, as usual, Angel Jo was in full flow,"... finally, someone on the BOAK Committee came up with a sensible idea for once, and that has worked great. They assigned a man who, although he is a Puritan himself, knows how to deal with the more awkward Puritans. Cromwell he's called but I suppose silly-little-you will never have heard of him. Good old Oliver has solved everything at a stroke by cutting out all the nonsense that was ruining the judgement system and driving St Peter astray. When anyone starts to argue over Cromwell's decision, he simply shouts *'You have sat here long enough, in God's name go - to hell'*. So Judgement Day is now working smoothly again and any misjudgements are just buried down below. Neat, isn't it. Now there is no point in you looking so dazed, Daniel Malachy, for you did ask your old GA to explain the heavenly goings-on, and the worries we've had there. Anyway, whether you've understood it or not, I must be off. It's been good to talk, and nice for me to get these problems out in the open, and not bottled up."

Since his explanation of the celestial crises appeared to have left the angel a spent force and almost speechless for once, Danny seized his chance to ask him again about his own big problem.

St Cecelia Wants an Answer

"Did you ask BOAK again about curing my stutter?" he ventured hurriedly in case the angel disappeared.

"I most certainly did not, and don't dare ask," said Angel Jo crossly. "I have told you we guardian angels are not allowed to *'tinker'* with you lot, and curing you would be tinkering. How are you getting on with your singing and music by the way? That was the best I could do for you. I hope you are putting it to good use?"

"I don't want to sing," Danny said emphatically, "it's sissy to sing," but when he saw the angry expression on the angel's face he said hurriedly, "... but mammy has got our Dorry a piano... so I might try to learn that... a bit, anyway... if I have time," though he had not the slightest intention of doing anything of the kind.

"I have said it before and I'll say it again, Daniel Malachy, you are a very ungrateful boy. When I think of the trouble I took to help you perfect your singing and music! St Cecelia is forever asking me how you are coming along?... and what am I to tell her? ... that you would rather roll stones up hills and lie about in the grass in the sun? It's really very disappointing."

"I'm sorry," said Danny, "I will try to sing but if you don't mind I'd rather sing very quietly so that nobody hears me. Would that be OK?"

"I suppose it might have to do for a start," said Jo, "but you know, I have my reports to write, and you will have to give me something to say about your singing or I'll be in trouble."

"I will try," said Danny.

"It's a deal, though I am still very disheartened. But I don't want to be cross with you for I must be off and it's not heavenly to quarrel... or it usen't to be anyway. I'll see you when I see you," and he vanished abruptly in the usual drizzly mist.

Danny immediately started to plot how he could keep his promise without having to keep it too much as he rose from his stone scrabbing himself badly on a whin bush.

Episode 11

Smuggling on the Sunday School Express

It was that time of year when the good Canon Pretyman of St Patrick's Church of Ireland, Ballybracken, and his three Sunday school teachers had to get around to organizing the annual Sunday school treat for the children. This year, the Canon had determined on a seaside excursion but choosing the best resort was not proving easy due to the resistance of his Sunday school teachers to the whole idea. Their resistance was unusually unanimous, for the three women seldom agreed on anything, but on this occasion they spoke with one voice; the thought of supervising wayward children let loose in a seaside resort could not be tholed[116]. What was wrong, they queried, with a well-conducted parish picnic in the rectory grounds as in previous years?

Quo Vadis?

But the Canon was set on the excursion justifying his decision, when taxed by his difficult helpers, by saying, *'travel broadens the mind, and sea air works wonders on young lungs.'* A trip agreed – or not agreed but now underway however grudgingly - there was now the thorny question of which seaside resort would be most suitable? On this, the three Sunday school teachers most unhelpfully split three ways, all of them equally convinced they were right. Mrs. Madge Alcorn, a tall thin woman of horsey appearance and who was, as it happens, Danny's Sunday school teacher, was determined that the destination should be Bundoran, a small seaside resort just over the border in the Irish Republic. As we shall see, Madge had her own good – or perhaps not so good -reasons for pressing Bundoran's case.

By contrast, Lavinia Ellis favoured Portrush on the north coast declaring it to be a 'good Protestant place' to take the children. Lavinia was holy to a truly incredible extent and so resisted having truck of any kind with Anti-Christ Catholics with which Bundoran, and indeed the Irish Republic generally, was literally crawling in her view. Phyllis Sproule, who was of such a nervous disposition that she had to steel herself even to go as little as two miles from

---

116 **Tholed** – *countenanced … endured… borne*

home, continued to plead for a quiet, well-conducted picnic with only the 'nice' children of Ballybracken Sunday school who were to get prizes invited. Phyllis had extreme discipline trouble of a Sunday coping with her own small group who tended to favour running up and down the church aisle, climbing into the pulpit and hiding behind the altar rather than attending to their catechism, uplifting hymns and the gospel message.

So not for the first time in his cure of souls in Ballybracken was the Canon facing a dilemma. Several stormy meetings with his three helpers had resolved nothing concerning the excursion's destination and, to his dismay, gave the three of them the opportunity to cast certain aspersions, and say more about each other's judgement than was either Christian or wise. After one of these unpleasant confrontations, when Miss Sproule had run into the vestry weeping and Mrs Alcorn had threatened to resign there and then, the Canon was sipping a restoring glass of sherry back in the rectory and steeling himself to call the whole thing off. He would give each of the children a nice Bible and Prayer Book as usual and perhaps a stick of rock to the few well-behaved ones to make up for not getting to the seaside, and that would be that. Broadening their minds and improving their lungs would have to wait. He was about to refill his glass when his wife came into the sitting room carrying the day's 'Times.' He told her his resolve. Mrs. Pretyman was made of sterner stuff than her husband. She now gave him one of her steely looks.

"Horace," she said throwing the newspaper on his lap, "you're a weakling! The houses around here are literally propped up with Bibles and Prayer Books. You dole them out to the hapless children every year, their parents before them got the same and probably their grandparents too. They can hardly get through their doors with the amount of holy literature cluttering up the place. I'll tell you what I want, I want to go to Bundoran! And I'll tell you for nothing why Madge Alcorn wants to get across the border to Bundoran? Smuggling! Lots of things still rationed here are not rationed there, and she wants to do a bit of honest smuggling. More power to her, I say. I may even join her. Now go ahead and arrange it."

"But, Dora, how can I decide we are going to Bundoran when the other two ladies are so determined that we won't."

"Overrule them, Horace, assert yourself."

"But surely you see that I need a reason I can justify."

"I'll give you the reason. Tell them you have told everybody there is going to be an excursion this year, and it is your Christian duty not to go back on your word. Well it is, isn't it?" Then say it has to be Bundoran because the train fare to Bundoran is far less than to Portrush. And for heaven's sake rule out Phyllis Sproule's stupid idea of a picnic. Sure it always rains and the children go home soaked. I wonder half of them didn't catch pneumonia in past years. Leave the train fare to me. I'll see to it that it's much cheaper to go to Bundoran by filling up every carriage on the train to reduce the fare. Next Sunday you can announce that there is an open invitation for anyone who wants to come with us, and they should give their names to me. I'll warrant there will be plenty of folk round here who will jump at the chance to do a bit of smuggling under the cover of your Sunday school excursion and, Horace, if that troubles your conscience, you surely can't be held accountable if some folk have motives for going to Bundoran other than broadening their minds and breathing in the ozone."

Thus guided and chastened, the good Canon turned to lose himself, if only temporarily, in the 'Times' crossword until he would be told what to do next.

Madge Alcorn Triumphs

It was indeed the lure of the Republic's ampler supplies of butter, cheese and ham, together with several other desirable items that had weighed most heavily with Mrs Alcorn in her preferred destination. So it was highly satisfactory from her point of view and, *'ony but right'* that the Canon should come down on her side and opt for Bundoran. As she told Effie McKnight in the shop a day or two later,

"Isn't he the gran wee man who cud bay brought tay hez senses when others wur trying tay lead him astray. But I seen tay it he wuz freed from under the skirts aff them that wur trying tay bully him. I wud niver bay a party tay that[117], fir petticoat policies is no policies at al! You know he relies on me tay tak sense when others is takin balderdash."

"If you happened to get the chance," Effie was bent over with her back to Madge filling her can with paraffin oil, "like if it came your way and wasn't putting you to a lot of bother, I wouldn't say no to you slipping me a pound or two of butter and maybe a quantity of that nice sliced ham they have down there... if it caught your eye like... not, of course, that I'm putting you up to smuggling, Madge."

"Yeh can leave it to me, Effie. I'm not fir doin anythin wrong but sure a pound or two aff butter, an' what have yeh, ill hardly sink the ship. An' sure isn't

---

117 ***'Niver bay a party tay that*** – never indulge in or support that kind of behaviour

it high time the rationing wuz aff here to?"

"Oh, indeed so," Effie agreed. "I was just saying the very same thing to the commercial traveller last week. We are poorly done by after all our efforts to back England up in the war... and no sign of light at the end of the rationing tunnel yet. But see what you can do for us anyway and if nothing comes of it... sure there's no harm done. Now, is there anything else I can get you?"

Danny Dons His Big Coat

Little did Daniel Malachy Dowdells know what a central part he was destined to play in Mrs Alcorn's smuggling venture as he prepared for his day at the seaside. Rosie couldn't go having landed a big job laundering many of the curtains in the McKendry mansion, Ballybracken House, which the old grand dame herself, Mrs. McKendry Senior, had declared must be done on the day she designated which happened to be the same day as the excursion. The fact that nobody had actually asked Rosie to accompany her children to Bundoran wouldn't have deterred her. The Protestant side in Ballybracken never invited her to anything even though she sent her children to their school and their church, but her critics put that down to Robbie's good influence even though he himself was generally regarded to be, as the Canon put it, *'a very loose fellow.'* Rosie just turned up uninvited when she could, and nobody ever turned her away.

But on this occasion she had no choice but to seek out Madge Alcorn to ask her if she would look after her three children on the outing? Madge agreed that she would look after Danny because he was in her Sunday school class, and Lavinia would look after Bobby with Phyllis taking care of Dorry. This caused the usual wrangle among the teachers, Lavinia saying that Bobby was the worst behaved boy in her class so… *'thanks very much for completely ruining her day'* … and Phyllis complaining in much the same vein about Dorry. Having thus lumbered her colleagues with charges they manifestly didn't want, Madge seized the opportunity to incorporate Danny into her smuggling scheme.

"He's a plump wee thing," she said to Rosie. "Make sure he wears a big warm coat with good deep pockets for yeh know yeh cud git a founderin at them sayside places, and we don't want the wee sowl comin back way a chill."

The day of the excursion dawned bright and sunny. All the excursioners were to meet at the railway station, Danny, Bobby and Dorry taken there in Mrs. Alcorn's Morris Minor which was itself a great thrill. Then there was the train which drew up at the platform with a shrieking of brakes, belching smoke, shrill whistling, and funny-smelling fumes issuing from the engine's every orifice. Madge found a carriage that had frayed but comfortable looking upholstery and settled herself and Danny in there. What became of Lavinia and Phyllis and their charges she neither knew nor cared for in this melee of children all screaming and shouting it was everyone for themselves.

"I'm glad tay see ye'r mammy took may advice an' sent yez al in nice big warm coats, Danny," she said looking at him for the first time that morning.

Danny was indeed swathed in a coat several sizes too big for him which Rosie had cut down, with only limited success, from one of Robbie's old army coats. He felt lost inside it and was already sweltered. He sunk deeper inside the ill-fitting cocoon of rough army material and started to suck his thumb. He would have liked to have been with Bobby and Dorry, but he loved the train and he was looking forward to getting to the seaside for he had never seen the sea. The train set off with a spinning of wheels, more dense smoke, and with specks of coal and soot drifting over him from the open window. All this was just great! How could Bundoran be better than this?

Hot-Gospellers & Hobby Horses

But it was, or as good anyway. Both their mammy and Robbie had given the children money so that was great too. To start with, the sea itself was a bit of a disappointment for the tide was so far out, added to which the Reverend Quigley and the small group of Ballybracken's intensely holy had got on to the beach first, had erected their *'Ye must be Born Again,'* banner, and were already well into a round of stirring religious choruses down on the sand.

'Wudn't yeh think he cud hiv left that owl banner at home. He's lettin us down a bagful'[118] *way that kerry on,'* was Mrs Alcorn's unsupportive verdict.

The sand on the beach was lovely and, before you knew it, the tide had started to come in and swept over the children's bare feet amid much screaming and laughing and then weeping when Dorry fell in the water and had to be taken away to be dried out. Mrs Alcorn had brought sandwiches and buns and cake and apples and oranges and nuts and fizzy lemonade in a big tin box which

---

118 **'Letting us down a bagful'** – embarrassing us dreadfully

she shared with everybody, warning Danny not to eat so fast or he'd be sick. Bobby was sick for that very reason but quickly recovered to eat ice cream and some sugary fluffy stuff on a long stick back on the promenade, and then he was sick again. Danny managed it all without mishap, and then they all went to something called the 'Amusements' where they spent their money on driving cars that bumped into each other, on a train that took you past terrible wild animals making an awful noise, ghosts that looked like they were going to eat you, witches with big teeth and pointy hats and screaming skeletons. Dorry came out of the ghost train tunnel as white as a sheet, and then she was sick all over Phyllis's best shoes but recovered to ride on painted horses that went round and round and up and down. Then it was on to something called swing boats that scared the wits out of Danny they went up so high so now it was his turn to be sick over the side.

Danny Boards the 'Duck'

But it didn't matter. It was all nothing short of great! When they went back for a final paddle in the sea, Danny noticed a big coloured boat with wheels on the beach with people getting out of it. It looked like you could go for a ride in it but Mrs Alcorn said no, it was something called a *'Duck'* that soldiers had used during the war, and it was famous for breaking down way out yonder and, *'the dear knows where you'd end up if you went on it – maybe Amerike.'* Danny was just thinking it would be great to end up in *'Amerike'* when, quite suddenly, Mrs Alcorn seemed to change her mind.

"Do yeh know, Danny," she said, "I think you'd be safe enough in yon Duck for a wee trip seein ye'r that keen. I'll find somewan for yeh tay sit beside an' look out for yeh for I hiv a wheena messages tay do up the town[119]. Wud yeh bay content tay go way out me?"

Danny was delighted. Mrs Alcorn, who he had always thought was an awfully cross woman especially if you hadn't learnt your hymns, catechism and verses of scripture for Sunday school, now soared in his estimation. But time was of the essence for the Duck was filling up fast. Neither Lavinia nor Phyllis could be persuaded to go for *'it wuz ony wan step up from suicide tay put a foot on that thing*

---

119 ***I hiv a wheena messages tay do up the town*** - *I have some shopping to do on the main street*

'and Phyllis declared that she felt funny even crossing Ballybracken bridge, so scared was she of water. Nothing daunted, Mrs Alcorn, with Danny running in front of her, made it over to the Duck and luck was with her for there was young Tommy Lyttle from Ballybracken Upper sitting in the boat with his arm round some girl - '*if yeh plaze... an' him no age tay bay runnin efter girls.*' Tommy wasn't the most reliable fellow she could have found but needs must. She clambered up the ladder into the boat and said to Tommy in a breathless whisper,

"Listen, Tommy, this wee lad, Dowdells, is mad keen tay go on the trip but I'm heart skared tay go way him. Wud yuz iver luk efter him an' I'll meet yez on the beach when yez get back. I'll get yeh a packet of fags for ye'r trouble?"

Without waiting for an answer, she shouted to the man who seemed to be in charge, "How long day yez think yez'll be?"

"About an hour at most, Mrs... ," came the reply and then, with a smirk at the passengers, "... al being well, that is."

Tommy didn't seem all that taken with looking after Danny since it didn't sit well with his intention to have a hot 'curt' at the back of the Duck when everybody was lookin the other way but before he could say yeh or nay, Mrs Alcorn was off down the ladder leaving Danny in Tommy's not too tender care.

Danny couldn't believe his luck. What a story he would have to tell Robbie and his mammy about the entire day but especially the ride in the Duck that only he had had.

Duck Drama

A few more voyagers clambered aboard, fares were collected, and then they were off. There were alarming clanking and groaning noises from somewhere underneath the boat as it lurched down the beach and off into the waves with a great thrust upwards at the front as it hit the deep water, spray flying everywhere and excited screams from the passengers. It levelled out, there was a chug-chugging sound from somewhere beneath Danny's feet and the Duck moved swiftly out to sea. Danny was beside himself with delight. Tommy's girl had made room for him beside her but apart from that neither of them said a word to Danny they were so busy kissing and cuddling which Danny thought was an awful waste of time when they could have been leaning over the side, tasting the salt spray from the big waves, and looking up at the seagulls following them and kicking up such a noise. He resolved there and then that he would never go in for 'kissin' and 'cuddlin,' even if Robbie said they weren't a sin, and he couldn't help wondering why a big boy like Tommy was wasting his time doing it?

They were far out now with Bundoran away back in the distance when the Duck's engine suddenly stopped. The man at the wheel looked round at his passengers with a worried expression, and even Tommy stopped kissing and fondling the girl if only for a moment. The Duck, now sitting sideways to the shore, jigged up and down on the waves. Some of the passengers crossed themselves and started to mumble prayers. Some of the men started to shout questions to the man in charge. Danny wasn't a bit scared for this could mean they would drift on to America, and wouldn't it be just great to write to his mammy and Robbie from there to tell them all about it, and wouldn't Bobby and Dorry be that jealous. Then the man at the wheel gave a great laugh,

"Ah ha, that put the fear aff God into yez," he shouted. "I was just givin yez a wee extra thrill for ye'r money," and, to Danny's great disappointment, he violently cranked a handle, the Duck's engine spluttered back into life and they were off back to the shore.

"Men-iez a man wuz kilt for less," somebody muttered from the other side of the boat.

"The ill-bred skitter, skarin the bloody wits out aff us," said another.

All too soon, they were rolling back up the beach. Danny wanted to stay on board as long as possible and was among the last to leave. Even Tommy and the girl had disentangled themselves, were down the ladder and on the beach before him, and were standing there still kissing passionately. Somebody helped Danny down the rickety steep ladder, and he was back on dry land.

"Thank you," Danny said to Tommy and the girl for, although they had ignored him, he might not have got going at all if they hadn't been there, and anyway didn't his mammy tell them that they should always thank everybody for everything?

"What for?" asked Tommy, who had clearly forgotten all about Danny.

"For lukin efter may," said Danny.

"Ach right," said Tommy and then remembering the deal struck with Mrs Alcorn, he continued, "be sure an' tell that woman she owes me a packet aff fags." With that he headed off up the beach with his arm round the girl's waist.

"I'll never do that either," thought Danny. "It's so sissy lukin."

Danny was not on his own for long. Bobby and Dorry came galloping down the beach demanding to know what it was like, and was there not still time for them to get a ride on it?

Danny said there wasn't for the 'drivin man' had gone for his tea, though he hadn't, but he was quite determined that nobody else must share in the great adventure that he had just had.

"Youz wud bay too skared tay go on it anyway… the waves out there wuz lake big mountains… an' the engine stapped… an' we wur nearly driftin on tay Amerike… we cud even see it way out far… but then the man got it started again… an' we come back at full tilt… I wuzn't skared a bit… but other people wur crying an' praying."

He broke off as Mrs Alcorn appeared carrying two very large brown paper bags.

"So yu'r back safe an' soun, love," she said. "That's good."

Danny was bursting to tell her all about his boat ride too but she cut him short.

"I've a wee job for yeh, Danny, but I need to get yeh on ye'r own. Yuz-uns run away back an' fin Miss Ellis and Miss Sproule… I think I can see them over yonner," and she pointed down the beach where the two were sitting on a rug well back from the sea.

"Danny, you come way me."

Danny's Big Burden

Danny followed her up the beach as she struggled to keep hold of the two bulging bags. When they got to the promenade, he saw with horror that she was heading towards the ladies' lavatory and clearly wanted him to follow her.

"Come on in, yeh boy yeh," she said, catching him by one of the big lapels on his coat. "This'll only take a minute," and she dragged him inside.

In no time at all she had filled his coat pockets with pounds of butter, square portions of cheese and packets of cooked ham. It weighed a ton, added to which Mrs Alcorn had not taken time to get his load of consumables well balanced so Danny was soon badly tilted over to one side.

"Now, you go on outside, son, an' for heaven's sake wud yeh try tay stan up straight," and she disappeared into one of the cubicles carrying what was left in one of her paper bags.

To say that our Danny was very glad to escape would be to seriously understate his frame of mind at that moment. As he emerged from the gloomy smelly interior he felt like one of those over-burdened camels he had seen in pictures of hot countries. Outside, he was further discomforted to find Bobby and Dorry and their two minders standing by the door, with Bobby saying he looked like that Eskimo in his school reading book and Dorry in an uncontrollable fit of the giggles. Lavinia and Phyllis looked as if they had each just swallowed a wasp, and their look of disapproval intensified considerably when Mrs Alcorn emerged with a sizeable bulge to the front which hadn't been there when she went in.

"I'll not say what that luks lake or what ye'r tryin tay hide," said Lavinia, "but I suppose yeh might get away way it if we're stapped at the customs for yeh look as if yeh might be takin a delivery any day."

"Ach, the customs will take no note of the wee fella, sure he looks like a wee waif, an' they'll not bother way me in what luks like may delicate condition. We'll get away way it the best, an' I'll warrant yez will not be saying 'naw' when I get al this cheap pruck[120] home!"

Platters & Maggots

"We'd better go an' get something tay ate before headin for the train. Did yez spot any nice eatin houses on ye'r travels, lake wan that's not clatty lukin[121]?"

They headed up Bundoran main street and into a restaurant that boasted ham salad 'platters' which sounded suitably exotic to drop into conversation back home. Danny went into a sulk when he was relieved of some of his money to pay for his brother and sister's 'platters' as well as his own and had to be coaxed, and then threatened, to get him to eat up when the platters finally arrived. He had the greatest difficulty with his overburdened coat, which Mrs. Alcorn had forbidden him to take off, and which seemed to have developed a mind of its own pulling him this way and that as he attempted to eat. The buttered bread that accompanied the platter proved a particular challenge, the long sleeve of the coat seeming intent on gobbling up the bread before he could get it to his mouth. All three women remarked loudly on how little there was on any of the platters, for the edibles comprised one thin slice of cooked ham hidden under a mountain of lettuce and little else.

"I'll swear that's margarine on the bread too," said Lavinia, "an' wudn't yeh think they cud .hiv stretched tay another slice aff ham!"

"Ach they seen us comin[122] al right… owl fools down from the Black North," Lavinia declared. She was about to make an assault on the salad when there was

---

120   **Pruck** – *here it means items not easily available in N. Ireland in the 1950s*
121   **Clatty lukin** – *dirty… grubby looking*
122   **Seen us coming** – *took advantage of us… took us for fools*

a piercing scream from Phyllis.

"Maggots!" she shrieked, and she held up a lettuce leaf from which one of the two hapless creatures fell unto the table. With her handkerchief to her mouth she bolted from the restaurant and was not seen again until they reached the station over half an hour later.

"Aren't you folk from the North very particular!" said the waitress as she removed the platter with the offending creatures. "It's a wonner yez come down here at al when yez is that hard tay plaze."

"That wuz hidjus[123]," declared Lavinia. "Didn't I say we shud niver hiv come near this Papish town. Didn't I advocate goin tay nice clian Protestant places lake Portrush or Portstewart, but sure yon wee Canon always agrees way the last person he's been takin tay. He'll hiv tay bay kep under stricter control tay stap him actin so foolish again. He drives me clian mad hez that aisy led[124]."

Madge Alcorn said nothing, for if you are infallible it's impossible to admit of error. Besides, she had got what she wanted out of the excursion and had no regrets, maggots or no maggots.

As they stood sweltering on the platform waiting for the train, Mrs Alcorn was busy putting the last stage of her smuggling plans in place. To her relief, when the train arrived the carriages had no corridors which suited Madge's plans admirably. If she managed to get herself and Danny into a compartment jam-packed with noisy kids, the chances of a customs man bothering with them would be slight. Holding on tight to Danny, who was lurching from side to side as if drunk, the butter and other items moving about alarmingly inside his coat, and disengaging from Lavinia, Phyllis and the other two Dowdells, Madge hoisted Danny into a compartment. There Danny found himself alone with the Reverend Quigley for Madge had remained on the platform to catch and shepherd as many children as she could into the compartment. Mr Quigley looked up from his Bible as Danny sat down awkwardly opposite him, avoiding his eye and looking bleakly at the carriage floor.

Reverend Quigley is Roped in

The Reverend was not best pleased to see our little hero. He cast a baleful look at Danny noting that the coat the boy was wearing seemed to have the strange quality of being able almost to stand on its own. Maybe the lad had been taken

---

123 **Hidjus** – *disgusting*
124 **Aisy led** – *easily influenced*

sick and was wrapped in a blanket beneath that strange coat, he thought. But whatever the explanation, he was not going to get involved. He returning to reading his Bible.

He was savouring some particularly harsh verses in Leviticus when the compartment door flew open again. This time Mrs Alcorn ushered in about ten more children telling them all to sit down, and that those that couldn't find room were to sit on someone else's knee, *'but not Danny Dowdells's'* she shrieked much to his relief. As the children flung themselves about in a most boisterous fashion shouting, squealing and pushing each other off the seats, Mr Quigley rose to go, intent on finding himself another carriage for the noise was intolerable made worse by the sand flying everywhere from the children's clothes, shoes and sandals. But Mrs Alcorn had other plans for him.

"Naw, naw, don't let these wee wans chase yeh, Reverend," she pleaded. "Sure we can al sing nice choruses al the way home. Wudn't yez al love that, children? Tay sing ye'r best for the Reverend Quigley?"

"Naw, we wudn't," muttered some of the bigger boys but Madge had made up her mind. A cleric with a Bible, a carriage packed to overflowing with noisy singing kids, what customs man with any sense would face in there to quiz them about any goods they had to declare? She felt she was on the high road to butter and ham heaven for the next couple of months.

The train started with a sudden jolt that sent two of the children flying into Quigley's lap, and another big lad spreadeagled over Danny.

"Danny Dowdells hiz pished hezself," declared the big lad as he pulled himself back unto his feet.

Danny's Mystery Stains

"I hiv not," said Danny. "I hiv not wet mezself," he repeated.

"Well, what's them big stains on ye'r coat there if it isn't pish?" demanded the big lad.

There were indeed damp stains appearing here and there on Danny's coat and the largest of all, as ill fortune would have it, was at a spot where he might indeed have been thought to have had the kind of accident that is not uncommon for small boys. Madge came to his rescue.

"Wud yeh min ye'r own business, Percy," she said to the big lad, "an' the rest of yez too," for the entire compartment had now turned to look at Danny, pointing and sniggering at his slowly expanding stains.

"Wud yez leave Danny alone. If hez had a wee accident, what's it tay youz? Now come on, what choruses are yez goin tay sing?"

Our little hero was mortified at the idea now generally gaining currency in the carriage that he had wet himself, no one stopping to ponder why some of the greasy stains were appearing in places remote from his supposedly offending member. All he could do was sink even further inside his large heavy coat and hope that the melting butter didn't start oozing down his legs, for what would his travelling companions not make of that!

With a chorus fixed upon and the train underway, the younger children joined in the singing with gusto. The older boys were less enthusiastic, one indeed produced a packet of cigarettes and another a pack of cards and were, with considerable difficulty, dissuaded for lighting up and playing poker.

The Fatherly Customs Man

The train stopped at the border and the customs men walked up and down opening carriage doors in a casual fashion asking if anyone had anything to declare. Never was *'Jesus wants me for a sun beam'* sung so loudly or out of tune, for Madge was determined not to lie when asked the fateful question. A customs man duly opened their carriage door, surveyed the Reverend engrossed in his Bible and the crowded carriage scene with a hint of a smile, said nothing, slammed the door shut and moved on. All was well! The butter was safe, or whatever of it could now be salvaged from Danny's coat and Madge's person, no lies had been told and the coast was clear.

Then to Madge's consternation the customs man returned!

"Are yez not very cramped in there?" he asked. "Do yez not know that there is a near empty compartment a wee bit further down the train. Why don't yez spread ye'rselves out a bit more."

"Ach naw, we're al right as we are," the words were not right out of Mrs. Alcorn's mouth when there was a mass exodus of children from the compartment led by the bigger boys.

"Are you not going too, son?" the customs officer asked the huddled figure in the corner. "Sure you would have more fun down the train with your wee mates."

Danny just stared at the man in terror. How could he move with butter now dripping from his coat?

"Are you all right, son?" The customs man had now entered the compartment and was standing beside Danny.

" Ach sure he's gran, officer. I think he's got a wee bit sick way the jowltin aff the train. Sure it's been a bumpy ride so far, hezn't it son? Day yeh know, I haven't been feelin that good mezself."

"Would you stan up, son," the officer said ignoring Madge, and Danny stood up with melting butter and cheese oozing from every stitch of his coat.

"Well, well, well," said the officer sternly, "and who put a wee lad like you up to the likes of this?"

"I'm not too sure," said Danny dismally for Mrs. Alcorn was frowning and mouthing something at him from behind the officer's back.

"Ye'r not sure, son?" queried the officer. "Ach, I think you surely must know. What's ye'r name anyway?... Danny, you say... come on now, tell me Danny? I'll say nothing more about it to you but some others might have a bit of explaining to do."

There was silence, and Danny started to cry quietly.

"Oh now, don't be crying there at all, son. Sure you're a big boy and big boys don't cry."

Then, turning to Madge and the Reverend, he enquired,

"Do any of you know who is with this wee fella? What's his surname anyway?"

Madge saw a possible escape route and seized it.

"What's this ye'r other name is, son?"

"Danny Dowdells," he mumbled.

"... an' I don't think ye'r mammy or daddy are with yeh the day on the excursion, are they?" she raised her voice as if Danny was hard of hearing.

"Naw," Danny said, "jist Bobby and Dorry."

His stammer was really bad now.

"And who might they be?" enquired the customs man.

"I think that's his wee brother an' sister," explained Madge pretending to help him out. "I believe they are somewhere down the train but I think they are on their own too, aren't they Danny?"

"Aye," said Danny, "except for the Sunday school teachers."

"Now Danny," said the customs man quietly, "I'm gonna ask you again, son. Who put yeh up to this?"

"I think it wuz... " Mrs. Alcorn had put a finger up to her mouth behind the officer's back and had gone so deadly white all poor Danny could think of to do was call on the name of his great hero to somehow help him even at long distance.

"... I want… tay see Robbie… please," he stammered."

The customs man now thought he was getting somewhere. "Is Robbie on the train somewhere?"

"Naw… he's back at home… he's a sodger… he bate Hitler[125] … an' maybe he's away… killin pigs… " Danny said, thinking all that would make Robbie sound big and fierce and not somebody the man would ever want to tangle with "… he's ofen away… killing pigs… an' things… way a big mallet an' butcher knife."

"An' who is Robbie, tell me, Danny?"

'But Robbie is jist Robbie,' thought Danny. *Sure iverybody knows who Robbie is.'*

"Now I come to think, it wudn't surprise me in the slightest if that Robbie fellow, who is living in sin with the boy's mother, put him up to this," Mr Quigley now intervened to say. "The lad comes from a bad family, you know, officer. Oh, very bad… sinful an' wicked. I pray for them to see the light constantly."

"I'm sure you do, Reverend, I'm sure you do," the officer turned in Madge's direction prompting her to say,

"Day yeh know, I can't mind that man Robbie's full name either," and she paused as if she was thinking hard about it. "Come tay think now wuzn't he a sodger lake Danny says that come through the war? Yeh know, that can be the ruination aff menies a decent man. They seldom come back the same," and she continued on in this pious vein, "Och yes, the Reverend's quite right. Very poor family… very poor indeed… nothing behin them at al… hardly the nails tay scratch themselves.[126]"

The customs man looked back at the poor distraught little figure standing in the corner, tears in his eyes, sucking his thumb, determined not to tell and trying not to cry. At that moment, his official officer's cap vanished and a caring father took its place.

"Ach Danny, I know when I'm bate. I doubt I'm never gonna get to the bottom of who put you up to this but whoever it was shouldn't have done it. Now, do you know what I'm gonna do with you?"

"Naw," Danny couldn't even imagine but it was sure to be something terrible. The very worst thing about it so far was to have mentioned Robbie, the man who was his very best friend, as if Robbie had had something to do with it but

---

125 **He bate Hitler** – *he defeated Hitler*
126 **Nothing behin them at al… hardly the nails tay scratch themselves** – *very poor people with no prospects for improvement*

all he had meant was that he wanted Robbie to somehow be there now to help him as Robbie always did. But it had come out all wrong.

"I'm gonna take you off the train," continued the officer. "I'm gonna take that old greasy coat off you and all you have in there... and I'm gonna get you a new coat... then you can get back on the train and go back to your mammy... and daddy," he added after a pause for he had found the Dowdells's domestic arrangements a bit hard to grasp.

"New... coat?" stammered Danny. "I hiven't... no money left... "

"That's ok, Danny. It's your lucky day. My son came down to my office after school and football today for me to give him a lift home. He's a wee bit bigger than you, and the coat he's wearin doesn't fit him anymore. His mammy has been at me to take her and him in to the town to get him a new one. Now wait till I tell yeh. You can have his coat. It's as good as new and will fit you to a tee. Come on now, get out unto the platform with me and we'll get you sorted out, son."

On the platform, and with every window on the train packed with on-lookers, Danny was relieved of his coat dripping melted butter worse than ever, and the officer appeared very soon with another coat together with his son.

Danny's New Coat

"Danny, this is Colin. Danny's a bigtime smuggler, you know, Colin. Customs men were all looking for him high and low, and it was your daddy finally caught him. What do you think of that?"

Colin looked at Danny astonished, and then said to his father,

 "But he's only the same age as me!"

"Oh, that Danny boy has been round a few corners, I can tell you. Anyway, we haven't time for any more coddin[127]. Here's the coat I promised you, Danny. Don't be puttin it on till you get home and have had a bath or you will get more of them greasy stains on it. There still some melting butter here and there on your shirt."

"Thank you very... very... very much," stammered Danny. "I... love... my... new coat."

"That all right, Danny, sure you're a fine fella," and he hunkered down to look Danny straight in the face and whisper, "I know, wee son, that Robbie or your mammy didn't put you up to all this, and I am sure your mammy and Robbie

---

127 **Coddin** – *fooling around*

are great people who you must love very much... so we will say no more about the butter and all that... Good luck to yeh, Danny. You're a fine big man, so you are, and it has been great meetin you"... and as he got up from his hunkers he muttered to himself, '... *and who cares a bucky who ye'r daddy is? Feck these owl hypocrites.*'

Danny held the lovely new coat out at arms-length in case it got stained and got back into the compartment. The customs man slammed the door.

"I hope all goes well with ye'r delivery, Ma'am," he said to Madge through the open window then paused and continued, "Yeh seem to be leakin a bit there ye'rself but it would be very indiscrete of me to enquire further for who knows what might emerge from that big bulge..." and he walked off down the platform whistling, his young son running ahead of him.

The Reverend Reveals All

After a few minutes, the train started off again, Mrs. Alcorn's face was now beetroot red, and remained so for the rest of the journey.

"I'll niver bay caught dead doin the lakes aff that again," she gasped when they were well clear of the border.

"Well, see you don't," said the Reverend Quigley standing up and taking several packets of melting butter and some ham from each of his own coat pockets. "I thought we'd niver get rid aff him but I think if we put this up here on the rack an' open the windows to give it a good airin, we shud get it home safe enough."

"Ye'r right, Reverend, that'll save what's left an' get it home in wan piece," said Madge beginning to unstrap her bulge while Quigley looked fixedly out of the window, "for I wuz beginnin tay feel lake a well-basted ham shank way al this meltin roun me."

When she had her burden safely up on the rack, she said knowingly to the Reverend,

"I'm surprised an' a wee bit shocked at you, Reverend, you so good-livin, doin a wee bit aff smugglin ye'rself!"

"Martha likes the South's butter and ham. Hiv tay keep the wife happy, yeh know. She thinks it's tastier than ours in the North. Ony for that I wudn't bay bringin anythin back from that God-forsaken country... an' besides," he continued, "didn't somebody wance say *'a smuggler is the ony honest thief.'*"

Having thus salved his conscience, he went back to studying Leviticus.

'Desperate Danny'

"You wur a great boy for not givin us away, Danny, for, day yeh know, I thought we wur for the high jump. We wur just unlucky that the whole jingbang aff them-uns raced out of the carriage the way they did, the rascals. I blame the owler wans for I think they are now up the train smokin and playin cards for money."

Reverend Quigley sniffed his disapproval without looking up.

"...an luk, yeh got a lovely new coat out aff it... what make is it? ... Ach 'Burberry'... ony the very best... I'm sure ye'r mammy will be delighted."

Danny stroked the front of the coat. It was smooth and had all its buttons and a nice belt and buckle. He felt content in spite of everything. It had been a great day. He had got a ride in a boat and nearly got to America. That man had been nice to him... given him a lovely coat... and called him a big man and a big-time smuggler. What could be better? The only thing he still felt sorry for was letting Robbie down. But then Mrs Alcorn and the Reverend Quigley had let him down far worse in that compartment, and they didn't seem a bit sorry!

So a great end to a great day out. It had indeed been fortunate for our little hero that an understanding customs man who knew instinctively how to deal with the likes of Danny and his world, had the decency to give him a nice coat knowing he needed one, and not just because of melting butter. But most important of all, he had said nice reassuring things to Danny about those he loved most in all the world.

Before long, Danny's fame... or better still, infamy... spread around Ballybracken by those who claimed to have witnessed his undoing on the train.

'... they had seen it way their very own eyes, the wee rascal taken out of the carriage unto the platform... stripped naked he wuz... arms up in the air... .. hez coat filled up way butther an' bacon an' cheese an' ham an' cigarettes an' whiskey an' brandy... an' God alone knows what else... an' the man had said he wuz as darin a smuggler as ever he'd come across... an' wuzn't it desperate tay see such cunnin in wan so young... but sure somewan had definitely put him up tay it... wuzn't that Rosie herself a cunnin rascal... an' her that plausible... an' wasn't the whiskey for that big hard man of hers that she's livin way... an' Rosie an' Robbie not even there tay look efter the cunnin wee rascal... an' sure wuzn't that the most cunnin part of their plan... an' what a bad example it had al been to well-brung-up wains in

Danny Dowdells

Ballybracken... for them Dowdells wur a bad rarin[128] *... an' what wud that Danny not get up to when he was owler... him the make-ins aff a criminal already...an' he had nearly got away with it ... but for the Reverend Quigley telling on him for Quigley can't bay havin sin of any kin as they al knew... an' the customs man wuz about tay arrest Danny but then discovered he was under age so let him aff with a terrible warning... an' he is niver tay darken the Republic again and Bundoran in particular...'* and on the story went around Ballybracken in various forms getting more and more exaggerated in the telling. But it was as a hero in Ballybracken school playground that gained Danny the most benefit, for wasn't he now *'up tay hez oxters*[129] *in smugglin'* with all the money that must be raking in. Our Danny was now the boy to know.

And it would all have been great, for wouldn't it have been something to go home and tell his mammy and Robbie all about, if Danny's one and only great hero hadn't landed himself in jail that very same day.

---

128 **Bad rarin** – *had turned out badly.*
129 **'Up tay hez oxters in smugglin'** – *up to his armpits in... i.e. deeply engaged in smuggling*

Episode 12

Crime and Punishment

Robbie had found himself at a loose end with Rosie away to work in Ballybracken House and the children off on the excursion. Having kicked his heels around the kitchen in the cottage all morning, he thought he would call in at what passed for Ballybracken's library, which was located in the old schoolhouse, to see if he could pick up something to read, and then he would drop into Cobain's for a pint or two to pass the time. His folk would be back with various tales to tell of the day's events, and he was especially looking forward to hearing about Bundoran having once cycled there when he was a lad, and had happy memories of his very first swim in the sea.

Maisie & the Master

When he arrived in the library, the only other book borrower was Master Blair, the retired headmaster of Ballybracken Protestant school. He was sitting in the library's one and only chair, and casually perusing a large book. The Master had been a pitiless old tyrant to both his scholars and his family. He referred to everyone in the school, clever or otherwise, as *'Stupid Goosies'* and caned mercilessly, especially the farm labourers' children for there would be no come-back from 'their sort.' When he didn't get the recognition he considered due to him by the local school inspector, and those were the days when results were carefully monitored and the Master's results were less than persuasive, he had attacked the inspector first verbally and then physically and had been taken to court. Only a well-paid barrister and membership of the Masonic Order had got him off. Now here he was, clad in his sartorial suit, bow tie and well buffed-up shoes ordering around the young woman, Maisie Trimble, who minded the library, and who was heart-scared of him as she had been since the age of five.

"Miss Trimmel," he was saying sonorously, for he specialized in mispronouncing the names of those he regarded as inferior beings, especially women, "Miss

Trimmel. You have brought me the wrong volumes, girl. I said Churchill's 'History of the Second World War' and you have brought me something on John Churchill, Duke of Marlborough, which is of no interest to me at all. Are you deaf, girl, as well as stupid?," and he brushed some pipe ash off his bulging waistcoat and gold watch chain.

Maisie Trimble was a good-natured timid girl of ample proportions whose one ambition in life was to marry Ballybracken's only single policeman, Constable McCrum. With little by way of personality, Ballybracken folk never took her under their notice except to agree that she baked the very best sponge cakes in the townland, and these they fought over at every church sale. These same sponge cakes played a major part in her wooing of Constable McCrum which, while they added to his girth, were so far proving to be unsuccessful bait in Maisie's pursuit of her man.

Robbie felt sorry for Maisie that afternoon as, yet again, she was being bullied and exploited. He decided to take a hand. He too was interested to read what Churchill had made of the war, and how his history of that eventful period matched his own first-hand experience. He now planned to grab whatever Churchill volumes were available from under the Master's nose. Having located them not on the library's rickety shelves but in a big wooden box lying open on the floor, he found Maisie anxiously scanning the bookshelves, her cheap steel framed glasses slipping down her nose as she frantically tried to find the Churchill histories for the Master.

"I think these might bay the books you're lukin for, Maisie," Robbie murmured with a smile.

"Och thanks, Robbie," she said quietly. "Thanks very much. I'll get them stamped out tay the Master."

She tried to grab the books from Robbie, but he held on to them.

"Ony yeh see," Robbie continued, "I want them mezself, an' I seen them first."

"What!" Maisie exclaimed. "But, Robbie, the Master wants them, and he got here first."

"But he didn't get tay the books first, did he?" Robbie said raising his voice for the Master to hear. "Wuzn't he puttin it up tay you[130] tay fin the books for him... tay act as hez skivvy lake iverywan else does round here."

Master Blair overheard this as he was meant to do.

---

130 **Wuzn't he puttin it up tay you** – Wasn't he expecting you to do all the searching… making demands

"What's that?" he demanded. "Who's there?" and he rose clumsily from the chair to squint down between the bookshelves.

"I was just saying to Miss Trimble here, Master, how much I have been looking forward to readin what Churchill has to say about the war, and what a great girl she is for getting all his books for me. So now if ye'll stamp them for me, Maisie, I'll get underway."

Maisie looked mortified and scared, and the Master was red in the face with anger. He was not used to being crossed.

Possession Nine-Tenths of the Law

"I had asked Miss Trimmel here to get those books for me," he said, "so I'll thank you to leave them there on the table for her to sign out in my name."

"I don't think so," said Robbie quietly. "What is it they say? *'Possession is nine-tenths of the law'* an' as yeh can see, Master, I'm in possession."

"You are a bad rascal and the breed of bad rascals," exploded the Master. "Now please hand those books to the girl, and we will say no more about it."

"I don't take kindly tay being called names by you or any man," Robbie said, trying to contain his anger. "So I will ask you tay take back that slur on my character and on my family, an' catch ye'rself on[131]."

"A slur on your character! What character have you? I know all about you and your manner of life. A drunken private soldier living in sin with a woman not your wife. That drunken father of yours over there on the Esker living in squalor. Don't talk to me about your character. You have a cheek! You will be parading your family's good name in front of me next." And he snorted in disgust.

Putting the library books down on the table, Robbie went across to the Master and, catching him by the lapels of his jacket and staring him in the face, said,

"You will take that back, Master, an' apologize to me for what you hiv said about me an' my father. Yes, I am a rough soldier and so was my father before me but we are dacent people. I was fighting for this country, an' so was meh father when you were sitting here in Ballybracken on your fat ass terrorizing the wee youngsters in school. My father in his war and me in mine went through hell, and what was it for? So that empty owl bastards lake you cud lord it over us an' if any proof wuz needed, just look at the way you hiv been treatin this woman here the day. Ridin roughshod over her lake you an' your sort round here ride roughshod over iverywan when yeh think yeh can get away with it."

---

131 **Catch ye'rself on** - *wise up*

Robbie knew that the anger that had been mounting in him since that day he had trudged up Ringsend back from the war had finally boiled over, had caused him to lose control, and all over this arrogant irrelevant old man and a pile of books. The furious words were no sooner out of his mouth than he knew he had broken his own taboos. *'Stroll don't Scrabble through life,'* and *'Whatever you say, say nothin'* were the wisest pieces of advice to follow in Ballybracken, and in the Ulster it mirrored. He must get out of the situation. He dropped the Master back in the chair with a resounding bump.

"I'll have the police on you, you villain!" shouted the Master when he had recovered from his shock and regained his breath. "You have assaulted me and you are a witness to this violence on an old man, Miss Trimmel. Elliot, you are a menace in this townland... clearly a dangerous socialist... a Communist even ... I'll have you lifted[132] by the police and up before the law." he paused to draw breath.

Robbie could not stop himself "...an' you are a cowardly bullyin owl mouth[133]," he spat out the words. "Go tay blazes where yeh belong. Do ye'r damtest. Divil-the-hair I care." And he headed for the library door.

Robbie Drowns his Sorrows

He perched himself on the stool in Cobain's pub not proud of what had happened back in the library. Cobain placed a pint of Guinness in front of him without having to be asked.

"I'll hiv a half'un[134] aff Bushmills as well," muttered Robbie,"... naw, make it a double."

He stayed drinking in Cobain's for the remainder of the afternoon mixing rounds of whiskey with beer of various kinds to drown his disappointment over his loss of control. He knew he was getting seriously drunk. Cobain was eying him oddly for he had never seen him in this state before. It was good for business, of course, especially as Robbie, in his increasingly drunken state, was treating every customer that came into the bar. At last Cobain was prompted to ask,

---

132 **lifted** – *arrested*
133 **Bullyin owl mouth** – *a loud- mouthed bully*
134 **A Half'un** – *a shot (of spirits)*

"What's wrong way yeh, man? Hiv yeh fell out way that woman aff yours or what?"

"She's the... best... woman in the... worl," Robbie said drunkenly. "Don't yeh bay takin hir name in vain, Sammy. Naw... I had... a run-in way[135] the owl school master... yeh know, Master Blair... an' I shud... hiv held may tongue... but yeh know how it is... the temper can git... git the better aff a man at times... I'm lake meh father, I'm aisy riz[136] ... but the Master provoked me way hez owl guff[137]."

Cobain began to say something, but Robbie continued in his drunken way, "Ach but sure... what is it Burns says? … *'A man's a man for a that'*… Great poet Rabbie Burns... same name as mezself... Rabbie... Robbie... same thing... listen Sammy… .listen tay me … " and now he caught Cobain by the lapels and, looking him in the eye, continued,"… *'That man to man, the world o'er... shall brothers be for a that'*… wudn't it be great if Burns' words iver come true... Sammy… wudn't it bay a better... worl... wudn't even Ballybracken be a... better place?"

"I'm sure it wud," said Cobain, breaking free from Robbie's grasp. "Now, I think maybe yeh hiv had enough for wan day. Yeh hiv a powerful feed aff drink on yeh an' need tay start goin canny[138]. Shud yeh not bay getting away home tay sleep it aff?"

"Away home... where wud that be, Sammy?... Yeh know where may real home is? I'll tell yeh, Sammy boy... may true home is lying way may dead comrades way out yonder on Dunkirk beach or... on wan aff the Normandy beaches... or whatever f***** battlefield yeh lake tay... name. I wuz at al aff them… so why am I still here when al may good mates is lying out there, Sammy, tell me that? That's where I shud be... at home way them what iver heaven or hell... they are in now… what smart man wuz it said, *'Life, tay be sure, is nothing much tay lose but young men think it is, an' they wur young'*… who wuz it said that, Sammy?"

He slumped forward on the bar counter for a few moments and then lifted his head again.

"I need another... drink... same again... an' treat every man-jack here... "

Cobain pretended not to hear, and started to mop the counter with a dish cloth.

"Did yeh... not hear me, Sammy? I need more aff the same."

---

135 **A run-in way** – *a confrontation… an argument with*
136 **I'm aisy riz** – *quick tempered*
137 **Owl guff** – *annoying comments… annoying talk*
138 **Goin canny** – *slow down… stop drinking so much*

"Naw, Robbie, I'm ony savin yeh from ye'rself. Now go over there an' sit in the corner an' I'll get yeh a glass or two of watter tay help sober yeh up... an' then we'll get yeh home to that woman of yours. She'll be fit tay dale[139] with yeh better nor me."

Robbie staggered over to an empty table and continued muttering to himself about dead comrades and arrogant school masters.

The jug of water Cobain brought him started to have some effect at sobering him up when the next blow fell an' put the final kybosh of Robbie's spree.

Retribution!

A small group of young men were playing cards at a table near the door, and they also had too much to drink, some of it paid for by Robbie. They were steadily getting noisier and more boisterous when an elderly man came in through the pub's double doors, tripped on the doorstep but steadied himself and went over to the bar. As far as Robbie could make out, the newcomer was talking to Cobain about leaving a collecting box for the 'British Legion' on the counter. He noticed the man had a terrible shake in his head, neck and arms which could only be the result of shell shock and, from the man's age, must have been an affliction from his service in the First World War.

The young card-players had noticed the man's shake too and, after a bit of whispering and sniggering, one of them got up and started to mimic the man's shaking head and body. This sent his drinking buddies into fits of laughter prompting another to rise to his feet and stagger about shaking arms and hands, his head to one side and mouth open in an insane toothy leer.

To Robbie this was red rag to a bull but he tried to tell himself that he had undertaken enough crusades for one day, and just to let it go. The lads were as drunk as he was, and the man himself seemed to be paying no heed to their antics. But as he placed his collecting box prominently on the counter and turned towards the door one of the drunken crowd lurched towards him and spat in his face saying, *'ony an owl coward got the shakes in the war... an' that wuz al you are... a f***** owl coward!'*

Robbie rose to his feet, crossed to where the man and the lad were standing and said,

"What did yeh jist say... tay this man here?"

"I said he wuz a f***** owl coward shakin lake he does, a skared owl woman.

---

139 **Fit tay dale with yeh** – *able to cope with you*

That's what may Da says about his kine an' may Da shud know. He wuz in the Home Guard. But what's it tay you anyway?"

Robbie clenched his fist and struck the lad such a blow that it sent him flying across the pub floor. "Tay hell way you an' ye'r Da," he roared.

The other lads jumped to their feet, and the melee that followed left two of them almost toothless, another with two bloodshot eyes and a fourth with blood pouring from his upper lip. Robbie had badly swollen cheeks and a right eye very bloodshot and steadily blackening. Cobain's pub resembled a battlefield when Constable McCrum arrived and arrested Robbie and one of the lads who hadn't had the sense to make good his escape.

Prison with Tea and Scones

The cell in Ballybracken Police station was small and far from hospitable. Robbie sat on the trestle bed with his sore head in his hands, reflecting ruefully on the afternoon's events. The arrogant old Master was bound to bring charges, maybe some of the lads too when they had sobered up and their fathers got behind them, and Cobain would doubtless want compensated for the damage to his pub. Yes, Robbie had had better days! He staggered over to the slop bucket in the corner of the cell and was relieving himself when he heard the key turning in the cell door. He buttoned up hastily, and just in time, for an attractive woman had entered carrying a tray with tea things and several scones.

"I don't think we have met before," she said briskly, "I'm Nora, the sergeant's wife. I thought you'd like some tea. Indeed, by the look of you, I think you need some!"

Robbie was taken completely by surprise by this kindly act.

"It will be very welcome, Ma'am, and very good of you." Then he added, managing a smile despite his sore face, "I wasn't expecting hotel service in here."

"Well," she said, "we all know what happened. Maisie Trimble has been singing your praises for standing up to that old tyrant, Master Blair, and Mr Cobain says you stood up for poor shell-shocked Willy McCracken. It certainly was your day for being a knight in shining armour! Mind you, you can be sure there will be repercussions. But in the meantime, you are not only a war hero but something of a hero in Ballybracken which, we all know, takes some doing. Now drink your tea before it gets cold."

Later the sergeant came to see him.

"A right mess you've landed yourself in, Robbie," he said sitting down on the end of the flimsy bed. "Predictably, your victims are all breathing fire and slaughter... but I understand George McKendry and young Jim McKnight are doin the rounds to try to get some of them pacified. We'll see how it goes. You know you said more than was good for you to the Master. If he goes ahead, and he's as hard as nails, I'll have to charge you and you'll need a lawyer. So you'll have to stay put here until we see if it can be squared[140]. I've left a message for Rosie. She should be round soon, and I predict she might be the hardest of all to square. I'd say she'll be givin you the rough edge of her tongue. Now I'll send Constable McCrum down with your supper. It's the same as I'm havin myself."

Robbie lay back on the uncomfortable bed bracing himself for the wrath to come. At that moment, the only wrath he really cared about was Rosie's. He resolved to listen in silence, go into the doghouse for a while, and make it up to her when she had forgiven him and calmed down. Or so he hoped!

What was bemusing him at this minute was the kindness, concern and understanding he was receiving from unexpected quarters. Perhaps he had seriously misjudged Ballybracken folk... or some of them anyway.

---

140 ***If it can be squared*** – *if we can draw a line under what happened... sorted out successfully and quietly*

Episode 13

China Tea with the Dowager

Rosie was having a very busy day at Ballybracken House but she was getting through the curtain laundering with her usual determination sustained by lots of tea and delicious food, for Hanna McKendry was generous both with her hospitality and her appreciation.

It was when Rosie reached old Mrs. McKendry's bedroom that things took a turn that were to have a profound effect on the life of young Master Daniel Malachy Dowdells though no one could have foreseen it at the time. The formidable old lady appeared to be fast asleep when Rosie entered so, after a moment's hesitation, Rosie decided that she could creep quietly over to the windows, unhook the curtains, and make good her escape without disturbing the huddled figure in the bed. She removed the curtains from the two massive bay windows to the front of the house and had one unhooked from the third side window when the sun emerged from behind a cloud and cast a beam directly unto the old lady's face. She awoke with a start and, realizing someone was in the room, started to mumble and tremble uncontrollably. Rosie dropped the curtain, went over to the bed and took both Mrs McKendry's hands in her's saying soothingly,

"Don't fret ye'rself, Mistress. I'm Rosie Dowdells, an' I'm jist launderin the curtains the day. I'm so sorry if I skared yeh."

The old lady's composure was returning.

"Rosie... yes, yes... Rosie. I know who you are. Would you find my spectacles please for I am lost without them? I think I dozed off, and they have fallen somewhere in the bed," and she ran a bony hand out over the coverlet to feel for the glasses herself.

"Here they are, Mistress," said Rosie, picking them up off the floor grateful she had not stood on them. "Can I get yeh anythin else?"

"You can tell Mina or Hanna to send me up my afternoon tea," she said firmly and now clearly back in control, "and tell them to send an extra cup."

Rosie went down to the kitchen by the back stairs and conveyed the old lady's request to Hanna who was just taking apple tarts out of the Aga.

"She's awake at last, is she?" said Hanna. "I'll get her tea. She's very frail but that's old age for you. I suppose she asked for an extra cup?"

"She did, Mistress," Rosie said, "she did indeed. I wuz wonnerin why?"

"She wants you to have a cup with her for she loves to talk to visitors about her extraordinary life and the old days… like most old people I suppose. None of us has time to sit with her… and she's hard to humour for one minute she's asking you to sit and the next she asking why you are not getting on with your work? She was always a hard goer herself, so I suppose it's understandable… and we'll all be old someday… though I doubt if any of us will have as great a story to tell as she has… for, you know, she had such an interesting life travelling the world with the richest of the rich and rubbing shoulders with great and grand people… and all of it is true, Rosie… don't think she is doting for she's not… it all happened as she tells it. Now here's the tea, and a cup for yourself… and two slices of my chocolate cake for the pair of you… she loves anything chocolate. You can sit with her for a wee while, and that'll humour her. Use the front stairs, Rosie, for the back stairs are a bit narrow when you have the tray to carry," and she held open the door to the main hallway.

The grand front hall and elegant staircase never ceased to impress Rosie as the most awe-inspiring room in a house of great grandeur and opulence. Hanna's casual talk back in the kitchen about old Mrs. McKendry's early life had made Rosie wonder about where all this wealth had come from? She had, of course, heard talk in Ballybracken of the old woman coming back from America years ago with a great fortune to her name… and maybe that was true for such wealth wouldn't have grown on Ballybracken's trees… but if it was true, how on earth had she come by it, and if she had hobnobbed with the wealthy and the great, what on earth had brought her back to Ballybracken?"

The tea tray had little folding legs which Rosie adjusted in front of the old lady who again took command. *'Did Rosie take sugar?... three lumps were dropped into her cup with elegant little sugar tongs... did she take milk or lemon? ...'* the milk jug was tilted with a remarkably steady hand until the cup was nearly half full… and the teacup and saucer then handed over. Rosie noticed that the old lady herself took her tea black with no sugar, and with a small slice of lemon. She made a mental note to wean her brood off so much sugar and milk for, if they were ever to get anywhere in the world, these things must be got right. Mrs McKendry then delicately tucked a linen napkin under her chin and began to toy with her slice of cake before remembering to pass Rosie her share.

"Forgive me, Rosie, I am so forgetful these days. Tell me, is the tea to your taste?"

It was not to Rosie's taste as it happened for it tasted smoky and musty, only drowning it with the milk, stirring up the sugar, and the taste of the nice chocolate cake making it palatable for her.

"In my view, it is the best China tea one can get, the delightful *'Lapsang Su Chang'*, and we can only get it when one of us visits London. So much better than Indian, I think. So much more character. Ah, it is one of the few pleasures left to me. I'm so glad you are enjoying it. It is a treat, isn't it?"

Rosie had never heard of China tea but made another mental note to spread it around the chapel people at Mass next Sunday how much she had enjoyed having China tea – *'an' al sorts'* - with her *friend* old Mrs McKendry Senior. That would make them all sit up and take notice!

"Would you by any chance know how to work the gramophone?" the old lady asked suddenly as they both finished, and Rosie had resisted the offer of a second cup. "It is over there in the corner. I am very fond of music... especially religious music... and the family bought me that gramophone one Christmas some years ago... and some nice records... They have long since bought more up-to-date gramophones for themselves but that old-fashioned one suits me well enough. I like its tone. Of course, it isn't a patch on attending a live performance such as I used to enjoy in New York and Chicago when I was a girl, but it has to do. Anyway, it would be a comfort to hear a favourite piece just now. I don't want to trouble the others and you are a smart girl... I'm sure you can work it for me."

Rosie stared in something approaching terror at the ancient gadget in the corner which had something sticking out of the top reminding her of a big Easter lily, only this was made of shiny brass. She approached the gadget cautiously as if the lily-looking thing might snap her hand off but she took hold of a handle sticking out of the side, and carefully started to turn it. When it was wound up, the old lady asked Rosie to bring her over the bundle of records from a shelf under the gramophone. She selected one and instructed Rosie on how to get it playing. Rosie listened in wonder to the beautiful music and singing.

"Isn't it wonderful, Rosie," said the old woman, lying back on her pillows with her eyes shut and a contented smile playing on her lips. "It's Bach's St Matthew Passion. Isn't it truly wonderful?"

After a pause, she opened her eyes, sat up and continued,

"Now, you have your work to be getting on with but when the music stops would you come back please, rewind the thing for me, and I'll give you another of my favourites to play."

And so the afternoon passed. Rosie could not think of anything that had given her so much pleasure as listening to the wonderful music as she worked her way through the upstairs rooms in the great house. When she had finished all that Hanna McKendry wanted her to do by late afternoon and was back in the kitchen preparing to go home, Hanna said she should go upstairs again to say goodbye to the old lady.

She found her sitting up in bed reading.

"Rosie," she said, "you have looked after me so well today, and I have been a great torture to you when you have been so busy. But I have enjoyed your company and the music. I can't even get out to church any more… and I used to so love hearing the hymns and the psalms, though I confess I do not miss our Canon's dreary sermons," and she gave a mischievous girlish giggle. "Do you like the beautiful old hymns, Rosie?"

"I go to Ballybracken chapel, Mistress, but we have nice hymns there too."

"Indeed you have… and such beautiful ones in Latin," the old woman mused. "I love your 'Ave Maria'… I used to listen to Miss Caroline singing it during her piano practice when I worked for the Niels-Christensen family in America… such a lovely Lutheran family… but Miss Caroline loved your Catholic Latin hymns… the enchanting 'Panis Angelicus' and the gentle 'Ave.' You know, Rosie, I often think the Protestant religion is so very hard and harsh and masculine whereas your Catholic religion is so much softer and feminine… like the beautiful Blessed Virgin herself… but when will I ever hear the wonderful 'Ave' sung live again? Never, I suppose."

This was Rosie's chance, and she took it!

Here we must pause again if only briefly for we are now to learn surprisingly that, although our little hero had been intent on concealing his singing abilities, inevitably his secret had leaked out. Ever since that morning when Big Bella had offered the Sunday school children a shilling bribe to 'sing up', the church organ having failed, and Danny having more than risen to the occasion, there were those present that morning who, for some time afterward, could talk of little else but the boy's amazing ability. While it took some time for his mother to hear of his triumph, Ballybracken is a small place and eventually hear of it she did, and also of her son's mysterious absences thereafter from church on Sundays, so pressure – on the nature of which we need not dwell - was brought to bear on him, and confession duly extracted. From then on, there was no hiding place. Soon he was roped in to singing in her chapel, then at services in the Canon's church, even the Reverend Quigley availed of his talent once he had carefully vetted the hymns on offer to avoid any danger of idolatry or any 'Papish' sentiments. And despite Danny's apprehensions, the outcome was not at all bad. Father O'Kelly gave him a pound, the Canon parted with two, and Mr Quigley a religious booklet denouncing the sins of the flesh. And secular commissions followed at which the whip-round afterwards harvested even greater bounty. We will recall that our hero's schoolmates had initially called him a 'sissy singer' but later, when news got around that his singing was a money-making enterprise, he found himself something of a celebrity. But, running true to form in this history of Daniel Malachy, when things appeared to be on the 'up,' for him they quickly took another twist to bring him down again. News that his singing was money-making soon led to him becoming the victim of an extortion racket organized by Tommy Morrison – one of the 'big boys' at school - who, for a monetary consideration, claimed he and his gang were 'protecting' Danny from unnamed others who were 'out to get him'. Such was the pressure brought to bear by Tommy that Danny felt he had no option but to pay the protection money even if, as far as he could see, the only person he needed protection from was Tommy himself.

So our little hero was now a singer of great repute and in ever-increasing demand across Ballybracken's many divides. It is this outcome that is emboldening his mother to offer his services to old Mrs. McKendry on the afternoon in question.

"My wee lad, Danny, can sing the 'Ave Maria', Mistress… he's a rail good singer… if you wud lake tay hear him, I cud bring him over some time that's convenient … if you wud lake that?"

"Do you know, I had heard something of the kind but had forgotten. Hasn't he been singing in church? It would be wonderful to hear him, Rosie, so bring him by all means. When can you both come? Bring him this coming week. What a glorious thing for me to look forward to."

"I hope he dizn't disappoint yeh, Mistress… " Rosie had a moment of doubt about what she had done but then continued, "I don't think he will, for they are al efter him roun about here tay get him tay sing."

"Tell Hanna and Mina you will both be here on, shall we say, Friday next, and tell them why. Now, where's my purse, for a little bit extra never goes amiss, does it?" And she handed Rosie a pound note.

Back in the kitchen, Rosie encountered both Hanna and Mina, and told them about the arrangement the old lady wanted for the following week. Mina pursed her thin lips and said nothing, but Hanna took up the idea with her usual enthusiasm.

"That'll be great. We'll all enjoy listening to him for the only time I have heard him was at the harvest service. He has such a beautiful voice. Bring him next Friday afternoon by all means. Now, Rosie, before you go, I have something to ask you. Our maid, wee Selina McKenna, has her heart set on going off to London with that cousin of hers that's home... what's she called?... Siobhan isn't it? Now we don't approve of this at all for the dear knows what those two flibbertijibbetts will get up to running around London but Selina is determined to go and so she'll be leaving us at the end of next week. I was wondering if you would be prepared to fill her place as a maid here full time?"

This was just the job Rosie had been praying for... a decent job with a nice generous family – sure weren't the Boss and the Mistress here known as the 'King' and 'Queen' of Ballybracken... and in such a beautiful house. She couldn't believe it was happening.

"Do you want to think it over, Rosie, and let us know?"

"Naw... naw, Mistress. I can tell yeh now. I'd love tay come an' work here for yez full time. When day yeh want may tay start?"

So it was with a spring in her step that Rosie set off up the McKendry's long tree-lined avenue to tell her family that a turn had finally come in their fortunes. She now had the prospect of a full-time job, Robbie was well-thought-of and nearly always had work of some kind, Danny was making a name for himself as a singer, and who knew where that would lead? Dorry had a piano of sorts. Bobby could nearly read. At last the Dowdells were on their way up in Ballybracken.

But her state of well-being was to be short lived, and her happiness bubble burst, when she met Minnie McFarland, Ballybracken's prime gossip and 'convoyer[141],' returning from the well with two buckets brimming over with spring water. Minnie now took considerable delight in telling her that Robbie

---

141 **Convoyer** – *a gossip who accompanies someone along the road to get news and indulge in gossip*

had '*riz a row*[142] *in Cobain's pub worse nor wuz iver witnessed in any disorderly shebeen*[143], *had left the place in smithereens*[144] *an' had landed up in jail... oh, an' hir Danny had been nabbed for smuggling on the train from Bundoran.*' With that Minnie lifted her buckets and set off humming with satisfaction.

The Prisoner is Sprung

Rosie and the three children stood at the cell door while Constable McCrum fumbled with his bunch of keys trying to find the right one. Robbie rose to greet them as they crowded into the small space. He avoided looking Rosie in the eye and made great play of tousling the children's hair as Dorry and Bobby grabbed him by each leg and Danny threw his arms round his waist.

"Ach well, at least some folk roun here still think well aff may," he said even though a quick glance at Rosie's very cross face made him feel he would rather be facing a German gun emplacement at that moment rather than the wrath to come.

And come it did! In a torrent! '*Cud she not lave him for even the start aff a day without him takin on tay fight the whole townlan... she had been let down a bagful*[145] *bay him gittin drunk an' fightin... an' she didn't know where tay turn now... an' the disgrace he had brought on her an' the three wains... an' there she was out slavin an' workin, an' al he cud do wuz cheek up the owl Master an' wreck Cobain's pub... an' now she wuz goin straight tay confession... an' she wud tell Father O'Kelly she wuz hivin nothin more tay do way him iver again... an' wud take the Father's advice an' quit living a life aff sin way him... an' he cud pack hez bags an' go... that is if they iver let him out aff jail... an' if they didn't let him out an' he wuz sent tay jail in Belfast, or someplace far away, how wuz she iver gonna get the fare together for them al tay go an' see him... an' did he niver stap tay consider how the youngsters wud miss him... an' what was he thinkin aff anyway?....*' and off she went again covering much the same ground only even more vehemently.

Robbie listened and hung his head. He knew he deserved it all. While their mother's tirade continued, the children clung to him sucking their thumbs. As far as they were concerned, they now viewed Robbie with awe for being in jail

---

142 **Riz a row** – *started a row*

143 **Shebeen** – *an illegal disreputable drinking den*

144 **Smithereens** – *wrecked*

145 **She had been let down a bagful** — *she had been dreadfully embarrassed and humiliated*

for that made him a really bad person that they could threaten people with in the playground when any of them were getting it tight[146] there. And anyway, they knew that their mammy would forgive Robbie like she always forgave them after a good scolding. But they didn't like the idea of Robbie not getting out of there and coming home for they wanted to tell him all about their momentous day at Bundoran, and Danny being caught smuggling, and the man giving him a new coat, even though our hero was now a desperate criminal… but that meant he was just like Robbie… an' sure that was great!

Rosie finally stopped for breath and sat down heavily on the edge of the bed a hanky to her eyes to have a good cry when the bed suddenly collapsed throwing her to the floor. Robbie disengaged from the children to help her to her feet. Once up, she struggled to free herself from his grasp but he held on to her whispering how sorry he was he had let her down… and much more besides that the children couldn't hear… then, after a final show of reluctance, she relented and hugged him long and hard.

"But I hiven't forgive yeh, so don't think I hiv," she said fiercely, breaking free, "… that Minnie McFarland able tay tell me al that had happened, an' hir that delighted… I'm scunnered… scunnered[147] … "

"Are you OK in there, folk?" It was the Sergeant in the cell doorway. "Well, I've good news for you, big man. The lads you had the fight with have all got offside so we'll hear no more from them, and the lad that got caught has been released without charge too so there will be no more trouble from him either I'm thinkin. Maybe, with a bit of luck, they will all have learned a lesson not to do anything like that again near a soldier in a temper. The Master took more convincing. It took the persuasive powers of young McKnight and the combined efforts of the Colonel and McKendry to win him over. I understand the Colonel offered him a couple of day's shooting on his estate and McKendry an invitation to the next big Unionist dinner to sweeten him up… oh, and Cobain wants his damages as you'd expect but apart from that your troubles are over… but wait now, there's somethin else, I must give you a caution, Robbie, which I now do. Considered yourself duly cautioned to keep the peace."

He paused, smiled, and continued,

---
146 **Getting it tight** – being bullied… coming under pressure
147 **Scunnered** – upset… annoyed… disgusted

"Now, Rosie, would you all be happy to take a cup of tea or a mineral or whatever's in the kitchen before I sign this man aff your's out?

As they walked home, Rosie began to feel something approaching a glow of pride. Now that she had heard the whole story, and though she would never say it, she was secretly proud of Robbie. He had stood up for that bullied girl in the library and for that poor shell-shocked man in the pub, and there could be no denying that was a good thing to do. All she said was, "I doubt there'll be few squarin up tay take yeh on at the fightin in the townlan from now on. They'll al bay skared aff yeh."

Robbie put his arm round her and said, "as the man says, 'if yeh get the name aff early risin, yeh can lie in ye'r bed tay dinner time'[148] but you're right, love, I'm expectin no more bother, and I'll not bay goin luckin for it ether."

Sponge Cake & Iced Buns

When they reached the cottage door, Dorry said, "There is a big tin box on the windey sill. Whose is that?

Robbie brought the box in and put it on the kitchen table. In it was a large cream and jam-filled sponge cake surrounded by buns with white icing on top. A note said *'To Robbie and family from Maisie Trimble. Thanks for showing me how to be brave, Robbie.'*

---

148 ***If yeh get the name aff early risin, yeh can lie in ye'r bed tay dinner- time***
– *Once you get a reputation for something it sticks however much evidence there is to the contrary*

Episode 14

'Strolling' and 'Scrabbling'

Small Talk - Big Issues

Danny, Jim and Robbie were walking along the Ballybracken river just below the 'Ladies' Bower' one Sunday evening following Robbie's brush with the law to see something Jim called 'ox-bow' lakes which he thought unusual and interesting, and thought Robbie and Danny might too.

"I owe you a drink or two, Jim, for standin my friend over my 'Barbarossa moment,'" Robbie said. "I must confess that I'm changin my mind about the folk of Ballybracken for it's not everywhere that you'd find the neighbours standing up like you, the Colonel, George McKendry an' even the Sergeant and the wife did for me. That said, I'm not sure Cobain will let me darken his premises again anytime soon."

"You do indeed owe me big time," Jim said laughing, "and I look forward to you standing me a few bevies. But you can leave Cobain to me. If he turns you away, he's turning me away too and, anyway, haven't you put manners on[149] half the countryside, and that can't be all bad."

"Believe me, I'm finished puttin manners on people. I've promised Rosie that I'm back 'strollin' through life, and now regret my lapse into 'scrabblin.'"

"You will have to translate all that for me," Jim said. " 'Strolling?' ... 'Scrabbling?' Decode this for me. Is it army talk?"

"In a way," Robbie answered. "It was a useful survival tactic for me on many occasions. Yeh see, when ye'r on active service al yeh can expect is the unexpected so how do yeh cope way with whativer's thrown at yeh? Well, I decided early on that yeh can either go one aff two ways – an' I invented these terms mezself so don't go lukin them up in an encyclopaedia – you can either adopt the 'stroller' or the 'scrabbler' approach, an' here's the definition yeh wanted. When doing anythin... an' I mean anythin, be it great or small... ye'r man who is a 'stroller' paces himself an' takes it calmly but he gets there in the end, an' finishes in good fettle always appearing in control of the situation. That man's confident

---

149 **Put manners on** – Taught them a lesson... forced them to behave differently... caused them to change their attitude

appearance means he is never seen as vulnerable, weak, and is seldom challenged. Now your 'scrabbler' approaches things differently. He tackles everything in a hurried breathless way an' in a near panic. So, even if he is on top of his game, he looks vulnerable, not in control, weak… an' the world knows only too well how to bully and exploit the apparent weakness of the poor 'scrabbler' even if he may be far more competent than ye'r 'stroller.' Now how's that for a sensible philosophy? You didn't think I was that smart, did you?"

"A sensible philosophy indeed," Jim mused. "So you are really a latter-day follower of the ancient Greek, Epicurus, who preached a calm approach to any situation if we are to enjoy life's journey. Epicurus must have been one of your 'strollers.' I'm telling you, if his approach and yours caught on, Robbie, you could save a good few folk from having heart attacks and nervous breakdowns. By the way, would you say I am a 'scrabbler' or a 'stroller'? Careful now! Friendships have come to grief on the answers to questions like this!"

"I'd say ye'r a bit aff a 'scrabbler' at the minute, young McKnight, but there is a 'stroller' in there trying to win ye'r soul. That Greek philosopher was right though, 'strollers' enjoy the 'journey' as much as the 'destination'; 'scrabblers' can't wait to get to the 'destination,' and when they get there are often disappointed or are too tired to enjoy it."

They were now sitting smoking on the high riverbank looking across at the ox-bow lakes partly filled by reeds and brackish water. Jim had explained how they had got marooned from the river when it had changed course centuries ago, and Danny had been listening with rapt attention wishing that school dealt with more interesting stuff like this, for it helped him to see familiar things in a different way, and he liked that. He was enjoying the afternoon listening and sitting beside the two big men. The only cloud in his sky was having to sing those Latin songs next Friday for some old lady that his mammy knew.

After sitting in silence for some time enjoying the sun and the birdsong, Jim lay back on the bank and said, "Can I now share with you my pseudo-philosophy of life? You have your 'strollers' and 'scrabblers,' I have my 'fluffies' and 'frowsties. Yes, you heard me correctly. I consider everybody in this world to be either 'fluffy' or 'frowsty'. The 'frowsties' are stuffy, buttoned up, mean spirited, that kind of thing. As for the 'fluffies,' they are soft, warm hearted, generous kind of people. Let me give you examples. Hanna McKendry is a 'fluffy' and so, in my book, is your Rosie. Now Quigley and Master Blair, they are 'frowsties.' Too many of the Ballybracken folk, men and women, are 'frowsties' in my view."

"So, yeh don't reckon on there bein too many 'fluffy' folk around in Ballybracken? I wud hiv agreed way yeh up until recently, but in the light aff the help I got with that recent hanlin[150], I am comin to the conclusion that there are more dacent people roun here than I used to think."

"What would you say young Danny there is?" Jim asked, throwing a small pebble playfully in Danny's direction. "I have him down as 'fluffy.' What do you think, Robbie?"

"Yea, he's a 'fluffy' wee fella al right… an' I'm workin hard to make him a 'stroller.' Do you know, he might be Ballybracken's very first 'fluffy stroller?' "

Danny was pleased they were talking about him, though he didn't understand a word.

"'Fluffies' and 'frowsties!' 'Strollers' and 'scrabblers!' We are right eediots, the pair of us," said Jim, slapping Robbie on the back. "But you realize you have just saved me from my mother who I now know is a quintessential 'scrabbler,' and will do all in her power to stop me becoming one of your 'strollers' if I don't watch out. No! I have seen the light. It's a 'stroller's' life for me from this day forth."

"I hope you manage it," Robbie said. "But don't think it's easy, it takes determination an' practice."

'The Luck of the Draw'

Jim said, "I've looked out Churchill's history of the war for you since you nearly started World War III over it in the library. But surely you could nearly write your own version of the war."

Robbie laughed. "You know, I sometimes look back and wonder to myself how the hell we won it? The other crowd seemed so powerful an' organized, an' had such great military leadership, determination an' equipment. I know well enough it wuz the Ruskies comrades produced most aff the men an' the Yanks, the money but, even so, we were in there at the beginnin and did our fair share. As for me, I can never figure out how I actually came through it with only a bullet graze or two, for there wur lads far craftier at keeping out of the road of the action, who niver come back. Al I know is that the rest of my life is a bonus.

---

150 *Hanlin - Trouble*

Some guys will say that God was lookin after them, an' good luck tay them if that is what they think for I'm tellin yeh when yeh come under fire, yeh hope there's a God lookin after yeh… but, for me in reality, I seen no sign aff God lookin after anywan on the battlefield an,' above al, when I seen the horrors aff the Nazi concentration camps, I couldn't help askin myself where was God tay do somethin tay save the poor craturs[151], many aff them wemen an' wee wains, when they needed savin? No sign aff Him at al, Him that intervened time outta number tay save folk, or so we're towel, in the Bible stories."

Jim said, "Well, why terrible things happen to innocent people is one of the great conundrums that nobody seems able to answer. About your survival though, maybe there's such a thing as fate, Robbie. Do you think it was just some men's fate to come through it, and others not? And if so, what is fate? What is it Shakespeare says? Come on… you know the quotations better than me… stop acting the ignorant squaddie when you're not. It's something about '*.. a divinity that shapes our ends… Rough-hew them how we will.*' "

"Aye but then what about the near opposite in another play when he says, '*The fault… is not in our stars… but in ourselves.*' How's that for an answer from an ignorant squaddie! I tell yeh, Jim, my war – an' I had a good war if there is such a thing – my experience of the war can best be described as semi-organized shambles, an' that's what it wuz lake for most ordinary soldiers."

The Tender Lesson for Our Hero

Danny liked to hear the men talking about the war since it involved guns and, since Robbie hadn't got shot, there was a happy ending like when people lived happily ever after in story books. He wanted to say that he would ask Angel Jo to explain why Robbie had not been shot by the bad men and why God hadn't helped the mammies and babies but Robbie had told him not to talk about the angel to anyone except him so he wouldn't bother bringing it up. Anyway, it would only mean the two men would sit there talking even longer and he was getting bored. He was idly poking a big stone with a stick when it dislodged and rolled down towards the river to reveal a family of woodlice whose home had been upset. Danny got to his feet and said,

"Luk, luk at them al. Shud I squash them way may shoe?"

Robbie said, "Day you know, wee warrior. I wudn't, if I wur you, for I don't think they are doin us too much harm."

---

[151] ***Craturs*** – victims

A gentle lesson that Danny occasionally called to mind later in life in other circumstances. But for now, he must get the big men to move. He decided he would pretend he was going to sleep so he lay back against Robbie and pretended to snore, which he was good at. It did the trick.

"This young comrade is gettin tired, I think," said Robbie, "so maybe we'd better make tracks..."

They rose to go. Danny scampered ahead of them up towards the ring fort and 'Ladies' Bower.'

Innocence & Experience

"To turn to more serious matters, I want to hear about all the women you've had," said Jim disarmingly as they walked up the back lane from the Bower to the yard of Grovehill Manor. "A virgin like me needs a few pointers from an experienced man-of-the-world like yourself."

"So it wuz al lectures an' studying an' no nooky at al up there at university?" Robbie said mockingly. "Ach come on, there must have been the odd bit aff hanky panky with al the good lookin girls about the place an' the whole big city of Belfast for a huntin ground?"

"I will only confess to one or two near moments that were also near misses. Dalliances that promised much but delivered little," Jim said. "No, like Caesar's wife I am *'beyond reproach '*- damn and blast - so, I need guidance, in fact lectures and tutorials would be good, come to think of it, from a master-lecher like you to set me on the right - but I really think I mean the wrong - path to successful sex and love making."

Robbie just smiled. If he'd missed out on education he was glad he hadn't missed out on that vital part of a man's experience, and he had no trouble recalling the urgency rough soldiering had given it.

"I'll get it out of you some day," continued Jim. "I'm sure that shooting Germans wasn't all you got up to from Paris to Berlin."

"I had my moments," Robbie conceded looking skywards with an air of innocence and grinning, "an' still do, if an' when opportunity knocks, an' duty demands that I rise to the occasion."

"You naughty fellow," Jim said slapping him on the back again. "You must tell me all about it... soon... and I promise I won't breath a word," and they walked on up the Roxborough's avenue towards the main road, Danny running ahead collecting dandelions and blowing the seeds all over himself.

Robbie's Epitaph

Just out of sight of the big house they turned into Grovehill Manor's private cemetery, home to the graves of the Roxborough ancestors set among gloomy yew trees, and now greatly overgrown with tall ling grass and rushes. They sat down on one of the grave slabs and lit cigarettes.

"Holy God," said Jim. "To think they couldn't even bear to be buried among the rest of us common folk. When the last trump sounds, God will know they were the gentry here below, and bring them up to the front of the queue. Would you credit such arrogance! And on the other side of the wall yonder their dogs, cats, horses and other pets are buried too. I suppose they will leap-frog into heaven ahead of us common folk as well."

Danny was scared in this gloomy place and imagined he could see dead people in long robes, their faces covered by big hoods, drifting in and out of the deep shadows cast by the yews. But he was curious to see the dog and cat graves and told Robbie so. Without a word, Robbie lifted him up and carried him to the back wall of the cemetery setting him down on top of it. He then jumped up on the wall himself and pointed out the animals' gravestones on the other side. There was 'Punch,' clearly a much-loved dog whose epitaph read, 'Faithful unto Death,' and 'Jemima' a cat who apparently was a terror of the kitchen mice and a 'Mr Clutterhead' who must have been a peacock for 'The beauty of his plumage now adorns heaven.'

He had been reading these out loudly for Jim to hear, when his friend shouted,

"And what epitaph will you have on your headstone, Robbie, that can match any of these grand folk, or even their cats and dogs over there?"

Still sitting astride the wall holding on to Danny, Robbie thought for a minute and then started to sing to the tune of 'Happy Birthday', *'How f***** are you now? How f***** are you now? How f***** are you now? Rob's really f***** now!'* he finished as Jim exploded with laughter.

"My army mates used to sing that when things wuren't goin too well an' I think the last line will sum up my eternal situation… *'yea, you're well and truly f***** now, Robert',* will be St Peter's greetin when I'm called up above to hear my eternal destiny."

The 'Liberty Bush'

To Danny's relief, they left the gloomy cemetery and dandered[152] on up the avenue to the gate house. Crossing the road, Jim was looking up at an ancient thorn, its leafless barren branches stretching heavenward as if in supplication.

Robbie went over to stand beside Jim. "Don't they call that the 'Liberty Bush'?" he asked, squinting up at it. "What is the history behind that?"

"During the 1798 Rebellion, the United Irishmen tied ribbons on a tree close to landlords' estates and called them 'Liberty Bushes,' just like in revolutionary France at the time. I suppose it was designed to scare the landlords so that they wouldn't feel safe and would up sticks and leave, but it was to no avail. That sad-looking dead old bush there is the rebels' only epitaph in this townland. I'm sure the grand folk lying down yonder in the cemetery saw to it the rebel lads were strung up or sent to Botany Bay for daring to challenge their wealth and power."

They all sauntered homewards under the beach trees. Even over the brief time of their acquaintance in Ballybracken, Robbie reflected that a real but unspoken bond had grown up between the two men – testament to which was the way they could talk so freely on the walk today - and Robbie valued this greatly, but he knew from army days that men's bonding, so valuable in life, came strangely out of nowhere, and should not be the subject of too much analysis lest it vanish.

---

152 **Dandered** – *strolled*

Episode 15

Danny Clams Up

Breakfast in the Land of Plenty

A soaking blanket of drizzle covered Ballybracken as Rosie and Danny slunk past Minnie McFarland's cottage on their way to Ballybracken House. Rosie was determined she was not going to be cornered again by Minnie with her apparently bottomless cauldron of bad news. Danny had been scrubbed up to look his best despite tantrums about not wanting to go, then phantom stomach pains, accusations that his mother didn't care if the drizzle would ruin his new coat, and other obstructive and delaying strategies.

The old lime trees overhanging the drive gave off a pleasant pervasive scent that wet morning but even the trees had it in for the Dowdells showering down on them the largest rain drops possible.

As the great house emerged from the drizzly mist, Rosie was soaked, and Danny was planning to bolt at the first opportunity. Once in the warm kitchen, things began to look up for Hanna and Mina were bustling about preparing large 'Ulster fry' breakfasts for the estate workmen who were milling around in the yard now that the morning milking was over. Rosie and Danny were bound to get a share of this morning feast.

"Ah there you are, Rosie," said Mina pushing her steam-covered glasses up her nose, "good and early. And this is Master Daniel. Are you going to sing for us today, Daniel?"

Danny said nothing burying his head in his mother's wet coat, and then peeping shyly out to take in this woman who looked to him very menacing.

"You can both have your breakfast with the men in the servant's hall, and then I will show you what needs doing today," Hanna said. "It's mainly cleaning. Keeping a big house like this clean is a full-time job. It was built for a different age when there would have been lots of servants. But we all have to do our best, and we are lucky now to have you to help us, Rosie. Young Selina was not very thorough nor was she a good timekeeper... well, maybe London will tighten her up... but you are both soaking wet... get those coats off and we will see if we can't get them dried before home-time... How's the men's breakfast coming on, Mina? When Rosie's ready she can start carrying it through… I hope there's enough for everybody."

There was more than enough. How could there fail to be in the 'land of copious plenty' that was McKendry's kitchen which young Daniel, perceptive boy that he was, could not fail to contrast with the Dowdells's 'land of near want.' Rosie carried the heavily-ladened tray through to the servants' hall and was surprised to find Mr McKendry sitting at the end of the long wooden table with a big mug of tea in his hand discussing the price old Mrs Ballantine's farm might make with his three farm labourers.

"Rosie," George McKendry rose to greet her in a gentlemanly way that took her completely by surprise, "and here is Daniel too, boys," he said, putting his hand on Danny's shoulder. "He's a wonderful singer, you know."

"He is that," said Aiden McGlinchy. "When are yeh comin back tay sing for us again in the chapel, Danny?" he continued. "The wemen hiv al fell for yeh, so they have. Maybe ye'll give us al a song now, Danny. What about it?"

Danny looked down at the floor.

George said, "Well, it a wee bit early for singing, isn't it, son. No man should be asked to sing before he's had his breakfast. You sit up here between me and your mammy."

The possibility that he was going to have to sing when breakfast was over now further horrified Danny until the big breakfast was placed before him, and that temporarily banished all such disturbing thoughts. He tucked in as only small boys can when they are wet, cold, and something tasty is put in front of them, and McKendry's breakfasts were certainly tasty. Plenty of bacon, eggs, sausages and tomatoes all sitting on a nest of potato, wheaten and soda bread. Rosie kept reaching over to wipe bits of breakfast off Danny's mouth and chin, but soon gave it up as a lost cause as Danny did justice to this bounty.

"The lad has a good appetite," McKendry remarked smiling. "I always think there's hope for a man that can eat up, Danny. Oh, before I forget, Rosie, would you tell Robbie that I'd like to see him about a couple of things in the next day or two."

Rosie hoped it wasn't anything to do with Robbie's brush with the law but from the casual way the Boss had put it, she didn't think so. She said Robbie would come with her any day that was convenient for Mr McKendry.

With that agreed, it was down to work for Rosie. Danny was given a few big books to read at the kitchen table, most of them too difficult for him. One had pictures of Kings and Queens in nice clothes and crowns, and there were gold coaches and boys dressed a bit like the funny people on the back of Robbie's pack of playing cards, and there were two girls playing on big castle lawns with three or four small bandy- legged dogs. He would have liked to have coloured in these pictures but there were no crayons, and he didn't like to ask so he just sat quietly sucking his thumb and slowly turning the pages. After a while, the lady with the stern face gave him a big glass of milk and two biscuits.

"My mother is longing to hear you sing, Daniel, so when you have finished your snack you can come up with me to her room when I'm taking her up her morning coffee."

Once again, Danny wanted to run away but he just said, "Thank you," through a mouth crammed to capacity.

He followed Miss McKendry up a long wide staircase with carved wooden animals holding shields on posts at the bottom and top of the stairs. They went along the landing and into a big bedroom. It smelt of powder like his mammy used on Dorry and Bobby when they were babies. A very old lady with a white face and dressed in a black nightgown with a frilly collar lay in a bed near the centre of the room. Danny was terrified.

"I have brought Daniel Dowdells to see you, mother, said Mina. "The boy you want to hear sing. Now, Daniel, you go and shake hands with that lady, there's a good boy."

Danny could not move so completely overwhelmed was he by the opulence of the big room, and the deadly appearance of someone so old. Mina put her arm round him and pushed him gently towards the bed as the old lady turned slowly in his direction. Her eyes were wet as if she had been crying.

"Don't be scared of me, little boy, I won't bite you. Come over here and shake hands," and she slowly drew a bony arm and hand from under the blankets and led it shakily out to him.

As he went slowly towards the old woman, tripping on a beautiful bed-side rug, he told himself, *'I'm a tarrible dangerous smuggler an' so I mustn't bay skared, for wicked bad people lake me is niver skared.'*

He reached the bed without further mishap and took the lady's hand. It felt like a cat's paw, hard, knobbly and dry.

"So, we meet at last, Master Daniel Malachy," she said, her voice now sounding strong and commanding, and not what Danny expected from a lady who looked to him nearly dead.

"I have heard so much about your singing in our church and your mother's chapel. I am delighted you have come to visit such a sad old woman who can't get out to hear you."

Danny was drowning, so far was he out of his depth. Even the lovely big breakfast couldn't make up for this torment. He wanted to escape to Bobby, Dorry, Robbie, his mammy, the hens and Tilly the goat. Yes, even being at home with their smelly goat and her new kid would be better than this. The old lady was smiling weakly at him.

"My, you look like a beautiful chubby angel, Daniel, do you know that? You are a very handsome boy with your curly hair. Mind you, I'm sure you are not an angel for few little boys are in my experience. I well remember Master Harald Christensen back in New York City... all the pranks he got up to... " she tailed off, and Mina took the opportunity to say,

"Daniel is afflicted by a bad stammer, mother, so he may not feel confident to say much by way of conversation to you just yet. You will have to excuse him... and he's shy too of course."

The old lady looked at her daughter sharply. "No need for explanations, Mina dear. Rosie has told me all this. It will not make him any less shy or tongue-tied if we talk about him as if he can't hear as well. Now, is that my coffee on the dressing table? Give it here and leave Daniel to me. We can have a little relaxed chat, and then maybe he will feel up to singing something for me... to please me. Won't you Daniel?"

But our little hero only clasped his hands and looking fixedly down at the delicate patterns on the bed cover. Even singing would be better than chatting, for how could he chat with his stutter and overwhelmed as he was by this scary old woman and the strangeness of this grand room?

Mina McKendry was used to her mother giving orders and taking control, so she did as she was told and left Danny alone swinging his legs and gently rocking to and fro on a leather chair at the side of the bed.

Stage Fright & Duets

Old Mrs. McKendry said nothing while she drank her coffee, indeed seemed to have forgotten that Danny was there for the moment. When she had finished and had wiped her mouth delicately with the linen napkin, she turned to him and silently pushed the tray towards him. It was large and silver but with big handles so Danny carefully took it from her and wandered off with it not knowing where to put it.

"Leave it on the dressing table by the door, Daniel… Yes, there… That's a good boy. Now I know you may be a little shy. When I was your age I was shy too, but I am a very old lady, and there is no one else listening. It will give me immense pleasure to hear you sing. Maybe it might encourage you if I give you a florin or half-a-crown in advance. A 'down-payment' that's called. Hand me that bag that is beside the gramophone and we will explore what coins I have there."

Danny handed over a large leather handbag from which the old lady took a dainty purse. She opened the clasp and tipped the contents unto the bed.

"I have only two-shilling pieces," she said. "Florins those are called, Daniel, and here is one as that 'down payment' to encourage you to sing for me."

She handed the coin to Danny, replaced her purse in the bag, and it fell off the side of the bed. Danny went round to retrieve it without being asked and put it back beside the gramophone. He had been paid, so now he must sing! He positioned himself at the top of the bed just out of sight of Mrs McKendry and opened his mouth. But he couldn't. The tune and the words just wouldn't come. But he must or he would have to give the money back. He burst into tears. With great effort, the old lady shuffled round to look at him then pulled on a long bell-pull that lay to her right hand. After a few minutes, Hanna McKendry appeared enquiring what the old lady needed? Danny was sobbing miserably. Hanna said,

"What ails you, wee love? Sure, we must have scared you, and you that shy. Come away and we'll find your mammy."

Rosie had been vacuuming just across the landing when she was hailed by Hanna and arrived in old Mrs McKendry's room looking flustered for she thought Danny must surely have broken something valuable or had transgressed in some other way. But all was well.

Hanna said, "Your wee son has got a bit flustered so maybe you'd keep him with you till he rallies."

At this good news, Danny wiped his eyes on his sleeve and ran to hide behind his mother. All was now well, and the singing threat had suddenly receded or so he thought. Forgetting that he was still clutching the old lady's florin, he now let it slip out of his hand and it careered across the wooden floor and went into a noisy spin when it encountered the bedside rug.

"Where did you get that?" Rosie whispered as Danny set off to retrieve it.

"I gave it to him," said old Mrs McKendry. "I said it was a down-payment for his singing, and so it still is when he feels up to it."

Danny and the errant coin were now back beside Rosie when an idea struck her that might solve what was increasingly becoming an embarrassing situation.

"Danny love," she whispered. "if I sing way yeh wud yeh sing for the Mistress? Wudn't that bay good? You an' me singin thegether for I have a nice voice too, yeh know."

Though not much appreciated in Ballybracken, Rosie had indeed a beautiful singing voice, and this would be a welcome chance for her to shine as well as her talented son. No opportunity, however unlikely, must be lost to get the Dowdells up Ballybracken's social ladder, even if only a little bit!

Danny thought for a moment, his desire to hold on to the florin – which he knew his mammy would insist on returning if he didn't sing – weighing against further tears and humiliation. "An' can I stan beside you tay sing?" he asked.

"Yeh can surely, love, an' you an' me will sing what iver Mrs McKendry wants if we both know it. Now, you tell the Mistress what we are gonna do since she has been so good tay yeh."

Chanteur Formidable!

"I want... tay sing... now," said Danny, "... an' Mammy... is goin... tay sing way me."

"Well, that will be just lovely with your mammy there to support you. I would like you both to sing that lovely Catholic Hymn '*Panis Angelicus*' for me for it brings back such happy memories."

With his mother in support our little hero had found his courage and, rather than tailing off like his mother - for Rosie could only remember the first verse - he sang on clearly and confidently to the end. When he had finished the old lady said nothing for several minutes. Then she murmured very slowly '*C'est simplement magnifique*' with her eyes closed and hands clasped. After a few moments, she awoke from her reverie, and said in a most decided voice, "That boy has real musical talent, Rosie, I knew from what my folk had told me about Daniel's singing that there was something special there, but I expected nothing like this. That was nothing short of heavenly! I know you are keen to get on, dear, but would the boy sing the Ave Maria for me now? I know these sacred Catholic hymns may seem strange choices for an old dyed-in-the-wool Protestant like me but, as I have said, they are so beautiful, and transport me back to such happy times in America. He can always sing good Protestant hymns for me next time, won't you, Daniel?"

Danny wasn't listening for now that he had overcome his fright of the old lady, of the beautiful room in this big palace of a house, he wanted to sing for her again and again.

"I'll start yeh aff on the 'Ave Maria', Danny," Rosie whispered, but Danny needed no further support. He was off on the 'Ave,' singing alone and at his very best.

"Such talent, such talent" murmured Mrs. McKendry lying back on her pillow. "We must do something about this for it is truly wonderful. What can we do to nurture such a special gift?" she mused.

Danny put his hand in Rosie's and squeezed it.

"Day yeh want tay sing something else for Mrs. McKendry, love?" asked Rosie literally flushed with pride.

"Aye, I do, but I need tay do a pee first."

It was ever so with small boys!

Episode 16

Tantrums and Betrayal

An Offer You Can't Refuse

"I am not gonna larn[153] the piana… I'm not… I'm not… I'm not larnin it!" Danny was throwing the mother–and–father of all tantrums when Rosie came home from the big house a week or so later and told them all about old Mrs. McKendry's plans for her talented musical son.

"Anyway, it's Dorry's piana. I hate it an' I niver wanted it. It's sissy playin the piana, I lake singin now… but I'm not… NOT playin the piana… PLEASE, mammy."

Danny worst long-held apprehensions about the presence of the piano down there in the lower room were now becoming a terrible reality. Rosie had been cleaning old Mrs. McKendry's room on the day after Danny's performance, and the old woman had immediately quizzed Rosie about the boy's singing, and what she might be able to do to help.

"He needs to learn to play a musical instrument, and I have decided, if you agree, that Mina could teach him the piano for she plays well but he will still need to practice between lessons and I don't suppose you have a piano at home."

We can only imagine with what pride was Rosie now able to announce to this grand old lady, "We have a piana, Mistress, we got wan….," she hesitated, "at… an' auction… an' I got it fixed up for our Dorry… fir it wud help hir get on in the worl if she could play… lake it hez helped other girls roun here."

"That is wonderful news," exclaimed the old lady clenching her hands together as if she'd just had an answer to prayer. "So it's settled, Rosie, young Daniel will come here after school once or twice a week, and Mina will teach him to play the piano. Hanna can play the piano too but she is far too busy and, anyway, I think Mina will be a better teacher… firmer you know… yes, Mina will do it."

So that was settled. Old Mrs. McKendry was seldom if ever over-ruled, and her

---

153 **Larn** – *learn*

offer took Rosie completely by surprise. What surprised her even more was the enthusiasm of Mina McKendry when she was summoned to hear her mother's plan. Mina was not a woman given to enthusiasms, and though she was as dutiful as an unmarried daughter - now indeed a bitter old maid in Ballybracken's eyes - was expected to be, she had no affection for her mother and with good cause. In the privacy of her own room, she would sometimes unlock one of the large wardrobes and run an ageing hand over a beautiful wedding dress, bought for what would have been Ballybracken's greatest event all those years ago, but never worn or seen the light of day since that fateful morning when all went awry. She had to fight back bitter thoughts about the role the old woman across the landing had played in her calamity and embarrassment. But duty required her to lock these thoughts away together with the wedding dress.

"Yes, that would give me great pleasure," Mina had said when the music lessons plans were revealed to her, "and would encourage me to practice more myself. I only hope I'm good enough for I have a feeling Daniel may be a natural musician, and I have always had to struggle to get to reasonable standards."

"Nonsense," said her mother. "You are more than capable of teaching the boy, at least the basics. After that, we'll have to see."

So Mrs. McKendry's hopes were now firmly fixed on our little hero! Escape would prove impossible. As Rosie and Mina were going down the stairs, Mina said,

"Do you know, I always wanted to be a schoolteacher but it was not to be, for I never got further than the seventh book at school when I was told I was needed at home. My music lessons continued, of course, but that was all. My brother got all the education in this family. My mother thought education beyond primary school was wasted on a girl. And I've always thought it strange, Rosie, considering what education in America had done for her, and the great benefits it brought her. As well as English, you know, she speaks two other languages quite fluently, all acquired at night school in New York, and of such benefit to her and her rich American employers on her many journeys with them across the length and breadth of America and Europe. So strange, then, that she saw education as of no real benefit to me, her only daughter. But when I think about it, I suppose that attitude to educating daughters is the prevalent one here in Ballybracken. And I am not alone in being denied a proper education, look at poor Helen McKnight. One would have thought such attitudes might have changed by now but resistance to change hangs in the Ballybracken air."

They were now standing in the kitchen, Rosie bemused at the frankness, to a servant, of this reserved woman whom she had always found strange and cold. Had the prospect of teaching Danny somehow helped her to unburden herself? Stranger things have happened!

Mina continued, "So please believe me, Rosie, when I say that I will be delighted to teach Daniel the piano. A chance to try out my teaching skills at last, to see if I really have any?"

"… and Mina will make an excellent job of teaching the wee dote," exclaimed Hanna when she heard the plan. "Did you mind to tell Robbie that the Boss would like to see him? … that's good… we'll expect him then. Thanks for all your hard work today."

The 'Wee Dote' turns Turtle

If Hanna McKendry had been privy to the scene in the Dowdells' establishment when Rosie broke the news about the piano lessons, she would have seen quite a different side to 'wee dote' Daniel Malachy! Now well into his tantrum, he felt it was doing the trick, so he decided to raise the stakes with a few threats.

"Yuz know yuz stole that piana… an' if yuz make me larn it I'll go an' tell the police on yez… an' if I'm playin it, the people passin on the road will hear… an' wonner how we can hiv a piana… an' then they'll tell the police… an' Robbie an' you will bay put in jail… an'…," he tailed off looking across at his great friend Robbie for the support he felt sure he could expect.

But what was this? Robbie was not coming to his aid. Instead he said, "Yeh niver know, yeh might lake larnin music, Danny. Sure give it a try, an' if yeh don't take tay it, we'll say no more about it an' yeh can give it up."

This was a disaster! Robbie betraying him now too! In his fit of rage, Danny rose from where he was perched on the outshot kitchen bed, went across and kicked Robbie as hard as he could on the shins, then thumped his mother on her back, rushed down to the lower room, banged the piano keys, kicked the piano which hurt his toes very badly, and then slumped in a heap in the corner howling with pain and rage.

Robbie followed him down, said nothing, lifted him by the one ear that was sticking out of his gansey[154] and marched him up into the kitchen. Bobby and Dorry were looking on with great satisfaction for now Danny was bound to get a good hammering, and seeing somebody 'for it' when it isn't you is always very satisfying.

---

154 **Gansey** – *a woollen pullover*

"Yeh wee scut[155], yeh," growled Robbie, "ye'll say ye'r sorry tay ye'r mammy this minute or I'll tan the hide aff yeh. Come on now, you'll do as ye'r bid,[156]" and he squeezed Danny's ear even harder.

Danny, now in considerable pain at both ends, knew the game was up.

"I'm sorry," he said sulkily, not yet ready to surrender completely.

"Come on, say ye'r sorry tay ye'r mammy, and main it[157], tell hir yeh'll niver hit her again, an' there'll bay no more twist'in an' thrawn'in[158] about larnin the piana."

Robbie released his ear, and Danny said what was required in as sincere a voice as he could muster in the circumstances. He then made a run for it, retreated to the bedroom and continued his sulk.

Bobby and Dorry were bitterly disappointed for they were more than half expecting to see Danny killed there and then in the kitchen before their eager eyes, and then Bobby could get his good coat and Dorry his schoolbag. True, Robbie or their mammy never gave any of them more than a slap on the ear or a smack on the legs whichever was handiest, but this seemed different for brother Daniel Malachy had succeeded in getting their mammy and Robbie into a temper such as they had seldom seen before, and that had boded well for the assassination to come.

But no! Danny sulked lying flat out on his bed, and Robbie and their mammy went on as if nothing had happened. In fact, they were now talking about a circus coming to Ballybracken. Danny was listening too. He knew in his heart that music lessons had been moved on to his agenda, and there was nothing more he could do about it. It was time to give in, make up and be friends again with mammy and Robbie, especially if the talk about the circus coming was right. If he continued to resist, there was just the possibility he wouldn't get going to it, and that would be disastrous. How could he get back on the right side of mammy and Robbie? He could sing… but what? It must be something that would make them laugh. He knew just the thing, for hadn't it raised a great laugh from Jim when Robbie sang it, though he still didn't know why? Surely it would work now with him singing in tune unlike Robbie's tuneless effort.

'How f***** are you now? How f***** are you now? How f***** are you now? You're really f***** now.'

---

155 **Scut** – *a despicable individual*
156 **You'll do as ye'r bid** – *you will do as you are told*
157 **Main it** – *mean it sincerely*
158 **Twist'in an' thrawn'in** – *being stubborn and difficult*

There was a dead silence!

"Where did yeh larn that bad language, yeh wee rascal, yeh?" exclaimed Rosie after a minute, "I niver heard such bad talk. If I iver hear yeh at that again, I'll give yeh a right trouncin[159]. Now where did he larn that?" she asked, looking suspiciously at Robbie. "If he come out way the lakes aff that down at the McKendrys, they wud sure hunt[160] him."

"He lakely larned it at school," said Robbie going over to the bed and winking at Danny. "Ye'r Mammy doesn't lake that kinna talk, my big champion. Was it Tommy Morrison or Guldy McFall or some other aff them bad rascals that taught yeh that?" He didn't allow Danny to answer and continued, "I doubt there's nothing for yeh now but the piana lessons to made it up to ye'r mammy. Come on, Sing hir somethin funny tay plaze hir."

Danny, knowing it was best to follow the lifeline Robbie had thrown him, thought quickly and began,

'*There's a hole in my bucket, dear Liza, dear Liza/ There's a hole in my bucket dear Liza, a hole...*' and, after a few minutes of this ditty, the whole kitchen rang with laughter. Harmony had been restored, in more senses than one, in the Dowdells household.

---

159 **Right trouncin** – *a good smacking*
160 **They wud sure hunt him** – *they would be certain to chase him... he would be unwelcome*

Episode 17

Revolution in the Air

The 'Royal Family'

"Big Bertie Stewart is an odd sort aff a fella," Robbie remarked one evening when Jim McKnight had dropped into the Dowdells's cottage for one of his and Robbie's frequent chats. "I know he's ye'r uncle, Jim, but he's always struck me as bein at war way the whole of Ballybracken an' most of the world niver tak aff the McKendrys. He seems tay detest them in particular. Why so?"

"It's simply jealousy," Jim remarked. "There they are with all that land, money and big house, and George and Hanna effectively the 'King' and 'Queen' of Ballybracken, George holding this outpost for the fast-vanishing British Empire here west of the Bann. He's a powerful County Counsellor, a Justice of the Peace so can vet all police summonses, he's Commandant of the B-Specials that can deliver rough justice to any cocky Nationalists, and then he's an Orangeman, Master of the Royal Black Preceptory and a prominent Mason, so all that means he has local power and patronage covered. Sure nobody round here gets anything, not even a school cleaner's job, unless it is filtered through George. And to top it all, he's recognized for his services to Britain with a most prestigious 'gong' declaring him to be a 'Commander of the British Empire', and entertained at Buckingham Palace. Is it any wonder Uncle Bertie is jealous?"

Trashing the Icons

Robbie knew that Jim was in one of his bitter iconoclastic moods, and there would be no stopping him. It was Rosie who thought she should try for she didn't like to hear people who were so kind to them being run down even by Jim, however much she liked him too.

"But Mr McKendry is a dacent good man, and so is the whole family as we know ony too well."

"They are," Jim agreed, "and can well afford to be, Rosie, for they have this place sown up. Boy, isn't Ballybracken a well-guarded and well-patrolled Unionist outpost! I wouldn't mind so much if only Unionists like McKendry showed some concern for Ulster's Protestant and Catholic poor. At best, they are paternalistic, and what does that amount to? Sharing out the crumbs that fall from their well-stocked tables."

"I've towel yeh that until recent events, an' my prison cell experience, I'd hiv been with yeh al the way, my friend, but Ballybracken's paternalism, as yeh call it, swung inta action tay save my bacon, so I can't say much agin it."

"That's because you are so well got[161] round here, Robbie, and, yes, we are good at looking after our own, but you surely must agree that the Stormont Unionist Government has resisted tooth and claw every social reform Westminster has introduced since the end of your war… in health… in education… they have rejected, delayed or watered down all the Labour Government's socialist policies. As far as they are concerned, the best policy is to keep the poor on both sides down and ignorant for if they are educated they will surely challenge the system… oh yes, and best to get rid of the poor Catholics to work in England or wherever for that'll mean there are fewer of them around to vote Nationalist, a good thing surely in any Unionist's book. Maybe they see that Nationalist haemorrhaging as helping to balance out the young Protestant renegades, the likes of me, who flee East selling out on the West-of- the- Bann Unionist cause. At election time, they have only to cry '*Union in danger! Border under threat!*' and the working-class Protestants fall into line, and vote for the status quo and, in effect, the continuation of their own poverty."

"Mind you, the Catholic Church isn't that keen on socialist reforms that wud help workin folk either," Robbie felt obliged to say. "What about this rumpus in the Republic over Dr. Browne's 'Mother an' Child' healthcare scheme? Sure the Catholic Church hez hounded him outta hez government job for even suggestin somethin that wud hiv helped the poor."

Rosie had left the men at the table to make tea which she now put in front of them with a plateful of ginger snap biscuits, regarding them as the sort of luxury you give a guest. She then went off to feed her few hens and milk the goat. The big issues the men had strayed into seemed to her a waste of time since there was nothing the likes of the Dowdells – or indeed Jim either - could do about them. Sure wasn't it great she now had her good job with the McKendrys and that wee Danny was getting on so well and hadn't she a good man beside her even if he was no saint. What more could any poor body want?

Back in the kitchen, Robbie dunked a biscuit in the hot tea and, trying to lighten the conversation a bit, said,

---

161 **Well got** - *highly regarded… respected*

"What about switchin over from 'scrabblin' tay 'strollin,' Jim, an' take a slug aff ye'r tay[162]."

Don't go East, Young Man!

Jim turned a very fierce look on him, for Robbie had forgotten for a moment what an intense and idealistic man his friend was.

"I suppose I am still resentful at some of the reasons – I'll call them 'Unionist reasons' - why my university education has been curtailed. I appreciate my mother's practical concerns. She and Helen would indeed find it very difficult to cope on their own but it's the underlying reason that is hard to stomach… Uncle Bertie's reason. The Unionist cause needs Protestant boys to stay here west of the Bann or Unionists will be outvoted by the Nationalists, and my mother is not behind the door[163] in putting that up to me too."

Robbie said, "but surely you yourself might be provin Bertie an' ye'r mother right! Bertie towel me wance[164] when I was workin for him, that more *fancy education,*' as he called secondary schooling, will bay the ruination aff the country… takin Protestants – the lakes aff you, Jim - away east to Belfast or outta the country altogether, while educatin the enemy among us – again, hez words - so they can rise up and destroy us. Now aff curze[165] you hiv come back. But wasn't that only because of your family circumstances? Will that be so in the majority aff cases? I main tay say[166], young Protestants go east an' they generally niver come back. I sometimes think Protestants, the educated wans anyway, aren't so sure they belong here in Irelan even after three or four hundred years… but Catholics know in their heart where they belong… they are Irish an' Ireland is their home, no question. Their pride in their Irish identity is bred inta them, an' good on them for they know where they stan." He looked his friend in the eye. "So maybe Bertie might hiv a point! Wud yeh be thinking al these dangerous socialist thoughts if you wuren't an educated gentleman an', as Bertie wud say '*losin the run aff ye'rself*[167],' as far as the Unionist cause is concerned here in Ballybracken an' indeed west aff the Bann?"

---

162 **Take a slug aff ye'r tay** – *drink your tea*
163 **Not behind the door** – *makes no secret of her view*
164 **Towel me wance** – *told me once*
165 **Aff curze** – *of course*
166 **I main tay say** – *what I mean is*
167 **Losin the run aff ye'rself** – *losing sight of your position… forgetting who and what you are*

They were both thoughtfully dunking biscuits in the tea.

Jim continued, "You're right. Higher education is a way up and, as my Uncle Bertie thinks, a passport out for young Protestant apostates like me, but surely you think the same as I do? You've seen other and better ways of doing things so surely you must agree that things here must change… must improve?"

"Well, I agree way yeh up tay a point. I've seen enough aff the world tay know there must be a better way but my nixt question has tay be, what is that better way? Were the Ruskies I met, an' drunk vodka with in Germany, any happier in their Communist paradise? Did Herr Hitler or Il Duce Mussolini bring great happiness to their folk with their Fascist utopias?"

'Liberty… Equality… Fraternity'

"But maybe **we** could actually make a better go of it," Jim persisted. "You've told me yourself that you think that if only Irish Republicanism was true to its origins in the French Revolution. If only it really meant *'Liberty, Equality and Fraternity'* for all Irishmen and not just the narrow Catholic Nationalism it has developed into which, let's face it, leaves no room for us if they ever get their united Ireland. If my mother was here she would be telling us in no uncertain terms to look at what's happening to the Protestant population in the Republic now. It's being wiped out with the Catholic Church's mixed marriage laws. My point is that Protestants in the six counties mightn't have a siege mentality if they had less evidence of actually being besieged, especially here west of the Bann. And while McKendry and Cobain, and indeed my own family, feel themselves and their religion and politics besieged by Irish Nationalism and Catholicism we can't move, we can't thaw out to our good Catholic neighbours. Oh yes, on the surface we are all very neighbourly in our day-to-day dealings – nothing worse in Ballybracken than to be thought a bad neighbour across all divides - but are we not almost complete strangers to each other? We besiege our Catholic neighbours here in the North; they besiege us in the all-over Irish scene. So we are all like rabbits caught in the headlights. Frozen and stuck! For you don't change things during a siege. Everybody must know their place against the day the walls look like being breached. That to my mind is so damaging to Irish society both North and South. But you're shaking your head, Robbie. Come on, tell me what you think?"

"I think yeh badly need a good willin woman tay take ye'r min aff al this," Robbie said putting his hand on his friend arm, "an' sure yeh know we can always depend on the English tay come to our aid," he finished with heavy sarcasms.

"Don't mention the English ruling class in the same breath as honest sincere people," Jim said. "Sure we all know their bizarre propensity for falling in love with people who hate them. I mean they despise us Ulster Protestants and the Unionists for being loyal to them yet have a love affair with Irish Republicans who hate them."

"What did I read wance?" Robbie said thoughtfully. "It was somethin about *'howlin your friends close but your enemies even closer'*…. maybe that is what the sly English buggers are up to."

"Maybe," Jim replied, "though I have to say that the great strength of the English ruling class, from my reading of history, is that they never know, or are so arrogant they simply can't believe, when they are beaten. They just muddle on regardless until they finally win a victory of some sort. Somebody once described them as '*scrawny wonders*' who organize the Scots, the Welsh and the Irish to do all the hard work, whether it's digging their canals, building their railways, fightin in their armies or adding to their Empire. And again, history would bear that out."

"Well, I have tay come clian an' tell yeh that I had no hesitation in joinin the army for it wuz the British Army not the English army so I wuzn't fightin for them but with them for I **wuz** them… British!... if that makes any kinna sense. By the way," Robbie continued, "I meant tay say during that long sermon of yours that you have left a Ballybracken family of great distinction out of your local Unionist hierarchy. What about Colonel Sir Thomas Roxborough of Grovehill Manor? Is he not the top of the Ballybracken hierarchy in your estimate of things?"

"In my estimation, the old aristocracy, like the Colonel there, are seen as yesterday's men. Not seen as reliable by the besieged. Why? They can up sticks and run… back to their broad acres in England or at least fall back on their rich relatives across the water. No, it's the Ulster Protestant bourgeoisie and the poor Protestant working class that are the besieged, the frozen, the stuck-here-for-keeps folk… not the lords and ladies and gentry of Ulster's big houses. The Roxborough's planter sword has passed down to the McKendrys and now takes the form of, well come to think, your B-Special rifle, Robbie."

"Well…. you did ask," Jim finished, for Robbie was looking a bit mentally frozen himself after this intense session with his friend. He smiled to break the serious atmosphere that had sprung up between them brought on by Jim's sincere intensity.

"Anyway, mate, yeh need a strong drink after al that, fir yeh hiv may head splittin[168], an' then a woman as soon as that can bay arranged. I'm on the lookout for yeh."

Jim produced a packet of 'Gallagher's' and offered one across. They sat smoking in silence.

"You know, the more I think about him, my Uncle Bertie really is the quintessential non-conformist, thoroughly contrary, the most awkward of the awkward squad. Despite his great loyalty to the Crown and the Protestant faith, he never attends church, he told me he wouldn't let a Protestant doctor or vet set foot on his farm nor would he deal with a Protestant accountant or chemist … for, as he put it, *'the Catholic Nationalists have no loyalty to the Northern Ireland state so they make it their business to know how to bamboozle it to get the best out of it by fair means or foul. The Protestants' loyalty to it means most of them toe the party line far too much to be any use to help the ordinary man.'* So he's a man who stands resolutely for the system and just as resolutely against it! He told me that when the Unionist big-wigs get up to speak on the platform on the Twelfth of July, he sits on the grass with his back to them for he has no time for 'blow-ins'[169] who only want the Orangemen's vote to keep them up there in big jobs in Stormont."

"Maybe ye'r uncle Bertie is the revolutionary ye'r lukin for, Jim?"

"God help us if he and his sort ever get their way," Jim said. "We will have even more of a right-wing state than we have already. No, Robbie, you are my best hope to lead the Ballybracken revolution and bring us to the broad sunlit uplands of liberty, equality and fraternity. I'll be behind you… but keeping well back… to write your history and tell you how wrong you have got it!"

"I doubt if I'm ye'r man either," said Robbie smiling. "Sure you know I've firmly resolved to become one of life's 'strollers.' The man you're lukin for wud hiv tay be a dyed- in- the- wool 'scrabbler'… just lake yourself, Jim."

Rosie appeared with a can of goat's milk.

"Well Rosie," said Jim, "me and this man of yours have just sorted out the world's problems in general, and Ballybracken's in particular."

Rosie said, "It wud fit yez better if yez had sorted out how we ur goin tay get a man for poor Maisie Trimble for, as God's may witness, I can't see any way tay get hir hooked up tay wee Constable McCrum, an' I know for definite that she's

---

168 **Fir yeh hiv may head splittin** – *you have given me a severe headache*
169 **Blow-ins** – *outsiders so regarded with suspicion… not trusted by the locals*

astray in the head an' hiz a while notion aff him[170]." An' it's no wunner fir he'd bay a good ketch for hir[171].

Rosie was ever well-grounded in Ballybracken realities.

---

[170] ***She is astray in the head an' hiz a while notion aff him*** – *she is driven mad by her deep affection for him*

[171] ***He'd bay a good ketch fir hir*** – *he would be a very suitable husband for her*

Episode 18

Money for America

"Rosie, would you finish what you are at just now, and then go and sit with Mrs Mary for a while. She has insisted on getting up this morning, and sitting in her chair, but we don't think she should be alone when she is out of bed. None of us can be with her all the time."

Rosie went across the landing to the old lady's bedroom. She was sitting upright in a high chair by the side of the bed beautifully dressed in shimmering black with a large cameo under her chin and her silver hair piled high on her head. She looked every inch the grand elegant lady with that day's newspaper on her lap.

"Ah Rosie," she said, "I am pleased to see you, but there is no need for you to leave your work on my account. I am quite content here on my own. They fuss and treat me like an invalid, you know, but I'm not… I'm not," and she took a pinch of snuff from a silver box, sneezed violently and let the newspaper fall to the floor. Rosie went to pick it up. "Don't trouble yourself about it, dear, for the newspapers are only concerned with bad news. So upsetting, and now another war, this time in Korea. Will we never learn from our mistakes? What cause have we to be fighting in Korea?"

Rosie said nothing but folded the newspaper and put it on the table beside the old lady.

"… and the last war barely over and Germany in ruins. I travelled the length and breadth of that great country with my American family at the end of the last century. Such a great Protestant nation. So cultured too. We have so much in common with them including our dear royal family. You know, I even admired Herr Hitler at first for, you know, in the early days, before he went completely mad, I thought he was the best the German people could hope for after all they had suffered during and after the Great War… and I also thought the strong efficient Germany he was supposed to be creating would save us from those dreadful atheist Communists in Russia. But there it is, he turned out to be a monster. 'Master Race' indeed! Such piffle! You must be so proud of the part your Robbie played in defeating the Nazis, and fighting for our stout British Empire."

The Ultimate Arrogance

She paused, and then turned a steady gaze on Rosie.

"Of course, I can't entirely approve of your relationship with Robbie, but the one thing I learned from such a long life, Rosie, is not to judge other people too harshly especially when you do not know their circumstances. It is wrong to try to live other people's lives for them, very wrong. It is a dreadful arrogance."

She paused again to pull on her bell.

"You will take tea with me, Rosie? No, no! Don't go. Hanna or Mina will bring it. I'm afraid I am boring you with my chatter, but I love to reminisce. You are such a kind listener and so tolerant of the ramblings of an old woman, though I fear I am keeping you from important work. I must meet Robbie too sometime… a hero in Ballybracken. I thought I'd never live to see it… otherwise such dreary boring men around here…" she tailed off to open her snuff box again.

Rosie had never thought of Robbie as a war hero though, of course, she could never forget that she and Daniel Malachy owed him their lives that day long ago down by the rivers. But what had the old lady just said about not trying to live other people's lives? Surely that is exactly what Miss Mina had hinted that old Mrs McKendry had done to her. But, then again, people are full of such contradictions, saying one thing and doing another.

Girls Don't Matter!

The old lady was continuing her reverie.

"You know, Rosie, my own life has been so varied," she said. "From rags to riches … oh yes, my family was very poor in Ballybracken Upper. A big family of us… four boys and two girls… and of course there was nothing for the girls as we grew up… the usual thing… the eldest boy, my brother James, who wouldn't do a hand's turn[172] about the farm, yet he would get the thirty hungry acres, my other brothers a miserable amount of money to give them some sort of start in life, and us girls… what great bounty could we girls expect?" and she gave a high-pitched laugh. "Well, if we married a local farmer, maybe a cow or a pig would accompany us to sweeten the bargain he was getting, and young wives thought of as little better than breading stock and farm chattels. And if we didn't

---

172 **Wouldn't do a hand's turn** – *was lazy and wouldn't help or do even the simplest job on the farm*

marry, to be hired out for six-month spells of pure slavery far from home. Can you imagine it, Rosie? To stand there at the local hiring fair – the well named hiring 'rabbles' - being looked over by the local yokels and farmers … thought of as little better than beasts of burden, calculating how much work they could get out of a girl for as little pay as possible… maybe never getting home to see your own people for months… maybe never getting time off at all except to scamper to and from church on a Sunday, and sometimes not even that. It makes me so angry to think of it."

"I know, Mistress, but don't you upset ye'rself now. Them days hiv gone. Things is better now, an' sure it worked out well for yeh in the end. Yeh married Mr McKendry an' sure luk at yez now in the lap aff luxury."

"No, Rosie," the old lady said more calmly now, "I married Hugh McKendry much later after I returned from America. But I might have been hired out had I not taken decisive steps to see to it that hiring was not to be my fate. If I tell you how I did it, I know you will be shocked, but I am so old now I don't care what people think of me. Well, one night, with my ear to the bedroom door, I heard our parents discussing what they planned for us. My father was saying that my sister ,Tilda, and I were at the age to be hired out, and that, come the next hiring fair, my mother must be prepared to part with us. What really made me very angry was our mother's reaction."

Here she paused, a lump of deep emotion in her throat as she recalled her hurt, then continued,

"… our mother was not concerned about us being hired out to the lord-knows-who or even if we sank to the lowest of the low and had to join the Irish potato gathering gangs in Scotland, the notorious 'tattie-hokers.' Perhaps that is going too far, Rosie, and she would not have allowed that but nevertheless it was clear to me at that moment that all that concerned her was the inconvenience to herself of our going away. How was she going to cope with the housework, with the young ones, with the milking, with winning the turf…and so on? No anxiety about our wellbeing or wherever we might end up. No regrets that she would miss us for ourselves. No show of affection or genuine concern. No pleading that we were still too young. Nothing, except our loss to her as skivvies. Those were tough times, Rosie, and I always knew she was a hard woman, but she was my mother. Until that moment, my love for her was unquestioning. I lay in bed that night staring at the ceiling crying bitterly, and for the first time in my life I was questioning everything. Why were the boys to get it all? What was wrong with being a girl? Why was our fate decided for us…? I fell asleep in despair, but I woke in the morning full of hope for somehow I then knew what I must do. I must take control of my own life whatever the cost. I would seek my fortune somewhere well away from Ballybracken… in England… in America… anywhere and anything but the indignity and uncertainty of being hired out. But, Rosie, how was I to get the money for the fare to that 'somewhere else' of my imagination?"

Marriage Impossible

She paused as if waiting for a suggestion from Rosie, then continued,

"Well, I was pretty in those days, Rosie, and I had seen some of the boys looking at me at church. One of them was Hugh McKendry, a presentable enough young man, and he had even cycled up to see me pretending to have come to borrow tethers or something of that sort from my father, but I knew the real reason. He wanted to see me and, since his family were said to be a little better off than most of us poor farmers, he would not have been a bad catch for a Ballybracken girl with no prospects. Well, he and I had a few secret meetings between his home and mine when we could both get away, which wasn't often, and I came to respect and maybe even like him a little. He was, of course, a dull fellow as only Ballybracken men can be dull, Rosie, but a girl didn't expect much from a man in those days, indeed I suppose still don't, which is just as well."

She paused as if to reflect on this and to take a pinch of snuff. "But you have a good man in Robbie… a good manly man… and so brave… so very brave."

Rosie thought of Robbie's scary nightmares when he roared in his sleep imagining himself once again under fire or in some other terrifying warlike situation half remembered in the morning, but this was neither the place nor the time to divulge such confidences. The old lady was continuing her story, and Rosie had come to realize that nothing was expected of her here and now but to listen.

"I confess it. I would have married Hugh there and then. I didn't love him, of course, but he was handy to us[173] up there in Ballybracken Upper and my one hope of escape if I stayed in Ireland… and he wanted me… but it was hopeless. We both knew that his widowed mother… well-known to be a cross old targe[174]… would never agree to sharing her home with any other woman. Despite all that, Hugh said he still wanted me… but we would have to wait

---

173   **Handy to us** – *lived nearby*
174   **A targe** – *a scolding woman*

for the old woman to die. Well, I was not prepared to wait! We might wait for years."

She seemed almost on the brink of tears as she recalled the anger and frustration she had felt as a highly intelligent young woman trapped by circumstance. When she had regained her composure, she continued,

"So do you know what I did, Rosie? I asked him to give me the money for my fare to America! Wasn't that brazen of me? I said I would repay him when I had earned enough in New York or wherever fate took me. I was touched when he said that he only wanted me, and that I mustn't go. That was the closest he ever came to saying he loved me. But then we all know that love is not in Unionist men's vocabulary round here. However warm-hearted and decent they might be, they are reared to present themselves to the world as hard, uncompromising, humourless, even if that is only skin deep for most of them. So sad… so destructive of the human spirit… they must never drop their guard or allow their hearts to thaw… and do you know why, Rosie? In case the 'other sort' think they are softening and take advantage of them, threatening their religion, their land, their territory… that is why. I understand it, I even value it, but I see it for the necessary evil that it is."

Scared of Shadows

It crossed Rosie's mind fleetingly that she must be one of the Catholics that they seemed to be so afraid of. Were they all scared of her and her kind? How could people so rich and prosperous as the McKendry's and the other Ballybracken farmers and her Protestants neighbours be scared of her and poor Catholic folk like her? It was like the bogey men she sometimes scared the children with to get them to behave. Maybe it was the same thing only it was powerful prosperous men who feared their own version of bogey men. It was beyond Rosie's comprehension.

But still the old lady was continuing, with Rosie only half listening, and wanting somebody to appear with a cup of tea to revive her.

The Stolen Wedding Ring

"… but Hugh couldn't get the money for my fare either. His mother controlled the purse strings and made it her business to guard every penny. He had to account to her for everything that came or went. There was no way he could slip such a sum past her. But nothing was going to shake my determination to escape and somehow get the money for the journey, and I needed it soon for the hiring fair was only a month away. Do you know what I did to get it, Rosie? I stole my mother's wedding ring and pawned it! Don't look so shocked. Did they not owe me? I, who had worked so hard for them in kitchen, byre, pigsty, during spring sowing and autumn harvesting, in the bog winning the turf not to speak of helping to rear my young brothers with all the washing and ironing and sewing that entailed… Oh yes, they owed me all right. And my reward was to be put up for hire! Well, I had other plans! My mother always hid her ring in the salt box in the hearth above the fire, and she never wore it for weeks on end. I knew that with any luck she would not discover it was gone for quite a while. I waited my chance, and when I had the house to myself I fished the ring out of the salt where it was wrapped in tissue paper, and I pawned it the next time I was in town."

Confession is good for the Soul

At this, she gave a heartfelt sigh possibly of relief at finally having told someone her guilty secret. Then she said, "I told Hugh my plans, though not how I had come by the money, and said I would return to him but, I must be truthful, I really never intended to. Fate and circumstances brought me home years later, and he still wanted me and I needed him, but that is a long way ahead and a different story. Do you know how I survived and prospered? I learned never to let life get the better of me, to calculate the odds, to harden my heart and to press home any advantage that presented itself. But the years are mellowing, and I see now the hurt I may have caused not just to my mother over that ring but to others too as I ploughed my own furrow. But you look tired, Rosie. You must be exhausted listening to the reminiscences of an old woman. I must not keep you any longer."

"So it was the money from the ring took yeh tay Amerikey, Mistress?" Rosie said, for the story of the ring had caught her imagination.

"It was indeed, Rosie dear. Miraculously, it turned out to be quite valuable, and was just enough, together with some I had scrimped and saved, to pay for my train fare to Londonderry and my passage, steerage class of course, from there to New York City. I was processed like an animal through that dreadful Ellis Island but I was free, Rosie, free for the first time of my life! Free to make my own way."

She paused, took a small embroidered handkerchief from her sleeve and dabbed her eyes. "You must surely be wondering what brought me back to this backwater having once escaped and seen such wonders? Well, I may reveal that to somebody someday but not now. I wish I could say I had a happy married life but I confess I have never been happy here and, worse still, I think I made Hugh's life a misery too in some ways. He who had waited for me so long and so patiently. Oh, I returned with all this money, and it bought this house and estate when the heir of the original owners bet it all on a Cowes Yacht race and lost. Did you know that, Rosie? It was pure chance that I arrived back as the former owners had to part with it to honour their son's gambling debts. As I said, I always had an eye to the main chance, and took it both in America and here." She sighed long and hard, "But Hugh was a good man and deserved better. But nothing in the past can be undone, and all that is left of me now is a soft prattling old woman. I hardly recognize her, but it hardly matters for she will soon be dead too."

Again she dabbed at her eyes with the beautiful hanky and, perhaps aware that she had bared her soul too much even to someone so out of her sphere as Rosie Dowdells, said, "They have forgotten about the tea, Rosie. Would you see what has happened to it?"

"Indeed, Mistress," Rosie said, rising and heading for the door. Before she got there, Mrs. McKendry called after her, "I should be very grateful if you would do me a favour."

"Ach aye, Mistress, Anythin within may power."

The Fateful Diary

"During all my years in America, I kept a diary and it and all my letters and journals, cards and so on are in that big trunk over there. My family are not interested in the contents at all or indeed in my life story, which I suppose is why I have inflicted so much of it on you this afternoon."

She paused, perhaps waiting for Rosie to disagree and Rosie didn't disappoint.

"Naw, Mistress, sure it wuz great hearin al that for I niver knew it before, but yeh can be sure nothin yeh tell me will go any further for I niver gossip."

"Rosie dear, I know you don't. I have no fear on that score. But all I've told you is true. And do you know, I feel a weight lifted from having told at least a small part of my story to you, dear Rosie. Our church does not have confession and I sometimes think it must be such a relief to confess things, even just little troubling things, to another human being. God can seem very remote at times when you try to confess to Him."

Rosie felt like saying that in her church Father O'Kelly could be hard enough with the penances when you went to confession, but she just said,

"Yeh mentioned a wee favour yeh wanted may tay undertake for yeh, Mistress. What is it, an' I'll surely do it?"

"Oh yes, I remember now," continued the old woman. "I have asked the folk below on so many occasions to send young Mr Jim McKnight to see me. That young man was, I believe, studying history at Queen's University until that tyrannical mother of his dragged him home. I don't know the young man at all, but I want to get my diaries and papers to him. I am hopeful that he will undertake to write up my adventures as a family record. But someone will first have to ask him if he will cast his historian's eye over them and consider drawing my story together?"

"I'll git Robbie tay ask him, Mistress, for Jim an' him is very great[175]."

"Robbie might whet his appetite by telling him that he is not to consider my diary and other papers the idle prattle of a silly young girl but the reflections of a mature young Ballybracken woman who faithfully recorded her experiences on travelling across continents, and indeed her encounters with Presidents, Popes and Kings. For, you know, I travelled the length and breadth of the United States and across most of the great Empires of Europe, Rosie. One year, 1899 it was, for that year in particular is emblazoned on my mind, I was at the second cataract of the great River Nile with my American family on their private river steamer and the next year, round about the same time, I was back in Ballybracken, a married woman, washing big ignorant Irish potatoes in the peaty burn[176] that ran behind McKendry's old farmhouse. But I rose above all that too, Rosie, I pulled us out of there. My money bought here and look at us now, the wealthiest folk in Ballybracken by a long shot. And, not that I should say it, but wealthier by far than the Grovehill gentry across the river there. Indeed, when Sir Thomas sells up or, from what I hear, is forced to sell, I hope to persuade my son to make a successful bid for those lands too! Carpe diem, Rosie, carpe diem! Seize the day… that has always been my motto."

Rosie had followed, as best she could, the old lady's long rambling monologue and wondered how much of it could be true? She had heard about this old woman meeting one of the Popes for hadn't she brought back rosary beads blessed by the

---

175 **Very great** – *very friendly… good friends*
176 **Peaty burn** – *a stream flowing out of a bog in which the water is peat brown*

Holy Father himself to give to some of her Catholic neighbours and was highly thought of among them for doing this. Hadn't one set of the Rosaries been a great talking point at Aggie Ward's wake as recently as six months back for there they were, the very same rosary beads, wrapped round Aggie's hands in the coffin with everybody touching them and saying that beads blessed by the Pope himself would surely do her a power of good speedin her through Purgatory. So maybe the rest of the old lady's story was true too.

"Ach, at last! Here's Hanna with the tea. Now I don't need a babysitter any longer. Rosie and I have had a great chat, but I want to enjoy my tea in peace, and read the paper if one of you will be so good as to hand it to me."

Rosie collected Danny from the music room at home time. Mina was tidying away the sheet music.

"He is doing very well," she said. "Very well indeed. We have a really talented musician on our hands."

Episode 19

The Donkey Derby

Protestant or Catholic Donkeys?

The arrival of Duffy's Circus in Ballybracken always caused great excitement. For the innocent at heart there were the horses and ponies, elephants and lions performing unbelievable tricks, the clowns acting in funny ways, and for those with somewhat less innocent and baser interests there were the scantily clad girls, baring nearly all, performing way up high on the trapeze or standing on horseback with legs the like of which were never to be seen at any other time in the townland. And the arrival of the circus this year coincided with a new fad sweeping the countryside, something called a 'donkey derby.'

The circus duly arrived, the big tent was erected, and the caravans and animal cages parked every which way in McKnight's field conveniently opposite the shop, and in the next field so too were the arrangements underway for this mysterious thing involving donkeys.

The Dowdells children could not contain their excitement, and neither could most other Ballybracken folk, though the great and the good pretended it was beneath them to take much notice of it. Indeed, for the very good and the very holy to attend, some speculated, might even be a sin. Those with such troubled consciences decided it would be best to consult the Reverend Quigley. There was no point in consulting the Canon for it was the general consensus that he seemed confused on the whole question of sin, and so couldn't be relied on to give them a definite steer. Not so Mr Quigley.

"Now tell me," he said, full of self-importance, and casting a baleful look over the two Miss Sproules, Maisie Trimble, Big Bertie's Janie, and a few others who had stayed behind to seek his guidance after one of his more terrifying sermons. "Tell may, day yez know if they are Protestant dunkeys or Catholic dunkeys?"

"They're a… mixture… I think," one of them ventured.

The look on some of the other faces told him he needed to rephrase his question.

"I main," demanded the Reverend crossly, "are the dunkey owners Protestant or 'RC'… mainly?" he paused, "for yuz surely don't want tay bay mixed up in some 'RC' affair maybe run for the good of the St Vincent de Paul or some other such outfit aff 'the other side'."

They all agreed that such an outcome would indeed be too terrible to contemplate.

"Fir yez know that yez hiv tay watch ye'rselves an' bay iver vigilant, for Rome is out tay take yez unawares an' decoy yez from the truth of the Holy Gospel. As for the circus, Duffy sounds like a suspicious name tay me, an' there's sure tay be a lot aff brazen hussies ridin about on horses an' doin stuff on swings way harly nothin on them to hide their nakedness an' bare flesh… al that cud inflame the senses an' knock yez sideways…"

He paused as if slightly overcome himself at these fleshy thoughts. He then surveyed his audience one by one, his gaze settling on one of the Miss Sproule's bare neck in such a way that unnerved her, and caused her to put a hand up to hide her shame. The others too were suddenly aware of any 'flesh' they might be showing at that very minute and hastened to cover up any offending parts.

"On the other han," he continued, "it wud surely bay a good opportunity tay han out some upliftin Gospel tracts… tay bring the ungodly tay their knees, an' tay repentance. The work of the Lord can prevail even in places of the darkest sinfulness… luk at Africa the way the missionaries are spreading the word an' makin conversions there even among the darkest heathens. So I think…" he paused for dramatic effect… "al things considered… I think it is al right for yez tay go tay both that derby an' the circus if that is where the spirit leads yez… but ony, mine, if yez take a bunnle[177] aff religious tracts an' distribute them as widely as yez ken. I'll even go mezself… tay the circus anyway… tay see what's what… I'm still not too sure about them dunkeys. Wud there bay gemmlin[178] at that, dey yez think? There must be no gemmlin, mind, for that is another aff Satan's snares. Look where gemmlin got the gran folk that used tay live at Ballybracken House. Al their lan an' fortune went on a boat race! So nothin more need bay said about that tarrible sin. In case there's gemmlin, I'll luk out some suitable tracts that'll stap the gammlers in their tracks. Aye, that what I'll do. This could be an outpouring aff the Holy Spirit for *'God moves in a mysterious way, his wonders tay perform'*. But if I load yez up way tracts, I want none kept back,

---

177 **Bunnle** – *bundle*
178 **Gemmlin** – *gambling*

mind. Fir amen't I efter tellin yez[179] tay see this as an opportunity tay spread the word with the tracts as ammunition in the war against Satan so fire them at the sinful like a broadside. As the 'Good Book' says, *'Cast yer bread upon the watters. It will return tay yeh a hunnerfold.'*" Whereupon he extinguished the mission hall gas light plunging them all into darkness.

The Keeper of the Watch

The news was not so good for the small Dowdells. Yet again, Rosie couldn't take the day off to take them to the derby and Robbie had to go for a full day's rifle practice now that he was in the B-Specials. This was the worst news ever, and the three set about sobbing loudly and plaintively, one taking over where the other left off until finally Rosie and Robbie could stick it no longer. In desperation, it was agreed they could go to the donkey derby but all three were to report together to Jim McKnight at the counter in the shop every hour to make sure they were safe. The three were so delighted that their weeping and wailing had paid off that they danced round the kitchen to celebrate.

The question now arose as to who was to take charge of Robbie's watch to make the monitoring arrangement work? All three knew that whoever had the watch had power and, human nature being what it is, all three wanted that power over the others very badly. Dorry laid claim to the watch on the grounds that their mammy always said she had more sense than the other two put together. A flaw was detected in her argument, however, when it was discovered she could not yet tell the time. Bobby then said he should get the watch because he was going to be a 'sodger' like his daddy, and it would definitely take a soldier to guard it properly from the thieves he firmly believed would be hiding behind every bush. But this claim did not prevail either for nobody could see the sense of it and, anyway, he couldn't tell the time either.

This lack of horological skill having been brought to light amongst Dowdells' youngest, the stewardship of Robbie's watch could then fall to none other but our very own Daniel Malachy. Needless to say, our hero was delighted by the outcome, his place at the top of the Dowdells hierarchy thus tangibly recognized. He now had the power – officially - to boss the others around all day and have the guardianship of Robbie's watch to boot. It remained an open question whether he was actually any good at telling the time either, but the whole plan would collapse if one of them didn't have the watch so no further enquiries were

---

179 ***Fir amen't I efter tellin yez*** – *haven't I just told you*

made about Danny's horological skills, Rosie and Robbie having had enough weeping and wailing for one day. As for Jim McKnight's part in the plan, in the event nobody remembered to tell him about his custodial role, so it remained a mystery to him why three small Dowdells heads appeared over his counter at intervals during the course of the afternoon and would then disappear again without saying a word.

Still to be resolved was the question of the circus, and could the Dowdells get going to that too? There was less uncertainty about allowing that for, unlike the donkey derby, everybody knew what a circus was, and Rosie even thought it might be good for their education *'what with them maybe bein able tay draw them wile animals afterwards for the teachers in school an' that...'* But again, the question was who would look after them? Only the Saturday night suited *'... what with the hannlin[180] it wud be gettin them up for school if they went tay bed late on a weekday night...'* so they would have to go on the Saturday night after the donkey derby. But Rosie had agreed to stay on at McKendry's to sit with the old lady to let the rest of the family attend some parish function that night, and Robbie couldn't be sure of getting back from his rifle drill to take them, the firing range being so far away and him depending on the police Land Rover to bring him home. So again, and entirely by default, it fell to Daniel Malachy, casting himself now as hero of the hour, to be given responsibility for getting them to and from the circus that Saturday evening.

"So, my big b-owl[181] comrade, you are in charge of this whole campaign," said Robbie running his fingers roughly through Danny's curly hair. "Make sure yeh bring al ye'r troops back tay barracks in wan piece, won't yeh."

A bright sunny morning promised well for the success of the donkey derby and the circus, the word from those who had attended the performance the previous evening being that it was the best ever. There was the greatest array of wild animals, deeds of wonderful daring-do by bronzed muscular stunt men all handsome and exotic looking, clowns whose antics had caused such gales of laughter as to nearly bring the big tent down, and very many lovely girls wearing

---

180 **Hannlin** – *trouble*
181 **B-owl** – *bold... brave... and it can mean very naughty in some contexts*

the tightest outfits ever and revealing acres of that desirable 'flesh' so feared by the Reverend Quigley.

Wayward Donkeys

The derby too got off in a blaze of excitement with much surreptitious betting from the outset adding to the thrill. Thus were the Reverend's worst fears justified despite the best efforts of the holy ladies and their tracts to persuade the crowd to resist such temptation. But even the most holy took time from the Lord's work to enjoy the colourful spectacle. Adorable little donkeys of every shape, size and hue, some as determined as their riders to win, some equally determined, amid much hilarity, to throw their riders, to head off in the wrong direction, wander to the side of the track and nuzzle spectators who tried in vain to help the riders get the wilful beasts turned in the direction of the winning post. One who had cantered promisingly at first, and looked like a winner, suddenly changed its mind and ambled off deep into the crowd coming to a halt where the holy ladies were standing in a bunch. It started to nibble at Jessy Craig's big handbag begging, not for the first time, the question as to what she kept in there?

Since the beast was standing still, Flo Lyttle, mindful of the Reverend's words to spread the word at every opportunity, took up position at the donkey's backside and, brushing aside some hair on its back, exclaimed,

"Wud yez al luk! It has the wee cross on its back provin that it carried Jeezus into Jerusalem… well, not this actual wan, yez understan, but isn't it proof that Jeezus took his last journey to die for our sins sittin on an ass."

Before anyone had time to support this visual aid to encourage belief, the donkey decided to relieve itself all over Flo's dress and shoes. Flo squealed and took to her heels towards McKnight's shop for 'a wee tidy' as she put it, shedding donkey dung as she went.

Disengaging her handbag finally from the donkey's mouth, Jessy struck the donkey such a blow on its head it staggered backwards stepping heavily on one of the Miss Sproule's toes causing her to let out an unmerciful squawk before she too fled the field clutching her hat and spraying her religious tracts in all directions.

Bobby Takes the Field

Back at the starting post, the organizers were looking for volunteers to ride in a line-up of donkeys in a children's race. Daniel Malachy found it easy to resist the temptation to have a go for he might drop Robbie's watch or fall off in the mud, and that would not sit well with his newly acquired position of supreme power. His great responsibility for timekeeping had weighed heavily on him all afternoon to the great annoyance of Dorry and Bobby for he missed no opportunity to boss them around, and not just at reporting-in times.

But now Bobby was volunteering to race on a donkey without Danny's permission. Much as he thought this would be fun, especially if Bobby fell off in the mud or came last in the race or the donkey bolted carrying Bobby away forever which would be great, Danny knew he must exercise his big-brother power, throw his weight around, and forbid it.

"Ach why not?" said Bobby and then, "your just an owl dunkey yourself… an' a wee shit," he added angrily, and with as much venom as he could muster.

"I will tell our mammy you said a bad word," Danny said drawing himself up to his full height. "Mammy said she would give yez a good skelpin[182] if yez give me any bother… so yez iz for it now… I'm…," Danny was striving to say something that grown-ups would say on such an occasion…. "I'm… I'm… puttin my foot down."

Nothing daunted by this terrible threat, Bobby began to race towards the line of donkeys and, by dint of heroic effort, got up on one of the hapless creature's back.

"Well done, son," the man in charge of the line-up said. "Ye'r the quare brave cub showing these other boyos up. Come on now, the rest of yez, an' folley wee Dowdells's good example or are yez al a bunch aff cowards?"

Slowly… very slowly… others began mounting the donkeys.

"I'm not startin till I hiv a full house here," the man said, beginning to push lads towards the donkeys that still had no rider. Danny had no intention of being coerced, for what would it do to his dignity if he fell off and Bobby didn't? Or worse still, if Bobby won and he didn't? He consoled himself by thinking it was a stupid race only of interest to big babies, so he turned away and headed over to the clump of trees that bordered the road. He didn't even want to give Bobby the satisfaction of watching.

---

182 **Skelpin** — *Smacking*

Danny Places His Bet

It was then Tommy Morrison appeared, Danny's self-appointed 'protector' for which 'service' we will recall he regularly relieved our little hero of some of his singing money.

"Hi, young Dowdells," Tommy said almost civilly, "hiv yeh got any money on yeh?"

Danny knew he should say he hadn't, but he had to weigh this against the fact that it would impress Tommy if he said he had charge of the money to pay the three Dowdells into the circus.

"What's it for?" he demanded. "I ony hiv our money fir the circus."

Tommy said, "Ach, that'll do well fir yeh see I'm a bookie for the day, an' I'll double it for yeh if yeh'll put it up front on a good tip I'll give yeh. Are yeh up for it or are yeh too big a coward?"

Danny didn't know what Tommy was talking about but with his power and dignity now reduced to such a low point because of Bobby's defiance, it would be great to end up with more money than he had been given. That would put Dorry and Bobby back in their proper place. He fished about in his coat pocket and handed over two half-crowns to Tommy.

"Ach, good on yeh, Danny," Tommy said, much to our hero's satisfaction for this had obviously impressed the 'bookie for the day.' "Now, what dunkey day yeh want tay bet on? Let me tell yeh that my wee brother is a dab han way the dunkeys. See, he's on that wan near the en aff the row. Aye, the wan that has just turned roun an' is pointin the wrong way. But he'll soon get it under control. I'd say yeh cud do worse than tay place ye'r money on him. He's a winner fir sure."

It occurred to Danny maybe he should be supporting Bobby, but he quickly put that out of his mind for Bobby had defied him and called him bad names. Wouldn't it be great to say he had got all the extra money by not keeping Bobby's end up? That'd show him.

"So, what's ye'r decision? Is it tay put ye'r five bob on Cecil or are yeh gonna do the wrong thing an' bet on wan aff them other losers? Hurry up for they'll soon bay aff."

"On… Cecil," Danny said, knowing full well he had no choice given the amount of pressure he was under. "Does that mean Cecil has tay win if I'm tay get more money back?"

"Yeh've made a wise choice," said Tommy pocketing Danny's coins. "For he's a sarrtainty[183]." And with that he strolled off into the trees.

Danny went back to the starting point. Cecil seemed not yet to have got his donkey completely under control... indeed, even Bobby at the far end of the line seemed more in control of his mount. Then, with the donkeys more or less in a row, though Cecil's still more at a side-ways angle to the others, they were off. To Danny's dismay, Cecil Morrison's donkey had not gone more than the length of itself when it turned sharply at right angles, threw Cecil over its head, and cantered off into the crowd. Worse was to follow. Bobby won! How was the great Daniel Malachy now to face them with Bobby triumphant and clutching a small silver-looking cup, and the money for their admission to the circus gone?

We need hardly reflect that Danny's day hadn't so far gone according to plan! He must find Tommy Morrison. Maybe he would give him the money back or… or what? He had no trouble coaxing Bobby and Dorry to report in at McKnight's shop counter even before the next hour was up for Bobby wanted everybody to see his cup, and Dorry was basking in reflected glory hoping Jim would give them sweets or chocolate or something to mark Bobby's triumph. Danny was strangely quiet even when Jim threw three bags of potato crisps over the counter for them to catch.

As they made their way back through the trees to re-join the derby, there was Tommy Morrison with two of his mates smoking and passing round a big lemonade bottle between them. Tommy winked at his cronies and said,

"Hev yeh any more cash goin spare, wee Dowdells, for we're the boys can spen it for yeh?"

"Yuz go back down the field ye'rselves," Danny said to Bobby and Dorry, trying in vain to re-establish some semblance of control over them. He then turned to stare at Tommy who was now not taking him under his notice.

"I want may money back," he said as fiercely as he could muster. "I need it for us tay get into the circus."

"Ach, f*** aff, yeh wee ganch yeh[184]," was Tommy's unhelpful reply. "Yeh've put it on the dunkey an' yeh lost it, so just f*** off."

Danny played his trump card. "It was Robbie's money, an' I'm gonna tell him that yeh'v stole it from us." Now, we know that this was not strictly true but in the circumstances truth was not a high priority.

Tommy pretended not to hear this and tried to go on arguing about the merits of some football team with his mates, but they were suddenly struck silent and were eyeing Tommy expectantly. All three knew that Danny's bombshell had

---

183 **Sarrtainty** – *he is certain to win*
184 **Ganch** – *you stupid boy*

changed things for it had put Tommy's reputation on the line. At that moment, his standing as a Ballybracken 'hard man', which he used so effectively to control his gang hung in the balance. Would he dare square up to Robbie Elliott? The events in Cobain's pub were now the stuff of legend among Ballybracken's youth making Robbie the most admired and feared man among boys like Tommy and his mates.

"Ach, go on ahead an' tell him whativer yeh want. Tell him I'm fit for him any time," Tommy blustered, taking what the others knew to be the most dangerously stupid path. It fell to Donald Bradley, the smartest of the Morrison gang, now to intervened to save Tommy.

Sappers not Sissies

"Sure why don't we show these wee buggers how tay get inta see the circus way out payin, lake we did las night an' are gonna try again the night."

With his leader's face saved, Donald must now put Danny firmly in his place. He said,

"Sure ony owl sissies lake this wee skitter wud think aff paying tay get in."

So it was settled. The Morrison gang would show the Dowdells how to get into the 'Big Top' without paying, and the price to be paid was to lose the hard cash.

Danny wasn't too happy but, weighing it all up, it was the only solution to hand. He didn't really want to tell Robbie and his mammy that he had lost the circus money to a big bully who had fooled him into putting the bet on a stupid donkey that had run in the wrong direction. Besides, it would be a great adventure to sneak into the circus without paying. Maybe it involved a tunnel or disguising themselves as clowns… or… who knows what? Danny's imagination was already working overtime. And they would be with these big boys doing big boy things and not paying money like a lot of sissy girls. Maybe that made losing the five shillings worth it after all.

Episode 20

Madam Catalina's 'Little Cherub'

Come teatime, Bobby and Dorry began to moan about why they were not all going to the tea tent since they knew Danny had been told to pay for sandwiches and lemonade to come out of the five shillings. Danny pretended not to hear them and then had a bit of luck when, on their last visit to the shop, Jim gave them another bag of crisps and a mineral each. That shut Bobby and Dorry up, at least for the time being. Danny had now to break the news to them that they were going to get to the circus all right but not exactly through the main gate *for iverywan knows that it is ony owl sissies that pay tay get in.'*

Dorry immediately started to cry saying she'd be too scared of getting caught, and anyway she was going to tell their mammy what the boys were up to. Bobby was delighted for he, now a world-famous donkey jockey, wouldn't want to be thought a sissy by paying to get in either. Dorry was finally bought off by Danny's half bag of unfinished crisps, whatever was left of his lemonade and the promise, which he had no intention of keeping, of finally handing over his schoolbag to her, the ownership of which had been for some time her greatest earthly desire. Negotiations thus completed, with fortunately no questions being asked about what Danny was going to do with the entrance money now apparently saved, he led the way to the rendezvous agreed with Tommy and the gang behind a big clump of whin[185] bushes at the rear of the circus tent.

"Now, dey yez see that loose flap over there? If yez pull it back there's enough space to squeeze through. When yez get in, head for a wuden[186] platform-looking thing at the far side, crawl in unner it an' we'll bay waitin for yez."

These instructions delivered commando style and taking no questions, Tommy and then Donald, disappeared through the tent flap. The other gang member was nowhere to be seen. It was agreed that Dorry must go first, then Bobby, and Danny would bring up the rear. Dorry's fears now returned so she started to wail and to say she was going home now this very minute to tell their mammy on them. Danny started to say that, in that event, the schoolbag deal was off when Bobby grabbed his sister by the arm, said he would thump her if

---

185 **Whin** – *gorse*
186 **Wuden** – *wooden*

she didn't *'give over an' stap cryin lake a big babby.'* He then propelled her still wailing across the grass to the tent flap into which they now both disappeared.

Daniel Malachy had had some misgivings himself when he saw what the plan entailed. But there was nothing for it but to go through with it for brother Bobby's flag was flying far too high for Danny not to assert himself to retrieve leadership of the Dowdells. With so much prestige to be lost, he too broke cover, darted across the open ground and squeezed through the flap which was far smaller than it had appeared from behind the whins. But he manages to crawl through on hands and knees to find himself in a broad grass-covered alleyway between the tent's canvas wall and the back of tiers of wooden benches. There was no-one to be seen, but across the way was a long wooden platform which he took to be their next hidey hole. Getting to his feet, he lost no time crossing the grassy space and squeezing under the platform. So there they all were hunkered down, the boys sniggering, Dorry sobbing and Danny well out of his depth.

"Now, we hide in here till some aff the payin people start sittin down on the seats up above, then yez crawl through between the wuden flure[187] an' the seat, just sit down an' ye'r in. Aisy![188] But yez must get in before too many folk take their seats or ye'r'll end up crawlin between somebody's legs an' then yeh'll bay caught on."

There seemed to be a lot going on now in the grassy passageway they had just crossed but they could see nothing except feet and hooves from their hidey-hole, and the sound of horses cantering round, the crack of whips, and people shouting in strange languages.

Danny was just waiting for someone to come and discover them by removing their wooden hiding place, but that didn't happen. Soon the noises in the passageway gave way to noises up above on the seating. It was time to make the next move.

"Yez can't squeeze through the low-down seats for there's not enough space," hissed Tommy. "Yez'll hiv tay swing ye'rselves up a bit higher, an' get through up there."

"Go on," he said to Donald, "I think there's nowan about now."

Donald pulled himself bodily across the Dowdells in the clumsiest way imaginable covering them all in mud and grass in the process. Standing on the platform, he swung on the back of the higher seats to pull himself up, and then promptly disappeared through the gap between them.

---

187   **Flure** – *floor*
188   **Aisy!** – *it will not be difficult*

"Hez done it," said Tommy. "Now wan aff yuz hiv a go."

"None of us is big enough tay reach high enough up," Danny squeaked, voicing, at one and the same time, a real difficulty and a possible way to end this escapade which was proving too much of an adventure after all.

"Ach come on, Yez wee cowards yez," Tommy said. "I'll stan on the platform an' if yez is quick yez can stan on my schaulders[189] an' then al yez hev tay do is squeeze through the gep[190]. Come on," and he grabbed Dorry who happened to be nearest to him.

She was now too petrified to cry so she just acquiesced, trembling. Without more ado, she was swung up on Tommy's shoulders, and she disappeared through the seating. Then it was Bobby's turn and he too quickly vanished. All seemed to be going according to plan as it came to Danny's turn. Up he went on Tommy's shoulders and, once he had steadied himself, there, at eye level, was the gap he had to squeeze through. It looked very narrow, but he consoled himself that the others had got through it so why shouldn't he? Launching himself forward, he promptly got stuck... fast... in the narrow slot!

Posterior Problems

"Get on way it, yeh wee slob," Tommy hissed unsympathetically from down below. "Ye'r wastin time an' yeh'll get us al caught."

But try as he might, Daniel Malachy was going nowhere either forward or back. Then, to his dismay, Tommy shoulders were no longer supporting him.

"Yeh shud hiv threw aff that big coat an' gansy"[191], Tommy hissed, "an' ye'r ass is too fat."

This tactless anatomical comment seemed misplaced in the trying circumstances in which Danny now found himself, but he still felt called upon to say something in his own defence.

"My bum's not fat," he said and then, "Bobby's is far fatter..."

But Tommy hadn't time to discuss the relative plumpness of the Dowdells brothers' posteriors for he was gone, disappearing into the tent through another opening in the seating. Hapless Danny was now dangling in mid-air, his head and shoulders under the seats and his backside, fat or otherwise, suspended out over the grass corridor. He was too upset to cry, and he knew that he would

---

189 **Schaulders** – *shoulders*
190 **Gep** – *a gap... an opening*
191 **Gansy** – *woollen pullover*

never hear the end of it from Bobby and Dorry, his 'Big Boss' standing with them now in shreds. He tried to rest on his elbows but there was no way to get comfortable in that confined space. His head and shoulders were getting very hot and his legs and backside very cold. Danny had never felt so helpless or indeed so exposed in all his short life.

People were beginning to occupy the seats over Danny's head. Deserted by all, what was there for our forlorn little hero to do but go to sleep and hope for rescue… and then jail… for he was now firmly convinced he would follow Robbie to prison when the circus people finally spotted him which could not be long delayed. Tearfully, he put his thumb in his mouth and, stretching out his left arm, rested his head on it.

At that moment, the younger Miss Sproule was reaching down for the twentieth time to confirm that her handbag was still safely at her feet, for there were bound to be thieves in such a wild place as a circus tent. Instead of the reassuring feel of her leather bag, she found herself touching something warm and fleshy. Glancing down, she saw to her horror an outstretched hand between her feet. She uttered a terrifying scream which fortunately was largely drowned out by the entrance of the circus's brass band leading the parade into the ring below. The other Miss Sproule now squinted down to the floor, and she too saw the fleshy hand. Like her sister, she was terrified at the sight. Was it… the hand of a madman… a dangerous criminal… or of a dead body? One heard such dreadful tales about these travelling folk. She and her sister might be involved in scandal, their names in the newspapers. What was to be done? One thing was certain, the Miss Sproules' possible connection with that hand, whatever its origin, must never see the light of day. Whoever liked could deal with it, so prompt action was required to get rid of the hand as quickly and as quietly as possible. The one Miss Sproule handed the other Miss Sproule her umbrella which had a very sharp point and motioned what to do with it.

Danny, who like most miserable small boys of his age, had removed himself from his current predicament by dozing off, suddenly felt a searing pain in his left hand as the point of Miss Sproule's umbrella struck home. Howling with pain, he jerked backwards, dislodged his backside from the seating above and, with a scream, was propelled into mid-air and then fell backwards towards the grassy corridor behind the tiers of seats. He knew he was going to die but strangely all that bothered him at that moment was the thought that Dorry would now get his schoolbag for keeps and Bobby control over Robbie's watch for ever more.

Madam Catalina's Performing Cherub

He landed feet first on something soft and moving at speed, his nose pressed tight against what seemed to him at first to be two large warm balloons but was in fact a woman's cleavage. He didn't know it then but he had fallen into the firm embrace of Madam Catalina, the circus's leading horse woman famed throughout Ireland and beyond for her deeds of daring-do on horseback.

Madam Catalina, who had encountered the unexpected in many guises in her distinguished career, was none the less somewhat taken aback to be holding in her arms a plump little boy, his scared angelic face now looking into hers, and who appeared to have dropped from the sky. Danny too was confused. Was he dead? Was this heaven? The lady was so beautiful she could only live in heaven. Avoiding her lovely face, he found himself looking at her long bare legs and above these her white tight-fitting outfit covered in things that sparkled like thousands of suns. He must surely be dead and, despite all Angel Jo had told him, this must be the heaven that they learned about in Sunday school.

For her part, and wherever this cherub had come from, Madam Catalina was now overdue in the ring where her equestrian partner was doubtless waiting to begin their famed double act. She was about to drop Daniel Malachy as gently as was possible from a trotting horse when a sudden thought occurred to her. She and her partner, Senor Vladko, had been speculating how to involve the audience a bit more in their act, for a dash of local colour went down well with the crowd. The clowns seemed to have no trouble getting volunteers but so far, she and Vladko had not, and had had to resort to planting a circus hand in the audience to join them in the ring. This proved less than successful for the whole point was to send the audience home spreading favourable comments about some local person's antics with the world famous equestrian artistes. Could this little cherub, who had literally landed on her lap, be just the 'volunteer' they were looking for? He was a little on the plump side but otherwise just the right size for what she and Vladko had in mind.

"Cherie," she cooed in Danny's ear when she had expertly turned him to face forward, "you gonna play with me and my horse. I make you big star."

And this was just the reassurance that Danny wanted to hear at that moment. He knew he should have been scared… terrified… but sitting astride this lovely horse in the firm grip by this beautiful heavenly lady, there was nowhere else in the world he would rather be.

They galloped into the ring. The ring master announced Madam Catalina and Senor Vladko then paused casting a puzzled look at Danny as did Senor Vladko.

"What your name, my little cherub?" Madam Catalina continued cooing in Danny's ear.

"Danny… Danny Dowdells," he said without a trace of a stammer.

"… and Senor Danny Dowdells… from Ballybracken," shouted Madam Catalina loudly.

The crowd roared and clapped such as the equestrians had seldom heard before, this dash of local colour doing for their act what they had long though it would.

And they were off! Danny wasn't entirely sure what part he actually played in it all for it was too terrifying to think about at the time. Most of what he knew he was told afterwards, and the story lost nothing in the telling. How the beautiful lady had set him on her shoulders and then, to the gasps of the crowd, passed him across to Senor Vladko who let him hold his horse's reins while he stood on his head on the horse's back, then bent over backwards to take the reins from Danny with his feet, all the while both horses galloping round and round the ring. Then back Danny went to Madam Catalina where she made him stand in front of her holding on to his legs and encouraging him to clap the crowd who were roaring their approval. Even the Miss Sproules were seen to remove their gloves to clap… modestly. Finally, Madam Catalina and Senor Vladko lined their two horses up in the centre of the ring, the horses knelt to rapturous applause, and then horses and riders galloped out as the clowns once again came tumbling in.

"Now, my little cherub. What you think? Will you join the circus?"

"What the hell do you two think you're doing?" A big man with a bushy moustache was confronting the two artistes obviously in a very great temper. "Who is that lad? You might have killed him… no rehearsals! … Never a word!"

"He fell from heaven into my lap," laughed Madam Catalina. "He was sent from God in answer to prayer. How could we let him go? Would you defy the Almighty?"

Whatever about the Almighty, the angry gentleman knew better than to cross Madam Catalina. The last thing he needed in the middle of a show was one of her dreaded tantrums. Not for the first time had she walked out at the last minute.

"Well, mind it never happens again… without tellin us an' plannin it… an' rehearsin… what about the insurance?… if anything had happened to the lad, we could be ruined."

"But nothing did happen," said Vladko, "and did he or did he not steal the show? They will now be talking about it for days… weeks maybe… I'm sure people will be disappointed if he isn't in every performance, and surely tonight's success will encourage others to participate with us, and not be afraid… "

"… and you were not afraid, were you, Danny Dowdells, my little cherub?" enquired Madam Catalina.

"Naw," said Danny, "I was too skared tay be afeared[192]!" and they all laughed, even the big man.

"Away way you now," the big man said briskly. "I'm not gonna enquire further anything about you or how you came to be in the show?" And he patted Danny on the head. "Oh, and here a pound for being such a game wee fella even if it wuz al the height aff folly," and he venture a glare in the direction of Madam Catalina.

Danny hastily stuffed the crumpled pound note into his pocket in case the big man changed his mind. A glow of well-being suddenly possessed him but then just as suddenly he felt faint, and that he was going to be sick. He turned aside from Madam Catalina and Vladko and was convulsed by violent vomiting. For it had suddenly hit him, delayed fright brought on by what he had just experienced on the back of those horses, and in the hands of the two riders. Suddenly he wanted to run away and hide.

Madam Catalina produced a coloured handkerchief and wiped the remains of the vomit from his face.

"Don't worry, little cherub. It has been a big adventure for such a little boy. But here is Blinkey, the best clown in the world. He will take you to a ringside seat for the rest of the show. Vladko and I must go and prepare for our next

---

192   *I was too skared tay be afeared* – *I was too scared to be frightened*

performance, and don't worry, we won't include you this time."

A clown in full regalia took Danny by the hand with his face now as ashen white as the clown's and led him towards the ring. As they appeared, the big tent erupted with shouts of "Danny, Danny, Danny Dowdells."

"You must bow to your audience, Danny," whispered Blinkey lifting Danny up on the wooden bench that encircled the ring. Danny stood frozen for a few seconds and then, as if to the manner born, he bowed very low several times to left, centre and right. Blinkey lifted him down and pointed to a vacant ringside seat at the end of a row. Danny was glad to go and sit down and, when he thought nobody was looking, he resumed sucking his thumb.

Danny's Big Plans

"Aff curse, they offered me a big job in the circus… way the horses… an' the lions… an' elephants an' maybe way the clowns too," Danny said grandly to Bobby, Dorry and Robbie, who had appeared to take them home after the show. "…an' they wud pay may a poun ivery week an' make me real rich… but I said I cudn't cos mammy needed me tay luk efter youz two, and Robbie needed me tay take care of his watch… an' things."

Robbie grinned down at him, and the other two were still too awestruck by what had happened to say anything. Even Dorry's designs on his schoolbag had vanished for the moment and Bobby, while he clutched his silver cup to his chest, knew that Danny was the real hero of the hour.

"I said I might join up later when I not too busy… an' that I cud play the clowns' trick piana… when I wuzn't workin way the horses an' lions… an' elephants… an' that."

Robbie said, "Ye'll bay sure a give us plenty aff warnin when you're headin aff, won't yeh, Danny, for the lord knows how we wud manage way-out yeh."

But this gentle teasing was lost on our triumphant little hero.

"Aff curse, I'll give up the piana lessons when I join the circus…," Danny continued, his self-importance growing by the minute, "… cos I can play enough already tay do in the circus… an' anyway I'll probably be too busy way the horses… an' teachin the lions to do new tricks… an' that."

So they proceeded home with Danny planning his future in the circus and steadily becoming a legend in his own mind. Ballybracken's youth were already buzzing with admiration for his exploits, some because of the nail-biting stunts he had been involved in on the horses, some because of the pounds he had allegedly been given - *'as much as a hunner they say!'* - and some, the older boys, because he had got into such close proximity to the acres of naked flesh displayed by Madam Catalina on her galloping horse.

Episode 21

The Knights of the Round Table

Angel Jo's Wing Colours

"Well, aren't you the famous boy!" Angel Jo had suddenly appeared beside Danny having mobbed him for a while in the form of a big black crow as he lay inside the fairy ring on the top of Ballybracken's highest hill, 'Croc-na-Shina.'

"Oh, it's you," said Danny rather grandly as if the angel appearing was almost beneath his notice now he was a big circus star.

"Yes, it's me, Daniel Malachy. Have you forgotten your old guardian angel now you're so famous? Well, that always happens when you 'earth-grubbers' think you can do without us. But I mustn't get cross. It makes my wings tingle. How is your music going by the way? I have a lot of catching up to do, I've been so busy crossing universes, visiting planets, writing reports… It can't go on."

"It's all right," said Danny cutting across Angel Jo's well-rehearsed moans in an off-hand way. "I don't like Miss Mina. She scares me and won't let me play by ear which I can do if I've heard a tune once, but she says I must learn to read music… so I can... it turned out to be very easy when you are as musical as I am … and now she says I'm better than her already. I'm going to play the funny pianos the clowns have when I join the circus. That'll be great."

He tailed off for Angel Jo was looking at him crossly.

"And who have you to thank for all this? Me! Yours truly! Old guardian here. Don't you forget, Danny boy, that I had to get the 'Awkward Squad' up above to agree to giving you this wonderful gift. Don't forget that… or I might just ask them to take it away again. What has been done can be undone! Now, I'm not threatening, and I know how pleased Saint Cecelia will be to hear about your progress for she has me tormented about you, but thanks where thanks is due… You owe it all to old guardian Jo."

Since he seemed to be getting angrier by the minute, Danny's off-hand approach evaporated as quickly as it had come. Time to butter-up the angel again before he did his usual disappearing trick, this time in a temper with heaven-knows what consequences.

"I'm sorry I said what I did. I love being good at music now, and sure I was no good until you got me the gift."

"Well, all right," said Jo, "I'll forgive you this time. But no more ungratefulness and high-and-mighty talk from you, my boy. Mind you, getting you back to being useless at everything would be such a pain… when I think of all the paperwork that would entail… duplicate this and triplicate that… and having to deal with Cecelia for I just know she'd take it very badly and begin weeping like that mystic Margery Kempe woman who never stops wailing in divine ecstasy and, believe me, one weeping woman up there is enough, any more and I'll get one of my headaches. Oh no, better to forgive and forget. We'll say no more about it… for now. By the way, I meant to ask you, how do you like my new-style wings?"

Without, as usual, waiting for an answer which was lucky because Danny hadn't noticed anything different about the wings, Angel Jo hastened on,

"I thought it would be the first thing you'd say… but there you are, you see, too busy boasting and annoying your old GA to notice my new coloured tips. I got fed up with the curly ends look… and I'm sure it slowed me down when I'm in transit… so I got Saint Michael the Archangel… he's still the patron Saint of Hairdressers… well just about, for it could all change in the flap of a wing the way things still are up there… now where was I?… oh yes, I got Michael to advise me… and I'm delighted with the result… though I think the Angelico Blue might just be a bit overdone… what do you think?"

"I think their lovely," said Danny, "especially the blue bits… it makes you look very… like heaven."

"Oh, you are a pet!" exclaimed Jo, "but still, I think the blue needs toning down a bit… old Fra Angelico took time out from a committee meeting on heaven's plumbing arrangements to touch up my blue tips… and I think he got a bit carried away. It took him forever… glad to escape for a while if you ask me… well, a man of that artistic sensitivity discussing plumbing… I ask you! No, I think a bit more emerald green…which I have to confess is the only thing I find at all agreeable about this Ireland place of yours… it looks divine from up above… like a lovely emerald ring swimming in a sea of blue and glinting in the sun, when there is any … pity about the people but as I always say, 'we are where we are.' I suppose it depends on whether I should go for the restrained look to tone it down… greys and browns perhaps or should I stick with my dashing look… go on, advise me."

"Green is very nice," said Danny, looking down from the vantage point of

Croc-na-Shina at the beautiful patchwork of small fields that was Ballybracken with the clouds and sunlight dancing over them and bringing out so many shades of green. He continued, "I think green would be better… painted in between the blue and the red."

"Green it is then," said Angel Jo decidedly. "Now, who should I get to do that I wonder? I think da Vinci is good on greens. I wouldn't want to let just anybody loose on the job… No, it'll have to be Leonardo…. Leonardo da Vinci I mean" for Danny was looking lost. "Surely even you must have seen pictures of his wonderful painting of the 'Last Supper'?"

Danny hadn't, but mention of the 'Last Supper' reminded him of something.

"Is that the time Jesus gave the other men wine in a cup and the cup is so holy, knights on horses have searched the entire world for it ever since?" he asked, for he had heard something about it recently on 'Children's Hour' on the wireless.

The Charm of 'Children's Hour'

We must now linger again if only for a moment to learn how the wonders of the wireless came to *'inform, educate and entertain'* the Dowdells home in general, and Daniel Malachy in particular, for its programmes, and one especially, were to leave their mark on him for the rest of his life.

Jim McKnight had arrived down one night to give them his big brown wireless for he had bought a new one on his latest visit to Belfast. He and Robbie had spent most of the night wiring up somethings called batteries to the brown box and fixing a length of wire out through the kitchen window to the crab apple tree at the back of the house. Then, at the switch of a big nob which lit up a small window on the front of it, a bit more tinkering with a wand-like thing that moved slowly across the window, and the Dowdells were linked to the outside world.

Rosie mostly listened to the Republic's 'Radio Athlone' *for the Irish music'* and Robbie to plays, a funny programme called 'The McCooeys,' and football and boxing matches that got him very excited. After the novelty of fiddling with the nob to make the wand hover over such exotic names as 'Allouis', 'Hilversum' and 'Luxemburg' that made the wireless make funny stomach-rumbling sounds, the Dowdells children lost interest in it. But then quite by chance Daniel Malachy discovered 'Children's Hour' at five o'clock every day. His life was transformed! There were plays about boys and girls his age doing all sorts of exciting things like visiting foreign lands on magic carpets, getting the better of bad men and their evil plans, plays about drummer boys in armies, girls who danced to lovely music Danny immediately wanted to be able to play, children who climbed high mountains and sailed on dangerous rivers, who discovered treasures on far away islands, who ran away to join the circus and had great adventures with the circus folk… and he was enraptured, couldn't wait to get home from school every day to hear more, and wanted so much to join in those adventures.

The play about the circus was great for, by chance, it followed hard on the heels of his own circus exploits but even that was soon overtaken by a weekly serial about a king called Arthur, a big castle somewhere or other and knights on horses who seemed to spend their whole time searching for some 'Holy Pail' thing. When asked, Robbie said he thought it was 'grail' not 'pail' and that it was something to do with Jesus's cup at the 'Last Supper' which rang a bell with Danny for they had been told about the 'Last Supper' in Sunday school, and it made sense for how could you have a supper without cups? Why King Arthur's knights spent so much of their time looking for this grail thing, however exciting their adventures were, remained a mystery but Robbie said the cup was so holy and could perform such miracles whoever found it would be world famous and very rich.

"Even more famous than the people in the circus?" Danny had enquired anxiously for he couldn't believe anybody could be more famous than that, especially since he now regarded himself as one of them.

The Holy Grail

"Aye, even more famous than that… than you, I mean, little comrade," said Robbie who was expert at playing along with Danny's imagination and dreams. "Whoever finds that Holy Cup will be the most famous man in the world, and it will stap iverywan nyamin an' nyerpin[193] fir they will hiv nothin tay girn about[194] anymore, nowan will bay starvin an' it will al be jist great. Are yeh gonna have a go at findin it ye'rself? Sure, they say St Patrick brought it tay Ireland, was passin through Ballybracken wan day an' was waylaid way pagan wizards down about the 'Meetin of the Waters' there, for that was where the pagans had their holy trees in them days. They tried tay get the cup aff Patrick tay get at its magic powers but he held on tay it, an' sez he *"Be Gob, yez'll not git it,* an' he threw the

---

193   **Nyamin an' nyerpin** – *whinging and complaining*
194   **Nothin tay girn about** – *nothing to complain about*

cup up over the sod ramparts of the fort up above the Meetins into the 'Ladies' Bower' as we now kal it, an' dey yeh know what happened?"

"Naw," said Danny now beyond excitement. "What?"

"The earth in the middle of the fort opened up into a cave as if by magic, an' into the cave fell the Holy Grail niver to be seen even tay this very day."

"Why did the wizards not dig it up?" asked Danny. "They could have got spades and dug for it."

"Not at al," said Robbie. "Sure Patrick cast a spell on them there and then, and they al went mad an' run helter-skelter into the water at the Meetins an' were al drownded[195]. Then Patrick went on his way tay make Ireland Christian an' that's why yeh have al these Christians – well, Catholics and Protestants anyway – in Ballybracken tay this day."

"Wud yeh quet blowin a pig's head[196] on the wee lad," said Rosie. "He'll bay hivin nightmares."

But the Holy Grail had now taken possession of Daniel Malachy, and who better to ask about it than Angel Jo? Was it in the 'Ladies' Bower' like Robbie said? He didn't doubt Robbie, but it would be good to have a second opinion about something so important.

Angel Jo was now looking at him quizzically.

"The Grail!" he said. "How does a silly little earthling like you know about the Grail? One of the most precious and holy things on this God-forsaken earth of yours."

Danny did his best to explain about the story on 'Children's Hour.' Angel Jo looked pensive.

"Yes, if it was found, and what it really stands for was finally understood, it might change everything for you earth idiots. Might even put your crazy world on the right track, and that would cheer God up a bit for there's no doubt about it, you all depress Him. I mean that was the whole point of Jesus being sent down here … and the 'Last Supper'… and the Grail… it was all designed to give you 'earth-grubbers' a second chance to be sensible and nice to each other and do the right thing for once."

"Everyone being nice would be really great," Danny mused. "What went

---

195 **Drownded** – *drowned*
196 **Quet blowin a pig's head on** – *stop filling his head with nonsense*

wrong? Was it because we lost the Grail?"

"Well, not so much losing it as losing the meaning behind it, but I can see that is a bit too complicated for your tiny brain."

"Well, Jesus coming was a good thing, wasn't it?" Danny thought he was on solid ground here for all the holy people in Ballybracken kept saying how great that was.

"Of course it was a good thing, the greatest thing but most of you have made a total mess of that too – those churches of yours fighting over who's right and who's wrong, and, I must be honest, Daniel Malachy, what most of them have to do with Jesus and his sensible teachings beats me. You have reduced all that to big buildings and men dressed up in funny clothes, BUT *you are where you are*. I mustn't interfere."

"Robbie says he thinks maybe the knights were not looking in the right place. If he's right and St Patrick brought the cup here to Ireland, but the knights never thought of looking here, no wonder they didn't find it. Maybe you could just ask St Patrick if it's in the 'Ladies' Bower' the next time you come across him up there.... when you are looking for that Leo man to paint your wings green."

"I can't ask St Patrick any such thing. First of all, he's a tetchy old boy likely to fly off the handle. Second, let me remind you that he's up to his eyes trying to sort out America which, let's face it, is a lost cause if ever there was one, but he can't stop trying. Mind you, he claims to be having some success if you can call getting Americans to march round and round in circles on his Saint's Day, painting their faces green and wearing leprechaun hats a success? If you ask me, his only real triumph there is getting them all to believe he is Irish when we all know he wasn't born in Ireland at all. Still, it gives us angels a much-needed laugh ... but NO, Patrick still has a mountain to climb State-side, so you can expect no help from that quarter."

Danny looked crestfallen for he felt his odd relationship with Angel Jo, and through him to the saints, might give him the edge over Arthur's knights when it came to getting clues about the whereabouts of the Grail.

"So you can't help me... again," Danny said pointedly trying to shame Angel Jo into parting with some useful clues. And it worked, even if it only prompted the angel to put in train a mischievous plan.

"Well yes... and then again, no," said the angel. "If your friend Robbie is right and the good Patrick had the Grail, how on earth do you think he could have got hold of it? Now, there's a question for you! How could it ever have got to Ireland never to mention this Ballybracken place?"

While Danny was thinking about this and wishing he had been brainy enough to ask Robbie, Angel Jo continued his teasing.

Angel Jo – Problem Solver?

"Of course," he said thoughtfully, and as if slowly working it out for himself, "the bold Patrick had been a student in a monastery on an island in the 'Mare Nostrum' – or is it the 'Mediterranean' you call it now? – anyway it was near where they say Jesus's mother arrived after her holy son was crucified by the Romans… terrible crowd those Romans… what I had to watch when they were around words couldn't describe… slaughtering tribes by the hundreds and animals by the thousands… but I digress… yes, well let's say His Holy Mother had the Holy Cup when she came ashore somewhere near the spot where some time later there was a monastery, and when she is about to be taken bodily up into heaven she's hardly likely to take the Holy Grail with her, is she? That would rather defeat the whole point, wouldn't it? So she gives it to someone… right… and who better than the monks in that monastery to keep safe for all of you… but when the Romans have finished massacring everything and everybody including themselves, and their empire fell apart, the holy monks and their holy treasure are not safe either… so they must send it somewhere safe… then along comes young Patrick to study so that he can go back to convert a bunch of wild heathens in rain-sodden Ireland and get them to stop worshipping trees and all that nonsense, and to see the light. Now, if you were one of those monks waiting for the next crowd of barbarians to attack your nice cosy monastery and make off with all your precious stuff including, God forfend, laying their savage blood-soaked hands on the Holy Cup, who might you give it to for safe keeping?"

"St Patrick!" cried Danny triumphantly. "So Robbie is right, and it must be here after all!"

"Well, you said it," said the Angel, "I didn't… but then again I suppose it's a possibility."

With his mischievous plan hatching out well, he continued,

"Those pagan wizards certainly worshipped groves of trees which they thought were very holy especially in places where two rivers meet… and remind me again what down there is called?"

"The 'Meetins,'" exclaimed Danny, "and there is a bunch of old trees down there all round the Ladies' Bower,'" he continued, "… and down below it two rivers meet!"

That clinched it for our hero. The Holy Grail was without question in the 'Ladies' Bower' and the sooner he got digging and found it the better. What was being a circus star compared to this? To succeed where King Arthur's knights had failed would make him the most famous boy in the world… and the richest… and then he would make everybody in the world rich too… and give Dorry his schoolbag … and buy his mammy a big car like the McKendry's for her legs get sore walking everywhere… and Robbie two packets of 'Woodbine' every day and maybe a football and boxing gloves since he never stopped talking to Jim about the matches on the wireless… and Bobby?… well, he'd have to think about Bobby… maybe nothin until he was nicer to him and deserved something… maybe something very small like a packet of chewing gum now and again. And so his mind raced on… for if he found the Grail, it might even make Ballybracken's holy people not be so miserable, and cheer them up, and stop them looking down on fun like reading comics or listening to dance music or just being happy like when it was home-time from school or even just when it was a sunny day?

"You are going to try to find it then?" enquired Angel Jo, breaking into Danny's reverie and in a tone of mock admiration.

He reflected that this small earthling was just like so many others on planet Earth who spent their lives on wild goose chases of one kind or another. Well, so be it! Better this silly hunt than many other things he might be doing, and he certainly had a great imagination, Angel Jo had to concede that!

"If you find it, be sure and let me know," said the angel. "I'll have to enter it in the lost and found bureau up above. St Agnes oversees that. Well, it keeps her busy. She was patron saint of virgins but, for reasons you are too innocent to understand, she is at a bit of a loose end these days."

"All King Arthur's knights were looking in the wrong places," Danny was on a roll, "and anyway the story on 'Children's Hour' says they were always running off to save girls who they heard crying and wailing, just like our Dorry, because bad men had captured them and kept them prisoners in big towers… and sure that was a waste of time and no good if the knights had really wanted to find the cup.

"So you won't save any maidens in distress… girls locked up in big towers, I mean?" queried the angel. "I need to note that."

"No," said Danny, "Well, I might if I happen to find any about to be tortured… and that. but only after I've found the Grail."

"Very wise," said the angel, "I look forward to hearing all about it and writing it up. Now where am I off to next?" He produced a scroll from under one of his wings and consulted it.

"Oh, not there again," he said frowning, "crossing all those asteroid belts, I won't have a wing left, coloured or otherwise. Still, needs must when BOAK drives! I've enjoyed our little chat. I'll be seeing you."

But Danny wasn't listening. Already he was Sir Daniel Malachy Dowdells, Knight of the Round Table, planning what he would do when he had found the Holy Grail in Ballybracken, was rich and famous, and had set the world to rights.

Episode 22

The Evictions

It was a sunny Saturday morning in early autumn and the Dowdells and Robbie were out early on their way to the McKendrys, Rosie to help prepare for a grand dinner party that evening, Robbie to meet George McKendry, curious as to why he wanted to see him, Danny for his music lesson with Miss Mina, and the other two because they could not be left on their own.

"An' if yez dizn't behave ye'rselves, I'll give yez a right skelpin[197] when I get yez home," Rosie warned. "Don't be lettin may down a bagful, an' don't bay touchin anything. If yez brake somethin, we'll be out a fortune. An' if yez is allowed out in the yard keep away from that fella, Packie's Ned, that works in the stables. He's a bad rairin I've h-erd[198], an' comes out way a lot aff bad language."

And so the dire warnings continued as they sauntered along Bobby sitting on Robbie's shoulders making provocative sign down at Daniel who wanted to be up there but had been declared too big now.

Rosie little sermon over, she felt happier. She admired the beech trees along the roadside that were just changing colour, the golden corn fields on both sides were looking lovely swaying gently under the last of the morning mist. She was just starting to hum a favourite of hers, the lovely *'The Mountains of Mourne'* when Robbie broke the tranquillity saying,

"What the hell's goin on yonner[199] at the gate lodge?"

And something dramatic indeed seemed to be happening in the front garden of the beautiful little lodge that stood at the entrance to the McKendry's driveway. There was a tractor and trailer parked at an awkward angle in front of the entrance gates, and Barney McGuigan and his son Seamus appeared to be loading furniture in great haste up on to the trailer. The McGuigan girls were busy too carrying more furniture and other family things out of the lodge and piling them up in the small front garden. Sinead McGuigan was sitting on the garden seat sobbing loudly.

---

197 **Skelpin** – *smacking*
198 **Bad rairin** – *someone who turned out badly*
199 **Yonner** – *yonder*

"What's goin on?" Robbie asked as they came up to the lodge. "Are yez flittin[200] or what, Barney, this early in the mornin, an' what wrong way Sinead?"

"Yeh may well ax," Barney said. "Sure al the Catholic cotters is in a c-owl sweat[201] the day. Evicted we've been, al aff us! That what! Towl tay clear out. McKendry sez hez cotter houses hiv al been condemned fir want aff proper sanitation, no piped water an' what hiv yeh, an' hez gonna spen no money putting them right. But I'll tell yeh the rail raison, an' we al know it. He lost his s-ate on the County Council at that damned election, that's the rail raison, an' that's what hiz took his toe[202]. So the story on the go now is that al Catholics must hiv voted Nationalist agin them Unionist an so McKendry is out, an' now we're out. Al aff us! … Mickey McSorley an' the woman an' wains too, them that hez the wee cotter house[203] down behind the orchard an' al aff the Catholics in hez row aff cotter houses down at the bridge… al aff us hiz got our walkin papers. Me that fought for them in the First War lake ye'r own father, an' still hiz a piece aff shrapnel bigger than ye'r thumb stuck here in may groin that keeps may fram sleepin iver since, an' nearly staps may walkin bay times[204]… me that hez wrought fir them fir years, we're put out on the road too lake al the others. He comes down here way a face on him as long as a Lurgan spade[205] jist when I've finished may day's work, an' puts us out on the road. Sure it's plain as God's in heaven that he now wants tay hiv no more Catholics an' Nationalists about him on the estate, an' that includes me an' mine… an' sure us cotters that dizent pay rates can't vote anyway so we'er not tay blame fir him gittin cow-uped aff the Council .Hez gone cl-ian mad if yeh ask me. The divil hiz got inta him."

"So where are yez goin tay? Hiv yez foun a place yet?" Robbie asked, helping Barney lift a heavy old battered armchair unto the trailer.

"Aye, Bernadette McManus, is lettin us hiv yon owl damp cotter house out in the 'Long Bog' till we fin somethin better. I'm sorry tay say we always thought aff hir as a bit aff an owl get-up. 'Lady Muck from Clabber Hill'[206] the people kalled hir for hir airs an' graces, suckin up tay the priest an' chawin the altar

---

200 **Flittin** – *are you moving house?*
201 **C-owl sweat** – *state of acute anxiety*
202 **Hiz took his toe** – *has annoyed him*
203 **Wee cotter house** – *small labourer's cottage*
204 **Staps meh walkin betimes** – *sometimes prevents me walking*
205 **Lurgan spade** – *an unsmiling and threatening look*
206 **Owl getup, Lady Muck from Clabber Hill** – *a proud pretentious lady with little to be proud and pretentious about*

rails[207] aff a Sunday, an' we al know it's them releegius wans yeh hiv tay watch. But fair play tay hir, she's bailin us out now… even lent us the tractor an' trailer for the flittin so we wur wrong about hir. Yeh niver know who yeh hiv tay turn tay when ye'r up again it."

They looked across to where Rosie was trying to comfort Sinead. "She's takin it very bad," Barney muttered. "Says she thought that the dark days aff evictions wuz long gone. But now we know tay the differs. She tried tay argue way him, but sure he wuzn't heedin a word she said… allowed he had no choice… said 'hez hans ur tied' bay the decision aff the Council's housin boyos… 'hans tied' bay damned… hez lying an' we al know it. Luk at the state aff Sinead over there, I doubt but she might go aff hir head[208] an' now en up in the asylum, fir hir narves hez always been a problem." He lifted a tea chest overflowing with children's clothing up unto the trailer and shouted to Seamus to hurry up with more from the pile in the garden. Another tractor appeared round the bend in the drive and stopped unable to get passed with Barney blocking the gates.

"I'll move now," shouted Barney, pushing some of the load further up his trailer to get the tailboard fastened.

"Take ye'r time, Barney," Mickey McSorley shouted back, "fir the divil knows where we're headin. We've got nawthin fixed up yet. Isn't this a tarrible hannlin[209]."

His trailer too was piled high with furniture around which were spread, at various precarious angles, the three young McSorley girls, one of them with the most recent arrival in her arms. Their mother, Peggy, was leaning on the tractor mudguard holding on with both hands. Mickey got down and came across to Barney and Robbie.

'Our Day Will Come'

"This is a holy tarra[210]," he said. "Ye'r quare'n lucky, Barney, hiz got someroad tay go. We've no place at al." Before they could reply, Peggy shouted across in a tearful bitter voice,

"Are yez men at al, lettin this happen? The landlords persecutin us again. Nothin iver changes in Irelan," and then in a still louder voice, "Up the

---

207 **Chawin the altar rails** – *putting on a show of great piety especially in church*
208 **She might go aff hir head** – *She might go mad… lose her senses*
209 **A tarrible hannlin** – *a terrible predicament*
210 **Holy tarra** - *A terrible situation*

Republic... God bless Irelan... God bless al true Irish Catholics an' the Pope aff Rome."

"Wud yeh howl ye'r wheesht[211], woman," said her husband. "Ye'll get us al lifted an' jailed."

"I'll not howl may tongue," she shouted. "Luk where howlin our tongue hiz got us now. Turned out on the road in our deshabilles[212] lake a crowd aff gypsies. We that hiz our true religion and our good owl Irish ways. An' what hiv they got? A king that can't put two words tegether. Fat Lizzy an' stutterin George. Well, let them hev it for now – '*Tiocfaidh ar la*' – 'Our day will surely come.' Up the Republic," and she launched into a high-pitched rendering of the Soldier's Song[213].

"I'll move the tractor," said Barney, "an' let yeh git away tay fine somewhere. In case ye'r stuck, day yeh want us tay ask Bernie McManus, when we get hir length[214], tay see if she'd let yez in tay wan aff hir farm outhouses for the night. At least ye'd bay in the dry[215]."

As his father started up the tractor, young Seamus McGuigan sidled up to the Dowdells children who had been standing in a dazed clump all this time trying to make sense of what was happening. Seamus was not much older than Danny.

"I'll bay joinin the IRA when I'm a bit owler," he hissed darkly to them, "an' then I'll bay back tay shoot al aff yuz Protestants, that's efter I've bate the shit out aff yez."

He went back to the load of possessions still piling up in the garden, squinting back at then ominously to drive home his threat.

The obstacles removed, Mickey started his tractor again, let out the clutch with a bang and away they went in a cloud of suffocating black smoke, the baby in the trailer crying loudly and Peggy still singing 'Ambran na bhFiann'[216]

"Peggy wuz always a bitter owl pill," Rosie said. "I donno why they ur voting anyway? Theze them that can niver leave well enough alone[217] in this country?"

Robbie said nothing, his 'strolling' stance shaken to its core and replaced

---

211 **Howl ye'r wheesht** – *hold your tongue... shut up*
212 **Deshabilles** – *underclothes*
213 **'Soldier's Song'** – *English version of the Irish Republic's National Anthem*
214 **Get hir length** – *arrive at her house*
215 **In the dry** – *protected from the rain*
216 **'Ambran na bhFiann'** – *Irish version of the National Anthem of the Republic*
217 **They can niver leave well enough alone** – *they feel impelled to change or challenge something that is working reasonably well*

with deep anger at what he had just witnessed. It brought back to his mind his soldiering days and fleeing refugees, their carts and barrows piled high with whatever they could carry, heading for God knows what kind of future, if a future at all. This was nothing like the scale of that but was just the same for the people concerned. Rosie glanced at him and read the warning signs.

"Now don't yeh bay for takin on tay fight[218]. Yeh've seen where that got yeh back that time in Cobain's pub. We'd be wise now jist tay keep our heads down. Don't forget they might be for getting rid aff me too for he seems tay bay for gettin rid aff al Catholics, an' then we'll bay back where we started. Promise me yeh'll keep ye'r opinions tay ye'rself jist fir wance[219]."

Robbie continued to stare straight ahead grim faced, and with his handsome chiselled chin thrust forward like a battering ram. Danny had managed to oust Bobby from the big man's shoulders and was now sitting up there triumphant. He didn't like the silence that had descended on Robbie, so he tried to break it with a bit of good news.

"Didn't she say the king hiz a stutter?" he began. "So it not jist me an' so since he's the king an' hiz it, it must be al right tay stutter."

Still nothing from down below!

"But maybe its ony good if ye'r the king," he finished, defeated for now.

Robbie was obviously not going to break his ominous silence even when provoked by Danny's giggling as he now ran his fingers round the beginnings of his big hero's bald spot, the mention of which on other occasions unfailingly threw Robbie into a rage to the delight of the children. Rosie now attempted to change his mood by raising more immediate and pressing domestic matters.

"How long day yeh think ye'll be way the Boss?" she enquired, "for I'll want yeh tay take these'ens home as soon as yeh'v finished so yeh can keep a good eye on them."

"I'll be as short a time as possible," Robbie replied. "Safest thing the way I'm thinkin about these gran landlords jist at present."

"There must surely bay somethin them evicted folk cud do?" Rosie queried. "Cud they not take it tay la[220] or somethin."

"They could," replied Robbie, "an' I tell yeh now, it wud get them no road. It's the big buck cats makes the laws an' they see tay themselves an' keep themselves right. What wud bay the point when ye'r landlord turns agin yeh. Sure they'd

---

218 **Takin on tay fight** – *starting a row*
219 **Just fir wance** – *on this occasion… this time*
220 **Take it tay la'** – *take legal advice… challenge it in the courts.*

git some smart-ass lawyer tay concoct some plausible story lake the houses bein condemned an' unhealthy tay justify why they wur al hunted, nothin tay do way the rail raison, so al they'd hiv to show fir it wud bay lost time an' money. I think the sooner yeh fin that Holy Grail thing, Danny, an' turn the world the right way up, may wee comrade, it will bay the better for al of us."

Danny was greatly alarmed at this sudden unexpected mention of the Grail. How did Robbie know of his imminent plans to go digging for it? Robbie, of course, knew no such thing, and our little hero had yet to learn about chance and coincidence. He was alarmed because he planned that this very day he, Sir Daniel Malachy Dowdells, would find the elusive Holy Grail but his quest must be a secret for the discovery to be the greatest surprise ever.

The Kitchen Battle

If a sort of peace had descended over Robbie by the time they reached the big house, the same could not be said of the McKendry's kitchen. They walked in to what appeared to be a battle royal. A tall strikingly handsome young man was shouting at George McKendry who sat head bowed at the kitchen table while Hanna and Mina busied themselves around the kitchen pretending everything was normal.

"This is unworthy of you, father," the young man was shouting, "to turn people out with a snap of your fingers and all because you lost your seat on the council, and now you are venting your anger on our good Catholic tenants. This is not the 19th Century, you know, but you are acting exactly like those tyrannical landlords. I am ashamed of this family this morning."

George McKendry had become aware that Robbie and the Dowdells had arrived, and that this was not a scene outsiders should witness.

"Well, Good morning to you all," he said affecting a calm voice, and then "I don't know if you have ever met my son, Edward. He is up from Dublin… from Trinity College to see his Granny on her birthday which is today… and to see all of us of course. These are the Dowdells, Edward, and Robbie Elliot. Robbie is our war hero… did remarkable things and won great distinction defeating the Huns in our latest skirmish with them."

He paused, and if he had left it there all might have been well, but he had been stung by his son's hard-hitting criticism and so could not resist making his own parry "… not like our neighbours in the Republic who sided with Herr Hitler and his murderous Nazis. I suppose we can only be thankful the

Republic didn't actually fight for them though their neutrality surely gave them great succour. And can anyone imagine a more craven and despicable sight than President de Valera offering the commiserations of the Irish nation to the German ambassador in Dublin on the death of their monstrous leader? It speaks volumes for what becomes of a people when they lose the run of themselves[221]… and His Holiness the Pope too… another fellow-traveller with the Fascists... "

"Let's not get down to berating the Pope," said Edward, interrupting his father in mid-sentence. "All I am saying is that what you have done to our tenants must immediately be undone for you are fooling nobody putting it about that all the houses are unfit and condemned. Everyone knows the real reason, and I know how hurt you are by the election result but most of our Catholic tenants can't vote in local elections. Can you not see how irrational it is to blame and punish them?"

"You completely misunderstand, Edward," said his father angrily. "It is not wounded pride on my part, though I confess I think I deserved better in view of what I have done for the Catholics as a counsellor, getting them good council housing and letting them our cotter houses for a pittance. No, it is the danger the recent election results pose to our union with Britain. You must realize that here in Ballybracken, and indeed everywhere west of the Bann, we are on a knife edge. We can only maintain our Unionist majority by…. careful management…."

"Oh yes indeed…," Edward had raised his voice again, "… by gerrymandering the political map locally and across the whole Province to manufacture a Unionist majority. That's how it is done, isn't it?"

"Well, whatever you think, Edward, I tell you I have learned my lesson. It is late in the day, but I am finally taking to heart the wise words of Lord Brookeborough when he said not so long ago that it was best for us Protestants not to have a Catholic about us for they wish us ill however plausible they are to our face, and regardless of how fair we try to be to them."

"So that greatest of old bigots, Brookeborough, is your guiding light, father. Well that explains a lot. A prime minister, the leader of this country, who hadn't even the wit to disguise his prejudices. Do you not see that it is him and his kind that has this part of Ireland in the embattled besieged state it is now in?"

---

[221] **Lose the run of themselves** – *forget who they are and what they are*

Defiance & Bigotry Rampant

"… and what is wrong with being prejudiced if you are prejudiced about the right things?" George exploded with renewed anger. "Were we not right to be prejudiced against Adolf Hitler, Benito Mussolini and all those other barbaric villains? Tell me that! As for your unwarranted criticism of the Brookborough family, their losses in two world wars fighting for king and country speak for themselves in terms of honour, duty and commitment to our cherished Britishness. And speaking of prejudice and bigotry, it is not to be found just on one side of the fence, you know. The Nationalist and Republican propaganda machine and indeed the Catholic Church in Ireland - and God knows it needs no lessons in the dark art of propaganda - would have the world believe that all virtue and rectitude lies on their side, and that we Ulster Unionists are just a crowd of prejudiced bigots because we stand up for our freedoms, our religion and traditions. But just look at the fate of our Protestant brethren in their glorious Free State, murdered in cold blood by the IRA in West Cork in 1922 and discriminated against in subtle and not so subtle ways ever since. Are our fellow Protestants not coming North in droves since Partition to avoid being wiped out completely through pressure on their farms and businesses, the imposition of the Irish language at every level and the Catholic Church's savage decrees on mixed marriages? There's prejudice in action for you! So don't come North preaching to us about the enlightened South of Ireland. Look around you when you go back to Trinity and I believe you will see a narrow… bigoted… priest ridden… poverty stricken… pathetic little country fuelled only by its venomous hatred for all things British… and that means us Unionists here in the North… the last bastion of decent Britishness on the island. And the Republicans' avowed aim is to drive us into the sea, but I tell you they underestimate the Northern Protestant spirit. We are a thran[222] determined people, and we are here to stay. They can shout 'Brits out' pretending they mean an end to British rule but we know they really mean driving a million and more Unionists 'out,' and they need to know that we are not moving anywhere. De Valera can't buy us and the English Government can't sell us. Despite our long history of resistance, how little they all still seem to know us and our determined dour[223] fighting spirit…"

This outburst had clearly exhausted McKendry. He looked ashen and tired

---

222 **Thran** – *stubborn*
223 **Dour** – *sullen and determined*

but continued, "... an, for the record, don't you dare think I did what I did today lightly or without a heavy heart."

He finished in such a broken way that Edward went across to him and, putting his hand on his shoulder, said,

"I am sorry to have so upset you, Father, and I know how sincerely you believe all you say. But I am very upset myself by what has happened both to your council seat and the action you have taken. I suppose I just see such lost opportunities if only Irish Protestants and Catholics had been able to stay together as one nation going back to the time of Home Rule. But that is water-under-the -bridge and irreversible, and of course you are right, all is not well in the South. They have indeed substituted British rule for Rome rule as our ancestors who signed the 'Ulster Covenant' predicted. They have sold out on the true republican values for narrow Catholic Nationalist ones. But Ulster Protestants too are deluded. They worship the British Empire, a shrine that no longer exists, and venerate an out-of-date vision of things English that also no longer exists. For England has moved on but Ulster has not, and I venture to say that the English are now embarrassed by Protestant Ulster's loyalty, and would rid itself of the Province tomorrow if it could."

George looked up at his son. "Oh, believe me, Edward my boy, I have no illusions about England... perfidious Albion! They would sell us down the river tomorrow if it suited them. Never more so than when they have a socialist government with their so-called welfare state and now this free secondary education…God knows where that will lead? To more Nationalist orators and malcontents whipping up decent Catholics against the Union I suppose. You know, in my more pessimistic moments, I reflect that the unravelling of the great British Empire worldwide began here in Ireland with that wretched Rebellion in 1916, and it may be here in Loyalist Protestant Ulster at some future date that the last Imperial bastion may finally be breached, the wheel of world-wide nationalist destruction having come full circle."

"Maybe so," replied Edward, "but do you not see that Mother England has cleverly transformed her vanished Empire into a 'Commonwealth of Free Nations.' A splendid example of the good old British art of compromise and muddling through. *'When the tempest rages, bend like the willow, don't fall like the oak.'* As I see it, the Unionist 'oak' is seriously endangered by Unionist intransigence, by the 'Not an Inch' mentality. As a firm supporter of British values and of the Union with Britain, father, do you not see that if true British values and indeed the excellent socialist welfare benefits were distributed fairly and evenly, the Catholic and Nationalist folk here might come to see the benefits of British rule, and the Union would be more secure than ever."

"That will never happen, son. What is it they say? '*A Nationalist would rather eat spuds and buttermilk in an Irish Republic than live one hour under Britain.*' That's the attitude we are up against. That's where the battle line has always been and will always be. Blind hatred of all things British, and that includes us."

Rosie had long since been dispatched to clean and dust, and Mina had removed Danny to the music room for his lesson. Only Robbie, with Dorry on his knee and Bobby at his side, and not knowing what else to do, had witnessed the battle between the two men, the son keen to try to redress a present wrong through reasoned argument and calling on the 'might-have-been' of history, the father, an otherwise decent and generous man, forced by malignant realpolitik to act so cruelly and out of character.

Now drifting into the kitchen was music of the most talented and magical kind which, for now, helped to calm the savage breasts and ease the tension between father and son. George rose and asked Robbie to follow him into the servants' hall. Hanna, clearly upset by the row, got the two Dowdells children glasses of milk and biscuits, and then paper and pencils to settle them. Edward disappeared upstairs without looking at his mother. It had been an unhappy chapter in a house more noted for its moderation, warmth and generosity.

A Grandmother's Pride

Rosie had just reached old Mrs. McKendry's bedroom to continue her dusting when Edward also entered the room.

"Rosie," exclaimed the old woman, "and my darling Edward! Isn't he the handsome boy, Rosie? And so clever! Not just an ordinary doctor, you know, but a distinguished lecturer in psychiatry in Trinity. We are all so proud of him …as you must be too about young Daniel for I have been listening all morning to his playing which is just enchanting, and not a wrong note. Isn't it wonderful, Edward dear, to have found such a talent here in poor old Ballybracken? And you should hear Daniel sing! Like an angel from heaven. Now, have you both come to help me up? It's my birthday, you know Rosie, and I always have Holy Communion on my birthday. The dear Canon will be here this afternoon, so

I must prepare. By the way, what was the cause of the rumpus downstairs for I could hear raised voices even here. I hope there has been no unpleasantness on my birthday!"

"There is no need for you to worry, Granny," said the young man, sitting down beside the bed and taking her bony hand in his. "Father and I had a slight disagreement over the outcome of the election. That is all. It has blown over now, and we have made up."

"Well, I'm glad to hear it," replied Mrs. McKendry, "for your poor father has suffered grievously at the hands of the Nationalists. So thankless! They don't know how well off they are under the British crown. Voting him out… voting so many Unionists out. and soon the Nationalists will control the council entirely. I suppose then the IRA will burn us out some night as they have done to so many fine houses and families in the South in that so-called 'War of Independence' of theirs. We need strong men again like Sir Edward Carson, but all we have now are a lot of shilly-shalliers who surrender at every turn. Well, I think your father and the others have learned a cruel lesson and now see the Nationalist danger for what it is. Fortunately, not all our best men leave us never to return. Look at Rosie's Robbie now. He has returned a hero and will guard Ulster for us as brave men have always done right from the time of Cu Chulainn."

Rosie blushed, but the old lady did not notice, and Edward just smiled and winked at Rosie.

"Well, you know, I might still come back, Granny, marry a local girl and have lots of strong sons to guard the 'Gap of the North' for you. Don't give up on me just yet."

"… and what job around here would befit you, and what local girl would be good enough for you?" and she ran a bony finger lovingly over his cheek. "The only one to come near is Sir Thomas's daughter, Caroline, across the river there who would do at a pinch for she would bring with her Sir Thomas's estate and, added to your father's, it would be a considerable asset to us. Now, if you garnered all that for the McKendry clan, that would show the upstarts round here what's what."

Edward took a fit of laughing as the old lady planned empires in her mind, both local and national.

"So you think I should set my cap at Caroline, Granny? Well, I will go about it in the next day or two for there is no time to be lost. But don't you think I would need a title of some kind before crossing the river to start wooing her? She is the daughter of a Knight of the Realm, after all."

"What do you mean, you would need a title? Aren't you a distinguished physician and lecturer, and hasn't your father been honoured by the dear king with a CBE, a very great honour? But I see now you are teasing your old Granny, you rascal. I fear you are lost to Ballybracken, but it is for all the right reasons. There isn't much need for such distinction as yours here, and all our best Protestant boys with talent head North, South, East and West and we are left with lesser men, and to the mercy of rampant Nationalists."

She paused, took one of her beautifully embroidered handkerchiefs from her sleeve and dabbed her eyes.

Attempting to ease his Grandmother's gloomy state of mind, Edward said, "I am told that young Jim McKnight has just come back from university to run the family business. Is that not good news? A clever man restored to good old Ballybracken."

"I think it would be truer to say that his dreadful mother dragged him back claiming she couldn't cope. Not cope indeed! When did anyone ever hear me say I couldn't cope? But your mentioning Jim McKnight reminds me that he has agreed to look over my diaries and papers from my time in America, and my travels with the dear Niels-Christensen family. It will be wonderful if he can do justice to my experiences in early life."

Edward brought her hand up to his lips and kissed it. "I'm sure he will do a great job, Granny, and expose all your guilty secrets. How is Jim to get your trunk? Is he coming to fetch it or do you want me to run it to him in the car? Either way, I would like to see him again."

"Would you take it to him, dear, and maybe even this afternoon for I fear my time is fast running out. Now help me up the pair of you, for I will not receive Holy Communion lying in bed if I can help it, and I owe it to my Saviour to be dressed to receive Him."

Dressing up for God

They eased her out of bed into her high-backed chair where she sat for a moment with her eyes closed as if even that little exertion had been almost too much. Eventually she rallied and said,

"Now Rosie, get me my dress… the black silk with the embroidered overlay I think… and my mantilla with the gold embroidery… Oh, and the gold locket that has my husband's photograph in it… and my fox fur. None of this so called 'New Look' for me, you see. Now, Edward, you can go, for I am an old-fashioned girl and need my privacy to dress. Rosie will dress me, won't you dear?"

"I think the locket I want is somewhere in my jewel case," she said when Edward had left and everything else was in place, fastidiously matched up and to her mind.

Rosie went to the dressing room and rummaged around among the beautiful jewellery in a finely engraved wooden casket which had 'MA' on the lid. Eventually she found a locket and brought it out to Mrs. McKendry. The old lady fumbled clumsily with the catch and the locket flew open. A small photograph of a handsome man fell to the floor. Rosie picked it up. Handing it to the old lady, she said,

"Ach Mistress! Wuzn't your Mr McKendry a r-ail good lukin man."

Mrs. McKendry fixed her gaze on the photograph, and then said slowly and deliberately,

"That is not my husband. That is a Mr Niels-Christensen who was…" she hesitated with an apparent lump in her throat, and then continued "… my American employer to whom I confess I had some attachment and to whom I owe… all that I am, and now all that I will ever be."

"I'm sorry, Mistress," Rosie said, "I've brought yeh the wrong locket. I'll go an' find the right one with your husband's photo in it."

The old lady carefully replaced the photograph, closed the locket and put it slowly to her lips, her eyes closed.

"No. Put this one round my neck. Though it was another I had in mind, you have succeeded in bringing me the right one, and I thank you for it. The memories it brings back are dear to me, and never-more-so as my life draws to a close."

The dressing complete, as Rosie left the room she glanced back at the old lady sitting upright in her chair immaculately dressed though marred, in Rosie's view, by the fox fur round her shoulders that reminded Rosie of a wild animal, its savage eyes glinting and with its tail in its mouth. But apart from that she looked beautiful in the steadily darkening room as the storm outside deepened. She had begun leafing through her prayer book to prepare herself for communion but suddenly the book fell from her hand. She had begun fingering the locket again, and was bringing it slowly up to her lips.

'Some are Born Great...'

Robbie had followed George McKendry into the servants' hall and stood waiting to be told why he had been summoned.

"Sit down, Robbie, make yourself at home."

George settled himself at the top of the table still red in the face, breathing heavily, and clearly upset by the row with Edward.

"I would appreciate it if you said nothing about what happened back there in the kitchen," he said looking Robbie squarely in the face. "These things happen in all families, and the lad is annoyed at what I felt I had to do."

Robbie nodded and said, "I know I shud hiv taken mezself aff, Boss, when I seen how things wur."

"Don't worry, man. I know rightly it will go no further. How are you enjoying your time in the B-Specials? I ask because I have it in mind to make you my sergeant. What would you say to that?"

Robbie was taken aback. He had been in the B-Specials less than a year, and there were other who had served in it half a lifetime and would be expecting the promotion. He had joined because he enjoyed keeping up his formidable shooting skills, and the regular target practice at the RUC range in the Sperrin Mountains kept his hand in. But otherwise, as a professional soldier, he had no great regard for the state of the Ballybracken B-Special platoon. They were decent enough men, Protestant farmers and farm labourers whose occasional nightly patrols mainly served to remind their Nationalist neighbours who was boss in and around Ballybracken. Robbie let all this drift over him, only taking the shooting practice seriously but otherwise enjoying the banter, the yarns, the effect the uniform had on the local girls but above all the male comradeship, such as it was, that he missed from his army days. But becoming the sergeant was a different proposition. What about the resentment his leapfrogging might have on the old timers and substantial farmers who would not take kindly to being given orders by a labouring man, living with a Catholic woman, whatever his soldiering record? There was the issue for him too of being sucked in too deeply to the Ballybracken view of the world with all its narrowness, prejudices and actions, something he had witnessed no longer ago than that morning, a view he had promised himself to resist.

While all this was flashing through his mind, Mr McKendry was continuing,

"I know you may need time to think about it, but you should know that there is reliable intelligence from the RUC that we can expect renewed intensity of the current IRA campaign in the near future. Their units are known to be drilling and preparing in the mountainy land in the North of the County and across the border in Donegal and Monaghan. The new attacks could come anytime, and they could strike anywhere in their usual cowardly fashion, good neighbours smiling to your face during the day and shooting us from behind the hedge at night. Their usual tactics! It is deplorable that we have to think so poorly of our neighbours but that is the way thing are and have always been in our embattled Province."

This explanation changed things for Robbie. If there was a real threat, then there was a proper job of work to be done by a trained soldier with the Ballybracken Platoon, and one which most of the B-men would accept without too much rancour. Quite suddenly he felt enthusiastic about the offer, almost as fired-up as that he had experienced when going into battle in the past, and that he had never expected to feel again. It would be good to get back to what he knew best, and that was the grounds for his self-respect.

"I accept, Boss," he said bluntly, "an' thanks for the opportunity, Sir"… and then… "I'll do my best."

"And that will be excellent, I am quite sure," said McKendry getting up and shaking Robbie's hand. "I'll notify the men at the next drill. I am sure the news will be very well received by all concerned. Now, let's see if there is any more tea on the go, and let us all pray that Edward has simmered down! We don't want him to ruin his grandmother's birthday."

Episode 23

The Quest for the Holy Grail

Daniel Malachy's Digging Team

Now, unseemly as it is to digress from this tragic story of wicked cottage evictions due, as we have seen, to the potent Ulster siege mentality and, yes, also to hurt pride and perceived betrayal, it is nevertheless timely to recall that this is, in the main, a history of our little hero, Daniel Malachy Dowdells and his preoccupations, triumphs and disasters. So we must rewind the clock a little to where we now find Danny perched – as a result of persistent pestering - on Robbie's broad shoulders approaching Ballybracken House earlier that morning. He has just heard the disastrous news that the Dowdells children are to be sent home early with Robbie. This would spell the ruin of Daniel Malachy's plans to go digging for the Holy Grail that very afternoon for he had a carefully worked out strategy which rested on the availability of the labours of his brother and sister. He reasoned that it wouldn't be right for him to dig for the Grail himself given that he was a Knight of the Round Table. No, he would supervise the others doing the digging by instructing them how and where to dig, keeping them hard at it, and casting his expert eye over all the other ancient discoveries they were bound to make before they would get down to the cave where the Grail must surely lie buried.

He had only got his diggers on side by dint of describing the wonderful treasures they would unearth and, when this was greeted by some scepticism, some straightforward bribes. Dorry was promised his schoolbag... again... and Bobby a considerable number of penny chews, and a promise of custodianship of Robbie's watch in the unlikely event that they were ever again given access to it. Danny also supposed, ruefully, that he might have to share the great wealth with them that would surely come his way when the Grail was his, but he didn't bother mentioning this in the hope he might be able to think of some way of keeping it all himself. Of one thing he was firmly resolved: neither Bobby nor Dorry would get going with him to meet the King and the Pope when he would be invited to their palaces to be thanked and rewarded for finding the Grail. Neither of them would know how to behave for Dorry would surely be sick with excitement and would probably vomit on the king's shoes and the Pope's slippers, and Bobby was sure to pick his nose and maybe fart. He, Sir Daniel, would go alone, apart from his mammy and Robbie of course, and he would tell the Pope about his mammy being a real good Catholic and maybe he would give her a prayer book or something holy, and he would tell the king about Robbie fighting Hitler, getting rid of him, and saving everybody from all that shouting. And now he knew that the King had a stutter like himself, he would advise him not to worry about it, and encourage him to try singing his messages to his knights and the nation.

But all these plans were now suddenly in jeopardy! The digging could not be put off any longer. It had to be done this very day but now there was talk of his diggers being sent home. He must act quickly.

"Miss Mina says I must have more practice on their big gran piana an' that I shud stay on for a while after may lessons tay practice... day yeh min her sayin that?"

Rosie didn't, for Miss Mina hadn't, but it sounded reasonable enough.

"Well, you can stay tay practice if ye'r good but I'm packin the other two home way you, Robbie, for I've enough on may hands what way havin al the silver tay polish an' whativer else they throw at me the day. They hiv some bigwigs coming this evenin for the birthday party. There's left-over champ[224] in a b-owl on the dresser but not enough so yeh'll need tay make them scrammeled eggs or something. I don't think there's enough eggs for a boiled wan each... so scrammell what there is, an' the champ an' that'll hiv tay do till I get home."

Scrambled Eggs to the Rescue

Now, if there was one thing the Dowdells children detested it was Robbie's scrambled eggs. He had acquired his culinary skills, modest as they were, using an army dixie over an improvised fire in earthen dugouts or similar improvised protection in lulls between gun battles, the eggs themselves usually the modest trophies of war and devoured in great haste. Pleasant taste or engaging presentation didn't come into it. So Robbie's scrambled eggs were more to be dreaded than enjoyed on the few occasions when Rosie was away and the Dowdells children were left to the less than tender mercies of Robbie's cooking.

However, mention of the dreaded scrambled eggs at that precise moment played right into Daniel Malachy's hands for, if carefully managed, the threat

---

224 **Champ** – *mashed potatoes with butter and scallions/spring onions*

would help him save his cadre of diggers for the excavations ahead. Desperate causes call for desperate measures, and Danny knew exactly what to do next. He made a rude gesture involving his nose and fingers in the direction of Bobby and Dorry behind his mother's back and mouthed,

"Ha, I'm gettin stayin. No owl scrammeled eggs for me. Youz-ins is for it."

This had the predictable and desired effect. The howl immediately went up from his brother and sister as to '… why rotten Danny always got what he wanted? An' why cudn't they stay an' come home way their mammy?…' and Dorry said she would die, or at any rate have to be hospitalized, if she had to eat even one mouthful of her daddy's scrambled eggs… and Bobby declared his intention to bring forward his plans to be a 'sodger,' would sign up there and then, and do his best to get killed at the earliest opportunity… and then they would all be sorry…' and so the process of wearing down went on that is so familiar to all good parents.

Danny now dealt his next deft hand:

"If they're allowed tay stay, I cud luk efter them two," he said in a tone that implied an onerous duty but one he was gallantly prepared to shoulder as befits a big and caring brother. This offer seemed to have fallen on stony ground, so he hastened on very quickly in case his mother called to mind his less than successful supervision of them at the donkey derby and the circus.

"Cos the teachers want us to do a thing on farm animals… drawins an' spellins … an' that… an' sure how can they do it if they haven't seen al the farm animals? … so I cud show them tay them… an' keep them well back from them in case they go too close. An' help them draw them an' spell their names" Then came his knock-out blow "Cos then they will do well at school and the teachers will be plazed way them…an' stap sayin they're no use at schoolwork… an' that."

This had the desired effect for if there was one thing Rosie wanted more than most it was for all of them to do well at school as the way up and out of their poverty. Maybe if they shone for once, like in this farm project, the teachers would stop doing them down, and begin to take an interest in their progress.

"Well, al right. Yez ken al stay even efter ye'r daddy goes home but min if I hear wan word out aff yez I'll skelp yez good and proper. I don't want to be let down due tay ye'r b-owl conduct. An' no gulderin an' gowlin[225] if yez is let out tay play in the back yard."

Success for Sir Daniel! Riding high on Robbie's back he began to pretend he was a knight on horseback digging his knees into Robbie and saying, *'Gee Up*

---

225 **Gulderin an' gowlin** – *bellowing and creating a commotion*

There,' until Robbie hit him a slap on the legs and dropped him unceremoniously to the ground.

Digging Difficulties

Danny had been delayed getting his workers mobilized for the afternoon dig due to Mina McKendry making him play and sing quite a lot for a big man she called Edward, and then Hanna McKendry had plied him with a sizeable portion of shepherd's pie and nice vegetables of various kinds followed by an equally large helping of jelly and custard. By the time this was all put in front of him, Bobby and Dorry had already been fed, and had escaped out to the farmyard with strict instructions to wait for Danny to supervise their visit to the various animals for their schoolwork. Neither of them could remember their teacher saying anything about drawing animals and spelling their names but since the teachers were always giving them things to do that didn't seem to have much point, they didn't query it, and anyway it had got them an afternoon at McKendry's with its warm kitchen, nice food, and the prospect of playing hide and seek in the big barns. Danny's digging plans and promised bribes were temporarily forgotten.

But not, of course, by Daniel Malachy. In fact, much as Danny was enjoying his dinner - even though it wasn't chicken - he knew he must hurry.

"Dear bless me, darlin," exclaimed Hanna as she swept past him at the kitchen table carrying a large tray of crusty bread, "have you finished already, love? You certainly don't futter[226] about. Is there anything more I can get you? What about a nice glass of milk?"

"Thank you," said Danny dutifully. "My dinner was very nice but mammy says I must luk after Dorry and Bobby else they will get inta trouble…for they are that bad mostly… an' I hiv always tay try tay stap them," he finished hoping the nature of his onerous supervisory duties would impress her.

"Well, love, you go on, like a good boy. I think I saw them disappearing into the stables a wee while ago. I think young Packie's Ned is there so I'm sure he is keeping them well back from the horses in case they get kicked."

Danny trotted across the yard to the stables as fast as his big dinner would allow to find his brother and sister being tutored in the art of smoking by Packie's Ned accompanied by an amount of unnecessary bad language which seemed to be Packie Ned's every second word. Bobby was spluttering violently from his

---

226 ***You certainly don't futter about*** *– you don't waste time*

single draw on Packie Ned's cigarette which that 'bad rearin', as Rosie had called him, now passed to Dorry. She had not yet taken a draw as she tried to finger the cigarette in a way she had seen film stars doing so seductively at the pictures house, when Danny appeared.

The scene before him was bad news for undoubtedly Packie's Ned had all the allure for the children of the naughty big boy whose gang they immediately want to join. Danny stood surveying them not knowing what to do next when fortunately at that moment Ned spotted Mr McKendry coming out of the house and heading in their direction. He hastily abandoned his plans to lead the young Dowdells astray, stubbed out the cigarette and disappeared into some inner sanctum in the stables.

Bobby, who had now turned a grey–green colour, was still spluttering and Dorry, who thought that Danny's arrival had been the cause of Packie Ned's disappearance, began to moan loudly that Danny always ruined everything. Their big brother now reminded them that their mission for the afternoon was to find buried treasure, and he could now reinforce this with a threat telling them that if they didn't do what he said, he would tell their mammy he had seen them smoking and saying bad words! Then he assured them again that the buried treasure would make them all rich, that he knew for definite exactly where it was, and that they were all going to dig for it this very minute. We will note in passing – and take time to deplore such barefaced deceit - that the 'drawing and naming animals' exercise had fallen off that afternoon's agenda largely because it had never been other than a clever ploy of our little hero.

Bobby and Dorry were looking at him with well-merited suspicion but 'treasure is treasure' though there now seemed to be some confusion about what it would actually look like? If there were any diamonds, brooches or necklaces, Dorry bagged them. Bobby wanted any watches and guns that might be unearthed, especially if they were canons. Danny didn't bother mentioning the Grail since only a Knight of the Round Table like him could possibly understand what it was, and it would certainly be beyond Bobby and Dorry. Anyway, it was unlikely they would be willing to dig to find a cup, however ancient and important, so better to let them think it was jewellery and guns, and that kind of stuff.

Now they must find spades and other digging equipment. Danny thought that these were kept in a shed near where the pigs lived so, marshalling his digging cadre and exhorting them to be quiet, he led the way to find the necessary items. There were plenty of spades where he thought they would be, but they were all hanging high up suspended on hooks well out of their reach. Nothing daunted,

Danny found a wooden box and ordered Bobby to stand on it to reach the spades one of which Bobby dropped, and it fell with a clatter hitting Danny a blow on the head. He would have cried if there had been time, and if he hadn't been a Knight of the Round Table but instead he gathered himself up, rubbed the bump on his forehead that was rising fast and gave Dorry and Bobby a spade each. He then headed for the shed door explaining that he didn't need a spade because he would have to supervise them and look down the hole for the treasure in case they would break anything valuable with the spades.

Both Bobby and Dorry seemed far from satisfied with this explanation but there was no time to argue so off they set down towards the Ballybracken river which they now had to cross and then make their way up to the 'Ladies' Bower' to start the dig. Things at that stage went a little awry when Bobby had to sit down on the river bank to be violently sick as a result of his unsuccessful experiment with smoking, then Dorry fell off the foot-stick[227] into the river and had to be rescued by pushing the handle of Bobby's spade towards her which promptly came off in her hands and floated away. Soaking wet, she reached the far bank where, because of his exertions to save her and the size of the dinner he had so recently consumed, Danny was violently sick while the other looked on without a modicum of sympathy.

It was in this state of dishevelment and disorder that the working party arrived inside the old earthwork. The fort was much bigger than Danny remembered so the next problem was to know where to start to dig? As he wandered round the fort, his deliberations were not helped by Dorry claiming she was too wet to do any digging, and Bobby claiming he was going to be sick again, and wanted to go home. Danny decided that prompt and emphatic direction was called for so he ordered Bobby to start digging at one end of the earthen ring and Dorry at the other, the plan being that they should meet in the middle. Surely that way they would quickly unearth the cave and the Grail.

The River Wizards Rise Again!

His instructions delivered, Danny clambered up the side of the earthen bank from that vantage point the better to supervise his diggers. It was then that the shot rang out. At first the children could not understand what it was. It sounded like a breaking branch, but then they heard the noise again only this time it was

---

227 **Foot-stick** – *improvised wooden bridge for pedestrian use only, often only a long flat plank*

repeated and was accompanied by men shouting. What could it be? Peering out over the rim of the earthwork, Danny could now see two rows of men one behind the other stretching right up the water meadows from the 'Meetings' heading slowly in the direction of the Bower. Every so often the line in front stopped, and a volley of shots rang out from the row behind. He slid down the bank and found Bobby and Dorry huddled at the bottom, both staring at him in terror.

"Them's guns," whimpered Bobby, "an' bullets. It's the army. We're goin tay bay shot."

This was not the most calming comment he might have made in the circumstances, though at that moment it seemed to have the ring of truth.

To Daniel Malachy too the situation did indeed seem perilous but, even in their plight under fire, his imagination was working overtime. He must stop trembling with fear like the others and act like a Knight of the Round Table. He tried desperately to remember what Sir Lancelot and Sir Galahad did when danger threatened for he, Sir Daniel Dowdells, must now do the same.

It was, of course, crystal clear to him that the men approaching were not the army but the old wizards that St Patrick had chased into the rivers and who had somehow got to hear that he was about to find the Grail, and had come to kill him and get it for themselves.

"What ir we goina' do? Take us back home," pleaded Dorry, abandoning with indecent haste her ambitions to find jewellery that would advance her aim to become a world-famous film star. "I don't want any jewellery now, I just want home tay mammy an' daddy." And she pinched Danny hard on his bare leg in case her message hadn't got through to him.

"I wanna go home too," cried Bobby, "an' I don't think I'll join the army an' be a sodger. It's too skary."

What indeed were they to do, besieged as they now were in the 'Ladies' Bower' with volleys of shots ringing about their ears and wicked wizards advancing on them?

"I know," said Danny bravely. "We'll surrender."

Like knights of old, Sir Daniel had swiftly concluded that 'discretion is the better part of valour', and he resolved there and then to tell the wizards that they could have the Grail, explain to them that unfortunately they hadn't found it yet but he would gallantly offer Bobby and Dorry's services to go on digging for it as the wizards' slaves. He would promise not to tell anybody that the wizards had it, would forget all about it, and just concentrate on his spellings, tables and music from now on.

That approach firmly decided, he started wracking his brains to remember how people in comics surrendered? It seemed to involve waving something white and then handing over your weapons and going to jail for a while until you planned how to get a message to the king to send the army to rescue you. The only weapons they could hand over were the two spades but maybe the wizards would accept these, and not hold them all up by the heels and shake them senseless to find any guns.

All this raced through Danny's fertile mind, but the first step undoubtedly was to find a long stick and something white to attach to it. Bobby was dispatched to find the stick which he did by sliding around the fort floor snake-like while Dorry was relieved of her wet white vest. Bobby returned with a suitably long branch to which Danny hastily attached the vest. Telling the others to lie low, for the shooting was now much closer, Danny gingerly crawled up the bank and nervously started to wave the soggy white flag.

The Wizard Queen?

The beautiful Caroline Roxborough had twisted her ankle the day before Sir Thomas's autumn shoot which was *'a bore'* but nothing could be done about it. She couldn't walk, but needs must and nothing daunted, she had saddled up her horse 'Midnight' and followed the line, pointing out quarry when the beaters put up birds that her father's distinguished shooting guests might not have seen. She was just heading up the steep slope that led to the 'Ladies' Bower' when she saw something waving uncertainly above the earth bank? It looked like a pair of white knickers on a stick, or was it paper or a white rag caught on a branch blowing in the breeze? But there was no breeze. As she narrowed her gaze, she could now see that it was a stick with something white attached to it and, just as puzzling, there seemed to be something like a mop that occasionally popped up and down beside the stick. It was a head of curly hair… a child's head! She fumbled about in her saddle bag to find her binoculars. It was indeed a little boy waving an improvised white flag!

"What on earth is going on?" she muttered to herself.

The beaters too had stopped on seeing Danny's flag. One of them shouted, "Ma'am, there seem tay be wains in the fort."

"Leave that to me," Caroline called back. "I think it's children playing up there, though God knows they shouldn't be there today. I'll go up and investigate. You carry on across the 'Owenreagh Meadows'. There should be a good bag there." With that she set off up to the fort on 'Midnight.'

Danny had peeped over the parapet from time to time to see how close the wizards were, and if they were getting his message of surrender. They were indeed much nearer now and those in the front row must be the wizards' slaves since they hadn't guns and were burdened with big sacks slung at their sides which undoubtedly were designed to carry away the Grail and any other treasures. Some of these men looked familiar but then he knew wizards could change shape, so this must just be their disguise. He wondered if they spoke English for it might not go amiss to shout out 'We Surrender' a few times just to make their position crystal clear but before he could try this a horse and rider appeared from behind the wizards and galloped up the slope. To his amazement, a beautiful lady dismounted and limped towards him. Could this be the wicked queen of the wizards going to cast a spell on them so they could easily be slipped into those sacks?

"Little boy," she said in a loud voice. "What are you doing here? I hope you know you are in danger of being shot. Who are you, and where are you from?"

Curiosity had got the better of Dorry and Bobby, and they were now gazing up at the lady in a state of terror.

"Oh, there are three of you! Are there any more hiding somewhere?"

"Naw… naw," stammered Danny. "Just… us."

"And who's 'us?'" demanded Caroline.

"Danny… an'…" he tailed off looking down at the others to come to his rescue. They were both sucking their thumbs and looking ready to take flight. Caroline could see immediately that they were terrified.

"Wait," she said in a gentler voice. "I'll come in to you, and we can have a nice talk."

"Is she a witch?" whispered Dorry "I think she must be with that funny hat."

"I think she might be a wizard queen," said Danny, wondering if there was yet time to leg it over the bank and make a run for the river. But, on reflection, that was not something a Knight of the Round Table would do… probably.

Miss Caroline had tethered 'Midnight' to one of the trees ringing the bower. She came limping across to them, her ankle hurting quite badly.

"So," she said soothingly, "tell me who you are?"

"Danny... Mistress," Danny knew that was how his mother addressed these grand people... "an' Bobby... an' Dorry... Dowdells," he added as an afterthought.

"Danny Dowdells," Caroline exclaimed. "Oh yes, I recognize you now. You are the wonderful singer we have sometimes heard in church."

This was better news, for Danny was almost certain wizards and their queens didn't frequent church much.

"Aye," he said and added, "I play the piana too... an' I'll soon be larnin the violin," hoping this display of skill would somehow also help to get them out of their present fix.

"Danny Dowdells!" Caroline repeated. "Well, I never! Now tell me, Danny, what are you doing here this afternoon?"

Danny thought this might just be a trick for he still wasn't entirely sure that she wasn't the queen of the wizards, so he said,

"Nothin... Mistress."

"Nothing," she said coaxingly, "nothing? With two big spades... I don't think you were here just for nothing surely?"

Bobby now decided to give Danny a helping hand.

"We wur lukin for buried treasure. He towel us there wud bay guns an' bullets... an'...." and here Dorry intervened "... an' jewellery... an' necklaces... an' nice stuff lake that."

"And what made you believe there was buried treasure here, Danny?" Caroline asked, remembering just such fanciful expeditions she and her dead sister had organised when they too were as young and innocent as these three downcast children.

Danny decided to come clean. On further reflection, she didn't look like a wizard queen or a witch, and anyway he could now remember her in church sitting in the grand seat at the front that had the little doors on it, and where he and the younger Sunday school children sometimes played 'hide and go seek' before their teacher arrived. So our hero now changed tack completely. Maybe if she was really a good person after all, she could help them find the Grail. So he told her all, hardly a word of which his brother and sister understood except that yet again their big brother, rotten Danny, had pulled the wool over their eyes. Dorry retrieved her vest and then she and Bobby sat scowling at Danny while he, as usual, stole the show, and now had the grand lady's rapt attention.

The Grail Unearthed!

Miss Caroline was indeed enraptured. As she listened to Danny stammer his way through King Arthur and the Knights and St Patrick and the wizards, and his determination to find the Holy Grail and make the entire world rich and happy, the innocent little boy stole her heart with his endearing belief that the ills of the world could be cured by finding an ancient mystical cup.

"An' I think maybe it is here," he was saying, "here... in the bower... but we wur jist about tay dig when the bullets started flying... so we won't fine it now."

Caroline was suddenly struck by an idea, for this unexpected encounter was much more fun than re-joining the shoot.

"I think if we all start looking," she said, "we might still find it for you have convinced me, Danny, that it really is here. I think the best thing to do is to divide the fort into three parts and each of you get down on your hands and knees and search your area very carefully. I will supervise you. So... Dorry, is it? Yes, Dorry, you take the part over there... and Bobby this part... and Danny... you over there. There are a lot of rabbit holes so it might be a good idea to just look in them when you are at it. I just need to get a drink of water from my saddlebag, and then I'll help you search."

"But we need tay dig," Danny was still determined not to have his supervisory position usurped by anyone be they ever so grand, "for St Patrick threw the Grail into a cave."

"Well now, Danny, there are caves and caves. It could have been a cave as big as a house or as small as a rabbit hole, couldn't it? They are all caves of a kind, aren't they?"

"I suppose so," Danny conceded grudgingly for he had envisaged this cave being like the pictures of Aladdin's cave in his school reading book. But now there was nothing for it but to give up on his supervising and join the workers on his hands and knees.

They all started to search through the ferns and briers and cow dung and nettles and thistles and indeed inside the occasional rabbit burrow. As Danny rubbed a nettle sting with a dock leaf, it occurred to him that the lady seemed to be taking a long time over her drink of water. Maybe she had forgotten about them already and had galloped off. He clambered up the bank and peered over. She was still there apparently having difficulty finding something in leather bags hanging from the horse's saddle. As she turned towards Danny, he slid down the bank again and resumed the search.

"Anyone found the cup or any treasures yet?" she called.

There was a chorus of 'Naws' from deep down in the undergrowth. The lady strode around, her twisted ankle all but forgotten, with the strap of the big bag round her neck and the bag itself clumsily bouncing in front of her.

"When we have found the treasures, we will put them in this bag so that you can get them home safely. Keep looking… now Bobby… no skipping parts of your area… that might be where the treasure lies."

In fact it was Bobby who found something first. Four… no, five cartridges lying among the roots of one of the old oak trees. They were empty certainly but… cartridges… real cartridges! All he needed now was a gun, and he would be well on the way to being equipped as a soldier. He leapt about the Bower in unrestrained delight running over to show his idea of treasures to Dorry and Danny, and dancing on top of the earth bank. While neither of them shared his enthusiasm for what looked to them like sticks of inedible rock, Danny was glad somebody had found something for to return to their mother so late and empty- handed would be bitter indeed.

Then he found it! He saw something colourful lying in the bend of a rabbit hole and putting his arm down as far as it would go, his fingers closed on a small metal handle. He pulled it out and there it was… the Holy Grail in all its glory! True, it wasn't exactly what he had expected. He had got a picture in his head from the 'Children's Hour' play that the Grail was… well, what was it actually? Now when he thought about it, the Grail was a cup certainly… and so was this… and it must be metal… and so was this… and it must be very beautiful… and so was this, for the metal of the mug in his hand was covered in a strange and beautiful mesh of coloured beads – orange and red and brown and white and green and blue - arranged in lovely shapes of squares and crosses. The beads glinted in the light of the afternoon sun.

"It's the Grail," he cried. "It's the Holy Grail. It wuz here al the time!" And now it was his turn to dance round and round until he got dizzy and fell headlong into a clump of nettles. But he didn't care. He would be rich, and the world would be rich and happy at last. And he, Sir Daniel Dowdells, would be famous, meet the king, and advise him about his stutter, and the Pope and tell him about his mammy having his picture in the bottom bedroom, and maybe ask him how he keeps his white clothes so clean…

Miss Caroline smiled happily on the scene before her. Only Dorry was not ecstatic for, so far, she had found nothing. Caroline gazed at the little girl who was now looking so sad while her thoughtless brothers ran around triumphantly carrying aloft their treasures. The circle must be squared! Caroline knelt down beside Dorry and said, "This necklace is too tight for me. Would you loosen the clasp, Dorry, please?"

Dorry awkwardly fumbled with the clasp on the back of Caroline's neck and eventually released it. The necklace slipped to the ground. Caroline picked it up and said,

"Do you know, I think the chain on this has always been too tight. I think it would suit a smaller neck better… like yours, Dorry… Let me try it on and see."

The silver chain had a pearl on the end, whether valuable or not who knows and who cares for now it was dangling on Dorry who was looking down at the pearl in wonder and fingering its gentle smoothness.

"Yes, it fits you much better than me, Dorry," Caroline continued. "Would you take it, and then I can get another that fits me properly."

Dorry threw her arms round Caroline's neck and covered her face in kisses.

Taken aback by this show of childish affection that she was not accustomed to, Caroline involuntarily drew back but then took Dorry in her arms, and the great lady and the little girl hugged each other as if they would never let go.

"Now children," said Caroline getting to her feet, "I think I had better get you home for I think your mother will wonder where you have got to. You say she is working over at Ballybracken House. Well, would you like to ride back on 'Midnight' here? You can take turns at sitting up beside me."

A Knight in Shining Armour

What could be better for a Knight of the Round Table, especially one who had in his possession the Holy Grail? So Sir Daniel Malachy Dowdells got to ride on 'Midnight' first. Happy beyond words, they went back to the river where, to get across dry, they all got up on the horse which was rather a crush but was just great! Then it was Dorry's turn to have a ride and then Bobby's. As if reading his thoughts, Caroline said,

"I think the Knight of the Round Table who has found the Holy Grail should have a second go," and so it was that Sir Daniel, still clutching the Grail tightly, was the Knight astride 'Midnight' as the party entered McKendry's farmyard in triumph.

Their euphoria was to be short lived! As Danny was dropped gently off the horse's back to re-join Bobby and Dorry, their mother appeared at the kitchen door.

"Where hiv yez been?" she shouted. "We hiv al been lukin everywhere for yez. I thought yez had been attacked bay the bull or that yez wur drownded[228] … I wuz at may wits en…" she was about to continue scolding when she spotted Caroline and the horse.

"Ach, Ma'am," she said, "wuz it you foun the rascals? Where on God's earth did yeh fin them? I hope they hiven't been givin yeh any bother? They're always up tay some sort aff rascality, wan worse than the other…"

She tailed off as Caroline dismounted and came across to the door, her limp forgotten.

"There is no need to worry. I take it you are Mrs. Dowdells?"

Rosie inclined her head and said,

"Yes, Ma'am, Rosie Dowdells."

"Well, Rosie, you can be proud of your children for they are as good as gold. I am delighted to have met them this afternoon."

Rosie glared at her offspring since 'good as gold' was not how she would have described them but she only said,

"Thank yeh, Ma'am. I'm ony gled they didn't give yeh too much bother."

"None at all… in fact…" Caroline tailed off as Edward and Packie's Ned appeared in the yard, back from their fruitless search for the children.

"Why Edward," she cried. "How long have you been home? Where have you been hiding?"

"Caroline! This is an unexpected pleasure. I was intending to call on you and Sir Thomas tomorrow, but you have beaten me to it. Delighted to see you," and he kissed her on both cheeks. "But what brings you across the 'Ballybracken Burn' this fine afternoon? I hope there is nothing wrong?" he added anxiously, for the thought suddenly flashed into his mind that she might have come to

---

228 **Drownded** – *drowned*

express her father's and her own anger at the evictions of the McKendry's cotters. Sir Thomas might be hard up but he was no Ulster Unionist and seldom missed an opportunity to express his dissent about the partition of what he called his 'raped country.'

"No, nothing wrong at all," Caroline reassured him. "I was only delivering these Knights of the Round Table back home."

"I see," said Edward, not at all sure that he did.

"Danny here was quite convinced that St Patrick had saved the Holy Grail from the evil wizards that lived down there at the 'Meetings' by throwing it into a cave in the 'Ladies' Bower'. Danny and Dorry and Bobby all set off to dig for the Grail this very afternoon and for any other treasures that might be buried in the old fort. I was a poor damsel in distress with my twisted ankle when Danny here took time out from his quest to rescue me as all good Knights should, so what else could I do but return the favour and help him search for the Grail?"

Edward gently eased the tin mug from Danny firm grasp. "So I am actually holding in my hand the Holy Grail." He was now enjoying entering into the spirit of this extraordinary fantasy.

"You are indeed," said Caroline, "and that is not all we found. Show Dr Edward your treasures, Bobby."

The little boy shyly produced the spent cartridges from behind his back clearly fearful that this big man would take them from him, as he had Danny's cup.

Dorry was now keen to show off her treasure which she valued far above smelly old cartridges and a stupid tin mug. She shyly drew attention to the silver chain and dangled the pearl for all to see.

"Oh yes," said Caroline, "to thank Dorry for caring for a lady with a sore ankle, I gave her that little token to remind her of our happy afternoon together."

Rosie looked mortified, for the chain and pearl looked valuable. "Och dear God, Ma'am, I hope she wuzn't beggin for she's that fond aff jewellery, an' doin hirself up[229]."

"Indeed she did not beg or ask for a thing," said Caroline emphatically. "She is a darling little girl. She rewarded me with a big hug, and she and I are now the very best of friends."

"I'm that relieved," said Rosie as she herded the children towards the kitchen saying, "Now I'll hiv tay get yez dried out some way for Dr Edward hiz tay do a message at McKnight's shap so hez kindly offered tay take us al home in the car but yez can't sit in it in that state."

---

[229] ***Doin hirself up*** – *Dressing up and experimenting with make-up*

Danny retrieved the Grail from the big man, and followed his mother and the others into the kitchen.

Meanwhile outside in the yard, Edward was looking at Caroline quizzically for he had never thought of her as anything but a haughty aristocratic young woman with airs and graces derived from her fancy English Public School topped off, with whatever was still lacking, in a Swiss Finishing School. There was the usual speculation locally as to how the supposedly impoverished Sir Thomas could afford all this 'fancy' expensive education for his daughters but, however he did it, now here she was, a beautiful elegant lady displaying a warm heart, and was obviously something of a romantic in the way she had played along with the children's fantasy. He was completely taken aback and even a little tongue tied. All he could think of to say was,

"The mug looks African. Am I right… South African possibly?"

She laughed. "You mean to tell me, Doctor, that you are querying the authenticity of the Holy Grail? Shame on you, you old cynic!"

"Indeed! How could I be so crass!" laughed Edward.

"But you are right," she confessed quietly, "African certainly. I got it in one of the villages near where my uncle used to have the farm in Kenya. It's pretty but worthless of course. I use it when I am out hunting since I do not like drinking from a flask or a bottle - not hygienic -as I am sure you agree. It was fortunate I had it with me today to turn it magically into the Holy Grail. Mind you, fantasies and facts can sometimes inexplicably collide. Did you know that what we call the 'Ladies' Bower' has the Irish name *'Rath Meadar'* on the oldest maps of our estate land?"

"Meaning?" asked Edward and continued, "I was never exposed to learning Gaelic in the Royal School I attended."

"I asked the Canon," continued Caroline, "and he told me 'meadar' in old Irish means a drinking vessel. So… for 'Ladies' Bower' read 'the Fort of the Drinking Vessel' Maybe it would be worth all of our whiles digging for the Grail down there in the fort! What does the Bible say, *'A little child shall lead them?'*

Rosie had reappeared at the kitchen door.

"Tell me, Rosie," said Caroline, "where on earth did Danny get this idea about the Holy Grail? He is clearly a highly intelligent little boy."

"He listens tay the wireless - a programme kalled 'Children's Hour'- an' there wuz a play or story about kings an' knights' an' horses an' them lukin for the Holy Grail. He tak-ed about it at home, an' Robbie spun him the yarn about St Patrick an' wizards, an' Patrick throwing the cup into the fort so it wudn't fall into the hands aff the wizards an' so on. Robbie shud have had the wit tay keep hez mouth shut for Danny believes ivery word he says."

Edward said, "A truly remarkable little boy, and then there is his playing and singing! Have you heard his talents in music, Caroline?"

"He has sung for us in church which is how I recognized him eventually in the bower, and he is simply wonderful… but no, I have not heard him play."

"Aunt Mina got him to play and sing for me this morning, and he played as well as I've heard some so-called professional pianists play in the National Concert Hall in Dublin. You have a treat ahead of you, Caroline, when you finally get to hear him."

Caroline nodded in agreement and made to mount 'Midnight.'

"Just hold on," said Edward in a tone of mock alarm. "We still need your prodigious imagination to get us out of the fix it has got us into! I assume you don't want the mug back, but in one small boy's vivid imagination it is the Holy Grail… that will cure his stammer… make him and the entire world sane and rich once he's got it to His Majesty the King and His Holiness the Pope. Now bring your considerable creative powers to bear on that little conundrum!"

"I am sure I can leave that to you, Edward. Aren't you psychiatrists experts on the human mind, its dreams, imaginings and its working. Surely you can get us all out of this dilemma on your own."

She mounted the horse and shouted over her shoulder as she trotted down the yard, "I look forward to hearing how you managed it when you visit us tomorrow."

Edward entered the kitchen where the three children were sitting in oversized dressing gowns drinking hot milk and eating chocolate topped buns while their clothes dried on the Aga.

"So, Sir Daniel Dowdells," said Edward earnestly. "What are you going to do now you've found the world-famous Holy Grail… and here in Ballybracken too… you will have put us all on the map."

Danny's Busy Schedule

Danny did one of his "Eeee, Aaaahs," and raised his eyes to the ceiling the better to appear to give this important matter deep thought, avoid any distractions and focus his undivided attention on it.

"I will hive tay go an' see the king first… since he lives closest… I think… an' then I'll take it tay the Pope… since he lives a bit further away… dizn't he? An' I'll ask them tay use the Holy Grail to make the whole world rich an' cure everybody of everything that's wrong way them… maybe even me an' the King's stutter…"

"I see," said Edward thoughtfully. "What a clever idea. So you think the Grail will cure people, do you?"

"It must cure iverything," said Danny emphatically. "Sure it's Jeezes's cup, an' sure He went about curin iverybody… so I think hez cup shud cure a lot aff things too… or else why did King Arthur an' the knights want it so bad?" He tailed off, now a little uncertain.

"Good," said Edward again reassuringly. "Now tell me, Danny, do you see the King and the Pope often?"

Danny reflected on this for a moment and was about to say he hadn't seen them that much recently, but now that he had found the Holy Grail they would surely be tripping over each other to see him. Before he could reply, Edward said,

"… because I see both of them very often dandering[230] about Dublin arm in arm so, if you like, and would trust me, I could hand over the Grail to them both the very next time I see them strolling together. That would save you a lot of time for I'm sure you are a very busy boy… and I'll ask them both to write to you to thank you for finding the Grail where all those other Knights of the Round Table have failed. What do you say? Would you trust me to do that for you?"

Danny thought for a moment. The big man was right. He, Daniel Malachy Dowdells, was indeed going to be very busy. How could he find the time to get over to meet the King and the Pope when he now had a spaceship to build to get to the planet 'Hesikos,' which was the current play on Children's Hour that had fired his imagination, and then he had his football team to organize for 'Evil Mickey' Gormley from over the Esker had declared all Protestants like the Dowdells were no good at playin football and were nothin but a bunch of owl sissies. Danny felt they must prove him wrong as a matter of some urgency.

"… so long as they sen me a letter tay tell me they hev got the Holy Grail," Danny said, "… an' that it's safe now an' nobody bad will iver get it… lake wizards… an' that… an' they will get on way plannin makin everybody rich an' happy everywhere… now they have it."

---

230 **Dandering** – *strolling casually*

"Oh, I'll make sure they write and tell you they have it safe and sound. They will almost certainly send you a reward for finding it for them too."

Now that sounded really good so, without further ado, Danny agreed. He fished the colourful mug out from the folds of the big dressing gown and handed it to Edward who took it over to the kitchen window where it caught the last rays of the setting sun. As he carefully turned it round, its coloured beads gleamed and were reflected for a fleeting moment in a pool of rotating light on the kitchen floor.

'Well, it might as well be the Holy Grail,' he thought, *'for doesn't the concept of the Grail represent something individual in each of our hearts, souls and imaginations… always inspirational… a cherished hope for a better life… a better world. Perhaps young Danny has captured its true meaning.'*

"Now, I must write you a receipt for the Grail, Danny," and he produced a note pad from a drawer in the kitchen table.

He carefully wrote, *'I, Dr. Edward McKendry, hereby promise Sir Daniel Dowdells of Ballybracken, latter day Knight of the Round Table, to deliver the Holy Grail to his Majesty the King and His Holiness the Pope the next time I see them taking a stroll through Dublin together,'* and he signed it with a great flourish.

"Are you happy with that, Danny?" he enquired, handing over the sheet of paper.

Danny took the paper, folded it and said solemnly, "Thank you, Sir. When you give the cup to the King and the Pope, will you say I would like them to use it to do good things lake feed boys and girls who hiv no mammies and daddies."

"I surely will," said Edward, "and I will remind them to send you Dowdellses a reward, for it is not everyday someone finds the Holy Grail…" and he ruffled Danny untidy mop of hair. "And now I must get you all home, and granny's treasure trunk to Jim McKnight."

Helen's Doomed Affair

The old lady was dozing when he entered her bedroom but woke with a start when she saw Edward lifting the trunk.

"Who is that? … robbers?... republicans?… who are you?… leave my trunk alone. Away with you or I'll call the police," she cried.

Edward rushed over to the bed to reassure her.

"It's only me, Granny. I am taking your diaries and papers to Jim McKnight, like you said."

He carried the trunk down the stairs and out to the boot of his car. The Dowdells children were now dressed in their dry clothes and, with much elbowing, squeezing and poking, got themselves settled in the back seat. When they reached McKnight's shop they left the trunk with Helen who explained that Jim and her mother had gone to a harvest thanksgiving service but said she knew that Jim was eager to see the papers and make a start on the work.

"Another beautiful girl hidden away here in Ballybracken," Edward mused. "Is she ever allowed out from under her mother's aprons? Does she have a boy-friend?"

"She's a very modest girl," Rosie replied, "an' very religious too I think."

This was the only comment Rosie dared say or even hint at for she knew, as no one else knew not even Jim, that Helen had had a boy-friend, a young policeman, but when her parents discovered he was a Catholic they forbade Helen to continue the relationship. But she, deeply in love, defied them, whereupon her father had beaten her within an inch of her life and her mother had then locked her in her room with only her Bible and bread and water for almost a week. When she emerged, the life-spark had been extinguished, and with it all hopes of marriage and family lost for ever. Guilt at having defied her parents and offended her God sealed her lips, and what was left was the modest, biddable shell of a girl trapped by ill-judged duty and narrow religion. To make doubly sure she would not transgress again, the McKnights had brought pressure to bear on the local police Inspector to have the young constable moved to a police barracks 'God-knows-where.'

"Modest, you say Rosie. I'm afraid I know what all that amounts to in this townland," said Edward wryly. "She can think what she likes so long as she never says what she thinks, Oh and always does what she's told. Isn't that what 'a modest girl' amounts to in this part of the world? I wonder Jim does not try to bring her out of herself a bit more, so quiet, so demure, so buried alive here?"

'If only you all knew,' thought Rosie.

The car drew up beside the Dowdells' cottage with its tin roof and its dangerously bowed back wall held up with three hefty wooden props. Rosie and the children got out. Edward got out too and, to Rosie's great relief, did not follow them into the house. He just stood looking at it as Robbie emerged to see who had arrived?

"So this is a house fit for heroes, Robbie. Not much changes, no matter how many wars we win!"

Robbie's Low Ebb

"It's not in great shape," Robbie agreed, and not for the first time thought that he really should be looking out for something better for them all. But truth to tell he had never been used to anything else all his life. Just tumbledown cotter houses, stark army barracks, and much worse on the battlefield.

Edward continued, "I think even my father's houses on the estate are in better shape than this but I won't insult you, Robbie, by suggesting you try for one of the vacated ones for I know you are a man of principle, and I suspect you deplore what my father has done to our Catholic tenants as much as I do. I am going to try to make him reinstate them when he calms down. Don't think too harshly of him. He takes the Unionist cause rather too seriously."

Robbie said nothing. On his own all afternoon, he had mulled over the events he had witnessed that morning and his former cynicism about Ulster in general and Ballybracken in particular had overtaken him. Worse still, in view of what he had agreed to regarding his new role in the B-Specials platoon, was the feeling that he was slowly but surely being sucked into Ballybracken's political and religious whirlpool, and allowing himself to be used by a system that in practice cared little for him and his class, be they Protestant or Catholic. He had only to cast an eye over their dark damp cotter house to see how little that class was valued.

But he must follow his own maxims - 'stroll' don't 'scrabble.' Now, facing Edward, this distinguished intelligent man who, like Jim McKnight, he knew shared his frustration, he could have let fly and revealed himself as a kindred spirit... but he didn't. He buried the thought, for didn't the great Stratford man say, *'There's nothing either good or bad, but thinking makes it so.'*

Edward was saying, "Take good care of Danny. An imagination like that is a rare commodity. God forbid that he ever loses his sense of wonder about the world. But now I must get back to help get my grandmother's birthday party underway."

The Doctor's Diagnosis

As he opened the driver's door, it suddenly occurred to Robbie that this was an opportunity, maybe the only one he would ever get, to ask Edward about something that bothered him a great deal on and off.

"I don't want to keep you," he said, "but can I mention something, Doctor?" He hesitated. "As you said yourself, Danny is a strange wee lad, an' he comes out with[231] some odd things at times… lake…" Robbie hesitated again, then continued, "He says he has chats with an angel who tells him things about heaven an' hell… an'… an' rubbish lake that… but it al seems very r-ail tay Danny," Robbie tailed off, sorry now he had brought it up for it sounded so ridiculous as he had voiced it.

Edward looked thoughtful.

"It could be a number of things," he said. "Small children sometimes invent an imaginary friend that they talk to, and who is in every way very real to them. They grow out of that as they learn to relate more closely to other children. It could just be that. On the other hand, and much more seriously, it could be psychotic episodes causing the delusions or an unusual form of epilepsy which can occasionally be an unwanted companion to extraordinary talent such as Danny's musical ability. Some famous musicians are thought to have suffered from it… Chopin I recall… and Joan of Arc's visions have been ascribed to it in this more secular age of ours. I hasten to add that it may not be directly connected to the sufferer's ability or genius at all… who knows? Certainly not medical science, as yet anyway. My concern would be that, if it is this form of epilepsy, it might develop into the full-blown thing, and that really is serious for there is no known cure. Tell me, did he experience any trauma, I mean a terrifying experience of some kind like a serious accident or traumatic event, that you know of when he was very young … as a baby even? Terrifying experiences in infancy or early childhood can sometimes trigger brain abnormality, if that is what it is."

Was the near drowning event at the Meeting of the Waters just the kind of experience the Doctor had in mind? But Robbie was letting no more cats out of any bags even after all these years. He just said,

"I'd hiv tay think about that."

"But let's look on the bright side," Edward continued. "It may just be the imaginary childhood friend I mentioned, only he or she has taken on the unusual

---

231 **He comes out with** – *he says unexpected things*

persona of a talkative angel. That may just have lingered a bit longer than most in young Daniel's vivid imagination. Such a talented boy will undoubtedly have difficulty finding a kindred spirit around his own age that he can relate to here in Ballybracken. The angel may be a substitute companion… someone he can relate to until a kindred soul turns up. Until then, if I may say so, Robbie, and even from our brief acquaintance, you and this angel are probably the closest he has yet come to finding his alter ego. But somebody sooner or later will appear and oust the angel from his imagination and indeed oust you too from his admiration. I will not even hazard a guess on how soon that may be but I will predict that the challenge for you then will be how to deal with letting go."

The car sped off leaving Robbie looking after it with a lot to think about.

Episode 24

Vengeful Fire!

Edward Reflects

As Edward turned into the drive now guarded by an empty gatekeeper's lodge, he joined a line of cars heading for the house and the birthday party. As he got nearer, he turned right taking the tradesmen's avenue leading to the back yards so leaving the front of the house free for their guests. As he parked, he mused over the day's events, and found himself thinking about the beautiful Caroline Roxborough, and the lengths she had gone to for the children's sake. It was a pity that relations between the two families were such that Sir Thomas and Caroline would not be attending this evening's party but maybe it was better so. Gentry like the Roxboroughs had largely bowed out of the Unionist 'struggle' and regarded the McKendry's as nouveau riche who had thrown in their lot with those the Roxboroughs regarded as the 'Orange bully boys.' So, with all his father's Unionist friends in attendance, his grandmother's outspoken views, the recent election disappointments and his father's evictions, it would make for a quieter evening to have everyone round the table of one mind.

Except him, but he would keep his mouth shut for the old lady's sake.

As he stumbled towards the kitchen door in the dark he thought he heard muffled voices and rustling over in the direction of the barns. Some of the labourers working late, he thought, or just those damned rats.

An Evening Fit for a Queen

The dining room looked dazzling. The canteen of silver cutlery from Tiffany's in New York had been a present from old Mrs. McKendry's American employer when she left his service. It was now laid out on the crisp white linen tablecloth alongside the Belleek dinner service and the 'Waterford Crystal' glasses. Two candelabra adorned each end of the long table, ranged around which was the beautiful set of Chippendale chairs while on the centre of the table was the elegant 18th century silver epergne displaying deep red roses.

It was a setting fit for a queen and, like a queen, old Mrs. McKendry had no sooner entered the room, supported by her son and grandson, to see that all was to her mind than she immediately demanded changes - *the napkin rings were not right, there were too many roses in the epergne… how was she to see all her guests through such a large bouquet?… far fewer roses would suffice… and there were not enough candles on the Georgian side tables to highlight the rest of her silver… and she did not want electric light anywhere in the room for candle light was more in keeping with the occasion, and would show off her rose-gold jewellery to best effect.*

Hanna hurried about making these pernickety adjustments while Mina just smiled wryly and disappeared into the kitchen. It was a hive of activity with three maids in starched white caps and aprons employed only for the evening. '*But why or why hadn't they asked Rosie to stay?*' thought Hanna, instead of depending on these clumsy girls who didn't know where anything was kept, would probably break some of the cut glass or '*chayney*'[232], and were only good at giggling, gossiping, and getting in the way.

These local lassies were indeed well out of their depth. There was talk of 'Fish Mornay', '*whatiever that wuz?*' 'Beef Wellington', another mystery…'Dauphinoise potatoes' – '*wud boiled or champ not hiv done rightly?*'… 'fancy cr*ame*'[233]… ingredients for four different deserts '*not wan aff them recognizable*'… smelly cheeses that '*wud turn ye'r stomach,*' and, to cap all these culinary mysteries, strange coffee beans to grind when the girls had only just got used to seeing bottles of 'Camp' coffee on the shelves in McKnight's shop and had never dared try it, '*in case yeh'd bay poshoned*'[234]. And where on earth did all this culinary bounty come from in the era of rationing! That was the greatest whispered mystery perplexing both kitchen staff and the guests all evening long.

But despite the disarray in the kitchen, the party was going well in the large elegant parlour. The guests were greeted with champagne in cut glass flutes and delicious canapes served on silver trays by Hanna and Mina, the maids having been ruled out as likely to drop things. Then it was into the dining room where the grand dame took her place at the head of the table, the Canon said grace in Latin which, despite being unnecessarily long, was undoubtedly in keeping with the required tone of the evening. The fish course was declared a great success, and, though much richer than most of the guests were accustomed to, all took note of the name, for the grand old lady had always been a trend-setter from her time with her wealthy Yankee family who '*knew how to do things right.*'

---

232 **Chayney** – *chinaware*
233 **Crame** – *cream*
234 **Poshoned** – *poisoned*

More frugal variations of Cod Mornay and some of the rest of the rich food that followed it, would shortly be on every self-respecting Tyrone Unionist dinner table to grace their own more modest 'state' occasions.

Dinner Table Diktats

The talk turned to the local elections, those who had been successful expressing great concern for George McKendry on his loss but venturing to say that maybe he had been too trusting, decent man that he was, of his Catholic neighbours in thinking they would ever vote Unionist, however well treated.

Edward had great difficulty restraining himself, and would have taken them on but somehow succeeded in holding back for this was not the evening for arguments that would upset his beloved grandmother. They then turned to discuss Sir Thomas and roundly agreed that he was their local 'Lundy' and was the only fly in Ballybracken's Unionist ointment for he was quite likely to 'sell the pass' by housing some of George's evicted cotters, so ruining their gerrymandering plans for the district if, 'God forbid', the local franchise was ever extended to include such people.

"Sir Thomas must surely be one of Ballybracken's great disappointments," old Mrs. McKendry declared. "A peer of the realm who should be giving a lead but instead selling us all short. I suppose we can only be glad he is not openly espousing the Nationalist cause! I think it is time for consolidation of all our Unionist efforts under good strong men… yes… like you, George, and our friends here tonight. It is not a time for divisions and wavering."

This little speech had left the men a trifle troubled. Unionist woman folk were noted for their ability never to seem to have opinions, and to always say the nothing they might say very quietly. But old Mrs. McKendry, with so much wealth at her back and knowledge of the world, could be excused from adhering to the code of womanly silence in public that prevailed in Ballybracken. In public, yes, but be assured a fair number – not unlike Effie McKnight whose manipulative powers we have already admired - though noted for their 'modest' demeanour, controlled their men with the skill of puppet-masters without anyone seeing the controlling strings.

Someone went to speak but she cut him short.

"Now that is enough politics for one evening. Let's have the cheese course… a la mode francaise," she added, for the Unionist wives were clearly taken aback by this latest manifestation of high sophistication, "I mean we will have the cheese before our deserts," she declared, her rose-gold locket and earrings glowing softly in the candlelight, "for the French way with food and wine was one of the few things I admired about them during my visits there. Now there's a shilly-shallying nation if ever there was one. Surrender indeed! How dare they let our beloved Empire down. Of course that's the way with the Catholic nations in Southern Europe… always compromising, running with the herd, temporizing, looking for the easy way out, cutting spiritual corners… so unlike the strong unflinching Protestant nations of Northern Europe… and indeed so unlike the Catholics one meets in North America who brook no compromise of their faith and traditions. Now that is what I really admire in any nation or religion… standing fast."

Yet again Edward had to bite his tongue to prevent himself saying that she was overlooking the fact that we had just had to fight - almost to the death and certainly the bankruptcy and breakup of the British Empire she so admired - one of those same great strong 'Protestant' nations of Northern Europe. But it was HER evening, and anyway he was quietly enjoying the effect this great old lady was having on the Unionists stalwarts round the table, unused as they were to a woman expressing strong views or indeed any views in public except on the low price they were getting for their eggs or the high price they were paying for their meat.

Cry Havoc!

The cheese and grapes arrived on two large platters that had just begun circulating round the table when there was an incessant ringing at the front door and then, to their utmost alarm, a banging on the dining room windows. George and Edward rose from their seats in alarm and ran into the front hall. The guests heard excited voices but could not make out what was being said.

"What is it, George? Whatever is the matter?" Hanna McKendry cried.

George had returned to the room looking white faced and anxious. He blurted out,

"It's the barns… and the gate lodge and empty cottages… they are all on fire… an arson attack doubtless. Edward is phoning the fire brigade and the police. In the meantime we must do what we can… to contain the fire in the barns at least… I doubt the cottages are done for."

He dashed from the room.

The old lady stood up and, gripping the arms of her chair for support, said in a calm collected voice, "Would you gentlemen all please go and do what you can to help our men contain the fire until the brigade arrives. And Hanna… would you please take the ladies into the parlour and serve tea, coffee, those nice dark chocolates and those pleasant liqueurs… and we must not forget about my birthday cake… but not until the gentlemen return to share it, and to drink my health. They will have to forgo their port on this occasion but we must not allow rabble to upset our evening entirely. I will join the ladies in a moment when I have steadied myself a little, and that would be greatly helped if someone would be so kind as to get me a little brandy from the decanter there."

The men rose hurriedly and followed the McKendry men out of the house. Mina McKendry quietly poured some brandy and handed the glass to her mother. The old lady raised the glass up to the candlelight and said in the same calm controlled tone,

"Isn't it beautiful, such a depth of colour in the glow of the candles, so alluring. Now leave me to enjoy it, and to steady myself… without an audience if you please." She gave one of her brittle little laughs and settled herself back in her chair.

The ladies heard the fire brigade arriving amid much indistinct shouting as they drank their tea and coffee in the parlour. They were, of course, dying to see what was happening outside but the curtains were never drawn back and Hanna did her best to keep the conversation going while trying to hide her acute anxiety. She abandoned them now and then to see for herself what was happening outside. All she could make out was an alarming red glow from the barns at the back of the house, and a more distant glow to the front which she knew must be the fire up at the gate lodge.

George did not reappear but Edward came in to tell them that all but one of the barns had been saved, and that there was nothing left of the cottages down by the river or of the gate lodge. He looked around for his grandmother but was told she had decided to stay quietly in the dining room on her own until she felt fully able to join them. Edward said he would now tell her the good news about the barns and help her into the parlour or, and this seemed to all much more sensible in the circumstances, get her back up to her bedroom to rest quietly. He did not return with any further news about the fires, so they assumed that they had heard the worst.

With their guests finally gone amid many protestations of sorrow and offers of help, the family subsided to recover and to take stock. It was obvious that the fires were revenge for what had happened earlier in the day and, as such, nobody would ever be brought to book for the Irish Republican oath of silence was unbroachable.

"Blow heaped on blow, son," George said, looking at Edward's soot smeared dinner jacket. "Maybe I'd have been better to accept my defeat, hang up my Unionist boots and join Sir Thomas across the river in his state of indifference and genteel decay."

"You had better not let granny hear you talking like that, father. Has anyone looked in on her by the way? I hope she has got over to sleep. Who helped her upstairs?"

"Surely you did!" exclaimed Hanna. "When she didn't join us here in the parlour, I assumed you had helped her to bed when you went to tell her about the barns!"

"No, I didn't," cried Edward rising from the armchair in great alarm. "I didn't go to tell her because, as soon as I left you, Aunt Mina said I was needed urgently to help round up some of the cattle and horses that had got loose and were going crazy in the far yard, scared out of their wits by the fire."

"Then where is she?" George exclaimed now getting to his feet too. "She could not have got back upstairs on her own. Surely she can't still be in the dining room?"

'Oh, my Lord!" Hanna cried as they rushed into the hall. "She'll be fit to be tied she'll be so angry with us for neglecting her. What an evening! And it the poor dear's birthday too. How will we ever make it up to her?"

But there was no need to worry! There she sat in majesty at the end of the great dining room table still presiding over the remains of her wonderful birthday feast, the last of the candlelight glinting on her gold and silver jewellery and with a half glass of ruby-red brandy before her on the table. She was as commanding in death as she had been in life not allowing even the great reaper to topple her from her perch. She died as she had lived - strong, determined, unflinching, and elegant to the end.

Episode 25

The Big Reward and the Bronze Halo

The King & The Pope Get in Touch

"... and the big doctor man gave the Holy Grail to the King and the Pope... cos I hadn't time to go and give it to them myself cos I'm so busy..."

Angel Jo was looking a bit sceptical so Danny hurried on,

"... and it's all true cos I got a letter from the King and the Pope... and a reward... though I had to share that with Bobby and Dorry which I didn't think was fair for they were no good at finding it... and it was me found it... but they said I had to share it... so I did... but I made Bobby give me his catapult... and Dorry has promised to stop bothering me about my schoolbag now she can get a new one of her own with the reward money. Do you not want to know how much the reward was?" Danny demanded in a note of triumph.

Angel Jo was once again sitting on Danny's stone rubbing his wings together in the middle of the Fort-of--Silk at the top of the Scroggy Brae. He said casually, "yes, go on then. You're going to tell me anyway."

"It was... fifteen pounds! Three big white five-pound notes. We'd never seen so much money. Mammy near fainted when we opened the letter!"

"About this letter you got. What did it say?" asked Jo with a hint of amusement.

"I have it here," said Danny triumphantly producing a screwed-up piece of paper from his trouser pocket. "It says... it says... here's what it says," as he finally got the wrinkles smoothed out on the flat surface of his stone, '*To Sir Daniel Dowdells, Latter-day Knight of the Round Table...*' (that's me, see) '*... To our trusty and well-beloved Sir Daniel... Greetings.*' I think that must be the way the King and the Knights talk at the Round Table, and in that place where the Pope lives."

"Would you mind getting on with it," said Angel Jo. "The excitement is nearly too much even for an angel to bear, and heaven knows patience is our second name!"

"*... To our trusty...* Oh, I've read you that bit... '*We, His Majesty the King and his Holiness the Pope, want to thank you for finding the Holy Grail where so many* others have failed in the past. It was great, and well done. We will share it and put it up on a high shelf in our palaces so nobody can get at it, and we will take it down now and again and put it to good use. So thank you again, and please accept the enclosed reward which we want you to share with Bobby and Dorry. We hope you are well as this leave us. The King says thank you for your advice about the stutter. He now sings everything to everybody and is doing great. The Pope says to tell your mammy that good soap and sunshine keep his clothes looking so white, so she should try that. Bye for now. Your friends in London & Rome. King George and Pope Pius'… and look they signed it at the bottom in red ink… or maybe it's even their own blood, the King with a nice crown and the Pope with a cross…"

Danny finished somewhat breathlessly, crumpled up the letter again and put it back in his pocket.

"So… I found it all by myself in the Bower above the Meetings… it was terrible hard… but now everybody in the world will get a five-pound note… and be rich… an' stop fightin each other… an' that."

He paused, and then continued thoughtfully, "Though mammy and Robbie haven't got their money yet… but I think that's cos the King and the Pope have a lot of people to give the money to first… but I've told them they would just have to be patient like mammy is always telling me and Bobby and Dorry to be when we want things."

Danny's Galactic Mission

"How very wise, Daniel Malachy. Now, what's your next big idea? Let me guess. You're going to build a spaceship."

"How did you know?" Danny cried.

"I know everything," said Angel Jo smugly. "So where are you off to in your spaceship? Anywhere nice?"

I want to go to the planet Hesikos. Have you ever heard of it?"

"No… can't say I have," the angel said thoughtfully. "But it might be in one of the galaxies I don't get to much. I'll ask around and see what I come up with. Why do you want to go there anyway?"

"Cos there's this play on 'Children's Hour'… an' it's all about Hesikos and it sounds like it's a great place but bad people there have these spacemen trapped in a cave… and I think the spacemen would like a Knight of the Round Table like me, to go up there and rescue them… they have been in a cave for two weeks now according to 'Children's Hour' and they are runnin out of things…

like chicken and buns and biscuits an' that… and the bad people are forever setting fire to the cave which nearly cooks them in there… so I'm gonna try to rescue them if I can get my spaceship built in time. I need two big bins tied together, a pointy lid for the front to push it through space nice and smooth, and lots and lots of fireworks stuck on the back to get me off the ground and up past the moon… Oh, and matches to keep lighting the fireworks to keep it goin on up. I should have it ready by Friday. Would you know whereabouts Hesikos is by then so I can point my spaceship in the right direction? Cos It would be very bad to go in the wrong direction and get lost in space. I don't know how I'd get a message to mammy and Robbie to come and get me though I suppose I could write a note an' let it float down to them." He finished thoughtfully, with yet another of his intergalactic problems solved.

Angel Jo said, "Now you know it's more than my life's worth to interfere, my little man, but would you ever think about postponing your space travel until you have thought a bit more about it. I'm sure there are books on space travel even in that dreadful library at Ballybracken crossroads that might help you get a bit better prepared. How are you going to breath for example? Once you get above those clouds, if you ever do in your flying contraption, there is no air and without air you'll croak it… dead as mutton… in an instant… snuffed out… and then what will your mammy say?"

"Well, you travel through space, so how do you do it?" Danny asked crossly, for he had laid out his plans to spend next Sunday getting to Hesikos to avoid Sunday school.

"Oh hoity-toity," said Jo. "We are getting above ourselves again, aren't we? I don't need air… because I am air… and when I'm in space, I am space. but you wouldn't understand. If I were you, I'd organize your football match instead… yes, I know about that too… for you don't want those dreadful Esker boys calling you Dowdells sissies all the time, do you? And you never know, you might even win, and wouldn't that show them?"

Football Diversion

Danny pondered this and, yes, the space travel might be postponed for now. The trapped men would just have to be patient, like mammy and Robbie waiting for their fivers, and maybe learn to put out the dragons' flames with fire extinguishers like had just been installed in Danny's school… or damp coats maybe would do too if they could find any water. Anyway, they seemed very smart people so should be able to think of something until he got his spaceship up and flying.

"I think I might get the match organised first," Danny conceded reluctantly, "for I don't have the bins or rockets just yet… though I can get a box of matches from Robbie to light the rockets," he finished, trying not to sound totally defeated.

"Hum… Yes, that might be best," said the angel, "but remember it wasn't my idea. You were going to get round to organizing the match sooner or later anyway … you are now just going to do it sooner than you thought… all right? By the way, speaking of footballs, how do you like my halo? It's a bit like a football, isn't it? Though it's flat of course."

Halo Hullabaloo

Danny had noticed something different about Angel Jo and, right enough, now he came to look at him properly there was something flapping round his head. He had just been about to say 'nice' but thought quickly and instead said "It's OK" which he had heard on the wireless, and thought that was a very smart new sort of thing to say.

"Just 'OK!'" cried the angel, "OK! Well really! But then again, if I'm honest, I suppose your right," he said, calming down just as suddenly as he had flared up. "Yes, that's what I thought too when they doled me out a bronze one. I mean after all those millions of years dashing from pillar to post across all those flaming universes dodging meteorites, nearly crashing into unmapped moons and planets, going without nectar, ambrosia or even the odd plate of your cornflakes… and writing all those wretched reports… to only get a bronze one… so very disheartening! Of course, I blame BOAK. They never give me anything challenging to do so I can never show off my true genius… never get a planet-shaking message to deliver like that Gabriel a while back… no shepherds to scare the wits out of… no big new star to paste into the firmament to give wise men something to chew on… Oh no! BOAK keeps all that for the favoured few… the rest of us are just plume-pushers and small-time messenger-boys… and of course being allocated guardians to little nobodies like you. No wonder I only got a bronze one… wait another couple of million years, they said, and you might… just might! ... graduate to a silver one. It a lottery up there, I tell you!"

And he reached up and stroked the halo with both hands. Danny thought it was time to say 'OK' again, so he did.

"Oh sorry, Daniel Malachy, I digress, but I had to get that off my chest, Yes, back to my halo. I suppose I must just do the best I can with it, and it does look rather like the sun if caught in the right light. Anyway, I got in touch with the good Fra Angelico again… he got the heavenly plumbing all wrong, by the way… took them centuries to get it sorted… well, of course after that they had to move him back to painting… So as you can see I got him to paint the top half of my wings blue so the halo looks like it's the sun rising in a blue sky with my face looking out of it… and what do you think of the light pink on my wings? Do you think he has got the tint right?"

He spread out his wings for Danny to admire… "and you know what I'll do if you dare say it's 'nice' or even 'OK'" Angel Jo warned.

Danny strikes the Right Note

"It's very… engaging." Danny had heard this word used on the wireless too and, though he hadn't a clue what it meant, he thought, like ok, it sounded good.

"Well, my darling little man, you have come on! Engaging is it! I love it. I'll quote you… yes… what could be better? … engaging… well I never!" and he spread his wings out even further for Danny to admire. "Now," he said, folding them up slowly and with a coy look, "my 'engaging' little chap. What can I do for you that you would find… engaging?... bearing in mind that I must not interfere in case you end up like…."

"… Like Hitler or some very bad person like that," Danny finished the sentence for the angel and thought for a minute. "Would it be OK if you helped us win the football match?"

"It most certainly would not be OK!" exclaimed Jo emphatically. "That might lead you astray entirely. You might start betting on the football pools and end up a dyed-in-the-wool gambler, squandering your five pounds and any other money on horses or greyhounds or racing pigeons… or, worse still, you might get very rich, and the dear knows what wickedness that would lead you into. Oh, dear me, no! Asking me to fix the outcome of your football match is outrageous."

"Even if I promised to try hard not to become a desperate gambler?" Danny ventured. "Would that make it OK?" … for he knew much was at stake if they didn't win the football match and fell prey to the boys from over the Esker.

"Most definitely not!" repeated the angel, and then seeing Danny lip go down, he said soothingly, "but I tell you what. You know I gave you just a little nudge to help you find the Grail, well here's another little tip… now mum's-the-word if I give you this clue… all right?" And he tapped his nose several times with a long elegant finger. "Here it is: think very hard who you want to be your goalie and then do the very opposite… OK? That nice little puzzle should 'engage' you, my little man!"

This sounded to Danny like yet another piece of the useless advice that he had come to expect from the angel, even if he could work out what on earth it meant but he just said 'OK' again and then 'Thank you,' though he didn't really mean it.

"Oh dear, is that the time?" said Jo looking up at the only blink of sun that day. "Well, must be off to beat the aurora borealis… sheer murder clearing that thing, and its colours come off on your wings, you know. Could ruin everything! So bye for now… my 'engaging' little friend. Good luck with the match."

And with a chuckle, he slowly vanished leaving Danny to wonder, not for the first time, what earthly good it was having a guardian angel at all if he couldn't even help you win a football match?

Episode 26

The Dangerous Diaries

'Hell hath No Fury…'

Jim McKnight gently opened the lid of old Mrs. McKendry's oak travelling trunk noting its elaborate brass ornamentation and locks and the monogram of the old lady's maiden name – 'MA' for Mary Anderson - on the lid and sides. He knew that her full name had been Eliza Mary so why not 'EMA' he wondered idly to his mother.

"Och 'Eliza' mightn't have sounded grand enough for her when she got far away, for she was always givin herself airs and graces, that woman, thinkin that she was a pop-above-buttermilk[235]. Maybe she thought 'Mary' sounded posher, more befitting the grand lady she thought she was… likely imitatin old Queen Mary. What are the McKendrys but poor folk that got on, and we are left to wonder just how it was done? If you ask me, Eliz Mary buttered somebody up[236] out there in America but nobody will ever find out her guilty secrets now. She took them with her to the grave."

"Really, mother, I'm surprised at you speaking so ill of the dead. You must sit me down some day and tell me why you feel so strongly about her? I just don't understand it."

"It's bred into me," Effie continued. "That woman did a great wrong to your own granny… a wrong that your granny always said broke her heart… and maybe you'll find out for yourself what it was she did in them papers there. Eliza Mary Anderson was a scheming determined bitch, may God forgive me for saying so."

She paused to compose herself, and then continued, "… She come home from America and got round Hugh McKendry with some palaver[237] of a story an' just blackmailed him into marryin her – there is no other word for it - sayin she'd waited on him when God an' the world knows fine well that if she'd got a

---

235 *Pop above buttermilk* – *feeling superior to those around her*
236 *Buttered somebody up* – *flattered somebody to deceive them*
237 *Palaver* – *a questionable story*

better offer out there we would never have seen hilt nor hair[238] of her back here in Ballybracken. And sure she put a hand in her own daughter Mina's life tryin to marry her off to a clergyman who didn't want her or any woman for that matter for he wasn't the marryin kind, and so ruined Mina's chances of makin a sensible marriage to some decent farmer round about. An', I'm certain sure it was her that was behind the evictions. George McKendry would never have done such a thing off his own bat. Sure he has no backbone. No, it was her ladyship was behind all that, you mark my words… and look where it got them… the place nearly burned down round them… and maybe the rest of us put in danger from the IRA too. And sure she treated Hanna McKendry like a skivvy… a slave… playin on her background as an abandoned orphan from Dublin… sure she had George all set to marry into the Roxborough gentry but the minute she knew Hanna was to inherit a power a money[239], from the Harrisons that had adopted her, it was a different story. She changed tack and had young George going after Hanna and the loot. So don't talk to me about Eliza Mary…that woman could bamboozle a regiment… there will be nothin you'll find in them trunks that'll surprise me… though I'm sure she'll have dressed all her badness up to show herself off as whiter than white… odjus[240] woman, odjus I tell you."

Jim had had enough. "You'd better let me at it. Ten and more years of her life lie hidden in here, and the sooner I make a start the sooner I'll be finished… and maybe… . just maybe… I may find something to alter your opinion of her, mother."

"I'm tellin you, nothin you'll find in there will do that, so don't try," said Effie, and she left Jim to unearth quite a remarkable story!

As expected, the chest contained a jumble of letters, travel guides and brochures, evidently of places Eliza Mary had visited when travelling with the American family. The letters were all dated, so that make putting them in order that bit easier, and the travel guides – mainly the famous 'Baedekers' that no self-respecting traveller in the late 19th Century would be without - were easy to deal with in their eye-catching Burgundy-red binding and gold lettering. Jim fished them out of the compost heap of papers and piled them up.

---

238 **Hilt nor hair** – *not a trace… she would not have returned*
239 **A power of money** – *a great deal of money*
240 **Odjus** – *terrible*

"The old girl certainly got around," he mused as he sat back on his hunkers and flicked through guides to the German, Austria-Hungarian and Russian Empires, of Italy and Greece, Egypt and Palestine and several more, all of them dating back to the 1890s. This heightened his interest in the task for he knew at once that these little volumes captured an age that had vanished forever, the great Empires overwhelmed by the catastrophic outcome of the First World War, the Italian and Greek governments overthrown, and many of the smaller countries changed beyond recognition, including Ireland. He then turned to locate the brochures and they also grabbed his attention. There were illustrated booklets on New York, Boston, San Francisco, Chicago, London, Paris, Athens, Jerusalem and several more, all capturing the spirit of the 'Roaring 90s' and the golden age of luxury travel for the very rich.

"Better make a start on the diaries," he said to himself. "They say 'Travel broadens the mind,' even if it's other people's travel in my case."

Golden Travel in the Gilded Age

"How's ye'r researches into the owl girl's foreign exploits goin?" Robbie asked Jim one evening as they shared a beer in Jim's office where Robbie had just completed some running repairs. Daniel Malachy was sitting on the floor playing with the McKnight's new puppy dog and drinking a mineral. "Discovered any scandal? Wuz she upta anythin she shudn't? How did she come by al that dough?"

"How long have you got? And, yes, there is a small conundrum about dates that could spell scandal or maybe I should call it a possible 'impropriety.' But I'll save that for later when you and young Danny there can help me with dates and sums. One thing is certain, if I have got it right, things are not quite what we are led to believe down there at Ballybracken House. It is equally certain, Robbie, that if what I've discovered is true, it had better never see the light of day here in Ballybracken. Your lips and mine must be sealed for there are big egos involved that could get dented."

"Go on then, tell me? What the hell wuz she upta? Did she run a high-class brothel in the States or what? Is that the source aff their money? Or did she butter-up some owl fella out there an' swindle him out aff a fortune?"

"Oh no, nothing like that… but just hold fire and we will get to the conundrum in time. First let me show you some of the more interesting documents. I've got the trunk here in the office so that I can work on it in spare moments."

"On yeh go, then," said Robbie taking a swig of beer. "We've got al evenin, hiven't way, Danny?"

The pup was busy chewing Danny's hand, and had just peed on his leg so he was too preoccupied to reply.

Jim went across the office, pulled the trunk out from a corner and opened the lid.

"Here's her story, and I will be as brief as I can. As you know, she grew up in Ballybracken Upper on that small farm on the edge of Collity bog. So, tiny farm and big family. Nothing for the girls but to marry a local farmer, hire out or leave and seek their fortunes somewhere else. So at 18, Mary made her way to Derry, took ship to America where she almost immediately fell on her feet, as they say. Somehow or other, and I haven't discovered how, she found employment with a millionaire family called Niels-Christiansen. They were Danish-American, and not only had Mr Anders Niels-Christiansen made a vast fortune during the railway boom in the States and Canada but he was a major shareholder in an oil company and several steel foundries. As if that wasn't wealth enough, he then married a close relative of one of the richest families in America, the Vanderbilts, and she brought with her another vast fortune."

Danny was now listening intently, not that he understood much that was being said but mention of money always got his attention for, as we know, his finances were almost always in a perilous state. Here was talk of America – where he had nearly reached in the 'Duck' boat thing at Bundoran – and of people there who apparently had plenty of money. *'What a great place America must be'* he mused. If he could get there and come home rich, the Dowdells could have chicken dinners every day. Wouldn't that be great!

"Holy Jeezes," Robbie said. "Now ye'r gettin tay it. Did the b-owl Mary stale from them? Is that how she come-by the big clunnion[241] aff money?"

"I'll ignore that," Jim said laughing. "Suffice it to say some of their great wealth did rub off on her but be patient, will you, and we will come to that. Eliza Mary was clearly a clever woman with an eye to the main chance, and why not? At first she was employed as a lady's maid to Laura Niels-Christiansen, a young woman just a little bit younger than Mary herself. The family had a luxurious mansion at the Hamptons on Long Island and a luxurious lifestyle to go with it. Listen to this entry from Mary's diary when the family are 'at home' on Long Island, which doesn't appear to have been all that often,"

'Spent early morning unpacking and sorting Miss Laura's ball gowns and sportswear. Then went with her for her morning swim in Lake Agawam, and then to

---

241 *Big clunnion – great amount*

afternoon tennis at the 'Meadow Club.' Returned home and helped Miss Laura dress for the 'Meadow Club' ball. The style was out of this world with Miss Laura the belle of the ball as usual. The Bowrich family were all there again, young Mr Matthew very attentive to Miss Laura, and no wonder! We joked on the way home that she might soon be travelling to church in a gondola for old Mrs. Bowrich comes to church most Sundays in her gondola paddled by four liveried footmen. Quite a sight!'

"Now, how's that as an experience for an Irish 'Biddy' from the edge of Collity Bog? And the whole diary reflects this lifestyle of elegance, affluence and extravagance. But we mustn't lose sight of the fact that Mary was, of course, the family's servant and worked extremely hard for them for she was at Laura's beck and call day and night. That said, she seems quite quickly to have been treated more like a member of the family, and she was trusted to manage the other servants and take charge of all the family's travels… and boy did they travel! Always of course first class - and Mary with them - on many of the luxury liners of the day… their own private carriage on trains… staying in private suites in only the best hotels across three Continents. The family were great Francophiles – that's admirers of things French to you, Robbie – so they visited Paris and the Riviera several times in the 1890s."

"Ach sure I'm a great lover aff things French mezself. Didn't I help free the country from the Krauts, an' saved many a French maiden from a fate worse than death."

"Huh!" Jim snorted, "I pity the poor innocent maiden that fell into your hands."

"Anyway, on yeh go, Jim. There's the makins aff a good story in al this. No wunner the owl woman had such an air about hirself when she had seen so much aff the worl an' in such company. The mystery tay me is, what brung hir home tay Ballybracken lavin behin al that?"

"Now that's the next conundrum," Jim said, "and I'm getting to it. As you say, she sure covered a lot of ground with them. The other member of the family, apart from Miss Laura, was a son, Harald, or 'Master Harry' as Mary refers to him. Harry was a law student at Harvard during her time with them, and they visited him there quite a lot and met his roommate and friend, the young Franklin Delano Roosevelt, later President of the US. But, as I say, Mary spent most of her time travelling, first the length and breadth of America visiting the Grand Canyon, climbing Pike's Peak in the Rockies on mules, visiting the family's ranch in California and attending the Chicago World Fair in 1893. Then there was the foreign travel. France, where they stayed in the Ritz in Paris and the grandest hotels on the Riviera. She travelled with them to Vienna and Milan where they attended the opera. There are programmes here for ballet performances in St Petersburg, and guides and souvenir booklets of all these places and the performances attended. The Baedeker Guides for these countries shed an interesting light on the lavish lifestyle these rich people expected to enjoy. But it is Mary's personal accounts in the diaries that are truly remarkable. She writes of an interesting occasion where the family were entertained by the Greek Royal Family in the Royal Palace in Athens – this was a 'thank you' for a massive financial contribution the Niels-Christiansens had made to rebuilding villages in Northern Greece after an earthquake – and Laura and her lady's maid, our very own Eliza Mary, were allowed to sit on the Greek throne *just for fun* as she puts it in that diary entry. The family met the Austro-Hungarian Emperor and Empress when they were all 'taking the waters' at Marienbad, she was with them during Cowes Week in 1896 where Anders and Master Harald won some prestigious sailing trophy, and the family was then introduced to the Prince of Wales and the German Kaiser who were also competing at Cowes. On and on it goes, Robbie. The family were great art collectors so they had a private viewing of the major treasures of the Vatican finishing off with a private audience with the Pope."

"That rings a bell," Robbie said, "There's them roun here that say they hiv Rosary beads blessed by the Pope an' that it wuz owl Mrs. McKendry that brought them tay them."

"I think the family's audience with Pope Pius X must account for that local story about those rosary beads," Jim said. Mary wrote home very often, and her letters and her mother's replies are all here. There is a real 'down-to-earth' funny moment in one of her mother's letters. Mary had written to tell the family about the Niels-Christensen's audience with the Pope and clearly, even as a good Ulster Protestant, she had been greatly impressed by the occasion, describing the uniforms of the Swiss Guards and splendour of Vatican City and St Peter's. When her mother writes back… here's her letter… she says,"

'Glad to hear you are safe an' well an' keepin ye'r end up with such grand folk as the Pope of Rome. You'll be glad to hear that the wee black cow calved on the back hill last night. It's a wee heifer calf an' your daddy is delighted.'

Robbie laughed. "Well, I suppose we al hiv our pressin priorities whether they are meetin great Roman Pontiffs or the safe arrival aff a wee heifer calf on the back hill in Ballybracken Upper."

"Indeed you're right. The arrival of that calf probably boosted the Anderson family's annual budget maybe by 100%. But the bold Mary's tale is not finished yet. The next diary entries were written in Naples when they are all about to climb Vesuvius, and, plucky as she undoubtedly was, Mary appears to have been a bit apprehensive about this for I found a note tucked into that entry of her diary that she had obviously given to the manager of the 'Hotel Bristol' in Naples and which he must have given back to her on her safe return. Listen...

'April 19th, 1900. Going up Vesuvius. In case of accident please address Mr Frank Anderson, my father, Ballybracken, Ireland.'

... so, adventurous but cautious too, our Mary! By far the most poignant entries are her accounts of the visit they made to Egypt and especially the Holy Land. As a religious woman, it is clear that seeing the holy sites, especially those associated with Christ, moved her deeply... listen," and Jim fumbled through the diary trying to find the entry:

'Today we visited the Church of the Holy Sepulchre where we saw the Calvary and the tomb where Christ was laid. I was so deeply moved to be standing where my Saviour died for my sins, where his precious body was laid, and where he rose from the dead to sit at God's right hand. Inside the tomb itself... I could not help it... I fell to my knees and wept at the debt I owe Him. After I had prayed, Mr Anders helped me up and held me for I was in danger of falling, so overwhelmed was I by that holy place.'

Both men were silent for a moment then Robbie asked, "Did she iver make it home tay Ballybracken for a visit durin the curse aff her years away?"

"She made it back for occasional visits apparently loaded down with gifts – and welcome cash - when the Niels-Christensens were grouse shooting on some of the big estates in Scotland. And although she doesn't mention it in the diaries, I think she must have kept up some sort of communication with Hugh McKendry for in 1900, of course, she gave up her job with the Niels-Christensens and returned to Ballybracken to marry him. Her diary records that in April 1900 she was at the second cataract of the Nile with the family on their private paddle steamer and by Christmas 1900 she was back in Ballybracken married and expecting her first child, our very own George."

True Love or Sordid Scandal!

"So when are yeh gettin tay the scandal?" Robbie demanded. "Al right, she got roun a brave few corners[242] aff the worl, and for a woman from that poor backgroun an' with as limited an education as mezself, she sure did herself proud, but what the divil, I ask yeh again, brought hir home tay marry a kitter-handed an' skelly-eyed[243] wee farmin man she had lef bayhin al them years earlier? There's a story there fir sure?"

"And for sure, there is," said Jim, "and it's for you and me... and young Danny here... to unravel it this very evening."

The pup had been busy licking Danny's face with its warm wet tongue which Danny was finding most agreeable. He would have quite liked a Mars bar, some bull's eyes or, better still, a packet of the new and desirable sweetie cigarettes so he could pretend he was smoking like the big men. But it mightn't be timely to intimate his confectionary needs given the apparent importance of Jim's conversation that was going on above his head, and Robbie's interest in it. He did make some play with the now empty mineral bottle just in case that would alert the company to his need for further refreshment but it didn't work so he contented himself with stroking the pup.

"You see," Jim continued, "as far as I can read within, above and between the lines, Mary and her Boss, Anders Niels-Christensen, were growing steadily fonder of each other. The relationship would seem to have developed slowly yet steadily. I mean it was no instant fling."

"So now we're gittin tay it," Robbie said. "Lake, how slow wuz it? When did he git hez leg over?

"You are such a crude man," Jim laughed. "Actually, I think ultimately they fell deeply in love. There is a discernible thread of their mutually growing affection running through the later diary entries. It may be partly or perhaps wholly explained by the fact that Mrs. Niels-Christensen was struck down early on in Mary's sojourn with them by some form of growing paralysis. She was increasingly confined to a wheelchair, and our Mary was assigned to tend to her as well as to young Laura. She records how Mrs Niels- Christensen was steadily growing ever more irritable both with her husband and Mary, and possibly that shared burden was drawing Anders and Mary's closer as they both tried to deal with the invalid's constant demands. Whatever the reason, increasingly Mary writes about her Boss in tender and eventually loving terms – of times when they managed to be alone, of the photo of himself he has given her in a gold locket, of other gifts he gave her on her birthday – and oddly, Robbie, there

---

242 ***Got roun a brave few corners*** – *visited a lot of places*
243 ***Kitter-handed an' Skelly-eyed*** – *awkward & cross-eyed*

are apparently no feelings of guilt at that stage on her part such as you might expect of a staid Victorian woman of that time. Given the worldly-wise woman Mary later became, here we seem to be witnessing, quite literally, an 'innocent abroad.'"

"But I suppose it cudn't go on an' eventually guilt got the better aff hir," Robbie said, "so that's what brung hir home tay Ballybracken. I suppose they wur al that religious there was no chance aff a divorce even if that wuz iver on the cards." He thought for a moment and continued, "so is that the scandal? It's not much aff a wan."

"No!" Jim exclaimed. "Here's your scandal... or possibly one anyway. Get ready to do some sums. The family are back in the States from their tour of the Nile and the Holy Land in early April 1900 and shortly after, Mary's diary, so balanced and observant until this time, suddenly goes into what I can only call over-drive. She is obviously in a panic about something to the extent that even her beautiful copper-plate handwriting changes to almost scribbles. If this means what I think it means, the mystery must be why she was committing it all to paper. She must have found some sort of relief in writing about it - even if it must have been decidedly dangerous at the time if it ever came to light. Listen to this entry....

'... I have been so foolish. This is God's punishment. The disgrace I have brought on myself and my family... What will my poor mother think of me? I must leave now before things get worse... but I can't leave him. I love him dearly and he says he loves me... He says he will care for us' – notice 'us,' Robbie – 'but it's impossible... I must get away... back to Ireland... no, not to Ireland... to England where nobody will know me for they will not want me at home... he says he will get me a home here... and look after things... he says he can't live without me being close to him... Oh God in Heaven help me... '

... and on it goes. She comes across in those pages as a woman beside herself with anxiety and, for the first time that I can detect, actual guilt. So, here it is! As far as I can judge, she has become pregnant, and the father of her child is Mr Anders Niels-Christensen."

"But what's she panickin about?" Robbie demands. "Sure the wain's father is this millionaire an', from what yeh'v discovered, he's mad keen on hir so he's offerin tay set hir up in a house an' keeps hir as hez fancy woman. Where's the problem?"

"Think about it, Robbie. There are problems galore not the least of which is the strong religious belief they both had. Mary leaves here a strait-laced

Protestant. From earlier entries, it is clear that Anders and his whole family are devout Lutheran and, although it appears he is prepared to do the decent thing by Mary, how long will it be before his conscience gets the better of him and she and the child just become an embarrassing burden, not to speak of what will happen if, or rather when, his wife and children find out, as they could scarcely fail to do. No! Anders' solution, though honourable, is built on the shifting sands of mutual guilt and fraught of course too with the danger of social scandal, which is equally real. Mary knows this even if Anders is trying to pretend otherwise."

"So are yeh tellin me that she comes home an' coaxes Hugh McKendry tay marry hir, pregnant an al? Shot-gun weddin, ony it wuzn't Hugh that fired the gun."

"I told you," Jim said, "we have sums to do."

'Scheming Bitch' / Shrewd Survivor?

"Evidently our Mary steadied up and decided on a plan. Remember, this is a clever woman now driven by pressing circumstances to quickly become a calculating one in every sense of the word. So, she leaves Long Island bound for Ireland within two weeks of the family's arriving back from their travels in the Near East. I can only assume she must have concocted some story about being urgently needed back home but, even so, her abrupt departure must have surprised the family, though not her lover who knew the reason all too well. Whatever his reaction, he certainly sent her home in fine style. Either from love or desperation, we will never know, he gives her £5000 – that's over half a million today – a set of Tiffany's solid silver cutlery and paid for her to travel first class on the 'Majestic.' Home safe, sound - and just in the nick of time if you get my meaning - within a month, she is married to Hugh McKendry because, as she puts it delicately – or should that be 'disingenuously?' - in the diary…

I want to honour the understanding I had with him before I left for America.'

"Hum," Robbie snorted. "What did ye'r mother kal hir, a schemin determined bitch, wuzn't it? Maybe she wuzn't so far wrong."

"But let's not be too hard on her." Jim said. "Isn't self-delusion a very powerful stratagem all of us use from time to time to get by, and here is a woman trying to make the best of a tricky situation, turning her back on the past however difficult that is… for, if we can believe her, she was deeply in love with the man she has left behind and whose child she is carrying, and who she will never see again. Calculating certainly, but I see her as a shrewd survivor who had every reason to be calculating. After reading all this, the woman she most reminds me of, even if she is only a fictional heroine of mine, is Thackeray's 'Becky Sharp', both of them great survivors."

"If she's tay trick owl Huey inta believin the wain's hez, she'd better not bay turnin her back on him when she gets him inta bed," Robbie chuckled.

Jim couldn't avoid a brief smirk at this crude glimpse of first-night married bliss but he hastened on to say, "Now let's see if our Danny here is any good at sums? How many months are there from April to October, Danny?"

Trading Arithmetic for Jelly Babies

Danny pushed the pup aside, said 'Eeeeee-Aaaaaa' a couple of times which, we recall, he always did when asked his opinion since he considered it added gravity to his answer, and then said, "I can always do sums better if I'm eating something," whereupon Jim hastened to get 'our mathematician,' as he put it, a handful of jelly babies and a packet of 'Spangles'. That trade-off did the trick and cranked our little hero's brain into action. "I think it's seven," he replied.

"Yes indeed, Danny's right," Jim continued. "Our George was born a little over seven months later with no questions asked as far as I know. Why should there be? Why would any eyebrows be raised? A respectable girl arrives home having made good in America. She was getting on in life so if she wants a family, delay in marrying is not an option. Anyway, Hugh McKendry has waited for her all those years so why delay? Their first child is born a bit early – but nothing out of the ordinary that would have Ballybracken tongues wagging... and it soon gets around that she has arrived home with considerable 'savings' though I don't think the extent of her wealth was ever fully known around here. And as we know, great wealth has been the great balm down the ages. It helps staves off any awkward questions, even if it had ever occurred to anyone to ask any."

"But what about owl boy McKendry? Did he not smell a rat? Or did he just congratulate himself on being quick on the draw? Lake, God knows he'd waited long enough – an' then niver doubted that George wuz hez when he arrived a bit early?"

"You have such a skill at getting down to basics – or even lower, Robbie," Jim laughed, "but I think you're right. I doubt if it ever crossed Hugh's mind. Why should he question his good fortune? He could survey the broad acres of the Ballybracken estate bought with Mary's American money, he had a son and heir, and then their bountiful life afterwards. It was success all the way for Hugh, and now for son George. Mary's judicious dash home served all concerned very well. Her diary entries end when she gets married. Well, compared with seeing and describing the wonders she witnessed in the Americas, Europe, Egypt, the Holy Land and much besides, Ballybracken just couldn't compete. But do you know what else I found here in the trunk? An invitation for Mary and Hugh dated 1902 to attend the marriage of Miss Laura Niels-Christensen at the Hamptons, Long Island to, you've guessed it, yet another millionaire. Here's the invitation," and Jim handed an elegant card to Robbie that read…

'Mr & Mrs. Anders Niels-Christensen request the honour of Mr and Mrs. H McKendry's presence at the marriage of their daughter Astrid Laura to Mr Werner Charles Olson on the afternoon of Wednesday the Sixteenth of September at half after twelve o'clock at Saint John's Church, Southampton, Long Island.'

"I suppose that just goes to show how much the family thought of our Mary, but also how little they apparently ever knew of the reason for her abrupt departure from their service. The early diary entries clearly show that the Mary and Laura relationship quickly became much friendlier than you would expect between a rich young woman and her lady's maid. The invitation was a great compliment though I wonder what Laura's father thought about it? Was Anders hoping Mary would come just to see her again or was he hoping and praying that she wouldn't come? I doubt if it took long for Mary to refuse. It goes without saying that she and Hugh didn't attend the wedding, but I wonder if the invitation didn't cause her just a twinge of sorrow for what might-have-been, and the rich elegant world she had experienced, and had been forced to abandon so abruptly?"

The Whirligig of Time & Fate

"It sure is a story an' a half," Robbie said, "an' I can see why yeh need tay sensor it. Wudn't Ballybracken revel in that bit aff news."

"… My mother most of all," said Jim, "for I have since discovered what she meant when she told me that Eliza Mary had done wrong by my grandmother. It seems Hugh McKendry had got tired waiting for Mary to return, with no guarantee that she ever would, so he was on the brink of marrying my grandmother when Mary reappeared out of the blue, demanded Hugh honour their earlier 'understanding,' and snapped him up. My grandmother was broken-hearted so it's little wonder my mother called Mary a scheming bitch who had 'bought' Hugh and then, according to her, had made his life a torture when he could have had the genuine love of a good woman, my granny. What I think I have discovered about Mary's reasons for returning abruptly to Ballybracken would give my mother the great satisfaction of spreading the news all around the townland, but it's a pleasure I will deny her. Of course, I can't be absolutely sure I'm right. I am still left with two unanswered questions even if I may have unravelled the mystery as to why she came back home. I am still mystified as to how a relatively uneducated Irish 'Biddy' - as humble Irish maids-of-all-work were called in the 'Roaring 90s' - got employed by such a wealthy family in the relatively prominent position as a lady's maid, and the second mystery is why did the old lady want someone outside the family to peruse her diaries and papers knowing that this indelicate part of her story might come to light? Or did she think I would be too stupid to appreciate the full portent of what I was reading or too dim-witted to do the sum that Danny there has solved for us this evening? Or did she no longer care so long as her wonderful experiences travelling the world in such state were catalogued and recorded. Which begs another question. Surely George McKendry can't know, can he, that he is half American with a half-brother and sister possibly still living in the millionaire paradise that is the Long Island Hamptons?"

"She seems tay hiv been gettin a lot aff her chest before she died for she towel Rosie stuff too that you'd think she wud hiv wanted tay keep tay hersel. But, about George, maybe I cud help yeh way that wan," Robbie said, for there's a wee clue staring yeh in the face that yeh'v missed. Tell me, what is George McKendry's other Christian name?"

"Isn't he George Andrew McKendry?"

"Now that's where ye'r wrong, smart man. When he signed my B-Special joinin papers, he signed his name in full an' it's not 'Andrew', it's 'Anders' fir I thought he had made a mistake and drew his attention tay it but he said it really wuz 'Anders.' He put it aff as a joke sayin it had been a mistake the doctor had made on hez birth certificate. But now we know divil the mistake it wuz. The owl girl called him after hez real Da. Day yeh think I shud put it tay the test nixt time I'm out on patrol way him? I'll say 'Howdy, partner. Hive yeh heard from ye'r millionaire Yankee family lately?"

"Thanks for that kind offer, Robbie, helpful as ever," Jim said sarcastically, "but I think not. I suppose it could be argued that Mary gave the baby that name out of respect and gratitude for her former Boss, but no... with all the other evidence that has stacked up from the diaries, I think we can say that

George A McKendry is really George Anders Niels-Christensen."

Robbie continued thoughtfully, "So many bloody quirks aff fate, when you think about it. George wudn't be here if she hadn't come back, you are only here because she did come back an' stole Hugh from ye'r granny, an' sure I ony survived the battlefield by pure chance."

"Your right, Robbie. The strange working of the wheel of fortune and whirligig of time and fate. We surely are only the stuff of dreams as the great man said."

"So given what you know, what's your next move?" Robbie asked.

"I'll write it up now and then return all the papers to them. It sure has been a wonderful exercise for me in so many ways, Robbie, causing me to resurrect some history skills I thought had gone. I have glimpsed the life led by the fabulously rich in the 'Roaring 90s', the luxury of first class travel, and the truly amazing experiences of an Irish girl of humble origins but great intelligence and determination who simply 'struck it rich' though at a high price. For since all good histories must end in love or tragedy, this love story has more than a tinge of tragedy. I might just drop a few hints towards the end of my account about that side of things, leaving others to draw what conclusions they like. But what am I saying! Now that the old lady is dead, I don't suppose anyone in Ballybracken House will ever read my account of her amazing story."

And history does not record if anyone ever did.

Episode 27

The Football Match

Danny had consulted Robbie about the best name for their football team since he read the football paper every Saturday night and knew about such things. Robbie said he should call it the 'Ballybracken Soviet Gunners Team' which seemed good especially the 'gunners' bit for that sounded suitably menacing.

The long-awaited football match between the Esker gang and the Dowdells's team was scheduled for the first dry Saturday afternoon so as soon as the weather showed signs of being clement the Esker Gang put in an appearance behind the Dowdells's cottage looking extremely hostile and clearly spoiling for a fight. Why the organization of the event had fallen to our very own Daniel Malachy nobody could quite fathom since, on past experience, his organizational powers were somewhat debatable, and indeed were immediately called in question over the venue he had chosen for the match. Dowdells's back garden was instantly declared unsuitable since it was covered in hummocks, nettles and thistles and anyway, being more or less triangular, was the wrong shape. So not a promising start, but these objections were as nothing compared with the national and political matters to be resolved before the game could get underway. For the Esker Gang, led by 'Evil' Mickey Gormley, declared that they were not going to play *'owl Englich football'* and would only go ahead if it was something that sounded like *'Gaylick.'* That was the only kind of football their fathers allowed them to play.

When pressed on the difference between Gaelic football – for such it was –and soccer football opinions were divided. Gabriel Donnelly thought you had to wear a green shirt with something written in Irish on it while Owen Grimley thought you had to play it with a wooden thing that looked like a 'bat' adding, with unpleasant relish, that the rules allowed you to hit people over the head with it. None of this was helping to get the game started and anyway the Protestant boys on the Dowdells's team then declared that they weren't going to play any 'owl Kathilic football' which they quickly construed the 'Gaylick' version to be.

If the game was to go ahead, Danny, who had decided he was going to be referee since he thought that would be less taxing, had now to find a way through this unexpected sectarian turmoil in his back garden. Leaving aside green jerseys and bat things, which they didn't have anyway, he latched on to something Evil Mickey had said which was that in 'Gaylick' you could handle the ball but not in *'owl sissy Englich soccer.'* Daniel Malachy could not see a problem with that so he declared that everybody could handle the ball as well as kick it *'but ony if they wanted to'* and everybody could either score goals or points, again *'if they wanted to'* since whether success should be measured in goals or points had emerged as another bone of contention. Amid much grumbling on all sides that, *'Them-ens always git their own way,'* coats, jerseys and other disposable items of clothing were set down to mark the goal posts. At Owen Grimley's insistence, there was also a cord running between two sticks across each goal mouth to satisfy the issue of scoring points that had weighed so heavily with the 'Gaylick' players. All that resolved by somewhat confusing compromises, the game, whatever it was by that stage, finally got underway.

Bobby captained the Dowdells's side with Danny running up and down the touchline - though seldom venturing unto the 'pitch' since proceedings there were developing a little on the rough side for his taste - in an illusion of keeping order. With less than twenty minutes gone, it had already become apparent that the Dowdells's goal keeper, Guldy McFall, was less than efficient since the score, even at that early stage, was three goals to nil against the Dowdells's, and more 'Gaylick' points than could readily be calculated give the inability of the players to do the sums.

Every goal scored by the Esker Gang was greeted with rowdy celebrations and cries of *'Up the Republic'*. Danny, who hadn't really grasped the fundamentals of impartial refereeing, was dismayed at the trouncing the Dowdells team was getting, and felt he had to do something to stem this tide of overwhelming defeat, but what? His options were limited. He could grab the ball and quietly try to burst it or he could say that he had forgotten to tell them that the game so far was only a "warm-up" - a term he had learned from Robbie – so they would have to start again... or he could try his hand in goals himself for surely he couldn't be any worse than Guldy …or, and here he cast a baleful look at the sky, maybe it would rain.

Two more goals had eluded Guldy when Dorry appeared in the garden, invaded the pitch, and insisted in a loud voice that she wanted to play too. This was greeted by much mirth from all sides, the unanimous consensus being that *'owl sissy girls cudn't play football'* though the Esker Gang did concede that she couldn't do any worse than the Protestant boys. However, and in an uncharacteristic show of unanimity, all agreed that the very idea of a girl playing was out of the question.

At this, Dorry, shouting that they were, *'al a crowd aff stupid skitters,'* grabbed the ball, and raced into the house with it. Much as Daniel Malachy had longed for something to occur that would bring an end to the Dowdells team's humiliation, this was not that 'something,' for allowing a girl to get the better of them was blow heaped on blow. That ball must be retrieved, and play resumed.

Dorry had barricaded herself in the lower bedroom and was making unpleasant faces when Danny and Bobby appeared at the window. A bargain would have to be struck. "Would she come out and give them the ball back if they promised not to stick plasticine in her hair ever again, stop pulling her plaits, not draw moustaches on her doll?"

"No"… "if Danny let her cog[244] his homework?"

"No"… "if they gave her back her store of treasured 'teesy'[245] paper recently hidden?

"No"… "if Bobby gave her one of his bullets?"

"Definitely Not!"… She would only give them back the ball if she was allowed to play.

There was nothing else for it but to agree and tell the others who were now standing around sniggering and sneering at the Dowdells boys' discomfort.

So she could play but only if she went into goals where she would be as little noticed as possible. Reluctantly, and with much unpleasantness, Dorry agreed, restored the ball and took up her position in the goal mouth. She did not get off to a very promising start for she fell face down over the stretched cord and cut her lip on a stone. This was greeted with more hilarity, the general view being that it served her right *'fir stickin hir neb[246] in tay the match.'*

Play now resumed, and Evil Mickey, a smirk on his face, took a long shot at the Dowdells's goal knowing that he was now more than ever leading his team in a total rout of the opposition. But Dorry saved the goal! Clearly a fluke! Now it was Patsy McFadden's turn. A hefty shot up close to the goal mouth. Again, Dorry saved it! And that was not all. Guldy McFall, now in mid-field, had discovered his national health glasses in his coat that had been serving as a

---

244   **Cog** – *copy*
245   **'Teesy' paper** – *sweet wrappings and other coloured paper collected and valued by some children in the 1950s*
246   **Neb** – *nose*

goal post and, since he could now see, was soon turning the tide dramatically in favour of his team, scoring goal after goal helped by Marshall Todd and Dezy Mulgrew both of whose will to win had recovered due to this unexpected turn of events.

Danny could only watch in amazement at his sister's sporting prowess and, since nothing succeeds like success, Bobby now managed to score two goals. The mounting score against his team was the bitter end for Evil Mickey. He kicked Marshall Todd viciously on the ankles. Marshall, who was a silent burly boy, punched Mickey in the face. Mickey appealed to Daniel Malachy who said Marshall was quite right for Mickey was *'off side'*. He didn't know what that meant but it added an air of authority to his refereeing which so far had been somewhat lacking. He followed up his ruling by declaring '*... an' yeh keeked*[247] *the ball too high*' which he thought would clinch the matter. It didn't. Instead Mickey punched him on the nose, and it started to bleed. It was when he proceeded to punch Danny in the eye that Bobby decided to take a hand.

Now, sad to say, it was not unusual for Bobby himself to punch Danny, indeed it was something of a regular occurrence, but to see his big brother getting punched by Evil Mickey was a different matter entirely, blood being thicker than water. While Danny was nursing his steadily swelling eye and wiping up the blood from his nose on his pullover, Bobby was leading the fray on the Esker Gang assisted by his team and by Dorry, fresh out of goals and busy pulling Gabriel Donnelly's hair.

Guldy McFall had lost his glasses again in the melee and, to compensate, had somehow got hold of a large stick and was laying about him though in a totally unfocused manner. This caused almost as many casualties on his own side as on the opposition, one of his swipes hitting Bobby's legs as one of his unintended victims. It was only when Rosie, alerted by the commotion in her garden, appeared round the gable end of the cottage with a yard brush in her hand that the Esker Gang decided that discretion was called for and promptly fled.

There was only time for a brief moment of triumphalism and celebration on the part of the Dowdells team before Rosie was driving Danny and Bobby before her swinging the brush from side to side the better to lay into their backsides.

Still, it had been worth it.

---

247 **Keeked** – kicked

Part II

Cupid Fires His Arrows

Episode 28

Love and Betrayal

Expert Advice on Romance

Jim McKnight was deeply in love but, like most shy young men at that time, couldn't for the life of him think what to do about it. He needed to talk. So on one of their Sunday walks, he confided his plight to Robbie.

"When I see her, she knocks me sideways. I feel the hairs tingle on the back of my neck," he said. "When she comes into the shop, I can't hear a word she says. I fumble over her order and I'm totally tongue tied. I tell you, Robbie, it's crippling me. I've never felt like this before about any girl. There she was in church this morning dressed to kill. I couldn't keep my eyes off her."

"Away ar' that[248], Why don't yeh jist put spake on hir an' bay done[249]," Robbie said tactlessly. Then seeing his friend was deadly serious and not in the mood for banter, he continued, "But I see ye'r in a bad way. Well, I'll give yeh that she's surely a fine lukin woman, an' I needn't remind yeh that *'feint heart niver won fair lady'* so you'd better close on hir[250] and see how yeh get on."

Danny was toddling along behind the two men with his hands clasped behind his back just like them for that seemed to be what big men did when they were talking over serious matters, and were talking about "it" but the conversation was bringing him no closer to understanding what "it" really was. He now understood that girls were involved, and it must be something to do with kissing and cuddling but if that was all it was, why would you be bothered with it? There must surely be something more to it. They were approaching the 'Meeting of the Waters' and the evening light had transformed the rivers into ribbons of sparkling silver.

"No, I can't approach her," Jim said bitterly "She is Miss Caroline Roxborough of Grovehill Manor, for God's sake, daughter of Sir Thomas, Knight of the Realm, Colonel of the Regiment and so on and so on. I don't think she will have her eyes set on marrying a country grocer."

---

248 ***Away or that!*** – *you don't say!*
249 ***Put spake on hir an' bay done*** – *talk to her and get on with it*
250 ***Close on hir*** – *approach her*

The two men sat down on the bank overlooking the Meetings, Danny moving in to sit between them. The smoke from Jim's 'Senior Service' wafted over him keeping off the midges. He was happy, and started to suck his thumb.

"You mean yeh want tay marry her?" Robbie narrowed his eyes, a smile playing round his lips' "an' here wuz me thinkin you jist wanted a hot date. Now I'm beginning tay twig[251] that yeh are deadly serious Well, if that's the way yeh feel, ye'd better summon up al ye'r pluck an' put a set on hir[252] lake I said. Sure ye'r intentions are honourable an', at worst, she can ony set the dogs on yeh, an' here's a man speakin from experience. An' sure if it dizn't work out, cut ye'r stick[253] an' move on."

"Marry her? Well… yes… of course I do… eventually. Ach no… I'm just being stupid. I don't know what I think or want, and whatever it is, I know I'm not within a bagle's gowl[254] of getting it so where's the point?" Jim looked away to hide the feeling of vulnerability having bared his soul to a man so much more experienced in the ways of the world. He went to rise. "Forget I mentioned it," he said. "It's crazy stuff. I shouldn't have… I mean I should have more sense. My mother keeps egging me on to marry uncle Bertie's Janie."

Robbie caught him by the arm to stop him rising.

"Well, Janie Stewart is ye'r cousin an' a good steady girl. But naw, it has tay bay said, the poor girl is no great beauty. Take my word fir it, yeh won't be content until yeh square up tay[255] hir ladyship an' see what she says. I main ye'r not gonna ask hir tay marry yeh first go aff. Ask hir tay the picturs[256] or somethin. What about tay a dance in that Floral Hall place in Belfast? I hear Dave Glover an' hez band put on a great show there… anyway, a pictur house or a dance hall or somethin at that Festival aff Britain thing goin on in Belfast… what I'm sayin is some-place well away from here fir if yez are seen thegither the Ballybracken folk's tongues won't stap waggin from there on, an' lukin at you dead sleekit[257] across the counter in the shap. I'm sure yeh don't want that."

"But how do I know she likes dancing?" Jim was first seized by Robbie's suggestion, and then almost immediately overwhelmed by difficulties and

---

251 **Twig** – *to understand… to get the point*
252 **Put a set on hir** – *start pursuing her*
253 **Cut ye'r stick** – *leave abruptly… make yourself scarce… get off-side*
254 **Not within a bagle's gowl** – *nowhere near*
255 **Square up to** – *summon-up courage and ask her*
256 **Picturs** – *cinema*
257 **Dead sleekit** – *slyly and knowingly*

doubts.

"Well, true, I've niver herd aff hir attendin any of the dances roun here in Ballybracken," Robbie grinned mischievously.

"No. I don't think the Ballybracken dances would be up her street. They might be a little too, shall we say, 'rustic.'"

But Jim's mind was already racing ahead. "Maybe I could get a couple of tickets for a show in Belfast or Dublin. I could say I'd got them from a friend who couldn't use them for some reason, and would she like to go? A play or the opera or the ballet? Yes… yes… it might work. Robbie, you have missed your calling, you should be a match-maker."

"Ach, sure I'm as wise as owl Solomon hezself, but don't git too kerried away too soon, Jim, owl son. Ye'r ony askin the woman fir a date. Don't rush ye'r fences. Take it canny[258] an' see how it goes."

They got up to go, Robbie lifting Danny by his arms. "What day you say, little comrade? Will yeh sing at Jim's weddin, an' maybe play the piana at his big fancy ball in the evenin, fir he'll pay yeh well, yeh know, he'll be that happy."

"When is it?" Danny asked, "for I might be busy that day," and the men chuckled swinging Danny by his arms between them.

Danny would indeed sing at Jim's wedding, but it wasn't quite the wedding either man had in mind that sultry summer afternoon as they made their way back from the enchanted 'Meeting of the Waters' up past the 'Ladies' Bower'.

"Not Belfast… Dublin it has to be," Jim was musing over his dating plans. "If I could only get two tickets for something she would like in Dublin. That would be classy and set the right tone," he thought.

He scanned the 'Irish Times', not a paper widely read in Ballybracken, but he had delayed the delivery of Father O'Kelly's copies for the last couple of days for a thorough perusal of what was on offer. Suddenly there it was! In the National Concert Hall! The Radio Eireann Orchestra performing Beethoven's 'Fifth', the symphony of 'Fate' … of triumph over adversity! What could be better or indeed more appropriate? Like most young men who believe themselves to be in love, Jim could already imagine himself settled down with the beloved at his side for the rest of their days floating on a cloud of music and song. He applied for two of the most expensive tickets which duly arrived in a large envelope with

---

258 **Take it canny** – *take it slowly… don't rush your fences*

Eire stamps that did not escape his mother's notice.

"It's from Trinity. I asked a friend some time ago to send me a copy of a history lecture on something that interests me," he lied to Effie, and threw the package with affected casualness behind the wireless. When the coast was clear, he retrieved and opened it. All was well. The two tickets for the required date were enclosed. Now all that remained was to ask the lady to accompany him.

The rest of his plan did not go so smoothly. Murphy's Law dictated that the next time Caroline came into the shop it was crowded with Ballybracken folk intent on lingering so as not to miss any gossip. But then his chance came; now all that was needed was courage.

"… and my car need's a fill of petrol, Jim," Caroline was saying. "I've noticed my father has let it get very low."

He followed her out of the shop and down to the petrol pump. It was now or never! She stood looking back at the shop where the Dowdells children were climbing on to its high windowsills and then jumping off amid screams of terror and delight. Rosie emerged from time to time to stop them but to no avail.

"Is that the dear little boy who is so musical?" Caroline said, casting her beautiful deep blue eyes on Jim and reducing him to jelly.

"Yes… Danny… Danny… Dowdells," he spluttered "He's very musical… and… yes… a talented singer."

But this was his chance, the opening he needed handed to him on a plate.

"Caroline," he said, steeling himself both to ask and to be rejected.

"Yes Jim," she was looking at him again, and boy was she beautiful!

"Caroline, a friend of mine… at Trinity… He's in third year… studying history… like I was at Queen's… only he's…"

She was looking at him somewhat bemused for he was undoubtedly wandering.

"Do I know him?" She asked, trying to make sense of Jim's garbled little speech.

He knew he had failed. He turned away from her to replace the petrol hose in the pump.

"I… don't think so… only he was planning to go to the Beethoven concert in the National Concert Hall next week… well, week after next really… and he can't go now… so…," he turned round to face her, "only he has sent me the two tickets… and I was wondering if you would like to go… if you're free that is… and if… you like Beethoven… and that kind of music… if not, I suppose Helen and I… "

She was smiling. "I'd love to go with you," she said calmly. "Can you remember the date?"

He staggered back against the car but managed to say "the 23rd… I think… I'd need to check… but I think it is the 23rd.

"Oh, I'm sure that will be fine," she said. "Yes, it would be lovely to get down to Dublin. Will you phone and tell me the arrangements? Now, I must go. Mark all the groceries I've got, and the petrol, up in our book. I'll remind daddy to pay you at the end of the month."

And she was off, her little Pekinese dog, wakened from his slumbers on the Wolsey's back seat, barking at Jim from the rear window. And as for Jim, he was in a daze. It had worked! It had been easy…well, not exactly easy but anyway, easy or otherwise, it had worked. For some reason his first thought was to tell Robbie - that man of the world, so experienced and so successful with women - that he had done it. It was with joy in his heart and lightness of step that he returned to the shop. Nobody noticed the change in him for they were relishing the joy that discussing bad news brings when we hear of other folk's misfortunes. Today it was the shocking if delicious news that a local farmer had been declared bankrupt in Stubbs Gazette; surely a moment to be savoured!

"That's wonderful," Caroline was saying on the phone. "We really should make a day of it and leave early. And it will be too late to come back home after the concert. I hope you don't mind, Jim, but I have phoned Edward McKendry to tell him we are coming down. He says he might join us at the concert if he can still get a ticket. That would be super, don't you think? And he suggests we should stay overnight in, say, the 'Gresham' or the 'Shelbourne.' I think that's a splendid idea too, don't you? He has promised to treat us to lunch in Trinity or perhaps at his Club in Kildare Street. He says it oozes history, so you would like it. What do you think?"

Jim wanted to think whatever Caroline wanted him to think so two days in Dublin it would be.

Great Expectations

"Caroline Roxborough! You and Miss Caroline going to Dublin. Did you hear that, Helen? Your brother is mixing with the gentry. Rosie, can you believe it?"

Effie McKnight was overcome with a toxic mixture of pride and ambition worthy of Mrs. Bennett in Miss Austin's imagining. Her mind was already racing ahead to a grand wedding, to the clothes she and Helen must get – *'New Look'* dresses ... *maybe even Mink coats...* nothing but the best would suffice. Just think of the Ballybracken noses it would put out of joint. Oh, Happy Day! And then there was the land… the 'Grovehill Manor Estate' to call it by its proper name... the McKnights marrying into the gentry... if all went well, her family would be made-up[259], and Effie resolved that it most certainly wouldn't be her fault if it all didn't go according to plan... her plan of course!

"Well, what do you think, Helen? Isn't it wonderful?"

"I think," Helen said coldly, "that it would be better if Sir Thomas would pay his bills more promptly. He is over six months behind in the shop."

"... and I think you are just jealous of your brother's success, my girl, and his prospects. You should be ashamed, shouldn't she, Rosie?"

But Rosie continued filling the Esse cooker with coal and said nothing. In the light of what she knew - as a servant girl warned by Effie to keep her mouth shut – about the cruel treatment of Helen, when she had fallen in love with a man from the 'wrong side', there was nothing to be said.

"Such a beautiful morning for the drive." Caroline was sitting beside Jim in his Jowett Javelin speeding down towards the border with the Republic.

When she had appeared at the front door of Grovehill Manor earlier that morning Jim thought he had never seen a more beautiful woman, not even in glossy magazines or on the cinema screen.

"So, tell me about this friend of yours who sent you the tickets. What happened to prevent him going tonight?"

It was time to come clean. Jim had not the makings of a liar, so he told her the truth.

"I got the tickets myself in the hope you would agree to go with me but sure I couldn't tell you that. You would have thought me so presumptuous."

---

259 **Made-up** – *going up in the world*

"Oh, you fibber," she exclaimed. "But it was a wonderful idea. Great to get away from Ballybracken for a couple of days. I have been telling fibs too. I told Papa I would be staying with an old school friend in Dublin. He might have felt the need to come the heavy-handed father if he knew I was staying in a hotel with a man… not that I think your intentions are anything other than honourable, James McKnight, or that you have wicked designs on me, but better not to raise papa's blood pressure."

She gave Jim a quizzical look that was not lost on him, and he constantly drew his eyes back to look at her when they should have been on the road.

"It's wonderful too that Edward can take time off to see us. I haven't really seen him since that strange episode with the little Dowdells children and the discovery of the 'Holy Grail'. I thought it wonderful the way he played along with that. Such a brick! And so clever… I have, of course, spoken to him on the telephone since but it will be lovely to see him again."

This admiration for another man, even so innocently expressed, was not really what Jim wanted to hear.

"Well, he's not bad… for a psychiatrist," he said smiling. "Guys at university had the theory that psychiatrists and psychologists were all mad, and only studied their subjects to find out what was wrong with themselves… but I'm sure that is unkind. Yes, Edward is a nice guy in no mistake."

If she had noticed that she had made him a little jealous, she did not show it. She was raking around in her handbag to find her cigarettes. She lit one for Jim and placed it on his lips. Her fingers brushed against his cheeks and he could smell her perfume. He was intoxicated. He wanted to stop there and then and take her in his arms… but he drove on. They crossed the border at Aughnacloy and then drove on down through Monaghan. She talked about her horses, her dogs, her cranky relatives in England and much besides but it didn't matter what she talked about, Jim was in heaven. He exclaimed, he laughed, he sighed, he grinned, he agreed, he reflected whenever and wherever that seemed appropriate, and there could not have been a happier man that day on the road to Dublin. Indeed, it was to be the happiest day of his young life though he didn't know it!

"Wasn't that superb!" Edward was holding open the taxi door outside the Concert Hall as Caroline and Jim piled in to escape a sudden downpour.

"You poor darling, you are soaked," Caroline exclaimed as Edward clambered in beside her. "You must come back to the hotel with us for a nightcap to help warm you up, mustn't he Jim?"

"Of course," Jim said good naturedly. He had been looking forward to getting rid of Edward and having Caroline all to himself, but he mustn't be churlish. Edward had treated them to a generous early dinner in his club, and undoubtedly was good company. Maybe he wouldn't stay long.

The bar of the 'Gresham' was crowded when they finally arrived.

"Would you be a darling, Jim, and get us the drinks," Caroline said. "We will never catch the waiter's eye in this throng… and, oh bliss… those people by the fireplace are leaving so Edward and I will dash across and grab their seats."

Jim pushed his way to the bar and ordered their drinks. While the barman was concocting Caroline's cocktail with an air of considerable drama and then, with much the same contrived ceremony, was pouring Edward and his pints of Guinness, Jim glanced across at Caroline and Edward. What he saw worried him. It was alarmingly obvious to him at that moment that both Caroline and Edward, as they chatted and laughed together in these elegant surroundings, fitted into this Dublin scene so naturally… it was just where they both belonged… in sophisticated society, or what passed for it in Dublin… with the 'in-set'… Caroline was top drawer… upper crust... that indefinable something called 'gentry'… and had the confidence and self-assurance that went with that even if her family was in genteel decay… almost broke by all accounts… but she was at that moment, in her elegant evening dress, coiffured hair and cigarette holder so beautiful, so desirable… and oh how Jim desired her.

"Great," said Edward. "We thought you had got lost. Caroline and I were just catching up on the goings-on at home. But enough of this idle gossip, however engrossing. The band has struck up again," he continued. "Would you care to dance, Mademoiselle?" He stood up and reached out his hand to Caroline.

"Oh, the foxtrot, how thrilling," Caroline beamed up at him. "You don't mind, darling, do you?" she pouted to Jim.

"Of course he doesn't," Edward said smiling. "Sure he will have the last dance. That's the one that counts, isn't it Jim?" And they glided onto the dance floor leaving Jim consumed with a mixture of doubt, desire and jealousy in equal measure. He sipped his Guinness.

"Oh darling," Caroline said to Jim, the foxtrot and a waltz successfully danced, "would you mind terribly if I slipped off to bed? What with our early start this morning and now the dancing, I am quite worn out. It has been such a divine but such a long day."

And with that she lifted her silk shawl, blew them both a kiss and swept out.

"See you in the morning, Jim," she shouted over her shoulder.

"Well," Edward exclaimed, sitting down at the table bringing a half'un of whiskey for himself and Jim, "quite a woman. Who'd have thought that Ballybracken could produce such a gem. Have you been seeing much of her, Jim?"

Jim wanted so badly to say "yes," and that they were virtually engaged but couldn't bring himself to swing the lead knowing full well Edward would see through him. He simply said,

"She is a very beautiful girl and I hope to get to know her better. There are none like her in Ballybracken, as you say, or indeed in the whole of Ulster and well beyond." Jim knew that this guarded remark had emerged like a paragraph in a university essay.

"Now there's is a guy who's got it bad," laughed Edward, immediately seeing through Jim's reticence. "She certainly is a stunner in no mistake. And, no, I won't enquire into your sleeping arrangements tonight."

He looked at Jim quizzically, a smile playing round his lips.

"Oh... No... No," Jim felt himself blush, "nothing like that... it's a lonely bed for me, I'm afraid. And I think I'd better hit the hay[260] too. It a long drive back tomorrow."

Edward stretched out his hand. "It has been such an unexpected pleasure to see you both here in dear old dirty Dublin. I hope to see you again very soon either up there or down here."

The two men walked together to the foot of the stairs and said goodnight. On the half-landing Jim paused to look back at the foyer. Edward was still there talking on the telephone at the reception desk, the receiver propped awkwardly to the side of his handsome face, his broad shoulders hunched to support it. As Jim continued up the stairs, he had to admit it... yes... he was jealous of this elegant man who glided with such confidence whatever the company, and

---

260 **Hit the hay** – *go off to bed*

who had talked with such ease and so engagingly to Caroline all evening. As he reached his room, Jim couldn't help wondering why Edward had asked him those personal questions about his relationship with Caroline? But why bother about that now? Sure Edward had gone, and he would now have Caroline all to himself at last. Life couldn't get much better than this.

'He Who Hesitates…'

"That whiskey was one too many," Jim was lying on top of his bed staring at the ceiling. What was it his old man used to say… *'Beware the demon drink! Remember boy, when you have one, you have quenched your thirst. When you have two, you have had enough. But when you have three, you think you haven't half enough. That the demon drink for you.'* He smiled ruefully, tried to get up and then fell back on the bed.

His body might be prone, but his mind was racing: *'Oh Caroline!… Caroline! … maybe she's waitin for me? What if she is and I'm disappointing her? …. Maybe going to bed early was her way of getting rid of Edward so that I could be with her … and here I am acting the gallant gentleman… or the shy innocent ninny more like… and me dying to make love to her… oh, what must that be like?… on the other side of that wall… all I have ever wanted… and maybe I'm what she wants… but what if she doesn't want me… what if I go to her and she screams the house down?… accuses me of taking advantage… maybe even rape… I'd never live down the disgrace… I'd have ruined everything… but maybe… I could always say I was drunk… didn't know what I was doing… no! no!… put it out of your mind… go to sleep… yes, sure I couldn't perform anyway… serious brewer's droop… better get my clothes off… easy does it.'*

He threw his clothes on the floor and got under the sheets naked, his mind telling him this was right… *'she will respect you for it,'* his mind counselled… but his naked body was telling him a different story. *'Och, but Holy God in heaven, you so want her! 'You are on fire for her,'* it screamed. If only… if only he could get over to sleep… put it out of his mind… wake up in the morning refreshed, clean, decent… but his hopes and dreams are all there on the other side of the wall… *'never mind that, you need to calm down … do the right thing, the honourable thing … get over to sleep NOW,"* counselled his mind … *get out of bed and go to her'*, coaxed his body…

… and he got out of bed…

'What the hell are you doing?' demanded his mind … *'Atta boy,'* said his body …

shirt on… tuck it in… never know who you'll meet in the corridor… 'Oh God, don't you wish you could go through the wall?' moaned his body … *'Get back from the door, get those clothes off and get back into bed,'* wailed his mind… *'You will regret this… what are you doing out here in the corridor?'…* 'Ach, go on man', screamed his body… *'sure you are only going to tell her she is beautiful and you love her to madness… sit on the end of her bed… don't try anything on and just tell her you can't sleep you are so much in love with her… sure where is the harm in that… it's the truth isn't it? And maybe she'll let you have more… a nice cuddle and a kiss or two… and maybe'* … *'You are doing the wrong thing,'* croaked his mind… *'but think of the paradise behind that door',* cried his body… *'think of the humiliation if she rejects you',* countered his mind… *'but think of the bliss if she says 'yes,'* pleaded his body. *'Come on. Act the man! Get in there. Take your chance.'*

"OK, OK, OK," he steeled himself. He was sobering up now and that helped him to see thing straight. After all, he would only be paying her a compliment… and one she had a right to expect… even such a beautiful woman could feel spurned if a man didn't at least admit to the spell her beauty cast over him… even at half past two in the morning… he would say he couldn't sleep… needed to chat… . what harm in that?

Body and mind thus reconciled for the time being, he continued along the corridor until he saw his reflection in a mirror hanging in a shallow alcove. He realized how dishevelled he looked so he paused to tidy his hair. As he stepped out into the corridor again, Caroline's bedroom door opened.

"Oh God," he thought, "all this time she has been waiting for me to make a move and now she is coming to me."

As his mind raced at the thought, he didn't know whether to feel happy or humiliated that this beautiful woman had had to come to him and not, as she had the right to expect, for him to come to her.

But the figure emerging from the bedroom was not Caroline. Although he had his back turned towards Jim, he could see clearly enough that the bulky figure in the doorway was Edward. He was holding Caroline in his arms and they were locked in an intense embrace.

Shattered Dreams

"You are very quiet. Not your old self at all," Caroline cast Jim a sidelong glance as he accelerated much too fast through North Dublin's suburbs. There was no man on earth at that moment keener to get home, and to be alone. "Is something the matter, Jim? Not a word out of you over breakfast either. Didn't you sleep well?"

"I slept OK," he grunted and then, remembering his impeccable good manners, "How did you sleep?"

"Very well indeed," she replied. "Once I get over to sleep, the last trump wouldn't waken me," and she laughed. "But yes, I sometimes have difficulty getting to sleep on my first night in a strange bed."

Jim felt like saying that he could suggest other reasons at that moment why her night's sleep had been 'restless' but he didn't and kept his eyes firmly on the road.

Clearly neither she nor Edward had seen him in the corridor so locked were they in their farewell embrace. He had been spared that humiliation at least. He felt used, foolish, betrayed but he didn't want to add to his own hurt by referring to the cause. It was already firmly locked away in a sealed compartment in his soul adding to the other humiliation that was locked up there already. He was now only a shop-boy after all, in thrall to his mother and to Ballybracken. How could he compete with a distinguished handsome psychiatrist when it came to bedding a beautiful gentlewoman? He was bitter, so bitter in fact that he felt sure this humiliation could, if he let it, colour his whole life. He swore a great oath to himself there and then as he clutched the steering wheel, his knuckles white, that it would not happen again. He would lower his hopes and expectations, finally reconcile himself to his lot and the limited horizons of Ballybracken. It was painfully clear that Caroline had used him to get to Dublin to see Edward. He had been made a fool of, and he knew it. They drove on in silence. How different from Jim's blissful journey down to the Capital, and the promise he thought it held.

On the Rebound

"Yeh want may tay do what?" Robbie was looking at Jim with a look of total incredulity.

"Would you ever do me a favour, an' be my best man," Jim said. "I'm marrying

Janie Stewart, so will you stand by me?"

"Wee Janie? Hiv yeh gone a wee thought saft?[261]." For a moment Robbie was lost for words but managed to ask, "yeh tell may ye'r for marryin wee Janie? Sure I thought yeh wur heart-set on curtin an' marryin that grand lady down at the Manor. What happened between yez?"

"What happened! I'll tell you what happened. That bastard… that two-faced deceitful bastard, Edward McKendry," Jim's anger, never vented openly until now, flared up and he could hardly get the words out. "… both of them made a fool of me…" He stopped for breath… "Sorry, Robbie, but I'm so mad, I am fit to be tied[262] … "

"Come on in an' I'll treat yeh tay a bottle aff stout," Robbie took Jim by the arm and led him round the gable end of the cottage and into the kitchen where Rosie was busy milking the goat with one hand while fending off the goat's newly-born kid with the other.

"Och my God," Rosie exclaimed getting up hurriedly from her stool, "what sorta Curze Christians[263] will yeh think us, Jim, me milkin the goat in here?" She rushed on, "I used tay milk her in the lean-to till it fell down last winter under that big fall aff snow… I've been at himself there tay fix it up again but sure nothin iver get done in this house unless I do it mezself… An' then the day way them desperate showers goin roun… I thought I'd no sooner start milkin outside than it wud start tay teem[264] on me…" She tailed off to untether the goat from the bedstead.

"Don't let me disturb you, Rosie," Jim had recovered some of his composure, "please carry on. I'm glad you are here for I want to ask a favour from you too. I wanted to ask you if young Danny would sing at my wedding? I've already asked the big man here to be my best man."

"Robbie tay be ye'r best man an' our Danny tay sing… at ye'r weddin! When is it tay be? … who's ye'r bride? … I niver herd…" Rosie suddenly realized she still had the goat on its tether in her hand, and it had just succumbed to a call of nature on the kitchen floor.

It was all too much to cope with. She headed for the door, the goat and kid in tow, shooed them out into the yard and shut the half door firmly behind them. If she had heard correctly her man, Robbie, was going to be best man at Jim Mc

---

261 **A wee thought saft** – *have you gone a bit crazy*
262 **Fit to be tied** – *in such a rage*
263 **Curze Christians** – *rough and tumble people but good-hearted*
264 **Teem** – *a downpour of rain*

Knight's wedding, Danny was going to sing at it and so it must surely be the case that she would be there too, for her mind was racing ahead. Rosie Dowdells, a guest at these grand folk's weddin! A dream come true… the Dowdells were surely on the way up when they were getting to attend big Ballybracken weddings. She started to mop the floor with a smile of deep satisfaction on her face.

"Take a sate, man, an' steady ye'r head[265]." Robbie pulled out a chair for Jim from under the kitchen table and perched himself on a stool opposite his friend. "Wud yeh get us them bottles aff porter, Rosie, that I brought home the other night. Jim here cud bay doin way a wee jorum[266]."

Rosie pulled a brown paper bag from under the outshot bed and, taking two bottles from it, handed them to Robbie. He pushed the jagged bottle tops off them using a well-experienced thumb, handed one to Jim and then started to drink from the bottle when Rosie, mortified at this display of crude behaviour in the house of folk that were going up in the world, speedily found two tumblers for the men.

"Tay think…", she mused as she gave Jim's glass an extra wipe, "… there hasn't been a weddin in Ballybracken for a good long while and now there's tay bay three close thegither maybe. The poor Canon will bay fair taivered an' run aff hez feet[267]…" She stopped, realizing Jim and Robbie were lookin at her curiously.

"Three weddings! What three weddings?" Jim asked.

"Well there's your own, Jim, an' hiv yez not herd that Constable McCrum has finally got roun tay askin Maisie Trimmel tay marry him? … Though there is a lot of gossipin on the go about that, an' I don't want tay be a party tay[268] any bad talk aff that kin. There's them in this townlan that wud fin fault way Christ an' hez blessed Mother if they landed here."

Robbie and Jim exchanged puzzled glances.

"Aye right," Robbie said, "so you're gonna keep us guessin on what's got McCrum jizzed up an' inta the marryin stakes. So whose is the other weddin?"

"Well, I don't know if I'm supposed tay say or not but it is definite… Doctor Edward and Miss Caroline is getting married roun the same time as Maisie and the Constable… or so I've heerd anyway."

Jim put his half empty glass on the table, pursed his lips, and took on a look

---

265 **Take a sate & steady ye'r head** – *sit down and compose yourself*
266 **Jorum** – *a quantity of alcohol*
267 **Fair taivered an' run aff hez feet** – *kept so busy he will be worn out*
268 **I don't want tay bay a party tay** – *I don't want to be associated with*

that Robbie had never seen on his friend's handsome face before. It was the face of a man whose humiliation and dejection had just been copper-fastened. Finally he forced a wry smile.

"One thing's for certain with all this news, Rosie. Constable McCrum will never be short of a sponge cake or two for the rest of his days, for we all know Maisie is a dab hand at the sponges," and he forced himself to join in the chuckles.

"Jim…are yeh sure ye'r not just on the rebound?" Robbie knew his friend was hurting badly so had persuaded him to take a walk along the lower Ballybracken road in the direction of Croc-na-Shina thinking it might be easier for him to unburden himself that way rather than face to face.

"So, what if I am," Jim said defiantly, "Ballybracken is my fate, and I have to be reconciled to it."

Robbie pursued it no further and they walked on in silence. Then Jim said, "… and do you know the worst thing… what put the kibosh on it? It was obvious that they both just took me for a country ganch[269] who could be easily fooled. Och she was as polite as get out on the way home but divil a hair she cared… " and he looked away to hide his deep hurt.

Robbie said nothing but put his arm round him and then, as was his way, he said, "ach well, it cud hiv been worse. Given what the folk roun here say about hir owl man's money problems, at leasht[270], she didn't tap yeh for any cash. Sur yeh know me, Jim, I was always wan fir lukin on the bright side."

At this Jim managed a rueful smile.

But Robbie knew there wasn't any bright side for his able and sensitive friend. The Ballybracken's trap had indeed snapped tight, as it had on Robbie, and was crushing Jim's idealism, his hopes and his dreams.

---

269 **Ganch** – *fool*
270 **At leasht** -*at least*

Episode 29

Wedding Plans

Danny Turning Cartwheels

Daniel Malachy Dowdells had just heard the disturbing news from his ecstatic mother that he was to sing at Jim's forthcoming wedding. He had immediately set out, running his hardest, to catch up with the two men and was now toddling along behind them hoping for the opportunity, which would be impossible if his mother was around - for she seemed to have gone completely mad over the Dowdells' involvement in this wedding thing - to somehow persuade Robbie to persuade Jim that Danny singing was a really very bad idea that would only bring ruin on the wedding plans. Not that he really knew much about weddings except what he had gleaned from photographs of them in old copies of 'Picture Post,' but what he had seen had alarmed him greatly. Lots of grand people dressed in strange clothes drinking from funny glasses with a fairylike creature all in white holding a bunch of flowers in the middle of them smiling at everybody. Did Daniel Malachy want to be mixed up in all that? He did not if for no other reason that it would give the boys at school yet more ammunition against him, and they had only just stopped calling him 'Sissy Singer Danny' when he had revealed what he had been paid for singing and playing the piano at this and that small function in Ballybracken's various churches and halls.

The news that singing and playing was money-making had got him off the 'sissy' hook even if Tommy Morrison had upped the stakes in his protection racket claiming that the more Danny earned from singing and playing, the more 'protection' he needed. Such was the blackmailing pressure that Danny felt he had no option but to pay up but singing at a wedding beside a fairylike creature in white would surely reopen the whole 'sissy' issue. He must get out of it come what may.

"So," Robbie was saying, "you think they jist used yeh to take Caroline tay

Dublin so that she and Edward could have a night thegether?"

"That's about it," Jim mumbled. "Sure, haven't we just heard they are getting married. What more confirmation do we need? I suppose getting to sleep together was well-nigh impossible when they met up here so me getting the tickets for the concert and asking her to go was their opportunity. How would you feel if it was you that had been so used, so duped?"

"No man lakes tay be made a pishin-post aff[271] but, if I ken spake plainly tay yeh, are yeh wise to commit yourself to another woman, to Janie Stewart so soon? Don't be doin this jest tay get back at them for if that's ye'r raison for doin it, it's you that'll will suffer an' may rue the day[272], not them. Wud it not fit yeh better tay wait a while an' take a luk roun? I'm thinkin a good-lukin fella lake ye'rself wudn't hiv tay thole[273] too long till another chance comes along."

"What do you mean, suffer?" Jim demanded.

"I mean that yeh cud jest bay doin this tay save face. I won't go any closer tay it than that, Jim, for the last thing I want tay do is tay offend yeh. I wud jist ask yeh tay think what ye'r doin, an' why ye'r doin it?"

"I know what I'm doing," Jim retorted indignantly. "Sure I have known Janie all my life, and I asked her to stay behind a couple of times until the shop was clear and, that way, I have got to know her even better. She…," he hesitated and then continued forcefully, "… she is a fine Ballybracken girl, no airs and graces. Not like these so-called gentry who have used and abused this country, and are abusing it still, certainly here in the North. No, Robbie, I am doing the right thing. When the coast was clear for a few minutes in the shop last week, I asked Janie to marry me and she agreed."

'I'm sure she did,' Robbie thought. *'The same 'Plain Janie' must have thought Christmas had come early',* but he said nothing.

"So, are you gonna be my best man or not, and stand by me on my Big Day?"

"Of curze I will, an' am honoured tay bay asked," Robbie replied. "How did Big Bertie take it or maybe yez haven't towel him yet?"

"Of course he knows. Sure I had to ask his permission. I went straight up there after closing time that night and spoke to him. It has all been done correctly by the book."

---

271 **Pishin-post** – *humiliated… being made use of… abused*
272 **Rue the day** – *bitterly regret*
273 **Thole** – *endure… wait*

"An' what did he say?" Robbie asked, curious to know how the most thran[274] man in all Ballybracken had dealt with what must surely have come as a surprise, to say the least.

"Well, you know my Uncle Bertie," Jim said. "He quizzed me up, down, and in all directions, and took the opportunity to air some of those bigoted if contradictory views of his" and here Jim started to mimic Bertie: *'Now, yeh know she's ye'r cousin… so that could be a snag, may boyo. An' ye'r not in any aff the Loyal Orders?… or the B-men. Well, yell not marry hir till yeh convince me ye'r gonna join the Orange at leasht*[275]*, settle ye'r head, stan by the loyalist cause bay' stayin put here in Ballybracken. No takin our cutty an' runnin aff anyroad lake back tay Belfast or tay that Queen's College place. Fir yeh know I don't howl way education for it is the ruination aff the country… educatin up Protestants so yuz young wans leave niver tay return, an' the Catholics gittin educated too but yeh may bay sure they'll not lave an' soon there'll bay no livin way them when they wance get their head… fir wance they git the upper han they'll hiv us sunk in the Republic sure as shootin… sure Tyrone and Fermanagh an' even Darry City come as near as dammit to being in the Free State at the time aff partition… only some smart loyalist heads fiddled way the numbers… that an' the threat aff the gun kept them counties in Protestant Ulster an' the British Empire…'* and on and on he went," said Jim, affecting amusement as he recalled his future father-in-law's interrogation and home-spun rambling.

"I knew I had finally crossed the Ballybracken Rubicon never to return as I sat across from him that night, Robbie."

"What day yeh mean?" Robbie asked.

"I mean that it has been inevitable from the moment I decided, or rather when I let my mother decide for me, to abandon university that I could not escape becoming chained to Ballybracken's Protestant and Unionist anchor, fitted into the various loyalist straight-jackets, swept up into the irresistible political and religious current that engulfs us all, but now I'm reconciled to being as hidebound as everybody else here. You above anyone, Robbie, must appreciate what I mean, so I'm resorting to your 'strolling' and abandoning 'scrabbling.' I could kick myself for my arrogance in thinking my lot might or could be different. I now accept that I am a prisoner but increasingly a willing one for I have steadily come to understand the 'realpolitik' that lies behind the West-of-the-Bann Unionists' view of the world. I have not, of course, abandoned my earlier liberal principles lightly or even entirely, and it was a terrible moment

---

274 **Thran** – *awkward… stubborn… contrary*
275 **Leasht** – *least*

when I heard the final bolt in my cell door being rammed home by my aunt and future mother-in-law. Big Bertie asked if she had any questions for me? Do you know what she said? *'Day yeh love the Royal Family an' are yeh washed in the blood of the lamb?'* So now my fate is to join the Loyal Orders followed by the holy brigade and the B-Specials if you'll have me." Oh, and one other thing emerged; they don't want our wedding to be in church but at home in their kitchen with Quigley presiding for, as my aunt said, they don't want people 'gawkin' at them and, anyway, she doesn't think the Canon is 'saved.' Uncle Bertie was adamant on that too but I know fine well that is just to save money in his case. So no church wedding and no fancy clothes. Now, how am I gonna sell that to my mother?"

Robbie was distressed to see his friend so unhappy but was relieved of saying what he thought by finding Daniel Malachy now walking between him and Jim looking very anxious.

Our little hero had indeed finally caught up and, since the men had been silent for a few minutes, he decided it would be timely to ask to be excused from singing at the wedding. He led up to it by asking if a wedding took very long? Were they over in, say, five minutes or fifteen? Were they like breaktime at school or an hour like lunchtime? "… Cos if they go on too long," Danny continued, "people might get tired and want out… lake tay sneeze… or get their dinner… or that… so lake anythin that kept them back would make them cross… an' cud spoil the weddin… so it cud."

"What are yeh getting at, my scheming little comrade?" Robbie demanded.

"Lake singin extra stuff… lake if you wanted out tay sneeze… or go tay the lavatory or that… singing extra things wud bay bad, wudn't it? … lake it is for us in Sunday school… lake when in Sunday school a while ago, Guldy McFall wet the choir cushions an' the sate an' the flure because the Canon wudn't stap readin from the Bible in time… an' everybody thought it wuz wile[276] … except for the big boys who thought it wuz funny…"

Danny looked from one to the other trying to judge which of them was getting his message.

Robbie winked at Jim and said, "So, yeh want al the other hymns cancelled so that you are the ony wan singin on Jim's Big Day. That's fair enough, Jim, isn't

---

276 **Wile** – terrible

it? That wud bay a nice weddin present from Danny here. Aye, Big Bella and the choir can stay at home an' our Danny here will do al the singin that's required. What day yeh say?"

"That's just great," Jim said. "That'll put everybody there in great humour."

Danny was thunderstruck. This wedding thing had now gone from bad to worse. He felt like kicking Robbie's shins in his frustration, but he decided instead to go back on the offensive.

"But I might be sick," he bleated, "… with a sore stomach, an' then there wud be no singin at al if the choir wasn't there."

"So yeh think Jim an' Janie shud limit it to one extra hymn from you an' then, if you're not well on the day, people will harly notice… an' they can get out early… to sneeze an' scratch themselves an' what not tay their heart's content."

Danny was beaten and, to show his displeasure at his big hero, he fell away behind the two men and consoled himself by sucking his thumb.

"Come on up here, Danny," Jim shouted. "I want to discuss terms with you."

Danny didn't know what terms meant but he sidled up, still sucking his thumb and glaring at Robbie.

"Now," said Jim, "how are we ever going to pay you for singing, Danny, now that you are such a big name. And, as I've just told Robbie, you will be the only one singing for the wedding is not going to be in church but up in Janie's house?"

Our little hero promptly removed his thumb and said, "ten shillins wud bay good."

"Och now man dear," Robbie exclaimed, "an' there wuz me thinking yeh wur well on the way tay bein a good Communist, little comrade. What about *From each accordin tay his ability, tay each accordin tay his need.*'"

"You tell Robbie to take a running jump," Jim said. "Ask him when he last did anything for nothing? I think we could strike a bargain at a pound note and, if you sing really well, we'll make it two. What do you say?"

"I'll sing my very best fir you an' Janie," Danny said, swiftly changing his tune, "an' if Big Bella isn't comin I cud play the piano in Bertie's house… but that wud be more… maybe five pouns."

"I don't think Uncle Bertie ever got round to getting a piano so your singing will have to do and will be just great, I'm sure."

"He can play the church organ at the christenin," Robbie said slapping his friend on the back.

Danny's gloom at singing had lifted dramatically at the thought of getting two pounds! As he trotted to keep up with Jim and Robbie when they turned for home, he now got to wondering how best to cope with his new-found wealth? It was important to let it be known that he was being paid to sing for that got him off the 'sissy' hook but when Tommy Morrison would get to hear of it, he would demand his share for 'protecting' Danny. He decided to lie about it. Yes, he would say he was being paid, but only, say, two shillings. That might put him in the clear. Why oh why was his life always so complicated?

"Well, so it's agreed, then, you'll be my best man?" Jim said when they reached the cottage.

"Way a heart-an-a half," Robbie said, "an' congratulations. I wish yeh al good fortune, ivery happiness an' half a dozen big strong sons. Now cheer up, owl frien, cheer up."

"Ach, isn't it great," Rosie said when Robbie and Danny arrived in the kitchen and Jim had gone, "an' when yez wur out it got even better. Danny love, you've been invited tay sing at the other two weddins. Mazie Trimble was here not half an hour ago tay ask yeh tay perform at hir's, an' aff curse I said yes. An' better still, the McKendry's wur hintin that Dr Edward and Miss Caroline's weddin wudn't bay complete if yeh didn't sing at it. Now, it's nothin definite as yet but I'd say it's as good as certain that they will ask yeh. Three weddins! Did yeh iver?"

Robbie sat down heavily at the table as Rosie rattled on "... an' Robbie, if you are gonna bay Jim's best man an' Danny's gonna sing, the lest they can do is invite al aff us an' maybe even ask Dorry tay get done up as a flower girl. I've seen flower girls at weddings in them 'Woman's Own' magazines, an' it's lovely...". Clearly Rosie was in the euphoria of weddings, dresses, flowers, singing, and there was going to be no stopping her.

"Indeed, I made it clear tay Mazie that we wud al expect tay be there if Danny wuz tay sing... an' I'll make it clear tay them'uns in the big house that if Danny is singin, we have tay be there too."

"But woman dear," Robbie interrupted her in mid flow, "first aff al, Jim an' Janie's weddin is not gonna be in church but will bay conducted bay that Bible-thumper, Quigley, in Stewart's kitchen so I can't see a fancy-dressed flower girl fittin inta that arrangement. Second aff al, gran folk lake the Roxboroughs an'

McKendrys wudn't want the lakes aff us at their big weddin. Jim's surely in yon kitchen …. Mazie an' McCrum's maybe… but not that big swanky wan. A sarvent[277] lake you as a guest at their weddin! Are yeh clean mad?"

"Well then, Danny will not sing at it… that jist the way it is… an' you'll hiv tay git a new shuit"[278] even if Jim's weddin is ony in Stewart's kitchen, something I hiv niver herd aff before an' can't help wunnerin if that means they'll be married at al… but you, me an' Danny must turn up cl-ian an' day-cent in good clothes, al aff us. Others there can plaze themselves"… and she was off again… dresses and suits… and maybe bow ties… and new shoes definitely…"

Robbie grabbed 'Ireland's Saturday Night' and buried himself in that. Danny retreated to lie on his bed in the lower room no longer to ponder how to escape from all this singing but to muse on how he could profit financially from being a pawn in his mother's schemes for scaling the heights of Ballybracken society using him and these weddings as the rungs on her social-climbing ladder. Clearly weddings might not be such dreadful things after all.

---

277 **Sarvent** – *servant*
278 **Shuit** – *suit*

Episode 30

The Canon's Conundrum

"I do not know how I can cope with all this," the Canon put down the 'Times' that he had been flicking through aimlessly and glared across the rectory drawing room to where his wife was engrossed in her knitting pattern.

"Well, whatever is bothering you, Horace, why not try prayer. Isn't that what you always tell the parishioners. Anyway, what is it? Who is running rings round you now?"

"What is it, my dear? You may well ask! What else but the three weddings in the space of the next fortnight… as the Bard rightly put it *'when sorrows come they come not single spies but in battalions.'*"

Without abandoning her perusal of the pattern, his wife said absentmindedly,

"I really don't know what you are fussing about, Horace. I think it is rather wonderful, this marriage blitz in Ballybracken. Shows there is still some life about the place despite all appearances to the contrary. Do you mean you're out of practice at weddings? I would have thought a quick scamper through the relevant pages in the 'Book of Common Prayer' would have refreshed your memory. And anyway, it not the coronation in Westminster Abbey your conducting."

"It not the service, my dear," the Canon rose to fortify himself with a glass of sweet sherry, "it's the … well the … embarrassment of… well at least one of the weddings, and the other two present me with some embarrassment as well, if truth be told."

"And why should you be embarrassed?" Mrs. Pretyman put down the pattern and let it and her knitting fall to the floor. "I mean it's not your fault if that fat little frog of a man, McCrum, has got Maisie Trimble pregnant."

"Well, that is just the point," the Canon dropped his voice almost to a whisper. "I mean big as she now is, she will manifestly be even bigger by her wedding day but, despite all appearances to the contrary, she will be standing at the altar dressed in gleaming virginal white. Does it not make a laughingstock of all the church stands for? Of all we try to teach?"

"Horace dear," Mrs. Pretyman's tone was that of one admonishing a silly schoolboy, "At the risk of repeating myself, is it your fault that yet again some Ballybracken folk are determined to make fools of themselves in public? It isn't the first time that a pregnant bride has stood before you at the altar. Granted perhaps never one quite so… advanced… quite so 'great with child' as the Bible puts it."

She thought that reference to Scripture might just help her husband keep things in perspective, but it manifestly brought him no comfort.

She rose to put turf on the fire. "You can count yourself lucky, Horace, if Maisie isn't delivered of her bouncing bundle-of-joy in the vestry when they are in there signing the register, and then processing down the aisle, newlywed, with the new-born screaming its head off in its mother's arms. Of course, they could always stop off at the font and have it baptized. Save them having to come back later."

Mrs. Pretyman was not a woman noted for her sense of humour, but she enjoyed teasing her husband when the opportunity arose.

The Canon eased himself limply from the armchair to replenish his sherry glass.

"… and that is not all. Mrs. Alcorn told me after Sunday school that she had heard Janie Stewart is not now getting married in white and not now getting married in church at all but in the Stewart's farm kitchen. She says that has set the tongues wagging too. They are busy adding two and two and getting twenty… now why on earth is Janie, a modest good girl, not having a white wedding here in church? That girl is pure as the driven snow. Everyone knows that. So I am faced with marrying one bride in dazzling virginal white when it is blindingly obvious that 'virginal' is totally inappropriate and another member of my congregation getting married out of public view when it could not be more obvious that she has nothing whatever to hide. What is the world coming to, my dear?"

"Well of course they will all be saying Janie too is in the family way as well, and that Jim McKnight HAS to marry her. Makes far better tittle-tattle than the real reason… that Janie's father and mother are such old oddities and skinflints that they want the wedding over and done with before anybody notices, and out of the way as cheaply as possible. The irony is they could not be laying the wedding more open to unsavoury comment than the hole-in-the-corner way they are going about it."

"What will the Bishop think if he happens to get any inkling of all this?" The Canon had taken on a haunted look. "What kind of cure-of-souls will he think I preside over? Heavily pregnant women pretending they are virgins and virgins dressing for their wedding as if they too have been up to no good, and have to hide themselves away. And his Grace has doubtless been asked to Dr Edward and Miss Caroline's wedding next week… and then there will inevitably be much talk about how many marriages we have had recently in the parish… and innuendos about the precarious virtue of the brides… leading on to talk of other of my parishioner's peccadilloes of which there are many… so, you see, my dear, the strange goings-on surrounding these weddings will be seen as only the tip of an iceberg… and what is the Church doing about it?"

Plotting, Planning & Social Climbing

Rehearsing this catalogue of the strange shenanigans in God-fearing Ballybracken had got the poor Canon worked up into a sorry state. But, by contrast, the possible appearance of the Bishop in Ballybracken had awakened in his wife a plan that could help alleviate her husband's concerns, and also serve her own longer-term ambitions. They must cover up the misdeeds of the Ballybracken parishioners so that the Bishop would never get a chance to hear of them. Consequently, they must take control of him from his arrival to departure. Her husband had his silly worries about tittle-tattle reaching the Bishop's ears casting doubt on his pastoral abilities. Mrs Pretyman too wanted only good tidings to reach His Grace but for a different reason. Her husband was a scholar and a sincere, humble man totally lacking in ambition. She more than compensated for him in the ambition stakes. Her main aim in life was for them to escape from Ballybracken to somewhere, preferably in the Republic where clergy of all persuasions were treated with respect, where their word was law, and where she could shine as a Bishop's wife in the Anglican community down there. No, they must get out… and up… and, for now, a contented Bishop… a happy Bishop… better still an impressed Bishop leaving the big wedding would be her and her husband's passport to greater things.

The Canon had taken comfort in yet another ample glass of sherry, and had promptly dozed off under the 'Times.'

"Wake up, Horace," commanded his wife. "There is no time to be lost. You must call on Sir Thomas and Caroline to see if the Bishop is indeed to be a guest at the wedding? If so, tell them we would be delighted if the Bishop would stay with us. Then you must contact His Grace and say how honoured you would be if he would conduct the service, with you assisting him of course, and if he would reside with us here at the rectory?"

The Canon looked at his wife in what might be termed stupefaction.

"But why, my dear? That wedding is the only one that I feel at all happy about and about which there surely can be no wagging tongues or opprobrium heaped on the oversight of the church… a wedding to be proud of rather than to dread."

"Nonsense," Mrs Pretyman said brusquely, "I take your point that it is highly undesirable for idle tittle-tattle about the parish to reach the Bishop's ears. Like Caesar's wife, we must be beyond reproach. Mind you, I am sure the goings-on here in Ballybracken are as nothing compared with what he hears on his travels. Try to see things in perspective, Horace. What about that parish near the border where the Rector seems to have gone off his head and put a curse on the whole congregation from the pulpit? How is that going to be sorted out? And what about the parish where the Rector has abandoned his wife and five children and run off with the organist? Those are the kind of things the Bishop really has to concern and worry him, not whether some silly girls decide whether or not to get married in a white dress… So, to business! Oh, and you must also try to find out what the Bishop's views are on current issues so that you can agree with him on all points when we have him all to ourselves."

"But my dear, it all smacks so much of scheming. It is worthy of… well, the wretched Macbeths."

"What ridiculous nonsense, Horace. You know I don't agree with scheming, but sometimes careful planning is necessary if goals, short and long term, are to be achieved. Comparing me to Lady Mcbeth indeed! You read too much and act too little, that is your problem. Count yourself lucky I am here to guide you and plan ahead."

"*I just wish,*" thought the Canon, "*that once in a while we shared the same sense of direction,*" but he said nothing, and went off to look for his forever mislaid wallet. He found the dog chewing it where he had dropped it at the back door.

Episode 31

Virginal White and Virginal Questions

That 'Peculiar' Wedding

"It is not workin out al that fine," Rosie and Mina McKendry were trying to fold great billowing white bed sheets at the clothesline in McKendry's back yard. Miss Mina gave one of her inquisitive little humourless smirks, keen to know more but not deigning to ask.

"Naw, Janie and Jim's Big Day wuz expected tay hiv been in the Canon's church, an' our Danny, aff curse, wuz tay sing, an' there wuz tak[279] aff our Dorry bein a flower girl lake yeh see in them fancy magazines in the doctor's waitin room, but now it appears they are goin tay bay married at home at Big Bertie's way no frills aff any kine an' it'll be the Reverend Quigley that marries them. Our Dorry's that disappointed that it's not gonna be in the big church. So there is tay be no white weddin fir Jim an' Janie, it's all takin place in Bertie's kitchen."

"Why have they decided to get married in that peculiar manner?" demanded Mina abruptly as if Rosie was somehow to blame. "That Quigley man is not a proper clergyman at all!"

"Robbie says it's al Big Bertie an' Mrs Bertie's idea. Poor wee Janie wuz niver axed what kina weddin she wanted, an' Jim dizn't seem tay care. Jist wants tay git it over way, accordin tay Robbie. Apparently, Bertie an' hez missus don't want the countryside gawkin[280] at them, an' right enough Mrs Bertie has always been very close[281]… sorta jukes[282] about anytime yeh see hir… doin hir best tay avoid people. I think it's a pity Jim an' Janie ur not hivin a nice ordinary sorta weddin in church. Lake it doesn't seem right."

Rosie had mentioned all this because of Dorry's disappointment and indeed of her's too. She would be attending Jim and Janie's wedding, of course, with Robbie and Danny if only to keep Danny in order before and after he sang, but

---

279 **There wuz tak** – *some mention was made*
280 **Gawkin** – *gaping*
281 **Very close** – *very private*
282 **Jukes** – *doesn't want to be seen*

sure it wouldn't be the same with no beautiful white wedding dresses, Dorry not a flower girl, and herself not needing to be dressed in the finery she had arranged to borrow from Cassie who had bought it recently from the Darkie, and that fitted Rosie 'to a Tee.' But now there would be hardly anybody to admire them, so what they would wear hardly mattered.

Back in the laundry, Rosie had started to iron the sheets and, even with her head bowed in concentration, she became aware that Mina had returned and seemed pensive as if she had something on her mind. She decided to try to lighten the mood.

"Well, sure hiven't we the other weddins tay luk forward tay. Maisie Trimble and Constable McCrum, an' then the best aff al, Miss Caroline's and Dr Edward's. Our Danny is singin at al aff them, an' they are gonna be proper white weddins with confetti an' iverythin. We are goin tay Maisie's but they niver axed Dorry tay be anythin at it ether. She got it intay hir wee head she wud bay gittin dressed up tay do somethin at wan aff the weddins with our Danny singin at them al but she wuzn't axed[283]. She's that disappointed but I towel hir sure there wud be other weddins sometime, but that didn't console hir. Yeh know how keen wee lassies is about dressin up."

The Old Maid's Shocking Questions

Mina, who was holding up the ironed sheets scrutinizing them for any flaws or blemishes, now fastened Rosie with one of her troubling looks, her chin thrust forward, and smoky grey eyes tightened.

"I understand," she said a little tentatively, "that a white wedding may not be entirely appropriate in Miss Trimble's case and, unlike Janie, with good cause. Is she not what is delicately referred to as 'expecting' just a little prematurely?"

At that moment, Rosie was glad to have the remaining ironing on which to fix her concentration.

"Aye, but the wee wain is…" she faltered and sprinkled some water on the linen… "it is Constable McCrum's al right… or so I heerd… that's what they are sayin anyway… an' I'm sure it is… for Maisie is a good girl really… jist maybe a wee mistake…"

---

283 **Axed** – *asked*

What came next, as she told Robbie later, nearly had her dropping the iron and burning the sheet.

"I've often wondered what losing one's virginity and bearing a child is like, Rosie?"

"Lake that's jist the way she put it," she told Robbie. "What wuz botherin an' owl maid lake hir that had put her in min tay axe such a thing, an' what wuz I tay say? I wuz put tay a stan[284] but she had axed meh straight out so there wuz no getting away from it."

"So what did yeh say?"

"Well, a-'ment I after tellin yeh, at the first I said nothin, I wuz that flushed an' embarrassed, lake how diz the lakes aff me explain such things tay an owl maid. I tried tay pretend I hadn't heerd right an' that there wuz somethin wrong way the iron so I futtered[285] way it but when I luked roun she was still lukin at me way that hard luk aff hir's an' she said somethin lake… 'Well, Rosie, are yeh goin tay tell this poor old maid – Aye, that wuz it, 'poor owl maid' - what it's like? You are the only one I can ask.' She said she had read in the letters in that 'Woman's Own' magazine that it seems to cause a lot of woman a lot of pain from beginnin tay end."

"When I had gethered mezself[286], all I cud say wuz, 'it's a bit sore the first time an' after that, if al goes well, yeh can feel very sick in the mornins for a while… but then it's al right… an' sure yeh git a lovely wee wain outta it tay love an' care fir so in the end it's worth it lake… but it's the men gits the most outta it… any pleasure that's in it… I then felt, for some raison, that I had tay say tay hir that my church seems tay think that sorta thing is real bad fir they don't allow the priests or monks or nuns tay marry an' hiv anythin tay do way it so I suppose it can't be right… but then again, sure as I said tay hir too, it's how we al come intay this world so, lake, we can't be doin without it, when yeh think about it that way. I towel hir that the nuns in particular are death on it. I repeated what wanna them nuns said tay me when I had tay go inta the Catholic nursin home an' I wuz in labour tay hiv wee Bobby… she says, says she, *'Ah, ha, may girl, ye'r payin fir ye'r pleasures now!'* I wudn't hiv minded that much for lake I suppose it is a sin sort'a but I had had such a tough time when I wuz cerryin Bobby that I cudn't mind hivin much pleasure or any at al at any stage aff it. I knew I wuz prattlin on in may embarrassment at havin tay discuss the topic at

---

284 **Put tay a stan** - *astounded… stunned… gob smacked*
285 **Futtered** – *fiddled*
286 **Gethered mezself** – *composed myself*

al way iny-wan, but worse still, way that strange woman."

Mina had started to fold the ironed sheets, but clearly she still had virginity, the loss of it, and the outcome on her mind.

"Queen Victoria told her daughters to *'close their eyes and think of England.'* You see, Rosie, at my time of life I sometimes regret not having married and had children. I suppose the desire to have a child is deeply ingrained in us women. However, there is no use thinking about it now. I suppose it's all these impending weddings coming fast on one another's tail that brought it to my mind."

Rosie had heard the stories about Mina being jilted at the altar, and by a clergyman too, or so they said, and it was that had made her such a bitter old maid, but who could say? She had the appearance of a woman who had never had, and had never given, much affection or who had let down her guard in any way. But today! That she, the ice-cold remote Miss Mina, should have unburdened herself to discuss such things and ask such questions of a servant girl! Rosie's feelings of shock and embarrassment continued long after the dazzling white sheets had been dealt with and put away. It was a conversation she would never forget. It was followed by something almost as amazing.

"Thinking it over," Mina said, and Rosie dreaded what might be coming next. "I think your little girl should appear at the church door and present the bride, Miss Caroline, with a silver horseshoe. Wouldn't that be nice? You know, a horseshoe for good luck," she explained, for Rosie was looking astonished.

"I know… I know," Rosie said, "Ach, Miss Mina, day yeh think yeh cud arrange that? Dorry will love it! A horseshoe! Och thank you… thank you very much… I can't wait tay git home tay tell hir. An' yeh can depend on me tay hiv hir al spruced up an' lukin lovely… an' our Dorry is not a bit through-goin[287] so there will be no rascality from hir… an' she'll play hir part great… Danny an' hir will bay lukin their very best on the day."

Rosie Soars with Icarus

Then she couldn't resist it! Betrayed by this unexpected condescending gesture, she now found herself angling for a place for them all at the great wedding. The stakes were high, but sure *'nothin ventured'*… an' what a triumph that wud be!

---

287 **Through-goin** – *boisterous*

The Dowdells at this grand wedding! … an' sure why shudn't they be! Wuzn't her Danny singin at it an' now Dorry would be presentin the bride way a horseshoe.

Still she hesitated, then blurted out, "… an' aff curze Robbie an' me will need tay be there tay keep the wains in order… "

"Oh Indeed you will be involved too, Rosie," Mina said, fastening the big linen cupboard door.

Rosie heart soared, totally disarmed and unprepared for what was coming next.

With her back still to Rosie, Mina said,

"I have told Sir Thomas and Miss Caroline that they can have you for the days around the wedding to help their staff prepare and, on the wedding day itself, to serve the guests at the wedding breakfast, and of course to help with the great tidy up afterwards which will, I'm sure, spill over into the following days, for four hundred guests will take a lot of looking after."

 She turned round to face Rosie, her eyes like Rosie imagined a snake's must be, and she abruptly extruded and retrieved her false teeth in that eccentric manner of hers.

"Thank you, Mistress," was all Rosie could say in her bitter disappointment.

"No need for thanks, Rosie, I'm glad you are pleased. Some extra pin-money will not come amiss, I'm sure. Don't mention it."

She headed for the kitchen with Rosie following, flushed and mortified.

"There you both are," exclaimed Hanna McKendry, "I thought you were lost. There is tea and apple tart on the go[288]. If Rosie will get us the whipped cream from the pantry, we can lay to[289]."

Rosie was glad of the chance to regain her composure as she made for the pantry.

'No fool lake an owl fool,' she thought. *'What wuz I thinkin on that we might be invited? I wuz clean forgettin our place. Sure Robbie wuz right al along.'*

Danny singing, Dorry presenting the horseshoe and Rosie skivvying would be as close as the Dowdells would be allowed to get to the great ones of Ballybracken. Like Icarus, Rosie had let her aspirations soar too high but despite her disappointment, the small Dowdells had made a breakthrough nonetheless. Rosie was not one to bear a grudge or grumble. Her lot was quietly to endure, whatever the circumstances or disappointments. As she said to Robbie after

---

288 **On the go** – *ready and waiting*
289 **Lay to** – *get started… tuck in*

telling him he had been right, "it ill-behoved[290] the lakes aff us tay bay gettin above ourselves. We hiv tay bay grateful."

---

290 **It ill-behoves** – *it is not appropriate for*

Episode 32

Robbie in the Doghouse

A Country 'Beatin'

Robbie had been expected home at the usual time, but it was growing very late and still there was no sign of him. The children had been in bed for over an hour when he did finally stagger through the door. He was covered in blood and bruises. And he was not alone. Behind him in the doorway Rosie could just discern three shadowy figures, one of whom aimed a kick at Robbie.

"What the hell are yez doin?" Rosie cried in a mixture of anger and apprehension. "What are yez about![291]"

"I'll tell yeh what we're about. We've just give this man aff yours a quare beatin fir not bein able tay keep hez hans aff other men's wemen. An' if he tries it on again, he'll bay good mate fir the same tratement[292]. Another good keekin will put manners on him[293]."

"I'll get the police on yez," Rosie shouted into the darkness.

"No need fir them bastards, Mrs," one of the assailants shouted back. "We hiv our own ways ah dalein way rogue men[294] lake him there, an' well he knows it."

With that they were gone, vanishing into the night.

"Put manners on yeh," Rosie cried as Robbie staggered over to the kitchen bed. "What are they puttin manners on yeh fir? Other men's' wemen! Ach Jeezus, Mary and Joseph, don't tell may yev been up tay ye'r owl tricks again. Who wuz she this time? I suppose yev got her in the family way!"

"Naw, I hiv not," Robbie managed to splutter, "but sure I jist took what was

---

291 **What are yez about!** – what do you think you're doing? Why have you done this?
292 **Good mate fir the same tratement** – richly deserve the same beating again
293 **Put manners on him** – bring him to heel… teach him to behave properly
294 **Dalein way rogue men** – dealing with promiscuous men

on offer… an' them'uns wuz hir man an' hir brothers… lying in wait fir me this evenin, so they wur, at the en' aff her lane they wur… they took may bay surprise or I'd hiv laid out flet the three aff them[295]."

The Dowdells children were now wide awake and out of bed standing awestruck at the lower bedroom door. With his bent body, blackened swollen face and matted bloody hair, Daniel Malachy knew at once who Robbie was at that moment… Cuchulainn!… the heroic Ulster hero currently the serial story on Children's Hour. He had no idea what Robbie had done but it must have been something heroic just like the great Cuchulainn.

But it was clear that Robbie was no hero at that minute in their mother's eyes.

"Yev done it this time," she was saying. "Me that depends on yeh an' does al I can fir yeh an' the wains. Well, I'm leavin yeh this very night an' takin the wains way me. Yeh can take care aff yourself from here on, an' see what them hures will do fir yeh after they have finished way yeh in bed."

Robbie, the bruises on his face shining bright blue and satin black in the glow of the paraffin lamp, just stared at Rosie's feet and said nothing.

"Come on, yuz'ens, pull them clothes on yez[296]. We're fir the road, an' we're leavin fir good."

"Ach woman, sit ye'r groun,[297]" Robbie ventured, "There's none aff us saints." But Rosie was already putting on her coat as the Dowdells children hurriedly burrowed their way into their clothes in the darkness of the lower room. When they emerged, Dorry was the only one properly clad. Bobby had his woollen ganzy on back to front and Danny had somehow managed to stagger up to where his mother was standing by the door with both his legs down one leg of his trousers. Clothing adjustments swiftly made, and flashlight[298] in hand, Rosie ushered them out of the door into the pitch darkness.

"An' don't dar come efter us or enquire where we ur fir from here on it's none aff ye'r business," she shouted over her shoulder to Robbie. "I'd as leif[299] sleep under the eye[300] aff Ballybracken bridge than spen another minute way yeh. Ye'r nothin but a bad hallion[301]."

---

295 **I'd hiv laid out flet the three aff them** – *I'd have knocked down all three of them*
296 **Pull them clothes on yez** – *get dressed quickly*
297 **Sit ye'r groun** – *stay where you are… don't go*
298 **Flashlight** – *torch*
299 **I'd as leif** – *I'd rather*
300 **The eye of the bridge** – *the arch of the bridge*
301 **Bad hallion** – *a good for nothing scoundrel*

Once outside, Danny looked back at Robbie from over the half-door and felt he should say something to his great wounded hero, although he had no idea what in the wide world Robbie had done to cause the bad men to nearly kill him and his mammy to leave him. So he said, "I'm sure ye'r sorry yeh did that now," half in rebuke and half in sympathy, whatever the 'that' was?

His mother was now hauling him by the arm away from the half door. Enveloped in the darkness, he could hear his mother crying. Whatever had happened, it must have been something terrible. They all wanted her to relent for it was scary to be out walking the road in the dark with only the faint beam of the flashlight to show them where the road was.

Danny took his mother's hand and asked, in as brave a voice as he could muster, where they were going? Rosie didn't answer for of course she didn't know except that it must be as far away from her man as she could manage that night. How she hated him at that moment. '*He was lucky she hadn't knifed him,*' she thought, '*and indeed she might yet.*' They walked on, the children anxious and scared, Rosie mortified, beside herself with anger and not caring what she was doing or where she was going.

At the top of the Scroggy Brae, Rosie had paused to draw breath when a light appeared in the distance. As it drew closer, to her amazement - for they could never be described as night-birds - she could make out the two Miss Sproules and behind them the form of Big Bertie Stewart.

"Ach it's ye'rself, Rosie. "Yeh hiven't seen a stray heifer on ye'r travels, hiv yeh? When these wemen wur fotherin their stock this evenin they foun wan missin[302]."

Rosie confirmed that she had not seen the stray animal but that she would keep a look out for it.

Ever curious about other people's business, Phyllis Sproule said,

"I suppose you are going up to Jessy Craig's… to say farewell to the poor soul?"

"Why?" exclaimed Rosie. "Where's she goin?"

"Sure she 'a-waitin-on'[303]," said Phyllis. "She has turned her face to the wall

---

302 **They foun wan missin** – *one of their cattle was missing*
303 **'A-waitin-on'** – *the watch kept by family and neighbours beside those dying or someone expected to die*

in best Biblical fashion, won't have a doctor near her, and is prepared and ready to pass over to her great reward. We were up seeing her this afternoon and took turns at reading her consoling verses of scripture. She is about to *'gather with the saints by the river that flows by the throne of God.'* We will miss her, you know," she finished somewhat unconvincingly.

"Did you know that Jessy Craig is a-waitin-on, Bertie?"

"Ach sure that owl heverel[304] hez been dyin regular since iver I mine," Bertie said unsympathetically. *'A creakin dure hings long*[305]*!'* She hiz been 'a-waitin-on' on three separate occasions tay my sartain knowledge. She hezn't a bit notion aff dyin, woman dear. She's ony doin it tay draw attention tay herself. I'm sartain sure neither God above nor the Divil below would want that owl hairpin[306]. She'd drive the angels an' divils clane mad. I'd surmise when she finally goes she'll en up somewhere good an' hot!"

"Yeh shudn't bay sayin such wicked things about the woman," Rosie said, and then to cover her tracks continued, " Naw, I hadn't h-eard that Jessy wuz a-waitin-on. Me an' the wains wur out on another wee erran the night but we must surely drap in on Jessy now we've h-eard."

News of Jessy's imminent demise helped Rosie to make up her mind where they were going. Jessy Craig might or might not be dying but it would only be neighbourly to go and sit with her in case she was and, anyway, there would be a good warm fire and maybe tea on the go. *'Sitting-up-with'*[307] someone 'a-waitin–on' was a regular Ballybracken pastime giving those not dying, but waiting for the *'Angel of Death,'* the chance to avail of the hospitality of the house usually, but not always, in sombre or sober mood. So to Jessy's Rosie hastened to offer her support and avail of a warm fire and a welcome mug of tea. There she would stay until she could think what she wanted to do next. Going back to Robbie was not an option.

---

304 **Heverel** – *an ill- disposed scandalmonger*
305 **A creakin dure hings long** – *in this context someone claiming to be ill/dying, being very demanding and stretching out their demise giving rise to the suspicion that they are not so very ill… done to get attention*
306 **Hairpin** – *an unpleasant person*
307 **'Sittin-up-with' someone 'a-waitin-on'** – *keeping a vigil with someone dying*

Episode 33

Awaiting the Angel of Death

"Will yez wheesht," Rosie said when they finally arrived in Jessy's yard for the children were beside themselves with tiredness, and getting really fractious. She peered through the kitchen window. The room was aglow from the blazing turf fire and the two oil lamps that hung at drunken angles near the rickety stairs. She could see there was quite a throng assembled round the room, the women in a huddle near the fire quietly gossiping, the men spread around with caps thrown on the floor, some with mugs of tea in their hands and others chewing tobacco and engaging in some sort of unseemly spitting competition apparently to see who could throw their spittle closest to the fire.

"There seems tay be ony stannin room[308]," Rosie muttered to herself, "but at laist it'll be in the warm. Now mind yuz behave ye'rselves for this poor woman's dying, so she is, so no noise!"

"Does that mane she's gonna heaven or hell the night?" Danny's curiosity was aroused, and from what Angel Jo had told him maybe he should advise the woman not to bother dying until heaven had got itself sorted out.

"Don't yeh bay askin them questions… an' jist keep quiet," Rosie said as she lifted the latch.

"Rosie darlin, it's ye'rself," she was greeted warmly by Teezie Knox who, together with her girls, never missed a good 'a-waitin-on' or indeed a wake or funeral largely, it must be said, for the prugh[309] that accompanied these occasions. "… An' the wee wains too," she added in surprise "Isn't it a powerful dark night, an' bitter caul[310] lake a step-mother's breath. Come on up bay the fire an' get ye'rselves warmed up. Yeh al luk real cauldrife[311]. Is Robbie way yez?"

Teezie's daughters Maggy May, Biddy and Annie were sitting behind their

---

308 **Ony stannin room** – *standing room only*
309 **Prugh** – *free items e.g. in this context food and drink*
310 **Bitter caul** – *very cold*
311 **Cauldrife** – *feeling the cold… shivering with cold*

mother half hidden in the shadows. Rosie thought she heard the girls giggle at the mention of Robbie. Surely he hadn't been cavorting with them trollops too! She ignored Teezie's question and instead asked, "How is the craythur[312]? When wuz she tuk bad[313]? Is there any improvement?"

Before Teezie could reply, a strange sound floated down the stairs like as if somebody was being slowly choked.

"Ach, sure there's ye'r answer," said Teezie. "Isn't that the death rattle. She'll be away before the mornin… Now yeh'll hiv a sup aff tea an' a wheen[314] aff Paris buns nicely buttered, Rosie, havin come this far. An' the wains… wud they like some goat's milk?"

Tea was exactly what Rosie needed, though what right Teezie Knox – who lived in a ramshackle hovel of 'ill-repute' in Ballybracken Upper with her three girls all of whom got the name of being 'loose hussies ' - had to be taking charge in the dying woman's house did cross her mind?

"Aye, a drap aff tay in may han[315] wud bay great, Teezie," she said, "an' a wee drap aff milk fir the wains way half a Paris bun apiece wud do them rightly too."

Danny was about to say he couldn't take goats milk for it brought him out in hives but his mother, sensing he was about to say something he shouldn't, stood on his toe. His squawk was drowned out by the dreadful scary noise still coming from upstairs which had suddenly got even louder. Then a pair of big boots started to descend slowly, a podgy hand clutching the rickety stair rail for support.

'Maybe it's the divil,' Danny thought. *'He might hiv the woman on hez back carryin her aff.'*

But the boots and the podgy hand turned out to be those of the Reverend Quigley whose grim face was now caught in the lamplight.

"I hope yez is al as well prepared tay meet the 'Man Above' as that owl woman up there is now," he said casting a searching look around.

They had all stood up to acknowledge the Reverend's presence and to offer the holy man a seat.

" … fir mind if yez is not," he continued with great menace, taking the seat closest to the fire, "it's hell bound fir the lot aff yez. 'Owl Clootie' is waitin fir yez

---

312 **Craythur** – *creature… the afflicted one*
313 **When wuz she tuk bad?** – *when was she taken ill?*
314 **A wheen** – *a few*
315 **A drap aff tay in may han** – *a quick cup of tea*

down below tay cast yez inta the fiery furnace. If yez wur tay succumb tay this faver[316] that's doin the rounds, an' is kerried aff unprepared… yez will hiv nowan tay blame but ye'rselves… yez hiv been warned offen enough."

On that less than comforting note, he took the mug of tea that had been poured for Rosie and launched himself at a Paris bun the butter from which was soon running down his chin unto his already heavily stained waistcoat.

The noise from upstairs had stopped abruptly.

"Ach, Holy Jeezes," exclaimed Tommy Leitch. "She a gonner."

Rosie crossed herself, and either that Catholic gesture or possibly Tommy's blasphemy caused the Reverend Quigley to splutter and spit bits of Paris bun unto the floor.

"Was that Rosie Dowdells I heerd yez mention down there?" croaked a voice from upstairs. "Fir I thought I heerd hir voice when that owl slippy-tit[317], Quigley, was up way may scarin the wits outta may about hell's fire. I hadda chase him fir he hizent a gleed aff sense between hez lugs. I don't think hez al there.[318]"

The Reverend looked thunderstruck, and attacked what was left of his Paris bun to hide his embarrassment. "If Rosie is there, sen hir up at wance fir a better craythur niver lived, even way hir bein a Papish[319] but she did more good turns fir me than any half dozen aff may own sort[320]. I want tay see hir before I go tay 'Glory'."

Jessy was lying staring steadfastly at the low ceiling, a frilly night cap on her head and her familiar capacious handbag clutched firmly in both clenched fists. Danny immediately had a fit of the giggles for he thought the woman in the bed looked like the grizzly bear in his current library book. A sharp clip on the ear from his mother abruptly arrested the giggles while he massaged his injury.

"Is that you, Rosie?" Jessy asked in a weak voice, turning her head slightly towards her visitor and squinting at Rosie with one eye. "Ach, aren't yeh the

---

316 **Faver** – *fever*
317 **Slippy-tit** – *a sly untrustworthy individual*
318 **Not a gleed aff sense between hez lugs. I don't think hez al there** – *not a glimmer of common sense between his ears. I think he is mad… unhinged*
319 **Even way hir bein a Papish** – *although she is a Roman Catholic*
320 **Aff may own sort** – *of my fellow Protestants*

darlin fir comin al this road in the glides aff the night[321] tay see me aff. They'll be no turnin back this time, Rosie, for I 'm heaven boun. I'll be way up way the 'Heavenly Host' before the morrow morn."

She gave a low cry and clutched her side. "Ach, the cramps, the cramps is clane tarra…niver knew the bate aff them[322]. The cramps is tryin may sore[323], Rosie."

"Yeh poor s-owl yeh," Rosie said soothingly. "Hiv yeh seen Dr Johnston? Is there nothin he cud give yeh? What diz he say? Is there no cure?"

"That sleeked wee glype[324]." Jessy raised herself on one elbow in a miraculously robust manner for one suffering so grievously and close to death. "He's ony a clift[325], an' knows nothin even if he hez the quare notion about himself[326]. Do yeh know what he said tay me? *'Get up outta that, woman, an' take a jorum aff 'Andrews Liver Salts' or a spoonful or two aff 'Syrup-aff-Figs' tay loosen ye'r bowels, an' yeh'll be as right as rain.'* Such tak tay a dyin woman. So that's al he knows! But sure what diz any aff them know, Rosie? Sure didn't I pay good money tay see that specialist up in Belfast at the tail en aff last year, an' when I cudn't rightly locate the pain for he'd got me that flustered, al he said wuz *'go home an' take a bath regular an' give ye'rself a good pummelling way plenty aff soap.'* Did yeh iver hear the lake? Ten Guineas he wuz gonna charge me! I towel him that he shudn't bay settin himself up as a fancy doctor charging a poor wuda-woman that sorta money. I towel him he'd bay well paid way a five-poun-note, an' that's jist what I give him. Take a bath indeed! An' me that takes a good warm bath before hivin 'Holy Communion' at Acester[327] time an' maybe again at Christmas if the weather is not too caul. An' I wuz nothin the better aff the tablets he giv may… sur I wuz ony throwin good money efter bad."

Rosie didn't know what to say but mention of 'Holy Communion' prompted her to ask if the Canon had been called upon to minister to the dying woman.

"Aye, an' he's another sleeked owl poultice[328]," Jessy exclaimed. "Comes up tay give me may 'Communion' so I can meet may Maker unblemished, not that

---

321 **In the glides aff the night** – *in the darkest part of the night*
322 **Clane tarra, niver knew the bate aff them** - *utterly terrible, never suffered anything like it*
323 **Tryin may sore** – *putting me through torment*
324 **Sleeked wee glype** – *a sly deceitful individual*
325 **Clift** – *very foolish person*
326 **The quare notion about himself** – *has a high opinion of himself*
327 **Acester** – *Easter*
328 **Sleeked owl poultice** – *a sly hypocrite… an insincere individual*

I wuz iver blemished, yeh understan, Rosie, fir I heff always done the right thing an' been clane and straight, no colloguin, convoyin or gettin anythin on tick[329] – an' then day yeh know what he says? He says, says he that he hopes I hiven't forgot the church in may will! Always efter the money them guinea-hunters way the turned collars[330]. Let me tell yeh, Rosie, they 'ur grippers[331] the lot aff them. 'No pockets in a shroud,' says he."

She drew the handbag up under her double chin, the cold leather feel of which seemed to comfort her for a moment until she exclaimed,

"Me, that wuz done out aff a farm aff lan bey that brother aff mine an' that heverel aff a woman aff his[332]. Bad rascals the pair aff them. I've prayed prayers on them iver since tay get the 'Man Above' tay strike them down lake he did tay that Pharaoh a while back. The 'Almighty' hezn't done it yit Him hivin that much tay luk about but I'll give Him a nudge when I get up there an' git Him on tay them, an' then they'll know what's stickin tay them. Och, It's a long road that hizent a turn in it, Rosie."

Having cleared her mind of at least some of her many hatreds, Jessy lay back on the pillow wearing her most pious face and resumed staring at the ceiling. The Dowdells children, who were now beside themselves with sleep, and had been trying to stay upright while Jessy ranted, were suddenly possessed by some lemming-like urge, and all three threw themselves unto the bed led by Bobby who landed on the dying woman's feet.

"Holy God," she said sitting bolt upright, "is that the undertaker fir liftin may inta may coffin? Wud yez howl on. I'm not dead yit."

Rosie did her best to grab the three children and get them off the bed but the dim light from the oil lamp on the far wall cast long shadows and she only succeeded in retrieving Dorry who fell to crying. The boys meanwhile had passed out as soon as their heads hit the blanket and were already fast asleep with thumbs firmly in their mouths. Rosie set Dorry on her knee and began apologizing for her sons' behaviour. She again tried to get them wakened and off the bed, but Jessy said,

"Let them be, Rosie, an' sure put the wee lassie up there too. They're doin no harm. What about Robbie? Is he down there in the kitchen? I know rightly what them'uns is about down there," she hastened on, "eatin may outta house

---

329 **No colloguin, convoyin or gettin anythin on tick** – *no scheming, gossiping or getting goods on credit*
330 **Guinea-hunters way the turned collars** – *clergymen looking for funds*
331 **Grippers** – *debt collectors who seize goods*
332 **Heverel aff a woman aff his** – *that ill-disposed scandal monger wife of his*

an' home. They're takin advantage aff a poor dyin woman. If I had the strength, I'd go down there an' hunt the lot aff them. Crowd aff gather-ups whose ony consarn is their bellies. Now, I hope you'll lay may out[333], Rosie, when may time comes fir I don't want any aff them others laying a finger on may dead body. Sure Robbie will help yeh fir I'm a brave weight[334]. I'd attend tay mezself ony I'll be dead so in no condition. I'd lek tay see Robbie if he's down there fir I always though well aff him. Bring him up, wud yeh."

Rosie, who was as tired as the children, could not stop herself and started to sob. Jessy raised herself up again, reached out and took Rosie's hand, mindful to hold on to her handbag with the other.

"Don't bay upsettin ye'rself on my account, Rosie. Sure I'm an owl woman, an' may time hez come."

"It's that surely," Rosie said somewhat insincerely, "but it's Robbie too. I've took the wains an' left him."

"Ach surely not," said Jessy, "an' you an' him such a good match. I was ony saying tay Minnie Hazlett the other day before I wuz tuk bad that you'd got such a good-lookin man an' that yeh desarved him, an' wudn't it bay great if yez wud quet livin in sin an' get married straight and proper."

"He's been… he's been frequentin other wemen," Rosie said amid her sobs, amazing herself that she was baring her heartbreak to this mean carnaptious[335] woman. "An' it's not the first time an' it'll not bay the last, so I'm done way him," she finished, continuing to sob.

Jessy turned her handbag away from what poor light there was, unclipped the substantial fasteners and squinted inside. She fished out a small grubby handkerchief which she handed to Rosie. When Rosie had dabbed her eyes with it, Jessy retrieved it, replaced it in the handbag closing its fasteners with a resounding jail-like click. She narrowed both eyes and looked at Rosie.

"Ach now, don't bay talkin lake that. Sure it wuz iver so, fir that's the men fir yeh[336], Rosie. Them runnin efter other wemen is no farn dizease[337]. There niver wuz a man yit, even the best aff them, but can stray. My advice is don't feed him too much red mate[338] for that puts the divil in them… an' give him a good

---

333 **Lay may out** – *prepare my corpse for burial*
334 **Brave weight** – *considerable weight*
335 **Carnaptious** – *cantankerous… quarrelsome*
336 **Ach now don't bay talkin. Sure it wuz iver so fir that's the men fir yeh** – *Oh now, don't be so surprised for that was always the way men conduct themselves*
337 **No farn dizease** – *nothing unusual or anything we haven't experienced before*
338 **Mate** – *meat*

bleachin[339] way an ash plant now an' again. I used tay take the yard brush tay Craig when I thought he wuz strayin an' I tell yeh that knocked the notion outta him. I had no bother way him efter that. So that the advice aff a dyin woman. Go back an' take the street brush tay him or whatever hard weapon comes tay han' an' he'll keep his trousers well buttoned up efter that. Mind you, even way al that I hiv always allowed[340] that if there wuz no bad wemen there wud bay no bad men. It's the women leads them astray, yeh know. Who wuz the hure he's frequentin?"

"I'm not jist too sure," Rosie said, now more composed that she had confided her unhappiness to somebody.

"An' he's got a hidin already bay hir man an' hir brothers. Sure isn't that Ballybracken rough justice fir yeh… give the keoboy a good doin an' bay done way it[341] … keep the la' outta it bay al mains fir them lawyers is the biggest grippers aff the lot… even worse than the clargy. But wuzn't it the quare mate fir him[342]. It's lucky they didn't kill him when they wur about it. What are yeh gonna do? Leavin him wud bay well- an'- good but yeh'd be a foolish woman tay do that jist cos ye'r man strayed. If ivery woman in this townlan up an' left when their man strayed, I doubt if there'd be a married couple left. An' there's even worse goings on in farin places or so I'm towel bay Minnie an' she gits al hir bars[343] in the 'News aff the Worl' that she buys aff the bread-cart ivery Monday. Yeh niver h-eard such shockin teed-reels[344] as ye'd read in that paper, but sure then again roun here's no better ony we don't know the half aff it."

Daniel Malachy, who had never got quite comfortable in the bed, had wakened up in time to hear Jessie's advice about beating Robbie with the yard brush before he fell on the floor with a crash. He started to cry until his mother drew him to her when he resumed sucking his thumb and staring at the big woman in the bed. Jessy now squinted at him which made him feel uncomfortable

---

339 **Bleachin** – *a thrashing*
340 **Even way al that, I hiv always allowed** – *despite that, I have always held the opinion*
341 **Give the keoboy a good doin & bay done way it** – *give the unreliable rascal a good beating and get it over with*
342 **Quare mate fir him** – *he well deserves it*
343 **Al hir bars** – *all her gossip and scandal*
344 **Teed-reel** – *shocking goings-on*

and very dizzy. He needed to escape from this death chamber, and he knew his mammy did too.

"I think I'm gonna bay sick an' vomit," he said. "Will yeh come way me outside, mammy, for it's very dark?"

Rosie got up, glad to make her escape with the children but Jessie didn't want to lose such a good listener to whom she could pour out her many hatreds.

"Ach, sit ye'r groun'," she commanded. "Sure he's a likely big lad an' ken take himself out. He doesn't need his mammy runnin efter him."

Danny made his escape down the stairs and, avoiding everybody's eyes in the kitchen, got outside just as dawn was breaking. The fresh air made him feel better and that fertile mind of his told him there were two things he had to do. He must somehow help his mammy escape from the clutches of that awful woman, dying or not, and then somehow get her and Robbie back together again. Mulling this over at the side of the barn, he decided the best thing to do was just to go back home now it was light. His mammy would soon miss him and get out of that house saying she had to go and look for him. She would surely know where he had gone and come home after him. Then she and Robbie would make it up but only after she had beaten Robbie with the yard brush. He did not wish his big hero any harm but if his mammy took the yard brush to Robbie maybe he would never do whatever he had done to make her cry ever again. So our little hero set off at a trot just as the sun was rising and chasing the night mist hanging over the bogs of Ballybracken. He could hear the music of that morning and, even in his exhausted state, it was somehow more beautiful than ever.

Horror & Hymns

Back at the cottage, Danny found Robbie still lying on the top of the kitchen outshot bed fully clothed. With Danny's arrival, he stirred in his stupor turning towards the wall away from the light of the open door. Danny was so tired he went straight to the lower room, threw himself across the bed and immediately fell fast asleep.

He had not been sleeping long when he was awakened by a dreadful dismal moaning sound coming from the kitchen. Tired as he still was, Danny tiptoed to the bedroom door and opened it a fraction. There was no one there but Robbie still spread-eagled over the top of the bed but now thrashing his arms around and moaning, crying and muttering to himself. Danny went over to the bed. He was very scared. Was Robbie dying from the beating the bad men had given him? Maybe he was just drunk for there were two empty bottles lying on the floor beside the bed. Whatever the cause, his big hero was obviously very sad and unhappy. Danny clambered on top of the bed beside him and tried to put his arms round him but couldn't. Then he tried putting his arms round his neck but got all twisted up in the St Christopher necklace his mammy had given Robbie a long time ago. He gave up and just rested a hand on Robbie's bare back. Maybe that would help him and let him know that whoever else didn't like him, Danny was still his friend.

At the touch of Danny's cold hand, Robbie suddenly sat up. He was staring but didn't seem to see Danny. He was pointing at the far kitchen wall as if he could see something there.

'*Not the wee wains,*' he called out. '*For f*** sake surely they cudn't do it tay the wee wains. Look at the bastards! Dey yeh see what they're doin? Cuttin the youngsters up, tryin out dizeases on them, poisonin their bleedin wounds, seein how long it'd take them tay die, gassing them, burnin them if it took too long… Jeezes Christ, burnin them an' them still livin. Surely not the owl men an' the wemen an' the wee wains! Ah but they did, the f***** bastards. Herded them aff trains as if they wur brute baists*[345]*, butchered them lake yeh wud a pig… stole al they had… beat them down yon alley coddin*[346] *them they wur gettin a shower… pulled the rings aff their fingers an' earrings aff their ears… grabbed their wee wains aff them an' knocked their brains out agin' the walls way their mothers watchin… an' in they went… an' come out the other en' as ashes. Them f***** guards wur no sodgers… a rail soldier way a gun in hez han hez a chance … an' the bastards wur still shootin them, even way us there, lake the poor starved craters wur target-practice… the evil bastards… 'Master Race' bay damned… '*

Robbie was now staring with his unseeing eyes at Danny, his face still covered in matted blood from his beating of the night before…and foam coming from his mouth. To Danny's dismay, his ravings were not finished '*… we shud hiv finished the f****** guards aff even though shootin wud hiv been too good for them. But then again, as Big Alfie Anderson said – sure yeh mine big Alfie, the Colour Sergeant, don't yeh? - 'yeh wudn't lake tay think aff ye'rself as bein as bad as them bastards or what wur we fightin for if we turned out tay be as bad as them? An' that's true but what justice wud the murdered folk iver git? NONE! I tell yeh, NONE!'* Robbie was roaring now. '*Judges wud let most aff them aff way a caution… what*

---

345 **Bastes** – *beasts*
346 **Coddin** – *fooling*

sorta justice is that? An' as I said tay Big Alfie, fir he wuz a religious fella, where wuz hez God when the bastards wur herdin the wemen an' wee wains into the gas chambers bay the million… where wuz hez lovin God then?'

Danny was scared and sobbing. This Robbie was a different man… He didn't know this Robbie at all or like him… What was this man saying about gas and pigs and people dying? He slipped off the bed, fell to his knees and, burying his head in his hands, said out loud….

"Please Jeezes, Robbie is sick. Make him better."

When he looked up, Robbie was now running his hand through his blood-soaked hair as if to recover himself, and then, totally unaware of his terrible nightmare, said calmly "Are yez back? Wherez ye'r mammy, wee son?"

Danny leapt up on the bed suddenly overcome with a wave of relief. This was the Robbie he knew. This was the Robbie who cared for him and who he cared for. The other strange scary man had gone away and that was all that mattered. Breathlessly he told Robbie about him running home to get his mammy to come back too.

Robbie listened to the youngster's patter and it brought him comfort, brought him back from the country of terrible nightmares… of bloody battle fields and the liberated prison camps… the essence of which was apparently still all too real to him and which, when it overwhelmed him, only Rosie's love had the power to calm… to briefly exorcise.

"… an' you wur in bed," Danny was saying, "an' sayin things about killin… .I think it wuz the pigs… an'… " He hesitated for he didn't want to mention some of the other dreadful things about shooting and burning that Robbie had said and that had so scared him. "… an' yeh said a lot aff other stuff that I can't mind[347] … but that dizn't matter now …."

"I wuz jist havin bad dr-aims[348]," Robbie said in a way that would convince nobody, not even his biggest fan.

"So you've decided tay be the bait in the trap, may wee comrade, tay bring them al back home. Well now, maybe it'll work and maybe it mightn't. But we need tay git yeh tay ye'r bed, may owl mucker."

And he caught the boy firmly by the chin and stared at him with unfeigned affection.

"While I'm tidying up, Way down tay the room there an' play me somethin on ye'r piana."

---

347 ***I can't mind*** – *I can't remember*
348 ***Bad dr-aims*** – *bad dreams… nightmares*

Danny skipped off happy that Robbie was like himself again, He fished out the first piece of music he could find in the piano stool and started to play. It was the hymn *'Dear God and Father of Mankind'* and he sang along, his voice echoing through the cottage. About the third verse, he sensed that Robbie was looking over his shoulder at the music sheet.

'Restore us to our rightful mind,' Robbie read out loud. "Yeh cudn't hive thought aff anything better tay serenade me way at this very minute, Danny. Then, as if talking to himself, he murmured *'... Rightful min it is... tay Hell way it al... Keep the show on the road an' stroll on... don't scrabble... isn't that how tay bait them*[349] *... muddle your way through it an' jist stroll on...'* Finally he pulled himself together saying, "Now, may wee mate, intay bed way yeh."

Robbie was Robbie again, and that was good. Maybe his mammy would now forgive Robbie for whatever he had done but probably only after she had beaten him with the yard brush.

---

349 **Bait** – beat... defeated

Episode 34

Jessie gets the 'Cure'

Things were not going well back at Jessy's. The Angel of Death had either been delayed or there had been a change of plan in the celestial realm, and Jessie had been condemned to earth for a while longer. The hub-bub from the kitchen below was continuing, getting more raucous in fact, since Teezie Knox, on the scrounge in Jessy's dresser for snuff or *'somethin tay aze our sorrah*[350]*'* emerged triumphant bearing a nearly full bottle of clear liquid recognized at once by all present as the best of good poteen. Continuing to rummage, she then happened on a large if mouldy seed cake.

"Now that will add a bit of variety tay the bread and Paris buns," she muttered, "though what the owl heverel wuz buying seed cake for bates may, for God-an-the- world knows seed cake is very bindin on the bowels. Mine niver moved proper for a good week the last time I eat it. But I suppose it will hiv tay do fir now. *'May God's givin han niver falter*[351]*'* she cried in triumph, waving the seed cake and bottle in the direction of the 'a-waitin-on' assembly.

Seed cake was in fact Jessy's only extravagance and, even then, was only bought when Jim McKnight had greatly reduced the price or, better still, she got it for nothing with mould on it. Teezie's girls now set about sawing at the hard cake.

"Sure we might as well start on the wake and rowel it an' the funeral drink al inta wan[352]. Sure it'll save yez al time later. Them cramps will do fir hir; sure as shootin she's a gonner this time." Teezie declared, expressing the general hope of all present for a sad outcome.

There was general rejoicing at finding the strong drink. The kitchen mugs, even those still half filled with tea, were now topped up with the crystal-clear liquid. The banter in the kitchen soon rose to a deafening level. True, the strong liquor caused Liam Owens and Packie McCrystall to fall asleep, their loud snoring adding to the rumpus but, in the main, the talk was increasingly warlike fuelled by the toxic brew. Long Tom Eccles remembered an old score he had

---

350 **Aze our sorrah** – comfort us in our grief
351 **May God's givin han niver falter** – may God's bounty never fail
352 **Start the wake an' rowel it an' the funeral drink al inta wan** – bring the food, drink etc customary at a wake and funeral, and roll all into one to save time

never fully settled with Dinnis Laughlin and considered it timely to resolve it there and then by punching Dinnis squarely on the nose with a cry of *'yeh cute hoor*[353]*, yeh. It's the last bloody time ye'll out-bid me at a lan' lettin.'*

Dinnis, the drink having affected his eyesight, lashed out and knocked Packie McCrystall off his chair. He fell on top of Teezie's Biddy who promptly threw the mixture in her mug over him crying *'Get away, yeh dirty baste, yeh,'* and pushed him unto the hot turf on the hearth where his nether regions started to fry as he tried in vain to get to his feet. Until now, the night's proceedings had passed largely unnoticed by a courting couple, Ruby Patterson and young Matt McCracken, who had so far been modestly and decorously holding hands on the settle by the fire but now they too, with passions inflamed, were getting more daring and indecorous by the minute.

While these unseemly drunken antics were taking place in the kitchen, a strange event, verging on the spiritual, was unfolding in Jessy's bedroom. Poor trapped Rosie was still in attendance on the nearly dying and had been joined by a very breathless Una Quinn, a devout Catholic woman who lived on the far side of Collity bog, and who had the *'cure'*[354]. She had been sent for as a last resort to see if this ancient remedy might prevail where modern medical science had failed or, more accurately, had washed its hands of Jessy's regular and protracted death bed scenes.

"Now dear, I hiv brought yeh the cure as promised," whispered Una, "an' if yeh hiv faith in it, it'll do the trick fir I've niver known it tay fail. Look at Mickie's Patsy that used tay live there unner Crock-na-shina hill. At death's dure, he wuz, an' Father O'Kelly had giv him the last rites an' al… well, he got the cure an' he riz from the bed an' niver luked back or had pain nor ache till he died three weeks followin. But yeh need tay hiv the faith in it, dear, for lake if yeh hiven't the faith, divil the bit good it'll do yeh."

The hairpins holding Jessy's night cap had somehow worked loose and the frilly edge of the cap had slipped down and was covering one eye making her look like the Gorgon or a one-eyed bullfrog.

"I trust there is no money involved for when Lizzy McCrumlish down the road got ye'r cure, I know fir a fact she payed yeh nothin. If there wuz anythin

---

353 **Cute hoor** – *a devious individual lacking in scruples*
354 **The Cure** – *'Cures' are ancient Irish folk remedies usually involving religious rituals*

tay pay, I wudn't hiv axed yeh."

"Ach, naw, naw, there is no money involved at al," Una assured her, "Money dizn't come inta it[355]. Sure the country cures is a charm from the angels up in heaven tay the Holy Saints here below in times past… an' then passed on from seventh son tay seventh son…"

"Well, how did you come bay it?" Jessy asked suspiciously.

Una gave an embarrassed little cough.

"It come our way… intay our family's safe keepin lake… indirectly… but with the blessin aff the church… so that makes it al right… lake I towel yeh, it hez done wonners fir manys a wan sick unto death jist lake ye'rself, Jessy."

"I'll go along way it so long as yez didn't stale[356] it… what diz it involve anyway? I hope there is nothin Papish about it… no crossin ye'rself or holy watter threw about or the lakes aff that… for I'd rather die than hiv any aff that Papish rigmarole or pishogues[357] goin on in a good Protestant house lake this."

She adjusted the nightcap and then continued thoughtfully,

"Min you… ye'r right, for it did wonners for Lizzy… when she cud harly get a breath… an' that scaldy[358] aff a doctor had giv her up… so that's why I'm givin it a try… not but that I'm ready for glory and the victor's crown… but nothin Papish, mind," she ended, mauling at the sheets as if tearing at the vestments of the Pope himself.

Rosie could see that Una was greatly taken aback by this for of course the cure would surely involve some act associated with her and Una's Catholic faith. She crooked her finger, and Una bent down to listen.

"I'll do the prayin an' whativer is required inta mezself," she whispered, "an' yeh do the other bits."

"But there is holy water on the hanky I hive tay use, an' I hiv tay make the sign aff the cross over hir an' say the Hail Marys."

Rosie stood up and bent over the old woman in the bed.

"Now fir this tay work, Jessy, yeh must close ye'r eyes tight an' not open them until Una tells yeh."

"Tell hir she's tay keep well back from may hanbag an' not bay fisslin[359] way it," Jessy warned.

---

355 **Money dizn't come inta it** – *no payment is required*
356 **Stale** – *steal*
357 **Pishogues** – *superstitions*
358 **Scaldy** – *bald*
359 **Fisslin** – *fiddling… handling it… rummaging inside it*

With that she closed her eyes tightly, screwed up her mouth and Una started to administer the ancient cure. Halfway through her muttered incantations she stopped abruptly and, looking at Rosie, whispered in a panic,

"Och Jeezes, sure I need tay know what's wrong way hir for the charm tay work. Is it hir appendix or the gall stones or what is it ails hir?"

A weak voice from the bed said, "Jist call it pains an' git on way it… fir the pains aff hell wudn't bay in it bay what I'm sufferin this very minute… an' me that hiz done nothin sinful iver… wuz niver a runagate[360] nor out oxter-coggin[361] nor main way money, so what has brought this affliction on may? That'll be may first enquiry when I meet the Good Lord up above this very night. Could He not go cannier[362] on a poor blameless widda woman?"

"So it's jist pains?" Una said much relieved, "sure that'll hive tay do… an' sure the Blessed St Ambrose will know what they are an' run his healin hans over yeh."

She continued her incantations but as the mention of the Blessed Saint slowly sunk in, Jessy sat bolt upright and snatching her errant nightcap off her head, threw it at the bedroom wall. She then put a plump varicose-veined leg to the floor shouting,

"No man be he saint, sinner or well-tay-do farmer is gonna run hez hans over me livin or dead."

Una sprang back, her eyes bulging and a look of wonder on her face.

"It's a merricle," she cried. "The charm hez worked! It niver worked that quick before. May God an' al the Holy Saints in Heaven be praised."

By now Jessy had reached the top of the stairs. Surveying the scene that met her eyes in the kitchen, she shouted,

"Wud yez al get outta may house, yez crowd aff drunken guttersnipes yez. Yez is very b-owl[363], takin advantage aff a poor widda woman an' hir on hir death bed. Go on, scoot[364]. Day yez think I don't know what yez is al up tay or that I'm not right wise. Bad cess tay yez al. I want tay see neither sight nor hair aff yez when I pull on may[365] an' get down there tay make myself a b-owl aff stirabout[366]. If yez is not well away, I'll take the yard brush tay the lot aff yez. The

---

360   **Runagate** – *a restless unsettled person*
361   **Oxter-coggin** – *walking arm-in-arm gossiping*
362   **Go cannier** – *go easier*
363   **B-owl** – *brazen*
364   **Scoot** – *scram… get out… away with you all*
365   **Pull on may** – *get dressed in a hurry*
366   **Stirabout** – *oatmeal porridge*

pity is I hiven't got a shot gun."

There was a hasty gathering up of coats and caps as the mourners fled.

Death's door having apparently closed for the evening and Jessy still in the land of the living, it was Rosie made Jessy her porridge. It was only then as Bobby and Dorry staggered bleary eyed down the stairs that she realized Danny was missing.

"He'll sure be in wan aff the out-houses. Didn't he go outside to relieve his wee self. He'll hev fallen asleep on the straw in the barn," Jessy tried to reassure Rosie.

"Sure I've looked in the barn an' ivery road. Yeh know, our Danny is that cunnin an' long headed[367] he jist mighta went back home fir he an' Robbie is that great[368], there no separatin them. I doubt there is nothin fir it but tay go home myself. Sure maybe I shud niver have left an' jist took the bull bay the horns an' threw that rascal Robbie out on the street. Sure it's my house...an' he hiz no right tay it."

With Jessy miraculously restored to life and devouring her third bowl of porridge, there indeed seemed nothing else to do but go back home. She would throw Robbie out, Rosie decided. He was like all the men '...*no good... he cud go an' live way wane aff them wemen he was so good at frequentin. She didn't care. Jist let him go.*'

Although the children were loudly demanding something for their breakfast, Jessy was back to her miserable old self in every way and was parting with nothing, not even a bowl of porridge for them. As Rosie confided to her friend Cassie later '...*an' hir that had al sorts - sowans, tatties, boxty an' even a ween'a fancy biscakes*[369] *- an' I donno what else hid unner the stairs, a wee gopin of iny aff them wud hiv done the wains rightly fir their breakfast, but divil the bit aff the tight owl hallion*[370] *wud part way anythin' an' efter me sittin way hir half the night.*'

So most reluctantly, Rosie set off for home with Bobby and Dorry. They were half-slept, very hungry and trailed along behind their mother moaning,

---

367 **Long headed** – *clever & calculating*
368 **Great** – *friendly*
369 **Sowans, tatties, boxty an' even a ween'a fancy biscakes** – *a sour fermented type of porridge, potatoes, potato pancakes and even a few rich biscuits......* **gopin** - *a small amount*
370 **Hallion** – *vulgar woman*

complaining and saying they hoped rotten Danny would never be found, and had high hopes he had fallen in the dams at the bottom of the Scroggy Brae where he would never be seen again.

War & Peace

Danny was wakened from a deep sleep by the row coming from the kitchen.

"That wee divil has decoyed me back," his mother was shouting, "else I wudn't be here. But now I am here, yeh can pack up ye'r belongings an' go… I hev no more time fir yeh… ye've broke may heart… "

Danny got out of bed and tip-toed to the room door. His mother was standing over Robbie who was sitting on the low three-legged stool which Dorry claimed as her's alone. He was looking into the fire, his head turned away from Rosie.

"… fir it's the last time yeh'll let may down. I'm right scunnered[371] way ye'r runnin after other wemen an' makin may a laughin stock. Hive yeh nothin tay say for ye'rself… ?"

Robbie still said nothing but threw a couple of turf on the fire.

"…fir min, I m-ain it… I don't want yeh aroun me or the wains any more… ye'r leadin them astray… yeh hev Danny owl before hez time… comin out way that owl-fashioned chat… so he diz… I know where he gits it from… an' it's doin him no good… an' the other two is nearly as bad…"

She tailed off as Robbie rose abruptly from the stool and, without looking at her, strode down to the lower bedroom nearly knocking Danny off his feet. He went to the far wall and unhooked his army kit bag which had survived because it was out of reach of the children. Back in the kitchen, he hastily started to throw his few belongings into the khaki bag. Rosie had turned her back on him and was filling the big black kettle from the bucket that held the spring water. Dorry and Bobby were now sitting up in bed bemused by the noise coming from the kitchen. It was then that Danny decided to take a hand and made his entrance from the lower room. He had a bundle of clothes under his arm and was sobbing loudly. Rosie looked round and demanded,

"Where are yeh goin? I niver giv yeh lave[372] tay go home from Jessy's?"

"If Robbie lay-vin…then I'm lay-vin[373] too," Danny cried without the trace of a stammer.

---

371 **Scunnered** – *disgusted*
372 **Niver giv yeh lave** – *I didn't allow you*
373 **Lay-vin** – *leaving*

Not to be outdone, and wanting to play some part in the drama, Bobby and Dorry grabbed Robbie by the legs, Dorry the right one, Bobby the left.

"We're goin too… we're going too," they cried in unison. "If daddy's goin back tay the army, I goin way him tay be a sodger," Bobby added sensing that this could be his big chance.

"Ach, wud yez wheesht," Rosie said. "Let go aff him an' come an' ate ye'r breakfast."

"Ony if daddy stays," Dorry cried, for her brother's mention of them all going off to join the army was now troubling her for she still had plans to be a film star.

They let go of Robbie's legs and all three children joined hands forming a human barricade across the door. Rosie said nothing but went about putting mugs of milk and bowls of porridge on the table. Hungry as they were, the three children did not move from the doorway.

"Can daddy stay?" And answering themselves, "daddy, yeh can stay."

Robbie unhitched his kitbag and, going down to the lower room, replaced it on its high hook. He went back to the kitchen. The three children were now seated at the table, and were eyeing him over spoonfuls of porridge and the overflowing mugs. What would happen next? It was down to their mother. No place had been set for Robbie but a bowl of porridge and mug of tea had been left by the hearth. Did that mean that things were slowly but surely thawing out? Robbie left the table, resumed his low contrite pose on the stool, and began to drink the tea. His mouth was still raw and sore but the lukewarm milky tea was comforting. Danny appeared at his side with a large, savagely-cut slice of bread covered thickly in jam. The war in Dowdells's was petering out, even if lasting peace had not yet been established.

Later that morning, the children watched as Rosie gently bathed Robbie cuts and bruised face. Though she had yet to utter a word to him, they knew of old that she would slowly but surely relent as she always did with all of them.

"Are you an' mammy friends again?" Danny asked Robbie a day or two later as they walked to McKnight's shop.

"Well, it is still al sight an' no sound," Robbie answered mysteriously, "but I think I'll be aroun for another while yet."

"So can I have some gob stoppers an' a comic?" Danny asked, always with an eye to the main chance and, anyway, didn't he deserve a reward for the part he had played in the Dowdells' drama.

"I think maybe yeh do desarve it, my calculatin wee comrade," Robbie said adjusting the bandage around his still throbbing forehead.

Episode 35

Maisie's Big Day

The 'Best Man' Bothers Danny

"What way yon big tent aff a white dress, will she not luk a right sketch[374]?" mused Rosie on the night before Constable McCrum and Maisie's Big Day.

Rosie had been asked by the bride's mother to come round early the next morning to help the bride get ready, and there were already severe doubts expressed that the dress, ample though it was, would not fit given that nature was taking its steady course. The term 'blooming bride' was never more appropriate than in Maisie's case on the eve of her wedding.

"For, Rosie, you're a great han way the needle an' thread, come early in case any wee eas-zin[375] might bay needed," Masie's mother was ever the practical soul.

"An' I'm takin our Danny way me", Rosie said to Robbie, "fir how in the world[376] can I get back here tay git him ready in time, him that hez tay be at the church singing his wee heart out."

"Might be as well," Robbie looked up from the paper and smirked. "The word's out that McCrum is swutherin[377], an' mightn't turn up at al. Our Danny might hiv tay sing a quare bit till take the bad luk aff things[378], an' they get a sarch party up tay try tay fin ye'r man an' get him nailed down at the altar. The dogs in the street[379] know McCrum's got caul feet[380] iver since he got hir in the family way."

Rosie had heard this bit of gossip herself but just could not bear the thought of the girl being let down at the last minute. She said,

---

374 **Luk a right sketch** – *look very foolish… a laughingstock*
375 **Eas-zin** – *easement*
376 **How in the world** – *how could I possibly*
377 **Swutherin** – *hesitating*
378 **A quare bit tay take the bad luk aff things** – *quite a bit to cover up the embarrassment*
379 **The dogs in the street know** – *everybody knows*
380 **Caul feet** – *has had second thoughts… is scared and will not go through with it*

"Ach, he'll turn up good enough but I ony hope he's sober when he diz."

Daniel Malachy had been listening intently and was smitten by a moment of anxiety. If Constable McCrum didn't turn up, would Maisie marry somebody else, for he sensed his singing fee might be in jeopardy if the wedding collapsed due to the absence of the main man. 'But then again,' he mused, 'wasn't there somebody at weddings called the 'best man,' so if he is the 'best man' why does the bride not marry him… like, if he is better than the other man she is supposed to be marrying?'

Our little hero was ever beset by trying to make sense of the nonsensical.

"There is a good bit aff logic in that, my little comrade," said Robbie when Danny raised the point. "An' if an' when Constable McCrum hiz a fit aff the head staggers[381] an' doesn't show up, I'll give you a fiver if you suggest tay Maisie that she alters course an' marries the other fella. Tell her it's any port in storm. Sure, as yeh say, Danny, what could be more logical than that the bride marries the best man?"

Danny was always pleased when his great hero agreed with him but his mother, as usual, was less than impressed with both of them.

"Quit takin rubbish, the pair aff yez. Surely McCrum wudn't let the girl down, an' him a policeman, an' as fir the best man marrying the bride… sure that's balderdash."

"It'd sure make history if the best man steps in an' marries Maisie the morrow," laughed Robbie. "I did hear aff somethin lake it happenin wanse when the groom an' the best man had the same name, and before anywan cud stap him, the priest hooked up the wrong wan tay the bride. They said she wuz content enough fir it wuz the best man she had always been after anyway. I donno how they got it sorted." Then, with a twinkle in his eye and in a low whisper to Danny, he said, "What do yeh say, little comrade, that we put them in the way aff it[382] again tay see what happens!" Raising his voice he said, "Danny an' me hez a wee errant tay run tay see Jim the night. We'll be back in a while."

With that he propelled Danny in front of him towards the door.

"Where are yez goin at this time a night?" Rosie asked. "Danny shud be in hez bed, an' anyway the shap will bay shut."

"Ach, sure a wee stroll in the good night air will strengthen hez lungs for the singin."

---

381 *Hiz a fit aff the head staggers* – goes crazy and changes his mind
382 **Put them in the way aff it** – set it up

Robbie's Revenge

"You an' me is on a secret mission, Danny," Robbie said as he strode out with Danny who was trying hard to keep up.

A secret mission! This was so great a prospect that Danny didn't even ask where they were going or to do what though it was soon clear they were not going to see Jim McKnight. Being out with Robbie well after his bedtime in the dark on a secret mission was all he needed to know. Now they were at the police barracks and there, parked at the side, was Constable McCrum's 'Austin Seven.'

"Day yeh know what we're gonna do, Danny?"

"What?" Danny demanded in a mixture of delicious expectation and downright fear for a policeman might come out and catch them at it, whatever it was?

Here we must pause to wonder what a former much-decorated Sergeant Major, Robert Elliot, was up to on his mission to the barracks that dark evening and, more importantly, why? Suffice it to say that he and Constable McCrum were not on the best of terms of late because of the Constable's failure to grasp the importance of turning a blind eye to the distilling of that important local commodity cherished by Ballybracken's humbler folk though deplored, at least officially, by its mighty ones and, of course, by its various holy brigades. Good-quality poteen was valued as a much-needed income supplement by its distillers, and as a source of good cheer by its consumers… though always purchased under the banner of *'great stuff for a bad chest an' keepin out the winter cawl',* and other alleged medicinal purposes. It was in this revenue-avoiding industry that Robbie Elliot had for some time been engaged in partnership with Packie's Ned, the rascal and 'bad rearin' we have met before in this narrative but who had the secret, passed down the generations, for making the best of good 'mountain dew.' With business thriving, Robbie and Ned were flying high until Constable McCrum, with too much time on his hands, decided to wage a personal crusade against Ballybracken's illegal poteen industry starting with a raid on the Crockins Bog. Among the first illicit stills to be discovered, dismantled and confiscated was Robbie and Ned's cherished poteen materials. The owners were not pursued since that would have required a degree of energy, and would have resulted in being more trouble than the good Constable could cope with. But the damage was done, a source of income removed overnight, and two angry men were left swearing vengeance. So as Robbie, with Master Daniel in tow, strode towards the police barracks that night, Constable McCrum's nemesis was approaching with the taste of sweet revenge on its lips.

"We're gonna make it a wee bit hard for yon fat Constable tay get tay hez weddin. Wee Maisie might en' up marryin the best man yit! Wouldn't that be the best aff craic[383]? Sure, it wuz you put the idea in may head, Danny, way ye'r questions about the best man."

To think that he, Danny, had given Robbie an idea, sure that was beyond great!

Robbie had dropped to his knees beside the Constable's car and started to let down the front tyre. Daniel Malachy fell to his knees too crawling after Robbie as he made his way round the car letting down all the tyres.

"We're gonna bay caught, an' you'll en' up in jail again," he whispered to Robbie as the last tyre gasped its final breath and the car gave a deadly creak and sank to its axels.

"Don't be skared, wee comrade," Robbie reassured him. "They're all over in Cobain's pub getting the wee man drunk tay see him through his ordeal the morrow. Anyway, we are nearly finished our secret mission, just wan wee item left."

With that, he crawled away from the car with Danny behind him until they reached the wall of the barracks.

"Now where are the other peelers' bikes?" Robbie pondered. "They usually lave them up agin the wall here. But maybe they're roun the back."

He rose and edged his way along the wall but at that minute Danny's courage failed him. Up until now, he had felt like 'Dan Dare' or one of the other heroes in the 'Eagle' comic out on a dangerous mission to blow up a spaceship, capture some villain or rescue somebody who needed rescuing from the evil Mekon, but enough was enough. Now he stood stock-still at the corner of the barracks

---

383 **Craic** – *fun; a good prank.* (**What's the craic?** - *can also mean what's happening? What's of interest is going on? What's the latest news?*)

wondering if he would ever see Robbie again.

"That's the job done, my little hero," Robbie said as he emerged from the back of the building. "That'll put manners on the wee blirt[384]. He'll 'll hiv a time aff it gettin' hez tyres in order the morrow mornin. Our nosey Constable might hiv to get tay the church peighin an' plucherin[385] on Shanks's pony[386]."

Danny didn't know about any ponies or anybody round about Ballybracken called Shanks, but this was not the time to enquire. This was the time to get back home, for it was one thing thinking how great it would be to be engaged in one of the adventures in his comics, but the real thing was far too scary.

The Wayward Wedding Dress

It was up with the lark the next morning in Rosie's household and, amid much protesting, crying, threatening to throw up and being generally awkward, Daniel Malachy got the scrubbing of a lifetime to get him ready for his performance.

"Yeh'll soon hiv that wain scrubbed away tay nothin," Robbie said between Danny's squawks, as the big man tried to concentrate on his porridge and the news on the wireless. "Sure that'll do him rightly, woman dear."

But nothing daunted, Rosie continued the unequal struggle starting with Danny's ears and steadily working her way down.

"They'll bay plenty takin a good skelly at him[387]. Day yeh want them tay bay sayin that I don't keep may wains klain an' that it is no wonner me being a Catholic an' clatty[388]. Och, I know rightly what them'uns bez sayin behin may back, an' I'm not havin it the day aff al day… an' stap scringin[389] ye'r teeth, Danny, yeh know it drives may astray in the head."

Eventually Danny struggled free and was standing dripping carbolic soap suds beside the fire.

---

384 **Put manners on the wee blirt** – *Teach the obnoxious constable a lesson*
385 **Peighin an' plucherin** – *panting & choking*
386 **Shank's pony** – *walking… arrive on foot*
387 **A good skelly** – *squinting*
388 **Clatty** – *slovenly*
389 **Scringin** – *grinding*

So it was a gleaming Daniel Malachy, dressed to kill in his best – well, actually his only – suit who followed his mother over to Maisie's to get her somehow into her virginal white dress whatever amount of pushing, pressing and shoving that might entail. And indeed a fair amount of pressure was required before Maisie was even three-quarter ways clad for her imminent nuptials. Rosie ordered Danny to settle himself on a chair by Maisie's bedroom window so that she could keep an eye on him, and so that he wouldn't get a chance to undo all her good work in getting him ready for his public.

"Fir I know yeh too well, Danny. Nixt thing yeh'll bay out rowlin in clabber[390]."

Nothing availed of his protestations that he would sit nice and quiet in Masie's mother's kitchen and not *'rowel in anythin.'* But no, he had to sit in the bedroom where his mother could see him as she tried to get Maisie wrestled into the gleaming white wedding dress, bought when she was considerably smaller in girth.

"Sure I ken harly get a breath," Maisie panted as her mother and Rosie worked to find what slack they could at the back.

Given Maisie's distressed state, it crossed Danny's mind that it might be a comfort to the bride-to-be if he were to reveal that the likelihood of Constable McCrum turning up at the wedding was now remote so she shouldn't worry about her dress not fitting, and that she could more profitably spend the day baking her famous sponge cakes.

While he pondered whether this information would bring even a modicum of comfort, to his consternation the two dressers had unzipped Maisie revealing mounds of white flesh which they pushed this way and that trying to even it out across her back. When they tried to zip her up again, they caught some of the flesh in the zipper whereupon Maisie screamed blue murder, disengaged herself from her dressers, and threw herself on her bed wailing loudly as the dress slipped, like an iceberg dislodging from the ice-sheet, round her plump legs to reveal bright lacy pink knickers. To Danny, this fleshy image called to mind the picture of a whale in his reading book. He couldn't help it. He got another uncontrollable fit of his notorious giggles. Rosie rose to her feet, dashed across the room and, lifting Danny by the collar, escorted him over to a dark corner and set him facing the wall with threats of a good 'skelpin' when she had time. With his mother soon otherwise engaged, our hero quickly re-orientated himself sufficiently to watch as the continuing wrestling match between Maisie

---

390 **Rowlin in clabber** – *getting covered in mud*

and her dress continued, but ultimately it was to no avail. The bride-to-be was sobbing miserably as her big front bump was now jerked way up to near her chin only to subside to very near her knees, or so it seemed to Danny, as the dressers continued to try every which way to get her zipped up.

"Meh head's away way it[391]," wailed Maisie. "I'm gonna kal the whole thing aff."

"Now don't yeh worry, darlin," Rosie was saying comfortingly. "I know it's maybe not tay ye'r min[392] tay hiv tay do it but sure it'll only take a minute tay sew a strip in here at the back an' that'll give yeh the wee bit a spare yeh need, an' sure I'm the girl can stich yeh up good an' proper an' nobody I'll bay a hair the wiser[393]."

"I'll get a shimmy[394] or a white poke[395] from the kitchen," Maisie's mother said, "an' we can cut a stripe outta that."

As she headed for the bedroom door, Danny too beat a hasty retreat to sit near the fire in the kitchen. In a surprising short time, the bride-to-be emerged from the bedroom now looking, to Danny eyes, like the large white sacks of flour that he, Bobby and Dorry often clambered over or hid behind in Jim McKnight's meal store. It was not an engaging sight and saddened his tender heart to think that if Constable McCrum could see her now he would not bother trying to get to the church but would catch the next train out of Ballybracken, and run away forever. Why did big people want to get married anyway?

A Deserted Bride & A Troubled Conscience

Picture the scene then: the church is half full, some are guests, some others are there to wish the happy couple well but some, sad to relate, have come just to gawp and giggle. The Canon, standing by the altar, is in a state of nerves in case his worst fears are realized and, in the excitement of the hour, Maisie might be propelled into labour. But where is Constable McCrum? Maisie has already arrived on her father's arm but there is no sign of the groom or the best man. Every minute seems like an hour to the Canon, and the folk in the pews are forever looking back to the church door to see what is happening… or not

---

391 **Meh head's away way it** – *I'm going mad*
392 **Not tay ye'r min** – *not what you want*
393 **Nobody will bay a hair the wiser** – *nobody will know*
394 **Shimmy** – *a chemise… slip*
395 **A white poke** – *a white meal bag*

happening. The organist, Big Bella, is banging out *'here comes the bride'* over and over, except that there is no bride gliding – well, more accurately in Maisie's case, waddling - up the aisle… or groom… or best man.

Danny and a few other choristers are in the choir ready to do their bit with Danny, as ever, the man of the moment. But Danny's mouth is dry, and his face flushed. He, of all those present, knows why constable McCrum isn't in his place, and probably why there was no best man either, whatever good he would have been, for our questioning little hero still hadn't a command of what that role entailed. Should he tell everybody they should all go home, Maisie to cry, some people to complain that they had been so put out for nothing and, of course, the cruel people to laugh. How he wished he didn't know what Robbie had done to the car and the bikes… but maybe it wasn't that at all… maybe Constable McCrum had just run off as people had said he would, as Danny had thought he should, and that he would never be seen again. Maybe the punctures had just given him the excuse he needed.

But despite his attempts at rationalization, Danny's troubled conscience continued to nag at him to tell someone and, anyway, hanging about in church to no purpose was not his idea of a profitably spent morning. But who to tell for, in the telling, he would betray Robbie, and he could never do that? Maybe he should just start to cry, a strategy he had quite often used to good effect in the past to get him out of a tricky situation. It usually got people enquiring what was wrong with him, and that would give him the excuse to tell all he knew, and he could then tell Robbie that they had made him tell.

With Big Bella blasting out *'here comes the bride'* for the umpteenth time, he could stand it no longer and proceeded to try his crying stratagem. Big Bella, who had been constantly looking round towards the church door, for even she was getting tired of the wedding march, spotted Danny's apparent distress. She could never have been accused of being a kind-hearted woman, but she had developed something approaching a soft spot in her otherwise impenetrable armour for our Danny. The soft spot stretched no further, however, than prompting her to hand him her hanky on which he now wiped his eyes and, to her annoyance, loudly blew his nose.

"Ye'll still git singin, wee Dowdalls," she whispered, for she mistook his tears for disappointment that he might not get his big moment. "Now don't bay joinin[396] tay cry, sure iverythin will be al right."

Having got somebody's attention, and so that she, Bella, would get the right message that there was something else amiss with him, Danny decided to turn up the volume.

"What's the matter way yeh?" she demanded, turning away from the organ to face him. "Day yeh need tay go tay the lavatory fir there's no way yeh can go here unless yeh go behin them bushes in the graveyard? I don't know why ye'r mammy didn't see tay yeh[397] before yeh come. Why day I hiv tay do iverythin for yuz brats in this choir. Yez hiv may heart broke."

"Naw, I don't wanna go. I want tay whisper something tay yeh," Danny said.

Whispering something to Big Bella wasn't as easy as it seemed for to get even in the vicinity of her ear involved removing her enormous 'hanging-gardens-of-Babylon' hat which, precious object that it was, had to be carefully removed to avoid shedding even one of its multifarious blooms, and positioned on top of the organ. That delicate manoeuvre successfully completed, Big Bella lent down towards Danny as if to hear his confession which, all things considered, just about caught the moment.

"Yeh see, it wuz me an' Robbie that… that must be why… might be why… Constable McCrum…" He tailed off, his attempt at confession not coming easy.

But just as he was picking up courage to continue, there was a flurry of activity down the aisle. Maisie had broken free from her father's arm to rush towards the altar screaming loudly. The Canon, ashen faced, his worst fears now apparently about to materialize, stumbled forward to cope as best he could, though nothing like this had been covered in his theological training. Maisie shoved him aside and turned to address the congregation.

"Ah jist want tay tell yez that I've been badly let down, as if yez didn't know. That scut, McCrum, hez decoyed me althegether, an' now hez up an' left may an' worse again hez desarted his own wee wain. I wudn't marry him now if he wuz tay crawl up that aisle there on his big belly an' plead way may tay take him. Me an' the wee wain will jist hiv tay make out[398] some way. I'm not the first girl tay bay jilted an' made tay luk foolish an' I'll not bay the last. If yez iver ketch up way the wee fat runt, tell him from me he's not worth chasin outta the kale

---

396 **Joinin** – *starting*
397 **See tay yeh** – *attend to you*
398 **Hiv tay make out** – *have to manage somehow*

garden[399]. I ony tuk him fir there wuz nowan else. There is nothin left fir yez al now but tay head home."

Then to the consternation of the Canon, Maisie threw herself on the carpeted chancel floor and sobbed uncontrollably. Danny was now beside himself for maybe Constable McCrum might -just might -have appeared if only Robbie and he hadn't gone on that secret mission. What a tumult of guilt was rattling around in the head of our little hero, we can only imagine?

What with Maisie still sobbing loudly and the congregation shuffling awkwardly in their seats reluctant to go home in case they would miss any more of the drama, the hapless Canon was at a loss as to what to do for the best. It then occurred to him that a rousing hymn might help defuse the situation somewhat so, by dint of mouthings and hand signals to Big Bella, she finally got the message and launched into *'Soldiers of Christ Arise and put your armour on'* which seemed to suit the occasion as well as any other, for Bella's musical repertoire didn't cover the most appropriate music to play for the comfort of jilted brides. The choir and most of the congregation, after a few moments hesitation, gave this all they'd got and at top speed which was very necessary since Bella had decided on speed too and was making no allowance for the fact that she was a good half verse ahead of the singing. The resulting cacophony, assault on Danny's sensitive musical ears though it was, at least had the effect of drowning Maisie's sobs.

While the organist, choir and congregation were pursuing each other at full volume, the Canon took the opportunity to try to lift the poor bride-to-be and get her into the privacy of the vestry. He managed to get her to her knees, but his frail strength was no match for her bulk so for the moment there he stood holding Maisie up by the arms, she now looking like an enormous dishevelled rag doll. A man sitting in the front seat finally wakened up to the fact that help was needed and started to come forward to help the Canon.

Belated Wedding Bells

At that very moment, the door of the church flew open and there stood Constable McCrum looking, it has to be said, even more dishevelled than his bride. But wet, crumpled and unkempt as he was, never was the arm of the law so welcome in any gathering. Maisie rose to her feet and, displaying the agility of a ballet dancer to the amazement of all, careered down the aisle where she threw herself

---

399   ***Not worth chasin outta the kale garden*** *– a worthless person*

at the constable. At first the congregation was uncertain as to whether she was intent on killing him or hugging him and, when it proved to be the latter, they were almost evenly split as to which they preferred. But hug and kiss him she did to such an extent and with such passion that Rosie's good efforts of the morning with her needle and thread gave way under the pressure, and the gusset so subtly inserted to expand the wedding dress, gaped open to reveal Maisie's fleshy back all the way down to the top of those large frilly pink knickers.

Eventually the couple disentangled themselves and stood erect all except Maisie's dress which now hung on her, or parts of her, like clothes crumpled by a gale on a washing line. Again it was Rosie to the rescue. She had been sitting at the back of the church and was only there to support Danny in case he got *'a fit of narves.'* She came quietly forward and with the benefit of several safety pins which, together with a supply of 'Mrs Cullen's Headache Powders,' she never left home without, somehow reinstated Maisie in her dress *'or enough tay cover hir up anyway'* as she said later. But the drama of the morning was not quite over yet. With Maisie's dress restored to some extent, the happy couple now linked arms but instead of heading for the altar they proceeded towards the church door.

"Excuse me," cried the Canon, "but there are a few preliminaries to be gone through if you don't mind," for he was determined he had not given up his morning sherry and battle with the 'Times' crossword for nothing.

"Ach, aren't we the right owl dopes," laughed Maisie. "Sure we're not married at al yit," and she and her groom did an about turn and processed in as dignified a manner as Maisie's wayward dress made possible back to the altar where, in accordance with the solemn rites of matrimony, they were duly joined together. When it came Danny's time to sing, he did so with gusto for sure hadn't he and Robbie nearly wrecked everything for poor Maisie that morning and, whatever Robbie might do or not do to make amends – and our hero thought he would need to do *'somethin real big'* - Danny had to do something *'big'* too so he sang his very best for the happy couple. And his singing that morning was declared to be the best ever; Maisie kissed him, Constable McCrum shook his hand, even the Canon said that Danny's rendering of *'Guide Me, Oh Thou Great Redeemer'* had transported him *'to another place'* which was pretty well where he had wished to be for most of that momentous morning.

With the church bells ringing out, the bride, groom and guests retired to Maisie's house to enjoy a nice wedding breakfast. Then the happy couple went off on honeymoon to Portrush from where postcards arrived saying that Maisie and her Constable were the proud parents of a bouncing baby boy, so their bliss was complete. The only sour, indeed alarming, note as far as young Danny was concerned was his mother's mentioning that she had heard that the Constable had vowed that if he ever caught the *'bastards'* that had let down the tyres on his car and punctured his bike causing him to have to trek through the rain to the church on his weddin day, he would *'cut them tay ribbons way his own bare hands.'*

Danny suppressed, as best he could, a squeak of terror, and cast a glance at Robbie on the other side of the hearth.

"Isn't that very bad chat fir a policeman tay come out way," Robbie said, a faint smile playing round his mouth, "But then again, did yeh iver think there was so much badness in the world, little comrade, as lettin down a man's tyres on his weddin day, an' did yeh iver think that such divilment is tay bay foun even roun here in God-fearin Ballybracken?"

Danny buried his head in his 'Beano,' swallowed hard, and resolved never to go on any secret missions again, however exciting it had been to follow his big hero in the dark that night to the police barracks. Real adventures were far too scary. Better by far to enjoy them in books and comics.

Episode 36

'Holy' Daniel Malachy

Moneymaking Miracles?

History does not record when Daniel Malachy made up his mind to found his own church. History does record, however, with dismal regularity, that our little hero's financial situation was regularly in a highly fragile state. We can conjecture, therefore, that whatever 'other-worldly' motives he may have had in terms of living the good life here-and-now and pointing the way for others so that all might establish a firm footing in the next world, sad to say… money! – or the lack of it – may have been at least one major motivating factor underpinning his ecclesiastical plans. In this context too, it may be that when he surveyed the coinage level on the collection plates in the Canon's church every Sunday, and the 'silent collection' called for by the Reverend Quigley in his mission hall, the matter was settled, and Daniel Malachy realized that 'church' was a money-making enterprise, whatever else it was.

But we would be unfair to our little hero if we doubted that there was also a spiritual element in his ecclesiastical ambitions. In pursuing an encyclopaedia in Ballybracken library, he happened upon the name 'Malachy' which reminded him that 'Malachy,' after whom he was named, was a holy saint and, not only that, but this Malachy could, apparently, foretell the future and tell peoples' fortunes. That sounded great to our Daniel Malachy; at last a saint who did something worthwhile. Wouldn't it be great if this St Malachy could be persuaded to share his fortune-telling skills with his namesake here below, and how could he resist if Danny had founded a church named after the good saint. And, while Angel Jo persisted in saying he was duty bound not to interfere in human affairs generally and Danny's in particular, St Malachy could have no such excuse.

According to Daniel's mammy's church, the Saints were constantly being asked to do things for people, as well as being really holy all the time. Danny knew that if it got around that as well as singing and being a good musician, he could also foretell people's fortunes, and if all these saleable qualities were somehow wrapped up in religion for, as far as he could see, everything in Ballybracken had to have something to do with religion to be any good, his church was bound to be an enormous success. Such a new ecclesiastical venture would face stiff competition for Ballybracken wasn't exactly short of churches but our hero, never one to be put off by difficulties, especially if he didn't foresee them until it was too late, determined to 'take cloth' and give the church thing a whirl.

It was while he was pondering on the logistics, the main focus being how much he would charge for his ministrations, that Angel Jo put in his next appearance. This fortuitous timing seemed like a terrific opportunity to try to get in touch with St Malachy, and also to get some advice from Angel Jo on the best way to get a church up-and-running for surely a heavenly body like Jo, with his intimate knowledge of the next world and all that, and who flitted between universes, could give Danny some useful pointers. But first things first, contact with St Malachy was a priority.

"You are a strange little fellow," Angel Jo said looking at Danny with something approaching interest, "and what, may I ask, are your motives for this noble ecclesiastical venture?" Seeing that this had gone over Danny's head, he continued, "Why are you doing it? I trust it is for high-minded other-worldly reasons?"

Danny knew not to say that he thought there might be money in it but instead said, "Well, I think fortune-telling would be good so if you were to get St Malachy to help me and I could tell people's fortunes, and if I could tell them they were doing everything wrong, and what would happen if they kept on doing what they are doing, it would help them people get into heaven… so that would be good, wouldn't it? Anyway, St Malachy is bound to want to help me this time to make up for how disappointed I was when he and BOAK wouldn't allow you to get rid of my stutter."

Given Angel Jo's earlier descriptions of the somewhat fluctuating and dysfunctional state of the heavenly realm at the minute, Danny's reasoning did not ring true so he hastened on "… , my church would be to just make people be better people and not hit each other… and wash themselves all over… and not pick their nose and… not steal other people's sweets… "

This last was currently a burning issue with Daniel Malachy for a small hoard of 'jelly babies' and 'penny chews' he had hidden under his bed had mysteriously disappeared, the main suspects being Bobby and Dorry whose fervent denials Danny had found unconvincing. If he got his church up-and-running he planned to lay great emphasis on the eternal fate of thieves if they didn't come clean, confess all, and give jelly babies and the like back to their proper owners.

"There's other things too," he continued, "like all those desperate bad things the Reverend Quigley never stops telling us about… I forget just what they are but they'll come back to me when I start preaching…" though he had at that moment run out of ways his church would try to improve the human race.

Angel Jo was pondering.

"I suppose it wouldn't really be interfering with you too much to help you with this daft idea -oh, I meant worthy ideal - and it would give me something to write about to put up to the BOAK Committee. Since I confidently predict that your church will undoubtedly have no beneficial effect on anybody down here, just like all the others, perhaps I could help you by interfering ever so slightly. So, what do you think you need, little 'earth - grubber,' to get this church of yours started? Spell it out, but nothing too elaborate, mind, like conjuring you up a cathedral, fancy vestments or anything like that. I could do it but that would be interfering big time."

Danny had already given this some thought. "Well, a collection plate would be good," he said, and then hastened on for that priority had Angel Jo looking at him rather quizzically, "and a few miracles now and again, and being able to tell fortunes just like St Malachy… if you'd ask him to help me."

"Just wait a minute! You are expecting me… ME! … to try to persuade holy, meek Malachy to help you tell fortunes! What are you saying!" Angel Jo looked thunderstruck at the suggestion but Danny persisted.

"Why not?" he said. "He told fortunes when he was down here. The book I read said he told the Pope's fortune and said that sometime shortly the Popes would be finished off and there would be no more Popes, which my mammy wouldn't like but the Reverend Quigley would be all for it for he's death on Popes."

Given Angel Jo's continued look of horror, Danny thought it best to lower the fortune-telling stakes considerably.

"Like, maybe he could help me tell ordinary people's fortunes… say, help Robbie with the football pools for he is forever getting them wrong… or maybe he'd tell me for definite if Bobby and Dorry have stolen my jelly babies… so then I could make them give them back if they haven't eaten them yet?"

Danny Dowdells

Saints Dissected

"My dear innocent Daniel Malachy," Angel Jo was in patronizing mode, "St Malachy, after whom you are named, has always been an example to us all of obedience, modesty and devotion in the BOAK paradise. I have to say, of course, that his positive attitude is helped greatly by the fact that he hasn't got a head at the moment. Don't look so puzzled," continued the angel, "Lots of the Saints have bits missing due to you superstitious buffoons hacking bits off them to make into relics, and what a money-spinner that is! Take St Anthony – no ribs! Or poor St Nicholas – hardly a bone left in his body, and there you all are believing he flits round this miserable bit of rock in the middle of winter giving out presents… as for poor St Theresa of Avila – hardly a drop of blood left in that woman's body so much has been drained to make relics and shrines… but then again I suppose that helps her to float so maybe it is not all bad. I could go on. Pure vandalism! … but the poor things just have to manage as best they can in the hope that one day heads, arms, legs, ribs, blood or whatever else is missing will be stuck back on them again."

While Danny found this litany of maimed saints a bit hard to follow, one thing Angel Jo had said did hit home - having something called 'relics' was a money spinner! He made a mental note to get a holy 'relic' from somewhere, put it in a jam jar, involve it in his miracles, and for that extra glimpse of the supernatural, he would charge extra. Yes indeed, this information about relics added a whole new dimension to Danny's view of his heavenly namesake. His expression prompted Angel Jo to continue,

"… Malachy died with his head on, of course, but it somehow got separated from his body when they dug him up during one of the ghastly revolutions you keep on having to make your world a better place, as if that's likely! I suppose his head might be in some shrine somewhere, but Malachy is so meek and mild he's never really tried to find it, and anyway he appears to be much happier without it. So even if he was willing to help you with fortune telling, having no head at present does present a problem."

Danny could well see that it would but, reluctant to give up, he said, "If I went on an expedition to find his head, and you could give it to him, maybe he'd appear in my church with his head under his arm. That'd be good."

"No, no, no," said Angel Jo emphatically, "that is out of the question. Even if you found it, and poor obliging Malachy could be persuaded to agree, BOAK would never allow it. You see a special visa is now required to get out of heaven even if you are a Saint, and quite right too for BOAK can't have Saints traipsing around the universe spreading peace and goodwill and foretelling the future, and all that nonsense with no agendas, minutes or records of any kind notifying BOAK what they are up to… in triplicate. So please leave St Malachy out of it, head or no head. If you want to tell people's fortunes, you will just have to make it up. Actually, between you and me, Daniel Malachy, I think that's what he did when he was down here. Now tell me, what else do you have in mind for this church of yours, and I'll see if I can help?"

Our little hero had long thought that as well as telling fortunes something sensational like miracles was what was most lacking in any of the existing churches of his acquaintance, which he thought odd for the Bible seemed to be full of them. And it had suddenly occurred to him that now Angel Jo was helping him for once in however small a way, maybe he could supply a miracle or two or maybe just appear once in a while even if only to flap the wings he was so proud of or maybe just sit polishing up his halo.

"No, I most certainly will not," said Jo when Danny suggested it. "What do you think I am, a circus turn?" Then more calmly, "where are you going to hold your church services, and when do you plan to hold them for it would be poor timing if they clashed with all the other rigmaroles going on in all the many churches round here on Sundays?"

Now our hero had thought this bit out too so he said confidently, "The best time would be on Saturdays… about two o'clock when Robbie is listening to the football on the wireless or away in Cobain's pub and mammy is doing her shopping… and there's no school, for its them'uns I want at my church."

"Oh, you mean both the Protestant and Catholic scholars will be your congregation… well, that will make a change round these parts since all the other churches work so hard at keeping you all separated… and you are not inviting older people… how very novel… so it's really a sort of Sunday school."

"No, it's not like Sunday school," said Danny firmly for there was no collection taken up at Sunday school and, as we have seen, Danny's hopes were mainly pinned on the bounty from that collection. "It is to be a proper church and older ones can come but only when I get it up and going so it's just people at my school and the Catholic school to start with. Oh, and nobody will have to learn anything off by heart like the catechism, hymns or bits out of the Bible."

"And how," queried the angel, "are you going to lure them in on a Saturday afternoon… when they might want to be playing that ridiculous football game you all play to what purpose I know not?"

"With the miracles… and the fortune-telling… and maybe a relic thing or two if I happen to find them," replied Danny. "There's going to be lots of miracles in my church but I've only got the first one worked out. It's about a dog and…. "

"Oh spare me," cried Jo raising his wings to his ears in mock alarm. "I don't think I can stand the excitement."

"Well anyway," Danny continued, "it's all about getting things up and going again when they're really dead. Wouldn't that be a good miracle?"

"Certainly would. I look forward to hearing all about it but not now. Where did you say this miracle, and all the rest, is going to take place?"

"In Robbie's shed, after Bobby and Dorry have tidied it up for me. Then I will need funny clothes and some candles. I won't bother with prayers and singing an' that… just read the Bible but only for a minute or two so as not to bore people, then a bit about the devil to scare them all, and then do the miracle… I am going to charge everybody a shilling before the start, for miracles are dear things done right… oh, and for anybody who wants me to tell their fortune, that's an extra sixpence."

"My, you have got it all worked out!" exclaimed the angel. "How I look forward to writing up my report on your ecclesiastical efforts. But now I must be off. Glad, as ever, to be of help to you, little earthling," and he vanished leaving Danny to wonder yet again to what 'help' the angel was referring?

The Church Militant

It was a wet Saturday afternoon when Danny got his church up and running. News of the venture had not been greeted with general rejoicing among Ballybracken youth, its attraction being mainly lost on his fellow scholars for who wanted the affliction, as sadly most saw it, of yet another ecclesiastical gathering in religion-saturated Ballybracken.

But in the event, turnout was quite respectable, and it would be gratifying to record that ultimately it was the lure of sanctity, devotion to the Scriptures and the prospect of a holy miracle or two to be performed by Danny - which had been his major selling point - that brought out such a goodly number on the day. But the reason is less up-lifting. In advertising his ecclesiastical venture, Danny had made it clear that a charge for membership was involved, and this had whetted the appetite of the Ballybracken Mafia - Evil Mickey for the Catholic and Tommy Morrison for the Protestant side - to get in on the act and get their cut out of Danny's takings. Both threatened a good 'duffin-up' of any non-attenders, and that had had the desired result that wet Saturday afternoon.

As befitted a pastor with a cure of souls, Danny appeared clad in a white sheet with his head through a hole in the middle for he thought it best to resemble, as much as possible, the Pope as depicted in his mammy's picture of the Pontiff. Thus clad, and with the belt from Robbie's B-Special uniform tightly doubled-buckled round his waist and Robbie's B-Special cap on his head, not at all successfully disguised by a white veil Dorry had worn at some function in her mother's church, he stood up to address the throng. On seeing this apparition, it was not encouraging to hear Guldy McFall describe Danny's appearance in his carefully considered ecclesiastical garb as *'lukin lake a seck aff oat mail*'[400], while other more scholarly observers said he reminded them of the scarecrow in the 'Wizard of Oz.'

Nothing daunted, Danny proceeded to collect the money, carefully monitored by Tommy Morrison on his right and Evil Micky on his left '... *in case yeh chait*[401] *us, Danny... so watch ye'rself...*' The stipend collected and carefully counted, it was reluctantly given to Morrison and Gormley at their insistence for *'safe keepin.'* Then, the congregation assembled, Danny made his way to the front to open proceedings.

"What day we kal yeh, Danny? Is it 'Father' or 'Reverent' or what?" Kathleen McGuire liked to be correct about such matters.

"If it's 'Father,'" Stanley Carson piped up, "I fir wan am hivin no daleins[402] way ye'r church, Danny, fir this must be an owl Catholic place so I'm goin home. May Da wud kill may fir bein in a Catholic chapel, him bein an Orangeman."

"Aye, an' if ye'r a 'Reverent', this is an owl Protestant church so we're leavin[403] too," chorused two Catholic girls at the front who had been clutching their rosary beads brought along in case they were exposed to just such heresy.

His ecclesiastical endeavours already threatened with schism and early withdrawal, Danny, who hadn't foreseen this problem, had to think fast.

"I'm kalled Holy Daniel Malachy," he said and, by way of further explanation, continued ".... cos from now on, yeh see, I'm very holy."

While the more thoughtful members of his congregation digested this information to resolve to their satisfaction if the use of the term 'holy' would

---

400 **Lukin lake a seck aff oat mail** – looking like a sack of oat meal
401 **Chait** – cheat
402 **No daleins** – will have nothing to do with it
403 **Leavin** – leaving

endanger their eternal destiny, Stanley again brought proceeding to the brink of schism.

"What's that white thingumajig floating about in the watter in yon jam jar, Holy Danny?" he ended amid an unpleasant ripple of laughter.

Alerted by the problem titles could cause, Danny sensed that he must not now refer to the bone in the jam jar as belonging to a saint so he said simply, "It's a holy realik. Yeh see, yeh can't do miracles or tell fortunes without a realik aff some kin. Yez don't know nothin about miracles or tellin fortunes if yez don't know that."

While he had thus succeeded in putting his audience on the back foot regarding the further perusal of titles and relics, he had now whetted their appetite for fortune-telling and miracles.

"When are yeh gonna git roun tay tellin our fortunes, Holy Daniel Malachy? I ony come tay hiv may fortune towel" demanded Madeline Beattie. "Ye'r goin that slow, we'll bay here tay Tibb's Eve[404]."

That was, at last, a helpful cue for our hero to extricate himself from the various difficulties that had so far beset his enterprise, so he said, "I can tell ye'r fortunes now I hiv got may realik." With that he lifted the jam jar, gave it a shake and peered into it.

Now the object in the water, so crudely and sacrilegiously referred to earlier by Stanley as the *'white thingumajig'* was indeed a saintly bone or so our holy hero had led himself to believe. After his discussion with Angel Jo, the necessity of getting hold of a saintly relic of some kind for his ecclesiastical foundation had been very much on his mind and, low and behold, didn't one turn up! Now we cannot ascribe his finding of the holy object to divine guidance, for he had found the bone in question in close proximity to the fox holes that littered the area around the Scroggy Brae, but Danny felt sure that it could easily have considerable holy provenance given that everybody knew the Scroggy forest was haunted – well attested by lots of people making their way home from Ballybracken pubs on Saturday nights - so what was to prevent the odd saint or two wandering about there scaring the wits out of people, rattling their skeletons and dropping their bones all over the place? It was thus that Danny acquired his 'realik,' so necessary for his fortune-telling and miracle working.

"Wud yeh git on way it," Madeline was getting impatient as Holy Daniel continued to peer into the jam jar.

Thus prompted, the holy one stretched out his arms and said in as other-

---

404 ***Tibb's Eve*** – *a folk expression for 'a day that will never come'*

worldly a voice as he could muster,

"I see al yuz-uns' futures. Unless yuz stap doin bad things lake stealin penny chews, jelly babies an' that… an' takin money from my church" - he thought this was a good opportunity to try to recover his church funds from his so-called 'protectors' – " an' copyin ye'r homework… an' al that sort aff thing, yez will al go straight tay hell tay be tormented bay the divil for iver… but if yez wud han things back lake money, jelly babies… an' that… yez wud bay alright an' might git inta heaven way a bit a luck… "

Having thus admonished them, drawing on these terrible examples of misdoing currently uppermost in his mind, yet finishing on a hopeful note, he threw a dishcloth over the jam jar and said hurriedly "so that's al… now yez know."

"Is that al?" demanded Madeline. "Sure that's no good! Sure we know al that. Isn't that what we hear ivery Sunday in big church. I want tay know who I'm gonna marry, and how many wains I'm gonna hiv?" Madeline was a large buxom girl of more mature outlook than the rest of the congregation.

"An' I wanna know who's gonna win the Gaelic match nixt Sunday between Tyrone an' Donegal fir may Da' is puttin big money on it?" demanded Seamus O'Kane.

"An' I wanna know when I'm gonna git picked fir the Ballybracken soccer team fir I'm far better than most aff them'uns on it?" said Walter Gillen.

With demands for personal fortunes to be revealed amid mounting clamour, Danny's had the presence of mind to say,

"Yez wud'nt want tay hear each other's fortunes fir sure it might be bad news, so I'll tell ye'r fortunes separate next week," adding, "if yeh bring me another sixpence."

That seemed to pacify most of the audience except for the extra sixpence bit which was universally challenged except by Tommy and Micky who let it be known that they expected their cut from this additional wealth fir holy Danny wud surely need even more *protection* if his soothsaying didn't match expectations.

With proceedings not going exactly as Danny had hoped, he now moved on to perform the long-awaited miracle which he felt to be so sensational it would surely retrieve the situation. Announcing this to his restive audience, he called for hush but not before Doris Lyttle side-tracked him again by demanding,

"What's that mangy owl dog doin there behin yeh, Holy Danny? It's stinkin an' it's boun tay bay covered in flays[405]… if I go home way flays may mammy will kill may… an' then she'll come lukin fir you."

"There's no flays on that dog," Danny assured her, "an' anyway its dead."

Some explanation is now required regarding the prone canine presence stretched out behind Danny which was indeed looking very dead. Robbie had found the creature, emaciated and sickly, wandering on the road a few weeks back. He had brought it home to try to restore it to health and strength but no matter how good his ministration, the poor creature continued to lie in front of the hearth semi-lifeless with Rosie continually tripping over it until she could tolerate it no longer and ordered Robbie to remove it to his shed. There it now lay, eyes shut looking suitably dead for Danny's purposes, and soon to form the centrepiece of his carefully planned first miracle.

"It can't bay dead," said Rose McGlinn whose command of anatomy seemed more secure than the others. "Sure it hez jist wagged its tail."

Yet again this afternoon Danny had to think fast to retrieve the situation.

"Dead dogs can still wag their tails," he assured her with what confidence he could muster and continued "… jist lake Robbie says dead people's hair an' nails still grow in the coffin long after they're buried."

This piece of gruesome information, whether true or otherwise, promptly split the congregation into those who speculated how great it would be to dig up a corpse after a suitable lapse of time to see if the coffin was full of hair and long nails, and those of more fragile disposition who clung to each other in something approaching terror at the very thought. Whatever the reaction, Danny felt his audience was losing focus so to re-engage them he thought he'd postpone the miracle and instead start to preach.

"Yeh see, Adam an' Eve ate an apple," he said, "an' God wuzn't fir that, an' towel them to get out of the garden, niver darken his dure again, an' that from now on they an' iverywan roun them were al goin tay hell after he'd drownded them al….except somebody come along at the last minute way a big boat an' saved some aff the good wans… an' the animals too fir they hadn't ate any apples

---

405 **Flays** – *fleas*

… includin lions… but they didn't ate Daniel either… but that was later on… an' that's why I'm called Daniel… an' so nobody called Daniel is iver ate bay lions so I can go to Africa anytime an' not be ate… but the rest aff yez wud bay ate so watch ye'rselves when yez go tay Africa… an' I wudn't ate too many apples cos God doesn't seem to favour people eatin apples…"

This seemed to bring his sermon to a satisfactory and logical conclusion, and, in Danny's mind, made as much sense as most of the Canon's sermons every Sunday. But his audience, who had not been at all attentive throughout his homily, now fell into yet more schism.

"We want tay bay nuns in your church, Holy Danny," demanded Roisin O'Neill and Brigid Heaney.

"I'm not fir havin no nuns," Danny said emphatically mainly because he didn't know what 'nuns' were.

"Yeh must hiv nuns unless it's an owl Protestant church," the girls continued "… an' yeh must hiv Jeezes's mammy, the Virgin Mary."

"I want tay play the Virgin Mary," pleaded Carmel McGuire, "fir I played hir at our school's nativity play hast Christmas, an' I wuz great."

"I'm not hivin the Virgin Mary ether," Danny declared.

"Yeh MUST hiv the Virgin Mary," shouted the Catholic girls. "Sure iverybody knows that without the Virgin Mary there would be no Jeezes."

"Yeh can hive Jeezes but no Virgin Mary… Protestants don't bother way the Virgin Mary," said Guldy McFall, taking upon himself the promotion of the Protestant cause.

Carmel McGuire retorted, "shut ye'r bake[406], Guldy. Hands up who wants Holy Danny tay hiv nuns an' the Virgin Mary?"

The Catholics all put up their hands as the Protestants shouted "We ony want Jeezes."

"There yeh are, Holy Danny. Most aff us want nuns an' the Virgin Mary."

"We do not," shouted the Protestants.

"Yuz'ens don't matter, fir may Da says yuz Protestants are al gonna hell anyway." Patsy Kelly's contribution, less than healing and settling as it was, immediately sparked a fist fight initially with Patsy and Micky Gormley championing the Virgin, nuns and other tenets of Catholic theology and Tommy Morrison and Guldy McFall battling it out for Jesus and the Protestants.

The 'Wars of Religion' thus rekindled at the back of Robbie's shed, the combatants were soon joined by several other youths thus turning the back

---

406 **Bake** – *mouth*

of the shed into a veritable battleground. As if that wasn't bad enough, the Catholic girls had now fallen out over who could best fulfil the role of the Blessed Virgin, and that despite the fact that Danny had ruled her out of his ecclesiastical canon.

"How cud you play the Blessed Virgin?" Carmel McGuire was now shaking Soibhan O'Neill in a most unchristian manner. "A big fat pahil[407] lake you. Sure the Virgin is lovely an' slim like the statue aff hir in the chapel. You'd niver fit into hir lovely white dress and blue cloak. An' sure it was me that wuz the Virgin in the school play the Christmas before last, an' I played hir far better than you, sure ivery wan said you were rubbish compared way me."

"Who are yeh kallin a pahil? Sure you cudn't be the Virgin, sure you're nothin but a wee trollop." Soibhan now had her hands round Carmel's throat and err long they had fallen off the bench and were rolling on the shed floor as yet another battle royal was joined at the front.

All the while, Danny was trying to convince himself that neither the structure of his new foundation or its liturgical essentials were yet in jeopardy or, put another way, that he was still in control of things in a loose sort of way.

"Day yez wanta see the miracle?" he shouted over the din.

When he had bellowed this at least three times, he succeeded in restoring some semblance of order if only temporarily for there was much unpleasant talk of the theological violence continuing outside after witnessing the miracle.

"Day yez want tay see me bring this dead dog back tay life?" he asked.

"Sure it's not dead." Rose McGlinn was determined to be awkward regarding the dog's physical condition. "Sure it hiz jist waggled its ears."

"They can do that too when they're dead," Danny reassured the doubters, "jist lake they can wag their tail."

"They can NOT," retorted Rose. "It's ether dead or it's not, an' it's not."

But her scepticism was lost on the congregation most of whom now wanted to see a miracle if only to get their shilling's worth.

"I can ony perform miracles in the near dark," Danny said and, raising his arms heavenwards, he started to chant in a high-pitched voice, "Sister Dorry, close the dure[408]. Brother Bobby, light the cannles."

Well-rehearsed as his sister and brother were, and mindful that they too expected a share in the ecclesiastical takings, Dorry promptly shut the shed door with a resounding bang which fortunately plunged the shed into temporary darkness

---

407 **Pahil** – stout; lumpen
408 **Dure** – door

for the noise caused the dog to exert itself more than it had since its arrival with the Dowdells. But all was well. This sudden exertion proved too much, and it promptly fell back to its prone semi-dead state, and so it lay as Bobby lit two candles placing one at its head and the other between its back legs.

"Go on, Bobby, shove wan up its ass," called Tommy Morrison confirming, if such were needed, what a very coarse fellow he was.

The candle glow had a soothing effect on the congregation prompting Danny to light a third candle. Then, holding it in both hands, he raised it above his head wailing and chanting in a high-pitched dismal kind of way and then, his audience stunned into silence, he steadily bent down over the dog slowly lowering the candle. Whether it was the hot grease dripping from the descending candle unto the dog's flank or the insertion of a large pin that Bobby had been instructed to stick surreptitiously in the dog's rear to effect the life-restoring miracle or a combination of both, it is idle to speculate. Suffice to say that thus stimulated, the dog gave an almighty howl, rose at least a good half foot in the air, bared its teeth, bit Danny savagely on the leg and bounded in a demented fashion round and round the shed to the consternation of the congregation. With screams of terror all round, somebody had the presence of mind to throw open the shed door whereupon the dog effected its escape and ran off down the road presumably in search of somewhere where it could lie down again and die in peace, well away from any attempts to resuscitate it.

The lobby of sceptics led by Rose had now grown considerably in the minutes following the dog's 'miraculous' resurrection with Rose now claiming that the dog had been drugged, and Danny should be put in jail for cruelty to animals. The same sceptics now demanded their money back or they would hand Danny over to Constable McCrum recently returned from his honeymoon, and this clamour for restitution was soon taken up by all the congregation some declaring that the afternoon's proceedings had just proved that Danny Dowdells should be in a mental asylum and was a bigger *owl fraud* than they all already knew him to be.

However, in demanding their money back, they had not taken account of the strong-arm tactics of Tommy Morrison and Evil Mickey who had no intention of letting their 'cut' slip through their fingers.

"Yez is gittin no money back, so yez isn't," Tommy said in a most threatening manner which Micky confirmed saying, "Sure yez hiv seen a real miracle way that owl dog an' yez hiv had ye'r fortune towel. What more day yez want?"

Though this was received with much dissent, the gist of which was that

Danny was *'for it'* at some future unspecified date, all knew not to cross the Ballybracken Mafia – especially since their threatening words were followed up with mention yet again of a 'good cloutin' being administered to those who persisted in seeking redress - so all made for the exit muttering darkly.

'Evil Mickey' said, "Yeh see what yev done, Danny. They've sure al got it in fir yeh. Boy, do you need protectin now! Sure Tommy an' me I'll divide the takins between us …. tay square us up[409] fir lookin after yeh, lake. Yeh know rightly that without us I wudn't give twopence fir ye'r chances."

And with that unsought promise of protection and leaving no room for negotiation, Tommy and Mickey were off acrimoniously dividing out all the takings as they went.

"What about us?" wailed Bobby. "Yeh promised Dorry an' me a share an' now there's nothin left. You owe us, Danny, an' if yeh don't pay us we'll tell mammy yeh got us tay stale hir cannles an' that it wuz you put that big tear in her sheet… an' we'll tell daddy yeh used his cep[410] an' belt an' hurted hez dog… boy, will you get the quare skelpin[411]."

It was indeed a truism Danny had reluctantly to concede – but only to himself - that his ecclesiastical endeavours had not exactly worked out as planned and, worst of all, that his financial situation was now in even greater jeopardy than before. His debts were mountainous, his physical well-being under threat from several quarters, his sanity in question, his leg bleeding, and how was he going to explain that tear in the white sheet to his mother and even worse the disappearance of the dog to Robbie? No solutions flooded in even to his fertile mind but, as we know, such tangled conundrums were not that unusual for our little hero and, as always, he found it soothing to take a walk up to his stone on top of the Scroggy Brae or down to the 'Meeting of the Waters' when his life became too turbulent and problems intractable. On this occasion, it was to the rivers he turned for solace, lying on the bank listening to the bird song and the wonderful river music that only he could hear. This was heaven on earth and, for Danny, always would be. He closed his eyes, sucked his thumb and fell fast asleep resolving to leave churches and all their attendant squabbling to the holy people.

---

409 **Square us up** – *pay us*
410 **Cep** – *cap*
411 **Skelpin** – *beating*

Apes, Evolution & The Big Cover-Up

"… Just passing," Angel Jo said. "I'm in a terrible hurry. On my way to the beautiful planet Verdantia but I was wondering how you got on? I suppose it's a bit early for your church to have started a war yet but give it time, in the end they all do. What happened, and what are you going to do next? I need full details for my report."

"It went OK," said Danny lying gallantly. "Just got to square up a few wee points and it'll be great," and not wanting to discuss the future of his ecclesiastical ambitions any further – for there weren't any - he closed his eyes and pretended to snore.

"How very rude," exclaimed Angel Jo. "Here I am dropping in on you at considerable inconvenience and all you can do is to fall asleep."

Danny said shamefacedly, "I am very tired after my church meeting… an' doing the miracle… an' usin my relic… an' that… "

Since, for once, Angel Jo didn't seem to already know what had transpired back in Robbie's hut, our little hero knew it was imperative to steer him away from embarrassing enquiries if he was to save even a modicum of face. He now deployed his considerable skill at diversion tactics. Robbie had recently said something about apes which intrigued Danny, and about which he had made a mental note to ask the angel. Now was just the time.

"Robbie claims we are really apes only without as much hair. And Robbie says when we apes decided to stop jumping about in the trees – which must have been good fun – and decided to live on the ground, we thought we needed to call God something so we called Him 'God' but we might just as well have called him 'dog'… for 'dog' is 'God' backwards so it's only a word and Robbie thinks we should now really call God 'Evil…' something. It's all to do with us being apes a while back, at least I think that is what he said. What do you think?"

The angel wasn't ready for a question on the origins of the human species so, in the absence of an immediate reply, Danny blundered on in the pursuit of knowledge, but mainly still pursuing the cover-up plans concerning his efforts at church building.

"… and Robbie says… " but he was cut short by Angel Jo latching on to the strange suggestion that the Almighty should be called 'Evil.'

"Evil!" he exclaimed, "Evil! ... that man reads too much. He is definitely dangerous... like your Ancient Greeks after we had foolishly meddled with them and made them too smart for their own good... and look what that has led to... ologies of all kinds, useless debates and discussions... everybody having a say... Ridiculous! No wonder we were told never to meddle with you lot again. Mind you, when I come to think of it, I suppose all those '-----ologies' keep your silly universities in business arguing and debating, and the democracy nonsense keeps you dunderheads from killing each other... well, some of the time." He tailed off and then, recollected what had started him on this diatribe against all that civilized humanity holds dear, said, "I don't think your friend, Robbie, could possibly have said that you might as well call God 'Evil'. Surely you didn't get that right, my confused little earthling?"

"It might have been 'Evil-u' ... something. Anyway, whatever it is, Robbie says it just proves God - or whatever you want to call him – is just far smarter than all the holy people think He is and even smarter than the Bible says he is because he invented that 'evil-u...' thing... an' we should all be calling Him that instead of calling him 'God.'"

"Oh, you mean 'EVOLUTION!'" exclaimed Angel Jo triumphantly.

"It might be that," Danny said, "but how can we all pray to God if He now should be called 'Eviluzhun.' My mammy says a decade of the Rosary and the Lord's Prayer every night and I don't think she would ever get used to starting the Lord's Prayer saying 'Our Eviluzion' who art in Heaven...'

Danny diversionary ploy was working brilliantly for the angel was now wearing his stern 'school-teacher' face so familiar to Danny when his class were having a bad day in school and getting everything wrong.

"The word is 'EVOLUTION,'" said Angel Jo in an exasperated way, "and of course you should not rename God 'Evolution'. Such a ridiculous idea worthy of you 'earth-grubbers'. Mind you," he reflected, "evolution brings us full circle to your question about you and the apes."

"So, are we really apes?" Danny repeated. "Only the apes haven't learned to shave like Robbie does before he goes to something special like a wedding or out on patrol with the B-men?"

"Well, what do you think, Daniel Malachy? Know anyone round here that looks like an ape?"

Danny pondered. "Jessy Craig looks a bit like one and Mickey Gormley from over the Esker looks like one too... so maybe we are apes only most of us have got a bit better looking now what with washing ourselves more and shaving the hair off our faces when we are big like Robbie."

"You are all apes really… only a bit cleverer… but only a bit, mind. I must confess, though, it was great fun watching you evolve but then of course it all went wrong. Still, there is no point in trying to improve things down here even if we were allowed to. No, you naked apes are a lost cause, so you will just have to muddle through as best you can, and I have to confess you have all become quite good at that. 'Leave well enough alone' must be my motto or as your Bard put it so beautifully, *'Striving for better oft you mar what's well'* … or something like that… though to say things are 'well' down here really does require an athletic leap of the imagination. But *'you are where you are'*… and now I suppose I have to tell you, my ignorant little ape man, that I'm quoting your great Shakespeare. That man said such a lot of sensible things, but do you apes listen? No, you do not, but then I suppose it was your stupid ape antics that gave him so much to write about so profoundly and beautifully. All in all, much better for him to turn up here on this piece of rock with you crowd and reflect on all your nonsensical goings-on than on one of the Almighty's perfect creations. Well, he'd have had nothing to write about if he had turned up on one of those."

This long reflection on the human condition was just what our crafty little hero had hoped for. He had successfully diverted Angel Jo from asking awkward questions about his attempts at church building, and all its attendant problems on that Saturday afternoon. While we must deplore such wilful guile, surely we also have to admire our hero's growing mastery of the art of the side-step, often so vital to a successful life.

And as for the apes… well… best forgotten! They had served their diversionary purpose!

Episode 37

Big Bertie's Bounty

The Kitchen Wedding

"Iniver wuz at a drier affair, well, jist short aff wan aff them dry holy folk funerals[412]." Robbie said in disgust and stone cold sober as he, Rosie and Danny trudged back home from Jim McKnight's wedding to Janie Stewart. "I'm dyin of drooth[413]. Wudn't yeh hiv thought that they cud hiv put on a better show than that. I wuzn't expectin a hooley[414] but a wheena bottles aff porter wud hiv been in order even if we hadda down them in the byre outa sight aff the holy crawthumpers[415]. Sure Bertie hez been known tay take a brave drap in Cobain's when he gets the chance."

And indeed Jim and Janie's nuptials had taken place in a spirit of dismal puritan gloom and an amount of unpleasantness in the kitchen of the Stewart farmhouse.

"Wuz it a proper weddin at al?" Rosie mused. "Fir lake is it right tay hive a weddin that's not in a church aff some kin? An' poor Jim… did yez not see how put out[416] he wuz throughout the proceedins. But at l-est they had Quigley there an' he's a great pretcher they say, so maybe they are married al right in the sight aff God. I hope so, fir lake it wudn't do fir them tay bay livin in sin."

"Sure we're livin in sin, as yeh cawl it," Robbie said taking her arm, "but yeh wudn't hiv it any other way, wud yeh?"

Rosie didn't reply. She was a woman used to living with contradictions. A bit further on she said,

"Yeh did great as Jim's best man even if ye'r joke wuz outta place in that holy getherin[417] … an' didn't wee Danny do great too way the singin… I'm

---

412 **Just short aff wan aff them dry holy funerals** – except for the tee-total funerals of the very religious
413 **Drooth** – extreme need of a drink especially alcoholic
414 **A hooley** – a lively party
415 **Crawthumpers** – very religious people
416 **Put out** – annoyed
417 **Getherin** – gathering; crowd

always that proud aff him," and she ran her fingers through Danny's hair which, although it was sissy, Danny didn't mind since it was dark and there was nobody about on the road. "Mind you," she continued, "in other respects yeh let may down a bagful[418], Danny. Cud yeh not hiv gone aisier on the atein[419], yeh wee gorb[420] yeh. I wuz fair crecked[421] watchin yeh ate iverythin before yeh at yon table when the releegious bit wuz goin on… cud yeh notta held aff till yeh were bid tay help ye'rself."

Robbie said, "Aye, wee comrade, Yeh didn't stint ye'rself. I thought yeh wuda ate the arm aff owl Quigley if he'd come too close tay yeh. But sure that'd hiv been the price aff him[422] an' maybe got him tay cal a halt[423] tay al that preachin. Anyway, Danny, sure a good singin-man needs tay keep hez strength up."

Danny said nothing. He was so full of good things his stomach ached badly, but he thought it best not to complain in the circumstances.

"Day yeh not think," Rosie mused, "that yon owl Mrs. Roulston shud bay at home in hir bed for sure she's clian dotin[424]. She hizent a gleed[425] a sense. Did yeh iver hear such owl lip[426] when it's hir prayers she shud bay sayin, an' as fir them duds[427] hir an' Annie wur wearin… niver seen the lake… luked as if they had jist threw on them[428] way whativer come tay han."

"The sooner the divil takes that owl woman, the better," Robbie said. "She's wan right owl heverel[429]. She had no need tay come out way al that bad chat about Catholics an' the rest aff it. It's a wunner yeh cud stick it[430]."

But Rosie was used to 'stickin it' in Ballybracken, so why would she be thrown by the ravings of a doting old woman when she had so much else to contend with on a daily basis? And anyway, wee Danny's great singing and musical

---

418 **Yeh let may down a bagful** – you embarrassed me greatly
419 **Gone az-ier on the atein** – you shouldn't have eaten so much
420 **A gorb** – a glutton
421 **Crecked** – driven half mad
422 **Hiv been the price aff him** – he would have richly deserved it
423 **Tay cal a halt** – to stop
424 **Clian dotin** – suffering from advanced senility
425 **Not a gleed a sense** – not a spark of common sense
426 **Owl lip** – offensive impertinent talk
427 **Duds** – poor quality clothes
428 **Threw on them** – dressed hurriedly without any thought of quality, taste or style
429 **Heverel** – an ill-disposed woman… a scandalmonger
430 **It's a wonner yeh cud stick it** – Its surprising you could bear it

abilities had got her family talked about in a good way by many Ballybracken folk though she knew rightly there were just as many, and maybe more, who thought the Dowdells were getting *'above themselves'* what with being invited – or at least asked to be present at – *'gran weddins, an' rubbin schaulders*[431] *way the big folk.'*

Daniel Malachy had come away with a different feeling about the kitchen wedding from his mother and Robbie mainly, indeed mostly, because the 'spread' already alluded to had been so good. There was his favourite chicken, of course, and lots of fancy iced buns, jelly stuff with cream on the top, nice short bread biscuits, big sponge cakes oozing cream, chocolate cakes and, as a centrepiece, a lovely big iced wedding cake. All this bounty was spread out on the big kitchen table set against the wall beside which Danny had been told to sit and behave himself while the wedding service took place in the middle of the kitchen. All the guests – and they only amounted to a few close relatives and some of the holy neighbours wearing funereal rather than wedding faces - were seated tight up against the kitchen walls. Sourest of all was Effie McKnight whose expression throughout indicated that this wedding, taking place out of public view in a farm kitchen, was not what she had envisaged for her son, and that she was only there because she had to be. What the beautiful Helen thought of her brother's nuptials we will never know. As usual, she sat demurely in the background at her most inscrutable.

Danny's removal from proceedings to sit by the table left him with a free run to get ahead of the field and make inroads on the feast. He knew very well that he shouldn't touch anything but, as so often happens to us all, desire overrode conscience, and he helped himself to an iced bun with a big red cherry on top.

The Reverend Quigley takes the Floor

The Reverend Quigley appeared to be in no hurry to get on with the marrying aspect of the ceremony for he felt it his Godly duty on this as on all occasions to remind all present how close they were to going to hell, and how it was anything but a picnic if you ended up there. As his rehearsal of the terrors ahead grew in length and volume, the Miss Sproules held hands and dabbed their eyes with

---

431 **Schaulders** – *shoulders*

dainty embroidered hankies, resolving there and then to get even more holy if that were possible. The good pastor had moved on to the 'Wedding Feast at Cana', his purpose being to remind everybody that when the Lord changed the water into wine, he had it on good authority it wasn't wine of the alcoholic variety. It was, he said, stuff made from black currants with not a touch of alcohol in it, which he proceeded to declare was the same alcohol-free stuff Jesus used at the last supper. This brought him neatly to the evils of drink, and he said he knew for certain there were still 'hellish' poteen-making stills scattered all over Ballybracken's bogs, the product of which was driving otherwise good men mad in the head and so anybody who knew of the stills' locations should report them to the police immediately so that the full rigour of the law could be brought to bear on such miscreants.

Robbie smirked for he and Packie's Ned had recently resumed production. Jinny Maxwell, however, felt a guilty flush sweep over her for she knew of a still on the mountainy land next to her farm but, hell or no hell, there was no way she could go running to the police about it since it was her father, Fat Jamie's still. The good poteen from it was the only thing that kept all her family's chests clear of the phlegm over a raw winter… or so this 'good-livin' family had convinced itself.

Then it was the turn of the rich and greedy to get a touch for the Reverend Quigley now proceeded to draw on the well-known story about a camel trying to get through the eye of a needle. For the life of him, Danny couldn't fathom that bit but anyway the Reverend's big message here was that, when the collection plate was passed round, he – and God – expected a 'silent collection' presumably to relieve some of the wealthy present of their bank notes, and so give them a fighting chance to tread the streets of paradise. It seemed a hopeful sign that, thus admonished and exhorted, Jessy Craig opened the noisy clasps of her big handbag - her constant companion as we have long observed - as if preparing to divest herself of at least some of the contents so as not to share the frustration of the camel and the dire fate of the rich. But no! The admonition had only prompted her to check that her bundle of white five-pound notes were still there and, thus reassured and ramming them even further down to the bottom, she closed the handbag with a resounding clang.

Danny, bored out of his mind for he had heard all of this before in the mission hall, was by now on his second, or was it his third, slice of cold chicken and ham having already devoured a further three iced buns.

But the Reverend wasn't finished yet. Hypocrites and heretics were next on the list by which he meant anyone who was not in full agreement with him on all matters spiritual, and that brought him on to the meek who clearly he thoroughly approved of, and then it was the whores' turn. But this was a Dantean Circle too far for the Miss Sproules who, trembling like delicate autumn leaves, had to withdraw to the back hall and prop each other up over a milk churn.

Round about the hypocrites bit, Rosie suddenly twigged what her Danny was up to since the lower part of his face was now covered in a mixture of fresh cream, icing and bits of chicken. Tempted as she was to go over and lift him by the ear, she had to content herself by gesticulating at him from across the kitchen to try to get his attention and exhort him to leave off. But by now the Reverend was waxing lyrical about the whores and, given her own questionable domestic arrangements, she dare not move in case he would use her as a visual aid of a local example of a woman 'taken in adultery', the Reverend's view being that the Saviour had gone far too *'aisy'* on that *'hure'* in the Bible.

The Danny Tucks in

Rosie's gesticulations from the far side of the kitchen were to no avail. Danny was now sampling the trifle and was just wondering where he could find a knife to cut a slice of chocolate cake when the bride's father, Big Bertie, spotted what was happening at his lavishly-spread table and said, for he was not a man to mince his words,

"Wud yeh fer feck sake get them pair married for they will bay ready tay draw the pension the speed ye'r goin at… an' if yeh don't hurry ye'rself up that caddy will hiv the leg ate aff the table the way he's goin at the burd[432]. It's well seen[433] yeh hiv no cows tay milk, stannin there tellin us what we al know an' ye'r two arms the wan length[434]."

Thus admonished by his host, the Reverend Quigley cut short his survey of the more chastening portions of Scripture and, without more ado, married Jim and Janie finishing in wringing tones, *'them that God hez joined thegether, let no man put asunner,'* whereupon Robbie muttered, *'not much chance aff that'* as he, in turn, rose to his feet to wish the newly-weds every happiness, tell a

---

432 **Burd** – *the food on the table*
433 **Well seen** – *obvious… quite apparent*
434 **Ye'r two hans the wan length** – *not getting on with the task in hand*

joke or two at which only Jim and one or two others laughed and, since there was no bridesmaid to thank for looking after the bride and looking beautiful themselves, he resumed his seat.

"I think we'll get Danny to sing to us after we have had some refreshment," Jim said taking charge, for nobody else was showing any desire to move things along, "… and it'll give his digestion a chance to recover for, like all small boys, I see he's keen on cake and buns."

"… an' chicken," said Danny, totally oblivious of the breach of decorum he had committed. This did raise a suppressed titter round the room.

Rosie now descended on the table and on Danny to drag him away and wipe his mouth.

Unsavoury Sentiments

"Wud yeh bring may somethin tay ate, for pity sake, fir may stomach thinks may throat's cut." Old Mrs. Roulston had fallen asleep during most of the Reverend's homily, her mouth wide open and dentures champing when she snored. Now refreshed, she was clamouring for sustenance. It was then she spotted Rosie for the first time.

"Is yon the Papish woman that's livin in sin way that big sodger fella?" she asked, wrapping her black shawl around her for protection in case the 'sodger fella' chanced to come her way with evil intent.

"Wud yeh wheesht[435], mammy," said her daughter Annie, "that's no tak tay bay comin out way here[436]." And then to the guests, who had now left their chairs and had flocked to the table in an undignified scrum, she continued, "mammy mains no harm, yeh know. She gets a wee bit confused these days."

"Well, what's a Papish doin here at a Christian weddin? Sure they're not Christians at al, them Papishes."

"Mammy, hir wee lad hez been brung up a good Protestant an' he's gonna sing tay us fir he's a powerful singer. He's that good, you'll die when yeh hear him."

"… with any luck," muttered Robbie, for his first thought was to take Rosie and Danny home before they had to endure any more insults, even if they were coming from a doting old woman. But he knew that would annoy his old friend, Jim, and anyway Rosie didn't seem to be taking any of this under her notice.

---

435 **Wud yeh wheesht** – *be quiet… hold your tongue*
436 **That's no tak tay bay comin out way here** – *Don't be talking like that here*

"I hope it's our hymns he's gonna sing an' not any Papish wans for way can't bay doin way them[437]," the old woman prattled on. "Them'uns is gettin in iveryroad. We had a Papish sarvant man wance; he wuz a right fella but sure yeh can niver thrust them. Cut your throat or shoot yeh from bayhin the ditch as quick as luk at yeh. Naw, I can't be doin way them, an' niver cud."

"Now mammy, I'll hiv tay take yeh straight home if yeh carry on this way," said Annie, handing her a plate of food salvaged from the wreck that was the remains of the wedding breakfast.

The old lady took a bite of a sandwich, and then spat most of it out.

"I don't think much aff that," she said. "Wudn't yeh think they wuda had a sit-down 'do' them that hez this big house way a dining room an' al. Ach, the Stewarts wur no better than wurselves times ago, hadn't the nails tay scratch themselves[438] more than other folk around here. Cud they not hive got the wee cutty a white dress tay get married in… or maybe there's something wrong an' white isn't suitable, if yez see what I main." and with that she leered at the bride whose turn it now was to flush pillar-box red, flee into the back hall and avail of the support of the milk churn.

"Towel yeh!" the old dame cried triumphantly. "She's fallen by the wayside[439]. Cryin an' hot flushes bees a sure sign that somethin afut[440]. Och, it'll not be too long till there's nappies on the line out there in the yard way no disguising them. This is a scannel that'ill surely finish aff the Stewarts an' it'ill bay the price aff them. I've waited long fir this day… Luk at Bertie yonner… him that fulla himself… but they'r good name is now down in the sheugh way yon wee trollop aff their's, sure as shootin. No white dress this weddin day clinches their disgrace. An' it's not before time. God an' the worl knows they al but stole a turf bank aff ye'r father… said it wuz theirs bay rights when it wuzn't… Bertie comes tay our dure an' says, sez he, b-owl as brass, 'I'll take it aff ye'r hans[441],' says he, an' stole it aff us… give us nixt nothin[442] fir it … an' then there's hir way hir tight lips, an' hir that main an' near[443] she wud skin a flea for its tallow… an' them

---

437 **Way can't bay doin way them** – *we can't tolerate them*
438 **Hadn't the nails tay scratch themselves** – *they were very poor with no surplus funds*
439 **Fallen by the wayside** – *become pregnant out of wedlock*
440 **Somethin's afut** – *something suspicious is going on*
441 **Take it aff ye'r hands** – *I'll relieve you of it as a favour*
442 **Nixt nothin** – *paid very little for it*
443 **She's that main & near** – *she is so mean and miserable*

pretendin tay be that releegious an' good livin. Och, it's a long road that there dezent come a turn in… and here they are now way their luck run out at last. Oh, there's nothin I don't know…" she tailed off as Annie brought her a glass of some temperance liquid in an endeavour to shut her up.

"Take that away outta that," exclaimed her mother. "I wudn't soil may mouth way the lakes aff that if may tongue wuz hangin out[444]. Wudn't yeh think they'd hiv stretched tay somethin stronger than coloured watter an' wake tay[445]. I niver cud bay doin way wake tay. Ye'r father used tay kal it 'scarred watter'. A drap aff brandy wud hiv gone high[446] …though yez know I'd ony bay takin it tay clear may chest… fir yez al know that strong drink is the ruination aff this country…. but wudn't yeh think they'd hive somethin laid in more than yez is getting."

It would be folly to assume that this unguarded outburst hadn't put something of a dampener on proceedings. Jim hastened to retrieve his bride from the back hall. Jinny Maxwell thought it was time to be going for *'the pigs needs feedin.'* The Miss Sproules looked as if a stick of dynamite, from which there was no escape, had landed on each of their laps. Jessy Craig, by contrast, her buffet plate still heaped with good things, which she continued to gorge on noisily, felt that there was a great deal of truth in what old Mrs. Roulston was saying, and indeed was hoping to hear more especially about disputes – verging on outright wars – over turf banks and farms of land, all battles that were close to her own heart.

Big Bertie's first impulse was to chase the Roulston couple home and tell them never to darken his door again especially if they wanted him to *'pull them out aff a hole'* which was a frequent occurrence since he had a tractor and they hadn't. But for once he restrained himself and only said,

"I hope yez is al enjoyin ye'rselves," which, despite the good spread, was, by this time, something of a vain hope. He continued, "now dig in, fir there's plenty left an' we want nothin goin tay waste."

Praise indeed!

Danny didn't understand what was going on except that in the midst of it he had feasted, and indeed was continuing to feast, rather too well. Better still, they now seemed to have forgotten all about him singing and if he got the money

---

444 ***If may tongue wuz hangin out*** – *if I was dying with thirst*
445 ***Wake tay*** – *weak tea*
446 ***Gone high*** – *it would have been very welcome*

without the bother of singing, that would be great. But out little hero was rejoicing too soon. With his bride disengaged from the milk churn and restored to the kitchen, the groom judged the time finally right to call for a song. So Danny, his stomach bloated but his face clean, delighted them – in so far as that audience could ever allow themselves to delight in anything – by singing, at their request, the hymns *'How Great Thou Art,'* and *'Be Thou my Vision.'* Jim suggested he sing *'Eileen Oge'* and a few other Percy French favourites but the holy brigade vetoed this as 'unsuitable' whether because such popular songs were Godless or smacked too much of Irishness… or both.

Mrs. Roulston had fallen asleep before Danny had finished but she woke up for most of the last hymn and, in an uncharacteristically charitable moment, said, "that caddy hez a voice that cud coax the birds outta the bushes."

Praise indeed from that quarter!

Episode 38

The Bishop's Table Talk

The Greasy Pole

"Yes, my dear, the Bishop has been invited to the nuptials, and, yes, he is coming and his wife also, and, yes, they will stay with us overnight here in the rectory."

"His wife coming too! Lady Lavinia, the daughter of an Earl! Oh Horace, what a wonderful opportunity for us to shine. You must call the palace at once, ask what part His Grace will play in the ceremony, and say how honoured you will be to assist him."

"All taken care of, my love, without me having to do anything, and behind my back. Grovehill Manor and Ballybracken House have asked His Grace to officiate, Lady Lavinia invited too as a guest of honour, and the rectory volunteered as their abode. I had no say in the matter. Many apologies offered, of course… no time to discuss it with us… knew we would understand'… so I have been side-lined, there is no other word for it. I feel hurt, but there it is."

"Now Horace, don't pout. We can now concentrate on the wedding that really matters. We will be dining with one of the greatest in the church. What an opportunity!"

The Canon said nothing as his wife prattled on about needing to get out linen tablecloths and napkins that hadn't seen the light of day for years, shining up the few pieces of silver they had, planning the flowers for the various rooms where they would entertain the Bishop and his wife, and on and on she went as he slowly progressed down the hallway saying 'yes' and 'of course' and 'very suitable' at appropriate moments.

When he reached his study door, he said gently.

"I know I can leave all the domestic arrangements in your ever-capable hands, my dear, but now I must have a little quiet to compose my sermon for Sunday."

"Compose your what! Horace, you are not taking this wonderful opportunity seriously! Resurrect one of your old sermons for next Sunday. Nobody will notice. You have much more important things to do. Telephone the Palace immediately. Tell his Grace how much we are both, emphasize 'both', looking forward to having them to stay, how honoured you are to share the conduct of the ceremony with him in however minor a role… " she paused… "I wonder if they prefer poultry or red meat or fish for dinner…. should you ask them? Perhaps not…. just have them all ready to be on the safe side… yes, we will offer them a choice on the day… that surely is the repast a Bishop would expect and that a bishop-in-waiting would be expected to provide… that should go down well" and then, "… Get along, Horace, there is work to be done… the telephone, Horace."

Not for the first time, the Canon was glad to seek the sanctuary of his study with the door firmly shut behind him. "Why," he mused, "had a woman, noted and valued for her pragmatic common sense, suddenly become obsessed with her place in the world and its baubles, and with Bishops and Earl's daughters and all that show that he detested and which, until now, she claimed to detest too?" He poured himself a large sherry, thought better of it, clumsily poured it back into the bottle spilling half of it, and then nervously lifted the telephone.

The Bishop was not available said a lordly voice at the other end. He would ring back when it was convenient.

No call came.

Enter the High & Mighty

So without confirmation of their intentions or preliminary courtesies of any kind, the Bishop and his lady arrived, chauffeur driven, at the rectory on the eve of the great wedding. Mrs. Pretyman was in full readiness to receive them, and had been from early breakfast time.

The Bishop rolled out of the back seat calling to mind illustrations the Canon had seen in his youth in 'Toad of Toad Hall' but he instantly banished such thoughts and tried to look suitably welcoming and grave at the same time. In contrast to her husband, Lady Lavinia was tall and thin her very posture spoke of imperial grandeur and hauteur. She looked, in fact, every inch what the Canon's wife thought the daughter of an Earl and wife of a Bishop should look like. Mrs Pretyman was taking careful note. This was how a Bishop's wife behaved to the hoi polloi. This was how she would behave if…. No! when her husband became a Bishop, the first step in that direction, she hoped, taking place this very evening. But just now she was in a dilemma. Should she courtesy or would a low bow have best effect? In her flustered state, she simultaneously tried both which unfortunately only gave the impression that the elastic had snapped on her underwear and that she was desperately trying to retrieve the situation. Not that it mattered for both Canon and wife were being totally ignored. Her Ladyship's first utterance was not a word of greeting to them but an imperious command.

"His Lordship needs a rest before dinner. He has been confirming snotty-nosed children all day and is quite worn out."

"Charles," she waved a gloved hand in the direction of the chauffeur, "take our luggage to the room. I assume there is one prepared?" She glanced at the Canon and his wife now for the first time.

Oh, indeed yes, your Ladyship," burbled Mrs. Pretyman, glad at last of recognition even if only to be of help. "Come this way, all of you please, and most welcome, most welcome indeed."

Her Ladyship followed Mrs Pretyman and the chauffeur into the rectory. The Bishop, having recovered his balance, offered his ringed hand to the Canon, whether to shake or to kiss, the Canon was uncertain. Upon limply shaking hands, the Bishop said in a breathless wheezy voice,

"Good of you to put us up, Canon. To travel back to the palace and then have the long journey back tomorrow… too taxing. And today was not without its disappointments. Very poorly prepared, those young people, for confirmation and first communion. Little grasp of their catechism or the scriptures. I'll have to write and admonish the rector. Such poor standards… too bad."

The Canon was about to agree, as indeed he had been tutored by his wife to agree with everything the Bishop said during his stay, but then recalled the battle he had to wage with his own confirmation class, so he just smiled weakly and found himself reaching out to carry the Bishop's briefcase. For him, it was already shaping up to be an evening of licking and lackeying.

Compromises & Contradictions

"I suppose you have good game in these parts being so very rural? Good shootin and fishin, I shouldn't wonder?" Lady Lavinia gravelly voice travelled the length of the rectory dining table accompanied by a matching stony eye which was now fixed on the Canon.

"Oh yes… lots of… game," he stammered.

"And I suppose you shoot and fish yourself?" she continued. "The trout you served us was…" and here Mrs. Pretyman strained anxiously to hear the compliment that must surely be coming. "… it was… fresh… and cooked… . another long pause "… adequately."

"Nowadays I neither shoot nor fish, I'm afraid," said the Canon who appeared to be gasping for breath.

"He used to fish down at one of our local beauty spots called the 'Meeting of the Waters,'" his wife volunteered. "Such a pity you won't have time to see it. A lovely spot. But the Canon has been so very busy of late, haven't you, Horace? So very conscientious about his parish duties, My Lord, no time for much relaxation, have you dear?"

"He shud try hez han at the farmin, that wud larn[447] him what it is tay bay busy." Huey Potter, his wife Aggie and their youngest son, Victor, had been invited to join the rectory party for dinner because Victor, an academically gifted young man, having given intimations of taking holy orders, Mrs Pretyman thought it would surely be a major plus with the Bishop to know that the Canon nurtured possible clerical recruitment for the ministry.

"The farmin tarrible poor at the minute," Aggie Potter said. "There's no livin tay bay got out aff it at al."

The Bishop paused as he was putting another large forkful of roast beef to his lips. "Life in the church is no bed of roses either these days, wouldn't you agree, Canon? So much to contend with… loose morals… poor attendances… not to speak of the financial upkeep of our real estate… churches… church halls… large ancient rectories… so many pressures… taking holy orders not a calling today for the faint hearted."

He stopped to utter a very audible belch, causing his pectoral cross to dance a little jig on his ample stomach all of which reduced young Victor to a fit of the giggles worthy of our own little hero.

So you are thinking of 'taking cloth,' are you, young man?"

Lady Lavinia's gaze had lighted on the hapless Victor as he attempted to hide his mirth behind a napkin.

"Indeed he is nat," said his mother. "His uncle Herbert is in the drapery trade, an' he allows there is no dazent livin tay be got outta it ether."

"You misunderstand me. I meant the lad aspires to become a priest," Lady Lavinia said with a condescending smile.

"Bae may Sowl[448], he's nat! Whativer giv yeh that idea, Missis?" said Huey.

---

447 ***He shud try hez han at the farmin, that wud larn him*** – *he should try farming, that would teach him what it is to be busy*
448 ***Bae may sowl, he's nat*** – *by my soul [an exclamation]*

"There has niver been a Papish priest allowed down our lane or over our durestep[449], niver tay spake aff us rearin wan. Naw, he wants tay be a Minister aff the Gospel. He got converted at wan aff the Reverend Quigley's wee gospel meetins in the Mission Hall, we al did, hirself here leadin the charge. So we're now al washed in the blood aff the lamb…no turnin back or back-slidin…"

He gazed accusingly at the half full wine glasses in front of the Bishop and his lady "… an' hivin no truck way strong drink or publicans an' sinners."

Lady Lavinia looked daggers at the Potters for having the temerity to parade all this crude fundamentalist doctrine in front of a Bishop but before she could muster her thoughts to put them firmly in their place, the Bishop said thoughtfully,

"Converted you say, yes, converted… though we Anglicans are of a mind that salvation is a more gradual process from baptism until we are called to give account… yes, salvation for us is more a process than any startling event like a blinding flash and getting converted of an evening. True, St Paul had such an experience on the Damascus Road but his was a sufficiently unusual conversion to be worthy of being recorded in Holy Scripture. Christ's disciples, by contrast, walked side by side with Our Saviour, their salvation being gently nurtured over the time of His earthly ministry. So I would be a little wary of the abrupt kind of conversion you describe… maybe the experience of a few but, for most, achieving salvation is a slower, more gradual and less dramatic process… wouldn't you agree, Canon?"

The Canon had been savouring his roast beef and clearly had lost track of the conversation, so he required a hefty kick on the shins from his wife which prompted him to say,

"Indeed"… and… "Oh indeed… a lengthy process… yes indeed, My Lord. The blinding flash… unusual!"

"Not… at… al," retorted Aggie emphatically. "There's wans roun here gittin a flash near ivery night up in the wee Mission Hall. The Reverend Quigley is a powerful praycher… he hez them al on the edge aff their seats pleadin fir mercy… an' givin their testimony tay save themselves from hell's fire… yeh niver herd such sin as they come out way tay git it aff their chest. Aff curse, we had no such dirty linen tay air when we wur al converted, an' giv our testimonies. But I tell yeh, wee Quigley puts the fear aff God in them an' hez them confessin wholesale. He's not a man that goes part aff the road way iverywan he meets an' agreein way the last wan he was spakin tay jist for a quiet life. Naw, you know

---

449 **Durestep** – *doorstep*

where yeh stan way Quigley for hez sermons is that powerful. There's wans wud prefer that kinna sermon aff a Sunday in your church, Canon, an' less tak about the history aff the Holy Lan… an' useless stuff lake that… sure that's niver gonna skar[450] the sinners inta seein the error aff their ways, confessin al an' seekin forgiveness in sackcloth an' ashes… I tell yeh, wee Quigley hez them skraikin[451] way fear an' pleadin fir forgiveness…"

She had been glaring across the table at the Canon who was now doing battle not only with a large Yorkshire pudding but also a dramatic onset of the hiccups.

"I knew it was a mistake to ask them," Mrs. Pretyman muttered to her husband. "You should have warned me they were so very… raw." The Canon too had been taken aback by Huey and Aggie's decided opinions now being voiced so robustly. He had never heard Huey voice an opinion or take an interest in anything beyond his farm gate. Indeed when, in 1939, he had met Huey driving his cattle along the road and had mentioned that Hitler had just invaded Poland, Huey's response, looking skyward, was "well, hez got a brave good day for it" so little interest did he take in world affairs, however earth-shattering.

Dora Pretyman had fixed a stern gaze on Aggie willing her to shut up, but she was clearly still in full flow…

" … An' that's another thing ye'r missin aff a Sunday, Canon, good rousin choruses an' hymns. Now, wee Quigley's the boy ken get them goin way 'Fight the Good Fight' an' similar… "

"Say something, Horace," whispered his wife. "Don't just sit there, for heaven's sake. This is disastrous."

The Canon, though greatly handicapped by his hiccups, now felt under duress from all sides to achieve a change of subject, divert attention from his alleged sins of omission and hopefully raise the tone. His approach, though typical, proved somewhat hapless.

"Skraiking with fear… you say. Yes, such an interesting local usage. Did you know that the Norwegian word for a scream is 'Skrik'? And did you know that Edward Munch's wonderful if terrifying painting "The Scream's" actual Norwegian title is 'The Skrik.' So similar to our local 'skraik' with the same meaning… yes really, it's true… I read it quite recently… so interesting for the etymologist to ponder… though we are not sufficiently aware of it, our local linguistic usages owe such a lot to our Norse invaders… as well as to the Irish

---

450 **Skar** – *scare*
451 **Skraikin** – *screaming*

language and Ulster Scots, of course, ... and then there's the local remnants of Elizabethan and Jacobean English from Plantation times colouring our everyday communication too... "

But interest in etymology seemed sadly lacking round the table. Indeed, if ever words of wisdom were falling on stony ground, this was the moment. With his wife glaring at him in despair, the Bishop stifling a yawn and the great lady casting on the Canon her stoniest of looks, only the entry of the rectory maid, Selina, carrying the puddings on one of the recently resurrected silver trays, saved the day. She put the heavy tray down with such a resounding clatter on the sideboard that the dining table visibly shook, and the diners were distracted from the finer points of etymological enlightenment by trying to retrieve their cutlery.

"I must say, you do yourselves proud," said the Bishop, eyeing the latest fare. "You must have a splendid cook, Canon?"

"It's Selina here. Did you hear that, Selina? You can take a bow... young she may be, but she is indeed a very talented cook, My Lord. London trained, you know." Mrs. Pretyman was pleased to get the chance to mention the maid's sojourn in London for it surely brought a degree of sophistication to the dinner. "We are a wonderful team when we cook together, aren't we, Selina?"

"Hir... that ken't harly boil an egg," said Selina back in the kitchen.

But Selina didn't linger on this loss of culinary credit for her attention had been distracted all evening by the presence, sitting at the kitchen range, of the Bishop's handsome chauffeur clad in his leathers. Every time she went near him to get to the range he pinched her backside which pleased her greatly though she pretended to be very cross with him.

"What do you think of this war going on in Korea, Canon?" asked the Bishop, abandoning his efforts to promote reasoned theology especially when it was clearly lost on the crude and ignorant below the salt.

Another sharp kick on the shins evoked "I think it is... a pity... that young men are yet again dying in foreign fields...," he tailed off, for he had given the matter little thought.

"But don't you think Communism must be thwarted at all costs?" suggested the Bishop.

"Oh indeed, My Lord, such a wicked system... yes, stopped at all costs... yes indeed."

"I think them Communists shud bay blasted tay hell whir they belong," said Huey. "Bunch aff atheists… sure the Yankees hiz the atomic bomb… what ir they waitin fir? Drap it on them good an' proper… an' wipe them aff the face aff the earth…"

"Such an action certainly shortened the war in the Pacific and saved a great many American lives to end the last conflict," mused the Bishop toying with the cream on top of his sherry trifle. "What do you think, Canon?"

The Canon, perhaps a little late in the day for his wife's satisfaction, was now fully concentrated on agreeing with his Bishop. He said,

"Yes indeed… Hiroshima, Nagasaki… blasted to bits… not a leaf left on a tree… not a tree left… nothing left… but many lives saved elsewhere… yes… the same now might solve things again in Korea… yes, the nuclear bomb… could be just the solution… quick and final."

"… and yet," mused the Bishop, "aren't we told to *'render to no man evil for evil.'* Isn't that in St Paul's 'Epistle to the Romans'?"

"Oh, it is indeed," said the Canon, turning another somersault. "So, no use of the nuclear bomb then… just… just fight it out… hand to hand… bayonets and that … like the First World War… best way… I suppose."

"Oh now, I would question if that is the solution either," replied the Bishop. "Surely we don't want to return to that kind of carnage."

"So, what are yez fir doin then?" demanded Huey. "Drappin Bibles on them? Sure they ken't read English… nay, drap the bomb on them, I say, an' bay done."

The Bishop pondered, and then said thoughtfully,

"In certain circumstances, the Roman Catholics can claim a conflict to be a just war… for which they have the word of St Augustine… and I'm sure they can, with justification, claim this one in Korea is a just conflict since it is to stop the spread of atheist Communism."

"The Catholics wurn't aff a mine tay[452] kal the war agin Hitler an' Mussolini a just war fir sure them two blackguards wur Catholics themselves," Huey said, "an' sure owl De Valera down in the Free State wudn't even join in fightin them but that wuz because it wuda meant sidin way the British Empire an' he was that much aff an owl bigot, he cudn't bring hezself tay sign up. Mind you, bay my way aff thinkin owl Dev an' that Archbishop aff Dublin, that McQuaid fella, between them is the best proof us Protestants hiz got on the need tay keep outta

---

452   ***Wurn't aff a mine tay*** – weren't prepared to

a united Irelan fir aren't they both livin proof aff the tratement we could expect livin under them, an' proof too that we wur right tay think that 'Home Rule wuz Rome Rule.'"

"Aye, an' there's another crowd yeh ken't trust, the Papishes," said Aggie with feeling.

"But dear lady," said the Bishop, "more Southern Irish Catholics fought in the British Army in the last war than Protestant Ulstermen. I think I'm right, Canon?"

"Oh, very true, My Lord… yes, I believe that is indeed the case," said the hapless Canon who again hadn't much considered the matter, and was still battling with his hiccups.

"And yet," mused the Bishop again, "how much of that was due to the chronic unemployment in the South or how much to conviction about the war being a just one is hard to say?"

He was staring at the Canon who consequently felt he had yet again to agree… but to what?

"Yes indeed, great unemployment at the time in Eire… so must have been the main cause surely… for so many signing up to fight."

The Canon felt a little flush of pride that he had got something right. But his confidence was premature.

"But surely you don't think the average man, when not compelled by his government, would put his life on the line, sign up for battle, face the foe, just because he can't get any other work. I find that a strange view, Canon, in truth I do."

"Oh, I didn't mean… I meant… some perhaps, yes, but most perhaps, no…" the Canon tailed off conscious that he was now sinking without trace in a slough of contradictions and compromises.

Lady Lavinia, who had risen from the table to survey the trifles on the sideboard asked, "Would your kitchen stretch to providing some cheeses? Sherry trifle is not for me nor can I have anything with rhubarb or gooseberries so a portion or two of cheese would be a delight. The Bishop is partial to cheese too. We usually have it before our desert 'a la francaise.'"

The Pantry Dalliance

Feeling suitably admonished for not serving things in the correct 'a la francaise' manner, Mrs. Pretyman rang the bell to summon Selina. She knew perfectly well there was only 'mouse-trap' Cheddar in the larder but she resolved to blame the lack of variety on the scarcity of any other sort in McKnight's shop, for that indeed would be the truth. She rang the bell again. There was still no sign of Selina, so she got up and went into the kitchen. She was greeted with alarming noises coming from the back pantry. She opened the pantry door and there, wedged up against the shelving were Selina and the Bishop's chauffeur... undoubtedly! ... unmistakably! ... in an intimate clench!' "But at least," as she said later as if it made a difference, "they were still both fully clad!"

The couple were so otherwise engaged that they were blissfully unaware of the presence of Mrs. Pretyman whose nerves, strained to breaking point both before and during her dinner party, now fractured to such an extent that she promptly administered her own version of the nuclear bomb. She grabbed a saucepan and brought it down on the chauffeur's backside. Now aware he was under attack, he turned to discover who or what had struck him. Seeing Mrs. Pretyman, he hurriedly tried to retreat but too late! Mrs Pretyman, still with benefit of saucepan, struck him again, this second assault sending him staggering backwards on top of Selina. Without a word, Mrs. Pretyman left them and returned to the kitchen. To compound her anger that such things should be going on in her rectory, made worse by the presence of a Bishop and an Earl's daughter in her dining room, she could now hear giggles and guffaws coming through the pantry door. She took the large chunk of Cheddar from the larder, placed it on a plate, miraculously found an actual cheese knife in the cutlery drawer and returned to the dining room.

"You look rather flushed, my dear," whispered the Canon after his wife had placed the cheese in front of Lady Lavinia with a mumbled apology for taking so long, and there being only one sort.

"So would you be if you had just seen what I've just seen," but this was not the time to elaborate.

"Oh dear, no grapes either I see," said her Ladyship through thin pursed lips.

As he stretched across to cut himself a large slice of cheese, the Bishop asked "What is your view on the ecumenical movement now gaining such strength, Canon? I think I need not seek Mr. and Mrs. Potter's views for I feel sure I can guess at it already," and he smiled indulgently in their direction.

"Is that joinin up way the Papishes, that ekkemenical thing?" demanded Huey. "We read about it in the truthful Protestant tracts, an' the warnins are there fir al tay beware. It's the nixt sly move bay the Church aff Rome tay delude

Protestants, take us over an' then wipe us out, as far as I can tell? Sure, how could any good Protestant link up way Rome in any shape ur form? Isn't the Pope aff Rome the Anti-Christ!"

Whatever about the alleged Anti-Christ sitting in Rome, the Bishop was feeling mellow after his excellent dinner so, even in the face of such crass utterances, he said calmly, "Ecumenism is indeed difficult to contemplate here in Ireland. There is before our eyes the whole vexed question of mixed marriages, an example of Rome's intransigence over the religion of the children in the mixed marriage situation. The Roman church here tolerates no room for debate about the matter. As a result, our population is vanishing in the South. I've often thought that there would be no greater advertisement for a united country if there was an expanding Protestant population in the Republic, but it just isn't so, and the Catholic Church is partly to blame for that."

"What am I efter tellin yez[453]," replied Huey. "Don't give them an inch for, bay Gob, thems the boys that'll move in on yeh an' take a mile, an' a whole lot more on tap aff it. Did I hear yeh right about unitin the country? Sure the ony time Irelan wuz iver united wuz unner British rule. I wud rether burn may premises tay the groun and slaughter al may livestock than give them-ins wan inch. Sure, we wud bay ruled bay Rome an' wudn't hive the livin aff a dog."

"Wud yez lake tay or coffee?" Selina had appeared at the Bishop's elbow, "bold as brass," as Mrs. Pretyman said later, "and with not a hair out of place."

"Is it ground coffee?" demanded Lady Lavinia, "for if it's that 'Camp' creation it goes for the Bishop's stomach.

"It's 'Camp'," said Mrs. Pretyman curtly. She was now well beyond the end of her tether.

"Give His Grace tea, then," she commanded. "He prefers China or peppermint tea but Indian will have to do if it is all you've got."

As Selina circulated round the table, everybody took tea except Mrs. Pretyman who made some play of asking for coffee even though she too detested 'the bottled stuff' herself.

"My dear Canon," said the Bishop, "I fear we stopped you keeping us right about ecumenism? Come along now, what is your opinion? Should we Christians all seek closer links?"

The Canon dragged up as best he could what could be ascertained from the Bishop's views on the matter from earlier, which wasn't much.

"Certainly, there is the problem here of mixed marriages… not here exactly…

---

453   ***What am I efter tellin yez*** – *haven't I just told you*

I mean here in Ireland.... in the Republic I mean... but here too at times... yes indeed, our numbers being eroded down there... too bad... "

He paused not knowing where to go next as his wife glared balefully at him. But he knew there was now no way he could seize victory from the jaws of defeat. The day was lost. There are only so many cartwheels an honest man can turn.

The day might be lost but Mrs Pretyman, as we have witnessed earlier, was made of sterner stuff than her husband and was not a woman to let the dogs, whatever their exalted pedigree, run off with her dinner. They were going down, the Canon and she, but would do so in style. She waited her chance.

"I think we'd better bay goin," said Aggie Potter, gathering up her handbag, removing a handkerchief and, with arm extended to display an array of expensive-looking bracelets that might not have been noticed during the course of the evening, blew her nose noisily.

"But wait," said the Bishop, "wait! We have not heard the young man's opinions all evening on any of the important matters we have been discussing. I am sure he has given some of these matters considerable thought."

He now turned an indulgent smile on Victor.

"Ach, sure he agrees way al we say," said his father. "His opinion, yeh'll fine, is the same as ours on al matters... isn't that right, son?"

'Oh Brave New World...!'

Victor rose from the table. He was a tall slender young man with his father's round face and mother's sharp nose. He was wearing his school blazer.

"No, it's not right," he said quietly. "I do not agree with much that you have said this evening, Dad, and very little indeed of what others have said either. About ecumenism, I think it is the best thing that has happened to the churches in years. I have come to the conclusion that we all, Protestants and Catholics, Unionists and Nationalists, richly deserve each other in this country. We are all equally to blame for the bigotry and divisions here, and it is time for it to stop."

He paused to take a sip of water while those round the table began to shift uneasily.

"Yev said enough now, son," said his father. "Them teachers hez put ye'r head astray. Ye'r Mammy an' me hez towel yeh tay stick tay ye'r Bible an' yeh'll not go far wrong. Sure that kinna chat ill becomes yeh[454] an' will bay the ruin aff us Protestants an' Loyalists here in the 'Wee Six'."

But Victor was far from finished. He continued,

" ... but ecumenism must be based on honesty with no side using it as a takeover. As you have just been saying, Lord Bishop, the use to which the Catholic Church in Ireland puts 'Ne Temere' especially in the Republic has all the appearance of a take-over. But may I ask what you and your fellow Bishops are doing to challenge them? As far as I can see, you are turning a blind eye to what is happening for fear of rocking the boat. Have you ever considered that many thoughtful Catholics in the Republic might welcome you Protestant Bishops showing more back-bone if your intervention were to curb the over-mighty power of the Catholic Bishops which looks increasingly like a tyranny and not just to the religious minorities but a tyranny over their own people? Well, you asked for my honest opinion, so there you have it."

... and the young man sat down to a stunned silence.

... But not for long.

"How dare you, young man," cried Lady Lavinia. "You have completely forgotten yourself. You want to become an Anglican priest and you speak like this to your Bishop. It is a disgrace. From what I have heard this evening, we have landed among a nest of vipers. We have never been so insulted. We will not stay in this locality a moment longer. Whoever likes can marry the happy couple tomorrow, but it will not be His Lordship."

Rising majestically from the table, and in the process upsetting the cheese board unto the Bishop's lap, she made to grab to retrieve her handbag and swept from the room.

"Now there wuz no need for that owl-fashioned chat, son," said Huey, "an' us good Bible-believing Christians." Turning to the stunned diners, he said, "Well, we'll bid yez al good night for we hiv a sow piggin' an' she'll need lukin tay." Rising from the table, he said graciously, "Ye'r dinner wuz as good as our last Masonic festal burd, Canon, or come near tay it any road."

With that they were off but not before the young man had gone around the table to shake hands and thank the Canon and his wife. No farewell greeting was forthcoming from the remaining mighty visitor.

"Do you know," the Canon said to him in an audible whisper, "I think there is hope for our church and our country yet." He stood up, put his arm round the young man and said in a loud booming voice *'Oh brave new world that hath such*

---

454 **Ill becomes yeh** – *it is unbecoming and you can't really mean it*

people in it'…," proud at last to have thought of something to say that wasn't false and orchestrated.

Mrs Pretyman said nothing. Her hopes of impressing her visitors had long since vanished, though she had to confess that she had thoroughly enjoyed the last few minutes. One thing she had resolved on, somebody had to pay for this evening's debacle, and the easiest victim was the hapless Selina. She would have to get her walking-papers[455] tomorrow.

She told Selina the next morning.

"That's gran, Mistress," Selina said. "Sure that big woman that sent the cheese flying last night come down early this mornin an' offered me a job as cook in her place so I'm goin away way them after the weddin. She says she niver tasted cookin lake it, so isn't that great. An' sure Charley, the driver fella, says he'll look after me an' show me roun. He says not tay tell but he hez plans tay go aff tay London an' he'll take me with him for sure then I can show him roun."

"I'm sure you will both have a lot to show each other one place or another," said Mrs. Pretyman acidly. She continued, "Did you say after the wedding? But surely after last night's events, the Bishop and her Ladyship are now not staying for the wedding?"

"Well, they musta changed their min. She towel me tay bring the two aff them up their breakfast tay bed, so I did, an' then she towel me tay pack their things, an' may own things too tay bay ready tay take aff way them so they'd bay no delay for she said they are goin away after he's done the weddin the day. Lake I wuz waitin fir hir tay give may a quare scowlin[456] fir… ," she hesitated not knowing what the grand lady knew about certain occurrences in the kitchen pantry last evening then continued "… but instead she wants me tay go tay work fir them-uns. Isn't it funny the way things turns out sometimes!"

"It's against my better judgement that we are still here," said Lady Lavinia sonorously a little later, "but the Bishop is a man of his word and wants to honour his promise to conduct the wedding. Then we will be off. By the way, I

---

455 **Walking-papers** – *dismissal notice*
456 **A quare scowlin** – *a terrible scolding*

have offered your girl a position which she has accepted."

"That's fine," replied Mrs. Pretyman. I have just sacked her anyway. I discovered your chauffeur and her up to no good in my pantry when I went to fetch the cheese last evening. She has shown herself to be a girl of loose morals, so I imagine she will fit perfectly into your establishment and the high life of the palace."

Revenge is a dish best served cold!

Episode 39

Danny's song of Love

Scrubbing Up for Greatness

"Why is it they hiv iverythin an' we hiv nothin?" Danny demanded as Rosie wrestled with him to get him well scrubbed up for the grand big wedding.

She had had permission from the McKendry's to use the bathroom at the top of the stairs to wash him and Dorry so they would be fresh-smelling when carrying out their roles the next day, Danny singing, and Dorry trusted with the safe delivery of the silver horse shoe as the happy couple emerged from the church. To keep Bobby quiet and involve him in proceedings somehow - for he was proving a torture about being left out - he was commissioned to shower home-made confetti over the happy couple as they took delivery of the horseshoe. This prospect pleased him greatly since it involved throwing things, was not as sissy as singing or fooling about with stupid horseshoes so he immediately hunkered down in the middle of the cottage kitchen and got busy shredding Robbie's 'Ireland Saturday Night' into confetti with Rosie's big sewing scissors.

"Wud yeh wheesht[457]," Rosie muttered to Danny. "Ye'll be tellin may nixt that you'd rether bay in the tin bath in front aff the fire at home. Sure, isn't this great," and she pressed hard on a pimple she had spotted on Danny's left cheek.

"I ony meant," Danny spluttered, trying to push her fingers away, "I ony meant why do we hiv a tin bath an' they hiv this big white bath way taps an' tiles an' nice fluffy towels…an' that? Robbie says when the red revolution comes here we will al hive nice houses… an' baths lake this… an' cars… an'… but I donno what the red revolution is or if it will be real soon? I must ask Robbie again."

He was stopped in his fantasy of the fabulous life to come by his mother applying a big yellow sponge to his face and scrubbing hard.

"Robbie shud quet fillin ye'r head way hez owl eediot chat. Now turn roun till I get at ye'r back. Isn't it jist great tay hive hot watter as yeh need it an' not

---

457 **Wud yeh wheesht** – would you be quiet

havin tay kerry it from the well an' fill our big kettle ivery time… now, out yeh come."

Danny hopped out unto the bathmat with water streaming down his glowing body. Rosie towelled him all over, firmly but gently, with the big fluffy towel warm from the hot press[458] making him giggle when she dried under his arms.

"Can I go out inta the yard tay play?" Danny asked.

"Yeh ken not," Rosie cried "Hi 'vent I jist washed yeh. Ye'll go no farther than the kitchen this day or I'll give yeh a right skelpin[459]. Now, get them clothes on yeh an' then away down way yeh, fir yeh niver know what Mrs Hanna might hive fir yeh yonner in the kitchen… an' Robbie still hez tay cut ye'r hair the night, fir it's got that long yeh luk lake an owl lukin outta an ivy bush[460]."

Thus, both chastened and encouraged, Danny skipped past Dorry in the bathroom doorway and down the grand mahogany staircase eyeing, as he always did with a mixture of attraction and fear, the four vicious looking griffins holding their shields to their chests that stood on the posts at the top and bottom of that great staircase.

Big Bella Crashes Out

Danny had never seen the church so bedecked with flowers. They sprouted from every step up into the pulpit, smothered the lectern, an enormous spray of pearly white roses covered the altar, bouquets were attached to the end of each pew, and there were large vases of them on every windowsill and just about every other flat surface including on top of the organ.

There Big Bella had taken up position and was sporting on this day-of-days a hat the floribunda on which was easily a match for any of the floral extravaganzas bedecking the church. However beautiful, the profusion of flowers was causing her eyes to water and commit to the occasional violent sneeze as she pounded the organ pedals and belted out nuptial music to get the wedding guests, now steadily filling up the church, in the appropriate mood.

Presently a swift movement in the aisle to Danny's left caught his eye as two of the most handsome men he had ever seen in his life, both dressed in jet black suits, gleaming white shirts and bow ties marched up the aisle side by side taking their places in the very front pew opposite the choir. Benny Wills, a fellow choir

---
458 **Hot press** – *an airing cupboard*
459 **Skelpin** – *beating*
460 **Luk lake an owl lukin outta an ivy bush** – *You hair is long and untidy*

member, pinched Danny's leg and, leering, said with reference to the somewhat severe haircut Robbie had inflicted on Danny, "Hi, scaldy turmit-head. That big fella over there ill hiv the quare night the night in bed way ye'r woman."

Danny was still trying to regain his composure from such a scandalous comment, for he simply could not envisage how the man across the aisle from him, looking so clean, so spotless, so like the Prince Charming in Dorry's reading book, could possibly be getting up to anything bad in bed, when someone, far more beautiful still, floated into his line of vision.

The two 'princes' – for that is what they must surely be – had now moved forward to take their places in front of the altar just as this vision in dazzling white, accompanied by a man Danny recognized as one of the important ones in Ballybracken, progressed towards the altar rails. Alerted a few moments earlier to the entrance of the heavenly vision of Caroline and Sir Thomas, Big Bella had greeted them with the familiar *'Here comes the bride'* belted out with something approaching bellicose ferocity.

As her assault on the 'Bridal March' continued, the older boys in the choir began to accompany it with low chants of *'here comes the bride, she's forty inches wide, see how she wiggles her big back side,'* accompanied by uncontrollable giggles. Benny Wills was so overcome with mirth that he fell forward off the choir bench and kicked one of the legs of Big Bella's organ stool. Bella turned round to see what had nearly unseated her and had reduced her choir to such unseemly mirth. Whatever the cause, it would be dealt with in her usual fashion. It was surely time to administer summary justice with the long metal ruler she kept on top of the organ for just this purpose. Without lifting her eyes off the keys, she let one hand stray to the top of the organ where she fumbled round blindly trying to locate the weapon. She was usually a dab hand at playing on with her other hand while smiting the choir members, both the evil and the good for she did not discriminate.

By now the beautiful princess had joined her handsome prince just like in the story books, a wonderful dream unfolding before our little hero's eyes. How he wished he could sing his song to her now and to her only… singing it with as much passion as he had been wishing all morning to get it over and done with. But not any longer. Now he wanted to sing his heart out for her, to lure the vision into touching him, smiling at him, kissing him, merging with him in a cloud of purity and happiness that would never end.

But, unfortunately, back at the organ things were not working in Big Bella's favour. She did indeed eventually locate the ruler but, in doing so, upset not one but two of the enormous vases of flowers which had been sitting precariously on the top of the organ. The vases slowly lent towards each other like two drunk men embracing in a momentary clumsy hug before falling backwards debouching their contents, both flowers and water, all over Big Bella before continuing their titanic journey to hit the stone floor of the choir with a resounding crash. All eyes, until now fixed fondly - for the most part - on the happy couple at the altar, turned to look accusingly at Bella and her nest of miscreants in the choir. For a moment she froze, then stood up, her flowery hat wobbling dangerously, looked to right and left planning her escape route and, giving out a loud expletive unworthy of the place or the occasion, as many remarked at the time and for a long time afterwards, ran screaming down the aisle and out into the morning sunshine.

What was to be done? Here was a bride and groom waiting to be bound in holy wedlock, a Bishop in full pontificals poised to perform, the massed ranks of the gentry of Ulster and further afield all present for the wedding of the year, a church full of expectant guests but now with no organist, quite possibly no workable organ… an occasion on the brink of ruin for lack of that most necessary ingredient at any wedding… joyful music and uplifting song. Who would save the day?

Miss Mina Steps Forward

Mina McKendry quietly left her pew from across the aisle and, picking her way carefully over the shards of broken glass, took up post at the organ. Without faltering for a moment, she embarked on the first hymn… *'Glorious things of thee are spoken, Zion City of our God.'* The congregation rose to its feet and were raising the rafters of the country church at a volume never before heard by any, least of all Daniel Malachy Dowdells. When the hymn finished, Miss Mina turned briefly towards him and gave one of her wintry smiles. Although he did not like her, never came to like her, and indeed feared her, he felt something for Miss Mina at that moment that persisted for the rest of his life, and that he later knew to call 'respect'. It wasn't for what she did that morning - for when he thought about it, he could have stepped in to play - but it was the way she did it….no fuss, no drama, no embarrassing break in proceedings, she just quietly took over. *'Look,'* she was declaring, *'the organ still works, the show will go on, so in life, Daniel Malachy, do what needs to be done however unexpected, difficult or embarrassing the circumstances. Just keep calm and carry on.'* Those who might be quietly delighted at the discomfort caused to the great and powerful on this 'Big Day' in front of a Bishop, an Earl's daughter, a Knight of the Realm, George McKendry CBE and all the other notables were to be sadly disappointed due to the prompt action of a strange woman with cold expressionless eyes, a wintery smile and ill-fitting false teeth.

When the events were related to Robbie, he said, "Ach sure I always knew it. In her own strange way, that woman was one of my 'strollers.'"

Danny now sat back to enjoy the spectacle and wait for his own big moment. Here he was, Daniel Malachy Dowdells, in the presence of a beautiful prince and princesses, in a church filled with the scent of a thousand flowers. Surely this must be heaven itself.

And it was buoyed up with intoxicating wonder that Danny went forward to stand and face the congregation to sing his heart out… but now it was for his princess, and for her alone.

As he finished the hymn and was about to step down from the altar rails, his princess and her prince emerged from signing the register in the vestry accompanied by a galaxy of beautifully dressed followers, the Bishop at their head. Danny realized too late that he was trapped. How could he get back to the choir now unless he dived through the prince and princess's entourage by crawling under their legs? But he quickly abandoned this idea as somehow not best fitting the occasion. As other equally ridiculous thoughts raced through his head, including making a dash to hide behind the altar, the party drew ever closer and then, to his amazement, the prince and princess stopped beside him. The princess bent down and whispered,

"Sing for us again, Danny. I won't move from here until you sing again so that Edward and I can really hear you properly this time. You have the voice of an angel."

Danny was blushing from head to foot and could say not one word, not even to ask this vision from heaven what she wanted him to sing? Then the Canon stepped forward and whispered something in his ear. At that moment a flickering beam of sunlight shining through the stained-glass window behind the altar settled on the Princess's tiara making it dazzle and sparkle, and casting over her what to Danny must surely be stardust. The Canon was right; there was surely only one thing to sing? Gazing up at her with the purest love in his heart, he offered to her in song his innocent young soul.

With Miss Mina following him immediately and expertly on the organ, out it came... *'Oh perfect love, all human thought transcending...'* When he had finished, he dropped his head, his love song finished but still the prince and princess did not move. The princess bent down and kissed him on the forehead... .

"Thank you, Danny," she whispered. "You have brought magic to my wedding day."

That kiss was to Daniel Malachy Dowdells an epiphany. In his simple way, he realized that music and song really could cast a spell, and he had the gift to cast it. No longer would that gift be unwanted. And it solved – if only for the time being - another of his puzzling conundrums. For surely the love he felt for this beautiful princess, and the kiss that had now sealed it, was what the elusive 'it' meant. So now at last he felt he knew, and it was too wonderful for words!

But like all such moments, it had to end, and who better to put a stop to a heaven-sent mystical moment than a Bishop.

"You have delighted us aplenty, young man, now you can resume your seat, and let us all rise and greet again our happy couple at God's altar.

Danny quickly made for the choir sensing, as well he might, for Bishops don't like being upstaged, that the man wearing the big hat and long dress was cross with him. Another of Miss Mina's cold smiles greeted him as he reached his seat... but, what was this? The congregation was beginning to clap! Who were they clapping? It wasn't the prince and princess for they were clapping too, and Miss Mina had turned round from the organ and was... clapping, even the Canon and Mrs. Canon were clapping, the Bishop was not clapping but that must be because he was holding that great big stick thing with the curly top... everybody everywhere in the church was clapping... and yes... yes, they were clapping ... Daniel Malachy Dowdells!

He stood up, and turning to face that sea of faces, he bowed as his mother had told him to do when people clapped... but still they clapped... with his blushes totally out of control, he bowed again... and then he started to cry... and he knew why he had started to cry. Not very much that was really nice happened to him, his mammy or his family... but this was just, well, a nice thing to happen to the Dowdells, a really nice thing... and sometimes something is so nice, it makes you cry. As he sat down behind Miss Mina who was now embarking on the recessional hymn, all that had happened that morning was overwhelming him. It was as if someone had just emptied a large mugful of creamy warm chocolate all over him in a delicious all-embracing shower. He was glowing, and, at that moment, it was the most glorious feeling in the world.

"Yu'r nothin but an owl show-aff, Danny," Benny hissed, nipping his leg savagely.

But Danny didn't care about jealous comments or pinched legs anymore. A strange feeling was blocking out everything but the 'niceness' of what had just happened.

Rosie's Rosy Glow

"He sung that well, the wee darlin," Rosie was saying to her friend, Cassy, as they made their way home from the chapel the next Sunday, "that they're saying he might get tay sing fir the Pope… lake not maybe anytime soon… but some day… lake, sure he wuz singin yonder in front aff a Bishop and a 'Her Ladyship'… so it cud well bay the Pope nixt."

"Aye, that'll be the quare day wheniver it comes roun," said Cassy dryly. "Way out yonner in Rome. I suppose stranger things hez happened. You'll hiv tay get the quare good rig-out[461] fir St Peter's, Rosie. Ye'll not bay borrowin the owl duds[462] I got from the Darkie tay wear in front aff Hez Holiness. There'll be no howlin yeh then."

But the sarcasm was lost on Rosie.

"An' Dorry!… now she near drapped the horseshoe she wuz that nervous an' excited but I jist managed tay catch it in time… an' she handed it over tay Miss Caroline… or I shud say Mrs. Doctor McKendry, so I shud… an' she curtsied… an' the bride and groom admired hir frock… an' then we al threw confetti… I hadda hurry back cos aff helpin way the weddin breakfast in the big marquee… an' yeh niver in ye'r life seen the like aff the style, Cassy… the dresses an' the hats… an' here, there must have been a good thousand pounds worth aff jewellery an' other figgairies[463] in the tent I was sarvin in. An' when the speechifying wuz over, ye'd niver believe it but the bride an' groom aked where wuz our Danny fir they wanted him tay sing again… an' sure the wee luv wasn't prepared… an' I cudn't even fin him? … but foun him at last out the back aff the tents playin way the other choir boys… an' he had got himself al iveryway[464] way hez clothes… but I got him squared up[465] an' in he comes… an' they al

---

461 **A quare good rig-out** – *a very expensive outfit*
462 **Duds** – *clothing of inferior quality*
463 **Figgairies** – *expensive fopperies*
464 **Al iveryway** – *untidy*
465 **Squared up** – *tidied up*

clapped… some aff them already with a drap too much, min[466] … an' Danny gets down tay singin' 'Danny Boy'… that got them clappin that hard I thought the tent wud fal down. An' then the 'Mountains aff Mourne'… the 'Green Hills aff Antrim'… al them Percy French wan's, yeh know. An' he kep the band way the fiddles an' a big harp back an' I don't think the band fellas wur too plazed… lake he wuz puttin their noses outta joint but sure, then again, yeh hive tay give the people what they want… an' what they wanted wuz our Danny… "

They had reached Rosie's cottage but there was no stopping her "…. niver wuz there a day lake it, I tell yeh… an' al them big swanky folk cheerin our Danny… I wuz that proud … "

… and, while nothing can exceed a mother's pride, we too must surely be proud of our little hero!

'Parting is such sweet Sorrow'

Well, there you have it… our Danny finally on the crest of a wave. So it is now timely for us to tip-toe away and leave him to savour his success as he lies in his favourite spot by the beautiful 'Meeting of the Waters' listening to the music of the rivers.

He has shared with us, with beguiling innocence, the challenges he has faced here on earth, which he dealt with in his own inimitable way, and so too has his Guardian Angel Jo shed light – if that is what it was! – on some of the challenges in the heavenly realm. But let us now say goodbye and good luck to our little hero…

… and of the many and varied 'brackish' folk we have met on the way? Well… let us close the lid on the Pandora's Box that is Ballybracken, mindful that folk just like them, with all their endearing qualities and virtues and, yes, also their manifest faults and failings are all out there scattered across the length and breadth of our beautiful country, and let us take comfort that the only thing left in Pandora's Box for us to cherish is… hope.

---

466 ***A drap too much*** – *had taken too much to drink*

Annex.

I found this material helpful in attempting to capture the richness of the Ulster dialect, and also many other aspects of rural life in Ulster in the 1950s.

- "Concise Ulster Dictionary" by Dr C I Macafee, Oxford University Press, 1996.
- "A Dictionary of Hiberno-English" compiled & edited by T P Dolan, Gill & Macmillan, 2013.
- "John Pepper's Ulster-English Dictionary", Appletree Press, 1981.
- "The Ulster Dialect Lexicon," Inaugural Lecture by J Braidwood, QUB, 1969.
- "Ulster Speaks" by W F Marshall, BBC, 1936; "Tyrone Ballads" by W F Marshall, Quota Press Belfast 1951; "Living in Drumlister, the Collected Ballads and Verses" by W F Marshall, the Blackstaff Press, 1983.
- "The Planter & the Gael" by John Hewitt & John Montague, Arts Council of N. Ireland, 1970. "Selected Poems 1961-2017 by John Montague, the Gallery Press, 2019.
- "The Academic Study of Ulster Scots". Essays by & for Robert J Gregg, UFTM, 2008.
- "The Hamely Tongue" by James Fenton, Ullans Press for the Ulster Scots Language Society, 2014.
- "Changing Times. Life in 1950s Northern Ireland" by Peter Smith, Colourpoint Books, 2012.
- "English as We Speak it in Ireland" by P W Joyce, with introduction by Terence Dolan, Wolfhound Press, 1979.
- "Slanguage: A Dictionary of Irish Slang" by Bernard Share, Gill & Macmillan, 2003.
- "The Dialect Vocabulary of Ulster" a paper by John M Kirk, School of English, QUB 1999.
- "Ulster Dialects" – an Introductory Symposium, Ulster Folk Museum, 1964.
- "Green English" by Loretto Todd, O'Brien Press, Dublin, 1999.
- "Traits & Stories of the Irish Peasantry" by William Carleton 1794 -1869.
- "Glossary of Words in the Ulster Dialect" by J. J. Marshall, Ulster Journal of Archaeology Vol. X (1904) and Vol. XI (1905).
- "BBC Northern Ireland Voices", 2016.

Printed in Great Britain
by Amazon